THE PERFUMIST OF PARIS

THE PERFUMIST OF PARIS

ALKA JOSHI

WHEELER PUBLISHING
A part of Gale, a Cengage Company

GALE
A Cengage Company

Wheeler Publishing Large Print Hardcover.
The text of this Large Print edition is unabridged.
Other aspects of the book may vary from the original edition.
Set in 16 pt. Plantin.

LIBRARY OF CONGRESS CIP DATA ON FILE.
CATALOGUING IN PUBLICATION FOR THIS BOOK
IS AVAILABLE FROM THE LIBRARY OF CONGRESS.

ISBN-13: 979-8-88578-595-2 (hardcover alk. paper)

Published in 2023 by arrangement with Harlequin Enterprises ULC.

Printed in Mexico
Print Number: 1   Print Year: 2023

For my brothers,
Madhup and Piyush Joshi,
who persuaded me to go further
than I could have dreamed.

And for anyone who thinks they can't:
You can.

Smell is a potent wizard that transports you across thousands of miles and all the years you have lived.

— HELEN KELLER

The beauty of fragrance is that it speaks to your heart and hopefully someone else's.

— ELIZABETH TAYLOR

CHARACTERS WHO APPEAR

In Paris

Radha Fontaine: 32, mother of daughters Asha and Shanti; lab assistant at House of Yves, a boutique fragrance firm in Paris

Pierre Fontaine: 42, Radha's husband; father of Asha and Shanti; architect working on the Pompidou Center in Paris

Florence Fontaine: 67, mother of Pierre; from a prosperous Parisian family; now serves on several boards and committees

Shanti Fontaine: 9, daughter of Radha and Pierre

Asha Fontaine: almost 7, daughter of Radha and Pierre

Mathilde: 32, Radha's oldest friend from Auckland House School; single; from a wealthy Parisian family

Delphine Silberman: 60, master perfumer at House of Yves

Celeste: Delphine's secretary

Michel LeGrand: senior lab assistant to Delphine at House of Yves

Ferdie (Ferdinand): lab assistant to Delphine at House of Yves

Yves du Bois: owner of House of Yves, a boutique fragrance firm

Agnes: Mathilde's mother; former hippie who romped through India until dementia forced her to return to Paris

Antoine: deceased, father of Agnes/ grandfather of Mathilde; former owner of an exclusive Paris *parfumerie*

In Agra

Hazi and Nasreen: 55 and 54, sisters and proprietors of a *kotha,* a renowned pleasure house

Mr. Metha: factory owner of an Indian *attar* factory

Hari Shastri: 51, Lakshmi's ex-husband; at 17 he married Lakshmi but she deserted the marriage two years later; now Hari owns an incense factory in Agra

Binu: teenager, kitchen helper at Hazi and Nasreen's *House of Pleasure*

In Jaipur

Kanta Agarwal: 45, wife of Manu Agarwal; adoptive mother of Niki, Radha's natural-born son

Manu Agarwal: 45, husband of Kanta; adoptive father of Niki; director of facilities at Jaipur Palace

Niki Agarwal: 17, adopted son of Kanta and Manu; Radha's natural-born son

Baju: an old family servant of Kanta and Manu

Sassuji: Kanta's mother-in-law; when addressing a mother-in-law directly, a woman would call her by the respectful "Saasuji"

Munchi: old man from the small village of Ajar who taught Lakshmi how to draw and taught Radha how to mix paints

In Shimla

Lakshmi Kumar: 49, Radha's older sister; director of the Lady Reading Healing Garden in Shimla; works part-time with her husband, Dr. Jay Kumar, at the Shimla Community Clinic

Malik: 27, used to assist Lakshmi with her henna business in Jaipur; now runs the Healing Garden in Shimla

11

Jay Kumar: 61, husband of Lakshmi; physician at Lady Bradley Hospital in Shimla; former Oxford chum of Samir Singh

Nimmi: 29, married to Malik; mother of Chullu and Rekha (from a previous marriage); lives in a joint family at Lakshmi and Jay's house

Madho Singh: talking parakeet gifted to Malik 19 years ago by Jaipur's Maharani Indira

In America

Parvati Singh: 54, wife of Samir Singh; mother of Ravi and Govind Singh; distant cousin of the Jaipur royal family; formerly a Jaipur society matron

Samir Singh: 61, husband of Parvati Singh and father of Ravi and Govind Singh; formerly a renowned Jaipur architect from a high-caste Rajput family; now runs a flourishing real estate business in Los Angeles

Ravi Singh: 36, son of Parvati and Samir Singh; married to Sheela Sharma; father of two daughters; works in the family real estate business in Los Angeles

Sheela Singh: 34, married to Ravi Singh; mother of two daughters; lives in Los Angeles in a joint family with her in-laws

PROLOGUE

"Imagine running amid a field of lavender bushes with your friends. Playing hide-and-seek between rows of jasmine vines." Antoine closed his eyes. "Your friend tickles your nose with a blade of grass and, just from its scent, you know it's from the farm down the hill, not the one up the rise. Imagine plucking a vine-ripened tomato from your mother's garden just to inhale its sharp aroma." He sighed. "That's what growing up in Grasse was like."

I didn't have to imagine. The delicate fragrance of the henna flower greeted me on my way to the village riverbank where I washed clothes. My mouth watered at the ripe melon scent of mangoes that Prem feasted on as his bulls ground wheat and corn into flour. And the moment before I offered my finest possession — the *peepal* leaf painting of Radha and Krishna that Munchi-*ji* had made for me — to Lord Ga-

13

nesh, I breathed deeply of the sandalwood incense as I folded my hands to pray for good luck.

Like Antoine, my memories were rich with scent. And so were my secrets.

PART ONE

PART ONE

Europeans once traded gold for cloves grown in South India so they could spread the spice across their floors to absorb foot odor.

Paris
September 2, 1974

I pick up on the first ring; I know it's going to be her. She always calls on his birthday. Not to remind me of the day he came into this world but to let me know I'm not alone in my remembrance.

"Jiji?" I keep my voice low. I don't want to wake Pierre and the girls.

"Kaisi ho, choti behen?" my sister says. I hear the smile in her voice, and I respond with my own. It's lovely to hear Lakshmi's gentle Hindi here in my Paris apartment four thousand miles away. I'd always called her *Jiji — big sister —* but she hadn't always

17

called me *choti behen.* It was Malik who addressed me as *little sister* when I first met him in Jaipur eighteen years ago, and he wasn't even related to Jiji and me by blood. He was simply her apprentice. My sister started calling me *choti behen* later, after everything in Jaipur turned topsy-turvy, forcing us to make a new home in Shimla.

Today, my sister will talk about everything except the reason she's calling. It's the only way she's found to make sure I get out of bed on this particular date, to prevent me from spiraling into darkness every year on the second of September, the day my son, Niki, was born.

She started the tradition the first year I was separated from him, in 1957. I was just fourteen. Jiji arrived at my boarding school with a picnic, having arranged for the headmistress to excuse me from classes. We had recently moved from Jaipur to Shimla, and I was still getting used to our new home. I think Malik was the only one of us who adjusted easily to the cooler temperatures and thinner air of the Himalayan mountains, but I saw less of him now that he was busy with activities at his own school, Bishop Cotton.

I was in history class when Jiji appeared at the door and beckoned me with a smile. As

I stepped outside the room, she said, "It's such a beautiful day, Radha. Shall we take a hike?" I looked down at my wool blazer and skirt, my stiff patent leather shoes, and wondered what had gotten into her. She laughed and told me I could change into the clothes I wore for nature camp, the one our athletics teacher scheduled every month. I'd woken with a heaviness in my chest, and I wanted to say no, but one look at her eager face told me I couldn't deny her. She'd cooked my favorite foods for the picnic. *Makki ki roti* dripping with *ghee*. *Palak paneer* so creamy I always had to take a second helping. Vegetable *korma*. And *chole,* the garbanzo bean curry with plenty of fresh cilantro.

That day, we hiked Jakhu Hill. I told her how I hated math but loved my sweet old teacher. How my roommate, Mathilde, whistled in her sleep. Jiji told me that Madho Singh, Malik's talking parakeet, was starting to learn Punjabi words. She'd begun taking him to the Community Clinic to amuse the patients while they waited to be seen by her and Dr. Jay. "The hill people have been teaching him the words they use to herd their sheep, and he's using those same words now to corral patients in the waiting area!" She laughed, and it made me feel lighter. I've always loved her laugh; it's like the temple bells that worshippers ring to receive blessings from Bhagwan.

When we reached the temple at the top of the trail, we stopped to eat and watched the monkeys frolicking in the trees. A few of the bolder macaques eyed our lunch from just a few feet away. As I started to tell her a story about the Shakespeare play we were rehearsing after school, I stopped abruptly, remembering the plays Ravi and I used to rehearse together, the prelude to our lovemaking. When I froze, she knew it was time to steer the conversation into less dangerous territory, and she smoothly transitioned to how many times she'd beat Dr. Jay at backgammon.

"I let Jay think he's winning until he realizes he isn't." Lakshmi grinned.

I liked Dr. Kumar (Dr. Jay to Malik and me), the doctor who looked after me when I was pregnant with Niki here in Shimla. I'd been the first to notice that he couldn't take his eyes off Lakshmi, but she'd dismissed it; she merely considered the two of them to be good friends. And here he and my sister have been married now for ten years! He's been good for her — better than her ex-husband was. He taught her to ride horses. In the beginning, she was scared to be high off the ground (secretly, I think she was afraid of losing control), but now she can't imagine her life without her favorite gelding, Chandra.

So lost am I in memories of the sharp scents of Shimla's pines, the fresh hay Chandra enjoys, the fragrance of lime aftershave and antiseptic coming off Dr. Jay's coat, that I don't hear Lakshmi's question. She asks again. My sister knows how to exercise infinite patience — she had to do it often enough with those society ladies in Jaipur whose bodies she spent hours decorating with henna paste.

I look at the clock on my living room wall. "Well, in another hour, I'll get the girls up and make their breakfast." I move to the balcony windows to draw back the drapes. It's overcast today, but a little warmer than yesterday. Down below, a moped winds its way among parked cars on our street. An older gentleman, keys jingling in his palm, unlocks his shop door a few feet from the entrance to our apartment building. "The girls and I may walk a ways before we get on the Métro."

"Won't the nanny be taking them to school?"

Turning from the window, I explain to Jiji that we had to let our nanny go quite suddenly and the task of taking my daughters to the International School has fallen to me.

"What happened?"

It's a good thing Jiji can't see the color rise in my cheeks. It's embarrassing to admit that Shanti, my nine-year-old daughter, struck her nanny on the arm, and Yasmin did what she would have done to one of her children back in Algeria: she slapped Shanti. Even as I say it, I feel pinpricks of guilt stab the tender skin just under my belly button. What kind of mother raises a child who attacks others? Have I not taught her right from wrong? Is it because I'm neglecting her, preferring the comfort of work to raising a girl who is presenting challenges I'm not sure I can handle? Isn't that what Pierre has been insinuating? I can almost hear him say, "This is what happens when a mother puts her work before family." I put a hand on my forehead. Oh, why did he fire Yasmin before talking to me? I didn't even have a chance to understand what transpired, and now my husband expects me to find a replacement. Why am I the one who must find the solution to a problem I didn't cause?

My sister asks how my work is going. This is safer ground. My discomfort gives way to excitement. "I've been working on a formula for Delphine that she thinks is going to be next season's favorite fragrance. I'm on round three of the iteration. The way she just knows how to pull back on one ingredient and add barely a drop of another to make the fragrance a success is remarkable, Jiji."

I can talk forever about fragrances. When I'm mixing a formula, hours can pass before I stop to look around, stretch my neck or step outside the lab for a glass of water and a chat with Celeste, Delphine's secretary. It's Celeste who often reminds me that it's time for me to pick up the girls from school when I'm between nannies. And when I do have someone to look after the girls, Celeste casually asks what I'm serving for dinner, reminding me that I need to stop work and get home in time to feed them. On the days Pierre cooks, I'm only too happy to stay an extra hour before finishing work for the day. It's peaceful in the lab. And quiet. And the scents — honey and clove and vetiver and jasmine and cedar and myrrh and gardenia and musk — are such comforting companions. They ask nothing of me except the freedom to envelop another world with their essence. My sister understands. She told me once that when she skated a reed dipped in henna paste across the palm, thigh or

23

belly of a client to draw a Turkish fig or a *boteh* leaf or a sleeping baby, everything fell away — time, responsibilities, worries.

My daughter Asha's birthday is coming up. She's turning seven, but I know Jiji won't bring it up. Today, my sister will refrain from any mention of birthdays, babies or pregnancies because she knows these subjects will inflame my bruised memories. Lakshmi knows how hard I've worked to block out the existence of my firstborn, the baby I had to give up for adoption. I'd barely finished grade eight when Jiji told me why my breasts were tender, why I felt vaguely nauseous. I wanted to share the good news with Ravi: we were going to have a baby! I'd been so sure he would marry me when he found out he was going to be a father. But before I could tell him, his parents whisked him away to England to finish high school. I haven't laid eyes on him since. Did he know we'd had a son? Or that our baby's name is Nikhil?

I wanted so much to keep my baby, but Jiji said I needed to finish school. At thirteen, I was too young to be a mother. What a relief it was when my sister's closest friends, Kanta and Manu, agreed to raise the baby as their own and then offered to keep me as his nanny, his *ayah*. They had the means, the desire and an empty nursery. I could be with Niki all day, rock him, sing him to sleep, kiss his peppercorn toes, pretend he was all mine. It took me only four months to realize that I was doing more harm than good, hurting Kanta and Manu by wanting Niki to love only me.

When I was first separated from my son, I thought about him every hour of every day. The curl on one side of his head that refused to settle down. The way his belly button stuck out. How eagerly his fat fingers grasped the milk bottle I wasn't supposed to give him. Having lost her own baby, Kanta was happy to feed Niki from her own breast. And that made me jealous — and furious. Why did she get to nurse my baby and pretend he was hers? I knew it was better for him to accept her as his new mother, but still. I hated her for it.

I knew that as long as I stayed in Kanta's house, I would keep Niki from loving the woman who wanted to nurture him and was capable of caring for him in the long run. Lakshmi saw it, too. But she left the decision to me. So I made the only choice I could. I left him. And I tried my best to pretend he never existed. If I could convince myself that the hours Ravi Singh and I spent

25

rehearsing Shakespeare — coiling our bodies around each other as Othello and Desdemona, devouring each other into exhaustion — had been a dream, surely I could convince myself our baby had been a dream, too.

And it worked. On every day but the second of September.

Ever since I left Jaipur, Kanta has been sending envelopes so thick I know what they contain without opening them: photos of Niki the baby, the toddler, the boy. I return each one, unopened, safe in the knowledge that the past can't touch me, can't splice my heart, can't leave me bleeding.

The last time I saw Jiji in Shimla, she showed me a similar envelope addressed to her. I recognized the blue paper, Kanta's elegant handwriting — letters like *g* and *y* looping gracefully — and shook my head. "When you're ready, we can look at the photos together," Jiji said.

But I knew I never would.

Today, I'll make it through Niki's seventeenth birthday in a haze, as I always do. I know tomorrow will be better. Tomorrow, I'll be able to do what I couldn't today. I'll seal that memory of my firstborn as tightly as if I were securing the lid of a steel tiffin for my lunch, making sure that not a drop of the *masala dal* can escape.

An ingredient found in almost every Western perfume, oil extracted from the roots of vetiver grass is woody, smoky, earthy — perfect for men's fragrances.

Paris
October 1974

I wave the scent paper under my nose. I've blended the formula three times, but I know something's not right. I scan the creative brief again. The client has requested a fragrance that's earthy but cool and light, like the middle, leafy layer of a forest — not its damp undergrowth. In the sample I blended eight hours ago, the pungent smell of decaying wood lingers. Delphine will not be pleased.

I look at the wall clock on the far side of the fragrance lab. Ten minutes to two. Delphine will be here precisely at two o'clock.

She's always on time. She's the only master perfumer at the House of Yves who insists on visiting her assistants in the fragrance lab to see what they've blended; the other two master perfumers ask their assistants to bring samples to their offices. In our tiny lab, over three thousand scents mingle to form a fragrance all their own, and I think that's what she loves. Every time she enters the lab, I see her close her eyes briefly. I imagine she's testing herself, trying to identify as many distinct scents as possible, before she approaches one of us. After working in the lab for five years, the deluge of scents is nothing more than background noise to me. I'm only ever focused on the formula I'm blending at the moment.

Directly across from me, Michel is organizing the tray of scents he's mixed for another of Delphine's projects. His workstation is spotless; it's as if he's always ready for inspection. He's in his forties, a decade older than me, and the most senior lab assistant. Delphine will approach him first. Michel's main job is to expand the fragrances that have been approved by clients into *eau de parfum, eau de toilette, eau de cologne* and *eau fraiche.*

Ferdie, whose proper name is Ferdinand, works to my right. His work area is cluttered and untidy, something I notice Delphine surveys but never comments on. Through the glass wall that separates our lab from the reception desk, I see him telling Delphine's secretary a story; Ferdie is an excellent storyteller. Celeste begins laughing even before he's finished. Her phone starts to ring, and she shoos him away, still giggling.

Each of our work areas resembles a church organ. In front of us are three tiers of scent vials in a semicircle — almost three hundred of them — leaving just enough space on the table for a tiny scale, a tray of pipettes, a jar of scent papers — each the width of a pencil — and a notebook on which to record our trials. I've organized my perfume organ according to families of scents. First, there are the powdery, narcotic florals — orange blossom, damask rose, lavender, lily of the valley. The next tier of bottles contains sweet, juicy fruit fragrances like lemon, bergamot, mango. There's a cluster of rugged green bouquets — pine needles and rosemary among them — and of course the enduring, profound gourmand family of scents like chocolate, vanilla and clove. The earthy woods take up the top row: vetiver, sandalwood, rosewood, cedar among them.

In the lab, each of us is assigned project

briefs. The brief describes what the client — be they a major perfume brand, fashion designer or a beauty products company — wants to create. For each project, Delphine, the master perfumer of our lab, designs several potential formulas based on her knowledge of thousands of scents. She may use anywhere from ten to fifty ingredients in her creations. It's our job as lab assistants to blend her formulas, using a pipette to accurately measure each ingredient on the scale and mix it with a small quantity of alcohol. If the ingredient is a solid, like musky, waxy ambergris (which, surprisingly, is a digestive by-product of sperm whales!) or a dark and spicy resin, like frankincense or myrrh, we must first grind or press it to a fine powder before adding it to the mixture. If an essential oil like rose or fennel is stored in the refrigerator to lengthen its shelf life, we must warm it to room temperature before using it. Once we've blended Delphine's formula, we dip the pencil-sized scent papers in our sample and sniff them to make sure we've created what she specified. That takes experience and time and an innate ability to discern aromas. It's taken me five years, and I'm still learning.

For the tenth time, I read the formula I've been working on to see if I've missed something. Could it be that my boss's preference for woody scents have led her to prescribe a higher density of vetiver than the fragrance needs? I check my scale one more time to make sure it's calibrated correctly. Even the tiniest difference in measuring a raw ingredient could change the fragrance. I chew my lower lip. Should I deliver the formula Delphine designed? Or should I experiment with a slightly different formula that might meet the client's expectations? I've never questioned Delphine's formulas before, and as the lab assistant with the least experience, I don't have a right to do so now.

I glance at Michel, the manager of our lab. When Yves du Bois lured Delphine from another fragrance house in Paris, he promised her a dedicated lab with her own assistants: Michel, whom she brought with her from her former workplace, and Ferdie, who happened to be Yves's nephew.

Michel has a degree in chemistry. He's worked with Delphine for nine years. In the five years I've worked here, he's kept his distance, only speaking to me when necessary. He barely looks me in the eye when addressing me. I've often wondered if he's resentful. I had only completed one year of chemistry before Delphine hired me and began training me as a junior lab assistant. I'm a thirty-two-year-old Indian woman — not French — like all the other employees of the company. Most have never been to India or expressed any desire to go. To them, I'm an anomaly, an oddity, and not necessarily a favorable one.

Ferdie is a few years younger than me. He also has a chemistry degree, but I doubt that becoming a master perfumer is his life's passion. He only works the hours assigned to him, taking off as many sick days as he is allowed, but he's a welcome contrast to Michel's gravitas. Ferdie is always in a good mood. He seemed happy to have me join their lab. Michel doesn't laugh at Ferdie's jokes. I do. Ferdie loves to sing and whistle and dance. When he gets nervous (which happens every time Delphine is scheduled to visit the lab), he whistles one of the disco tunes he's so fond of. Today, he's whistling "Lady Marmalade." To the scents he's mixing, he asks, *"Voulez-vous coucher avec moi ce soir?"*

Michel clears his throat, reminding Ferdie that the lab is no place for frivolity. With a guilty look at Michel, Ferdie whispers, *"Désolé,"* but then catches my eye across the room. He smiles and winks. I return his smile. He's harmless. Sometimes, when we

33

lunch together, he shows me his latest dance moves and tells me about his newest crush. Last week, it was Sergio. A week before, it was Miguel.

"Radha?"

I startle, almost knocking over the open bottle of vetiver oil, which costs more than what I make in a week. I turn to see Celeste hovering just above my right shoulder, her hands clasped together. She has limp, light brown hair just past her shoulders. Today, she's wearing a long-sleeved brown knit dress that does little for her bony frame.

"*Zut alors,* Celeste! How many times must I ask you not to sneak up behind me when I'm mixing?"

The young woman flushes a deep pink to the roots of her hair. "But it's the second time he's called. It's Pierre." She leans closer to my ear and whispers, "It's about Shanti."

My heart plunges to my stomach. My palms start to sweat. What now? Of my two girls, Shanti is the one who never quite accepts my authority as her mother, always questioning *why must I* and *who says* and *why do you get to tell me what to do?* When she was little and I would pick out a yellow dress, she would insist on wearing a blue one that wasn't in her wardrobe. She'd say no to *kheer* — something all Indian children are fed because the sweet rice pudding is soft on developing gums — and insist on Nutella, always Nutella. Just yesterday, I was going over her English vocabulary test (she's in an international school). Despite my repeated corrections, she kept spelling *friend* as *f-r-e-n-d*. I know she knows how to spell it — she's a smart girl. I'm convinced she likes being a contrarian to exasperate me. Is this how I was with my sister? A fleeting memory floats across my consciousness: resisting Lakshmi's attempts to enlighten me about the ways of the world, Jiji's brows furrowed, her lips drawn tight.

I turn away from Celeste and murmur, *"Merci. J'arrive."*

At times like these, I find myself reaching for the necklace in the pocket of my lab coat. On it is a pendant, a small vial, filled with a private scent — something I created just for me. Unscrewing the top, I inhale deeply. Within seconds, my heartbeat slows. I take another breath and let the tranquility bathe me. I screw the cap back on and drop it in the pocket of my coat. The necklace is always with me; I never know when I might need it. But I dare not wear it around my neck; Pierre might ask me what's in it.

I push my chair away from the desk and

wipe my damp palms on my lab coat. Michel glances at me, then at the wall clock. I nod to let him know I'll be back. He returns to his work.

Celeste is at her desk again, typing a letter. She's the receptionist for Delphine's department, handling Delphine's phone calls, correspondence, calendar, and welcoming clients to the studio. Celeste is good at her job, dependable, and sweet. I feel bad for snapping at her earlier. She's my age, but far more timid than she should be, which irritates me. In my crankier moments — especially after I've been dealing with Shanti, I have the urge to yell *boo* and watch Celeste jump out of her skin. Because of her nervous nature, she's the perfect foil for Delphine; Celeste needs an authoritative hand to direct her, and Delphine obliges.

I approach Celeste's desk, pick up the receiver and push the blinking button on her gray phone, which sits on one edge of her desk. If any of us has a personal call, this is the phone we must use. As a result, Celeste knows everything that's going on in our lives. But what choice does she have? And as far as I know, she keeps our personal business to herself. I've never asked her, but she may wish she didn't have to listen to me talking to Pierre or overhear Ferdie laughing with friends who call him for a drink after work.

I turn sideways to give myself some privacy. *"Chérie?"* I keep my voice low and calm.

Pierre's panicked voice is in my ear: "Did you not get my first message?"

My eyes flick to Celeste gratefully. I'll ask her to lunch tomorrow to make up for my testiness earlier. I ask Pierre, *"Qu'est qu'il ya?"*

"Shanti's school called. She pushed a girl — actually pushed her! — and ran from the classroom. They found her by the Trocadero fountains again. She's only nine, for God's sake! What is Shanti thinking going off by herself like that?"

Hai Ram! I wish I knew. For the past year, Shanti has been lashing out at other children, refusing to answer the teacher's questions and even skipping class to play with the boats in the Jardin du Luxembourg. She never offers any explanations. Just frowns, purses her mouth and disappears into the bedroom she shares with her sister. If only there were someone to tell me how to be a perfect mother. If only I could ask my closest friend, Mathilde, or my sister, Lakshmi, but neither of them have children. I tell myself not to panic; at least Shanti's safe —

37

this time.

I massage the two frown lines that have deepened on my forehead in the last few years. "What would you like me to do?" I ask Pierre.

"The school wants to send her home. Can you go get her?"

I start to ask why Yasmin can't go. Then I remember Pierre fired her. Were I still living in India, I, too, might have slapped Shanti for misbehaving, as Yasmin did, as Maa did so freely whenever I burned the rice or took too long at the farmer's well to draw water. I've tried to be a kinder, more loving mother to my girls. Still, I've failed with Shanti.

From the corner of my eye, I see Delphine walking toward the laboratory door. My mind drifts back to the scent I was mixing. What if I substituted one of the milder accords containing vetiver instead of the intense essential oil itself? Would that solve the problem with Delphine's formula?

"Pierre, I can't leave work right now. Delphine —"

His words are a hot hiss. "Always Delphine! Do you think my work is less important? You play with fragrances, for heaven's sake. I design buildings people need!"

I close my eyes and shake my head. *"Mais . . ."* When I open them, I see Delphine looking at me pointedly from the glass doors of the lab. I've kept her waiting.

"*Écoute, chérie.* Please take care of it just this once! I'll explain tonight." I hang up but I leave my hand on the receiver as if to apologize to my husband.

Celeste offers me a sympathetic smile, which makes me want to confide how awful it's been at home for the past year. My long hours in the lab. Shanti's behavior. The revolving door of nannies. I walk away from Celeste's desk and open the door to the lab.

Delphine likes for all three of us to be present during her lab visits and to participate in the evaluation of each project. We sniff the scent papers on Michel's desk and discuss which of his samples are working, which are not and why. Delphine suggests modifications to the formulas to bring them closer to the client brief. I hang on her every word, in awe of her knowledge, her absolute belief in her assessment.

Next, she concludes that Ferdie's project, which is late (it's been in development for six months), is ready for a second presentation to the fashion designer who commissioned it. Delphine tells Ferdie, *"On se vend comme des pains!"* These days, more and more renowned designers are requesting custom scents to enhance their clothing brand. Fragrances are big business; even if the season's fashion offerings are a bust, the brand's scent will keep the business afloat. I would love to be present at the client meeting to see the designer's reaction and Delphine's handling of it. So far, I have not been invited to client meetings.

Now Delphine turns to me and raises her eyebrows. I make no move to return to my work area. My palms are damp again, and I slide them down the sides of my lab coat.

"*Désolé, madame.* I'm not yet finished." I pray my voice isn't trembling.

Delphine Silberman cocks her head to the side and raises her pencil-thin brows. As always, she's well-groomed. Her dark curly hair, shot through with lighter brown, is cropped close to her scalp, unlike the longer hair favored by French women. If I were to guess, I would assume her hairdresser must excel at *balayage à coton* to give her hair that sunkissed look in winter. Her makeup is barely noticeable, save for the pink lipstick that always lines her thin lips. Today, she's wearing a Chanel tweed suit in red, white and maroon. She told me once how grateful she was to Coco Chanel for making it easy for women to get dressed in the morning with minimal fuss. Her Gucci pumps match her suit.

Delphine is still gazing at me, waiting for an explanation.

To tell her I suspect there's something wrong with her formula in front of Michel and Ferdie would be imprudent. I fight to keep my hands from sliding down my coat again. I say nothing.

She nods. "See me before you go home." She offers a pleasant smile to Michel and Ferdie. *"Bien fait."* Ferdie's face flushes with relief; Delphine doesn't usually compliment him.

Her smile has disappeared by the time she glances at me. I've disappointed her.

At my station, I select the bottles I need to tone down the intensity of the vetiver, a scent as familiar to me as my own skin. Back in India, Jiji and I used to cool ourselves with dampened fans made out of *khus,* the Hindi word for vetiver grass, during the sizzling heat of Jaipuri summers. The society ladies whose hands Jiji decorated with henna hired servants to continually sprinkle water on large *khus* screens over the doors and windows, which released vetiver's cool, woody fragrance into the rooms. I remember when Antoine, my first boss in Paris, told me that the first women's fragrance to use

41

vetiver was Chanel No. 5 in 1921, and here Indians had been using it and exporting the scented grass to the world for thousands of years!

I've never known Michel to challenge one of Delphine's formulas (maybe he only does so in private), but I sense that if an assistant is going to question the work of her master perfumer, she must be able to back up her claim. I mix the formula again, this time decreasing the vetiver and adding a smidgen of vanilla. I record my measurements. I follow the same process with a few other scent combinations that simulate the woody scent. I try oak moss. Then lichen. I avoid vetiver oil altogether.

Four hours fly by. I rub my eyes. I glance at Celeste's desk through the interior window of the lab. The typewriter is covered. She's gone for the day. I barely noticed when Ferdie left. Michel murmured *bonsoir* as he passed my desk on his way out. Here I am, the only mother in the group, still at work, neglecting my daughters and my husband. A pang of guilt slithers up my spine: *You forced Pierre to deal with Shanti!* Just then, another voice — where did it come from? — reverberates through my brain: *Pierre has never had to leave work to get the girls. It's always been me. Shouldn't he be able to do it sometimes?* Lakshmi told me that when she and Jay fight over household chores, their guiding proverb is: *If we are both queens, who will hang out the laundry?* I smile, take a breath, feel a little calmer. I'll talk to Pierre when I get home. I'm sure it'll be fine.

Yves du Bois, the founder of the House of Yves, pops his head into the lab. He's an attractive silver-haired man in his sixties. I think he prefers three-piece suits so he can dangle a Victorian watch chain from his vest pocket. In deference to the style of the times, however, he's let his hair grow long enough to graze his collar. I suppose it makes him more *au courant.* I've heard other employees speculate whether he has something going on with Delphine; they get along so well, lunching together frequently. But we've never seen any evidence of it. As for me, I doubt he even knows my name. I've hardly spoken five words to him in all the years I've been here. He usually only talks to his three master perfumers.

"Is Ferdinand about?" he asks.

"He's gone for the day."

He digests this information with a few blinks of his eyelids. Then checks his watch. "I thought we were meeting for dinner tonight." He stands there a moment longer.

43

"Hélène will be disappointed." I know that to be the name of his wife. Yves looks fairly disappointed himself. *"Alors . . . bonsoir."* He raps his knuckles on the doorframe and disappears.

Ferdie must have forgotten a dinner date with his aunt and uncle. It's not surprising; Ferdie has a busy social calendar. I remember the time he promised to take us all out for Celeste's birthday and instead left to meet his new friend Christophe. Celeste looked so crestfallen that Michel and I took her to her favorite bistro. I don't know if Ferdie ever apologized to Celeste; he never said anything to us.

Once Yves is gone, I return to my work. But worries about my older daughter now flood my thoughts. Shanti was a difficult baby and became more so when Asha's birth — just a few years later — took my attention away from her. Pierre tried to make up for it by taking Shanti for special outings while I was busy with baby Asha, but Shanti wanted my time more than his. Have I ignored my older daughter in favor of her easier, younger sister? They say *a guilty conscience is a lively enemy.* The battle is always raging inside me.

What was I like at Shanti's age? I remember bristling at the village women's taunts when I walked past them on my way to the farmer's well; I wasn't allowed to use the village well or talk to anyone in the village except for old man Munchi, a pariah himself with his game leg. Was it really my fault that my father, who was once a brilliant teacher, drank? Or that my mother went blind? Or that my older sister ran away from her marriage? Can a little girl cause such upheaval? Of course not. But we live in Paris, not an Indian village, and Pierre and I are hardworking parents. Shanti has no cause to be acting the way she has been.

The phone on Celeste's desk rings, and I wonder if it's Pierre. Did he know I was just thinking about him? I leave my station to pick up the receiver.

"Working late again?" It's Mathilde, my oldest friend, the one I roomed with at Auckland House School for four years in Shimla. Cigarettes have deepened her voice over the years, giving it a languorous, throaty quality.

"No, I'm drinking wine and eating oysters," I tell her.

"Charming. *La Reine* asked me to join your family for dinner, so I figured you were still at work." Mathilde calls Pierre's mother, Florence, *La Reine,* because every request from my mother-in-law's mouth sounds like

45

an order from the queen. We've joked about Florence's blatant attempts to push Pierre and Mathilde together when I'm not around. I wouldn't be surprised if she's suggested that Pierre have an affair with my best friend. Mathilde is Catherine Deneuve with blond bangs, and that space between her front two teeth only seems to make her more attractive to men. Except for the incessant smoking, my *saas* adores Mathilde. I wonder if it's because Mathilde doesn't work outside the home, as I do. But then, she doesn't have to; Mathilde has an inheritance, which Florence never acknowledges. Instead, when Mathilde is at our apartment, Florence will ask *her* where the spatula is or if the girls have been getting enough exercise on the weekends — as if Mathilde is Pierre's wife and not me. I suspect she does this on purpose to irritate me.

"Florence is cooking at my apartment?" I ask.

"Exact." I hear Mathilde exhale a stream of cigarette smoke.

Zut! Instead of picking up Shanti and Asha from school, Pierre must have foisted the task upon his mother, the only family we have here in Paris. Pierre is an only child; his father, Philippe, left the family when

46

Pierre was eight. My husband thinks Philippe lives in Spain now, but he's not sure. Florence is a staunch Catholic; she's never consented to a divorce. This past year, as Delphine has demanded more of my time, we've occasionally had to rely on Florence to help with the girls, something I don't like doing. She's quick with veiled barbs designed to make me feel like a bad mother for working outside the home. Sometimes I wonder if Pierre's resistance to my job is fueled by Florence's ideas of what women should and shouldn't do in polite society.

I stretch my neck and let out a sigh. "Thanks for the warning, *chérie.* Are you coming for dinner, then?"

"*Non.* I'm already spoken for." I can almost taste the tobacco of her Tigra cigarette through the receiver as she inhales. "I'm meeting Jean-Luc at eight at La Petite Chaise."

I chuckle. Mathilde has a line of suitors that would put Cleopatra to shame. Whenever we meet for lunch, she regales me with stories of the men who couldn't meet her expectations. However, I think this might be the same Jean-Luc she's been dating for three months — quite a stretch for her.

"And your mother? Who is looking after

her tonight?" I ask my friend.

A few years ago, Mathilde got a call from a woman down the street from her apartment building, saying that Mathilde's mother, Agnes, was looking for her daughter but couldn't remember her address. That was bizarre because her mother was constantly dropping in on Mathilde without prior warning. One time she walked right in on Mathilde and a man she was entertaining — in bed. Mathilde was mortified, but her mother casually said she was out of caviar and did Mathilde have any? Several visits to the doctor led to the diagnosis that Agnes was starting to lose her memory. It became clear that Mathilde would need to bring her mother to live with her. Now Mathilde only sees men at their apartments or in hotels and hires a nurse for her mother two evenings a week.

"Basira is already here. She's *maman*'s favorite. They watch *Les Shadoks* together."

"The cartoon?"

"*Maman* loves it. It's — ooh, I better get dressed!" She must have just noticed the time. *"A toute a l'heure, ma petite puce!"* She hangs up. Mathilde's nickname for me from the first day we met at boarding school has been *little flea.*

■ ■ ■ ■

Mathilde is the reason I met Pierre. In our senior year at Auckland, we often skipped the school's Sunday tradition of writing letters to family and hiked to the Catholic Nun's Graveyard in the cedar forest. We didn't have any need to write to family. Lakshmi and Jay lived only a few miles away, and I saw them often. Mathilde's mother was always following a different guru to Varinasi or Cooch Behar or Kerla so she never had a fixed address.

One Sunday we were sitting cross-legged in front of a grave Mathilde had selected, smoking the Galloises her cousins sent her through the local post office. The smell of moss, of cool earth, of ancient headstones, was comforting. Salamanders peeked at us from behind rocks before scurrying down to the ground. A lone partridge chittered amidst the crickets hiding in the thicket.

Solemnly, Mathilde crossed herself and began: "Sister Marie, we thank you for your service and smoke this cigarette in your honor. You, who may never have tasted tobacco on your own lips, would love the rush that comes with that first drag. Perhaps you tippled wine from the Sunday chalice, but you were kind to leave enough for the other worshippers. You were strict with your charges, but you prayed for them in your spare time. Not that you had much, what with all the polishing of the candlesticks, prostrating before Jesus and eating dry bread in silence with the other nuns. Still, we salute you and your life. Amen."

She wanted me to say something, too, but I didn't believe in talking to the dead, so I merely said, *"Jai hind."* Long live India.

A choking sound made us turn around. A twentysomething young man was trying to contain his laughter, a hand pressed against his chest. When he saw us looking, he made a sign of the cross. A Catholic. He said, *"Désolé.* Perhaps she was a relative of yours?"

Mathilde rolled her eyes.

He walked closer. "May I share one of your sacred Galloises? I'd like to pay my respects to Sister Marie, too."

That made us laugh. He told us his name was Pierre Fontaine and he was working on Le Corbusier's design of the city of Chandigarh, three hours by train from here. He liked coming to Shimla on weekends from time to time to escape the heat and fierce winds of Prime Minister Nehru's ideal city.

As it turned out, both Pierre and Mathilde were from Paris. They started chatting in

French. I was used to the attention my friend's blond hair, frosted pink lips and black mascara (*à la* her idol Sophia Loren) usually drew. But, eventually, Pierre smiled at me and said, "Your eyes are amazing. So beautiful."

My blue-green eyes were a source of curiosity to many. Did I have a British parent? Was I Anglo-Indian? Almost twelve years had passed since India's independence, and I didn't want to be associated with either. I blushed and looked away. But his deep-set amber eyes, lips the same color as his pink-olive skin, the way his light brown hair fell to one side of his wide forehead — these were burned into my brain as if I'd just taken his photograph.

The next day, he called the school and asked to speak to me. Not Mathilde, but me.

I was smitten.

Now, I yawn and glance at the wall clock above Michel's station. It's almost dinnertime. I'm finally ready to present my findings to Delphine. I would rather wait until tomorrow, give the blends time to mature, but I don't have that luxury. I pull the necklace from my pocket and inhale deeply from the glass vial. Calm once more, I gather the scent papers from my various trials on a stainless steel tray. I've labeled each blotter with ingredients in my own shorthand system. I push open the laboratory door and head to Delphine's office at the end of the corridor. I knock.

"Entrez."

Her office is a study in 1960s modernism. The walls are paneled in walnut from floor to ceiling. She's seated on an Eames aluminum group chair behind a sleek walnut desk that seems to float on the floor; the legs are almost invisible. On her side of the desk are long drawers, which spring open with the push of a finger, leaving the center — and her shapely legs — exposed. White Carrera marble crowns the desk. Against the wall behind her is a Charlotte Perriand bookcase in yellow, brick red and beige. To the left of the room is the antique perfume organ she inherited from her mentor and still uses to this day. On the opposite wall hangs an abstract in blue, mustard and black that she once told me was a Joan Miró; there are no other paintings or photographs in the room. The industrial carpet is a marigold yellow.

I would guess Delphine to be in her early sixties. She's the only female master perfumer I've ever met, which is probably why the lab assistants and secretaries at the

House of Yves say her name with reverence.

She looks up briefly and sees me. She taps the ash from her Gitane on the large triangular ashtray and finishes a letter she must have been writing in longhand. When she's done, she sits back in her chair and gestures for me to come forward. As usual, the ashtray is full of lipsticked filters, and the room is covered in a haze of smoke. When clients visit, they're ushered into a separate room, painted in white with a Saarinen quartz conference table, white Tulip chairs and a white rug. No hint of cigarette smoke anywhere.

At first, Delphine's chain-smoking had shocked me. Wouldn't it alter her sense of smell? I asked Antoine. He said that master perfumers, *Les Nez,* not only have innate talent but they've memorized thousands upon thousands of scents the way a musician memorizes notes, chords and melodies. It's a muscle they constantly exercise. Antoine said Delphine was the most extraordinary *Le Nez* he knew — despite her addiction to cigarettes.

I place my tray on Delphine's desk but remain standing with my hands clasped.

"Don't do that," she says quietly.

I start to remove the tray.

"Leave the tray. Don't clasp your hands.

Makes it seem as if you have something to hide or you are about to pray." She takes a long, slow drag of her cigarette, narrowing her eyes against the smoke.

Oh. I set the tray back down.

The corner of her mouth lifts in a small smile. "Are you going to tower over me or take a seat?"

I sit down hurriedly in one of the plush leather chairs in front of her desk.

"That's better." She taps the cigarette against the ashtray. "Now tell me what's wrong with my formula."

My mouth falls open. Was I that obvious in the meeting earlier?

She waves her hand at my tray to encourage me to continue.

I swallow. "*Alors.* I mixed the formula six times. Each time the vetiver was overtaking the blend." I clear my throat. "Perhaps I misunderstood the brief, but —"

She startles me by suddenly rolling her chair forward until her midsection is pressed against the desk and points the cigarette at me. "Don't. Ever. Apologize. Tell me what you think."

I can feel my face burning. My armpits are damp. "*D'accord.* The brief asks for a scent that's as light as air but your — the formula is far denser." I hurry to finish the last sentence before I lose my nerve. My heart is beating as if I've just run a mile at top speed. "I'm sure they'll make us redo it."

"Why do you think so?"

"The vetiver oil — it's throwing off the formula."

She stubs out her cigarette, releasing a stream of smoke through her mouth. Decades of heavy smoking have left a hundred fine lines fanning from her upper and lower lips. "Now take a breath. And show me what you did with it."

Once again, I wonder how she knew I would present alternatives. I walk her through my process, explaining the ingredients I substituted, and offer her the scent blotters.

Delphine takes her time with each combination, waving the paper blotters in front of her nose. She frowns, then repeats the process. She puts her elbows on her desk and leans her elegant chin on the bridge of her hands. Her nostrils flare as they move across the ten new offerings I've created.

"Leave it with me."

I turn toward the door but steal a glance at her before closing it. She's lighting another Gitane.

It's almost nine o'clock by the time I emerge from the Métro stairs and head to our apartment two blocks away. I want to see my girls before they fall asleep, kiss their smooth cheeks good-night, trail my fingers through their hair, but the dread I feel about confronting Pierre — how I left him to deal with Shanti — is like a weight on my chest. I used to love coming home to Pierre. In the first few years of our marriage, before I was pregnant with Shanti and when I'd started working at Antoine's, I couldn't wait to wrap my arms around his neck when he came home and inhale his peculiar scent — so exotic to me — a combination of Gauloise tobacco, tangy lemon, fresh rosemary and a hint of vetiver (he wore Dior Eau Sauvage, but I didn't know my fragrances then). Our clothes would come off before we made it to the sofa or the bed. Sometimes we'd fall asleep after sex and wake up hours later, ravenous for dinner. When did all that change?

We live in the heart of Paris, in Saint-Germain-des-Prés, the sixth *arrondissement,* in an apartment Pierre inherited from his wealthy grandmother. We even inherited her

Le Corbusier furniture — all tubular steel and black leather. We're three blocks from Café de Flore, where writers like Jean-Paul Sartre and Simone de Beauvoir (both of whom I had to read at Auckland) composed their seminal works and where poets and writers still mingle with Parisian glitterati over coffee. Pierre's *grand-mère* often joined their discussions and bought drinks for starving, creative types who frequented the café.

The door to our Haussmann apartment building is left open until ten o'clock at night. I wave at the concierge, Jeanne, who lives on the bottom floor, just to the left of the entrance. When she's not sweeping the front entrance or the stairs, she keeps an eye out for strangers from the window of her apartment. My footsteps echo in the musty stone stairwell as I mount them to the third floor (as in India, the first floor in France is the level after the ground floor). On each landing, as I pass another apartment, I catch snatches of mumbled conversations from the Blanchets, the smell of browning onions from Madame Reynaud's kitchen, a lonely piano melody from the flat directly below us (Georges is melancholy by nature). My front door key makes a distinctive, albeit satisfying, click. Inside the foyer, the warm hardwood floors creak under my feet. I recognize the scents of garlic, fish, butter, Galloise and Florence's perfume, Miss Dior, a floral mélange she has been wearing, it seems, her entire life. Her Dior handbag and scarf lay on the narrow console.

I close my eyes. All I want to do is hug my children, take a bath and get some sleep, but dinner and *La Reine* await.

I take my time hanging up my coat and removing my shoes (I still insist on the Indian custom of leaving them in the foyer before stepping farther inside the house, a practice Florence considers uncivilized). I place them next to Shanti's pair of red Pom d'Api, the latest boutique shoes on the market and ones which Florence insisted on buying for Shanti's ninth birthday. Like Kanta back in Jaipur, Florence has money to spend on children. Niki was better off with Kanta because she and Manu had the means to raise him. Does that mean I could lose my children to Florence as I lost Niki to Kanta? I close my eyes and brace myself against the wall. The dizzy spell passes.

Our apartment is large by Paris standards — about eight hundred square feet — with high ceilings and floor-to-ceiling balcony windows that flood the apartment with light in the daytime and make it seem bigger. It's large by my standards, too, growing up as I did in a hut just under a hundred square feet in a tiny village in India, before sharing the cramped lodgings with Lakshmi in Jaipur and, finally, boarding in a narrow room with Mathilde at Auckland House School in Shimla. Sometimes, I marvel at how different my life is today. Back in Ajar, I slept on a hard-packed dirt floor instead of a down mattress. I had to draw water from a well and heat the water over a clay hearth. Here, I turn on a tap and hot water magically appears. After thirteen years I've grown used to these daily comforts.

My mother-in-law comes out of the kitchen, an apron around her midsection and an empty plate in her hand, her high heels clicking on the floorboards. The corners of her lipsticked mouth are turned down. Florence's brows are perpetually raised, the way Delphine's are when she's displeased. Smiles are rare for Florence. I can tell she is annoyed that I didn't call out a *bonsoir* upon entering the flat.

She's rubbing the plate vigorously with a dishcloth, the yellow rubber gloves preserving her manicure. "Pierre asked me to pick up Shanti from school. I had to cancel my meeting at the Beaux-Arts." Florence is on several boards, including the celebrated art school, the École des Beaux-Arts. "I gave the girls sautéed cod and a salad." I can hear what she leaves unsaid: *French children need better food than you usually feed them, Radha.* Florence doesn't like Indian food; she thinks the spices harm the delicate digestive system of her granddaughters.

I swallow my irritation at the unspoken reprimand. "I'll finish up." I don't thank her for coming.

Florence's hand stops moving on the plate. Her nostrils flare (she has the most impressive nostrils I've ever seen). She presses her lips together as if she'd like to say more. But she turns abruptly on her heels and disappears inside the kitchen. I hear her slam the plate on the counter and strip off her gloves. She's unknotting the apron strings behind her back as she comes out again. She places the crumpled apron in my hands. I realize I haven't moved from the foyer, and I step aside as she grabs her handbag from the hall table. She doesn't kiss my cheeks the way she does Pierre's. Before closing the door behind her, she says, "If you want me to find a nanny, you just have to say —"

"*Non, merci.* Mathilde told me she knows someone," I lie. If I leave it to Florence, the

60

nanny will be a French matron who will take ownership of my children and my household. In my desperate moments, I almost want to beg Florence to do that, but my better sense usually prevails when I realize how completely my mother-in-law might cut me off from Pierre and the girls.

Pierre's half glass of white wine is on the dining table. Miles Davis's *Kind of Blue,* one of Pierre's favorite albums, plays softly on the record player. It reminds me that Pierre is taking all of us, including Florence, to the Festival d'Automne in a few weeks so we, too, can appreciate the jazz greats. The door to the girls' room is partly open, creating a soft triangle of light on the floor. I can hear Pierre's voice, deep and soothing.

I lean against the wall to the right of the door and listen to the rhythmic hum of his storytelling.

"The ship has the whitest sails. It's such a bright day. And the air smells so fresh, so clean. The wind is mild and is moving the sailboat slowly, smoothly, across the water. You are the ship. You are gliding across that calm water. *Doucement, doucement.* You are just floating on the water, letting the wind move you first one way, then another. You are peaceful. So peaceful."

Then it's quiet. Shanti must have fallen

asleep. Ever since she was a baby, Shanti has had tantrums that might last for hours — screaming-crying, her face wet and red, blindly pummeling everyone with her tiny fists. She would reach for me, but then push me away when I came closer. She would get overtired and need to nap but would refuse the slightest comfort. I tried to push the thought out of my mind, but it would only come snaking back: Was Shanti my punishment for having abandoned baby Niki?

One afternoon, when I was so exhausted and desperate for a solution to Shanti's cries, I phoned Jiji in Shimla — not caring about the price of a long-distance call. She told me how she used to soothe me to sleep with the lullaby that our father always sang to us: *Rundo Rani, burri sayani. Peethi tunda, tunda pani. Lakin kurthi hai manmani. Little queen, thinks herself so grand. Drinks only cold, cold water. But does so much mischief.* So I tried it. The first time I sang to Shanti during one of her tantrums, she fought me. Then I remembered that Lakshmi used to recommend saltwater baths to her ladies as a way to release anxieties and toxins. I prepared a warm water bath with salt while Shanti bawled, and then eased both of us into it. It startled her. She ceased crying and frowned, as if to ask what was happening.

I locked eyes with her and, while singing the lullaby, I tried to reach that part of her deep inside that was me, the difficult me who had responded to Jiji's singing and to my father's singing before that. Shanti watched my face intently. She stared for so long that I started to add new lyrics, making them up as I went along. Ten minutes later, her lids started to droop. I pulled us out of the bath, bundled her in a *rajai* and sat with her in the rocking chair until she fell asleep. That worked for two years until Asha came along. Shanti would no longer be soothed by the lullaby or saltwater baths. That's when Pierre asked Shanti to imagine she was a sailboat or a hot-air balloon or a bird so she was in control of how she moved through her environment. It worked. Gradually, she would fall asleep. I worried these sessions would keep my younger daughter awake, but Asha succumbed to her dreams after only a few minutes of listening to Pierre.

Pierre has a lovely, melodic voice. He used to read the *Notre Dame de Paris* to me in bed when we were first together. A peculiar choice, but it had a significant role in our courtship. Our first date had been a walk

63

along the Ridge in Shimla. He stopped to admire the Gothic architecture of Christ Church, praising the pointed arches, the stained-glass windows designed by Rudyard Kipling's father, the rib vaults. "But it's nowhere as grand as the Notre-Dame Cathedral in Paris. Have you seen it?" he asked.

When he turned to me, I realized I'd been staring at him. But in his place, I'd seen Ravi extolling the virtues of great architecture, me listening — back when I was thirteen and Ravi was seventeen. Without thinking about where we were or whether anyone was watching (public affection may have been acceptable in France, but it was frowned upon in India), I stood on my toes and kissed Pierre. Was I kissing Pierre or the memory of Ravi?

Without pulling away, Pierre's lips grazed mine as he said, "Notre-Dame must have made quite an impression on you."

I was breathing hard. "We read Hugo's *The Hunchback of Notre-Dame,* the English version, in literature class and then watched the 1939 American film. When it was over, I couldn't stop crying. I had fallen in love with Quasimodo."

Pierre kissed me harder. I didn't want him to stop.

Five months later, on a return trip to

Shimla, Pierre asked me to marry him. Instead of an engagement ring, he presented me with an antique copy of the Victor Hugo novel.

Now, I hear the girls' bedroom door closing, and I realize I've almost fallen asleep leaning against the wall. When I open my eyes, Pierre is facing me, but his face is shadowed; I can't read his expression, but the set of his shoulders tells me he's angry.

He skirts around me, heading to the kitchen. I follow him. The kitchen is only large enough for one person to occupy, so I wait at the threshold.

"Hungry?" He unwraps the dishtowel from the plate Florence has left for me: the cod and a salad of haricots vert and pimento. Usually, Pierre and I take turns cooking. He's good with omelets, fish and salads. I make the Indian *subjis* and *chappatis.* Luckily, the girls like both Indian and French cuisine.

My mouth waters at the sight of the food and my stomach rumbles. Until I went to my boarding school, I'd never eaten meat or fish. The diet of some Auckland students — they came from all over the world — required meat at school three times a week, and Matron allowed both a veg and nonveg option for dinner. I prefer mostly vegetarian but have grown to like the occasional fish and egg dishes.

"Are you having some?" I ask.

He brings my plate to the dining table and sets it down where I usually sit. "I've already eaten with *Maman* and the girls." He pours himself more wine. There's an empty glass at the table waiting for me, and he fills it. Now he takes a seat. So do I.

I don't know if we fight like other couples. But we do have a pattern. We begin politely. Then one of us starts to get heated. The other listens until impatience or anger or exhaustion gets the better of them and shuts the argument down. For a week afterward, we put our focus on the girls instead. Gradually, the intensity of our disagreement wears off and we're back to where we were, not having resolved anything, but we can be pleasant to one another again.

I wait for Pierre to start; he needs to blow off steam. Ever since I started working for the House of Yves five years ago, I've been counting on him to help with the girls and with the cleaning and shopping, and I know it confuses and frustrates him. He may think himself an enlightened French male, but he was raised to believe men and women had distinct and separate roles. He hasn't yet adapted to the fact that I, too, have a full-time career, not just a part-time job.

I chew my cod. It's cooled off and the butter has congealed. I sip my wine (it took me several years to get used to the taste of dry white wine, and I still only pretend to enjoy it because Pierre does). Pierre lights his cigarette, swirls his wine in his glass.

"We haven't seen a lot of you lately," he starts.

How do I explain to him that since Delphine took me on, it's not her who's asking me to prove myself. It's me who's struggling to show her that I'm worthy of her trust — and investment. Not every person with a year of chemistry and four years working in a boutique *parfumerie* (as I did at Antoine's) is given a job in a fragrance lab. Several years ago, a new perfume school was established in Paris where only students with two years of chemistry are admitted and trained to eventually become master perfumers — a process that takes a decade. Such a specialized school would never grant me access without the chemistry credentials. But I met Delphine through Mathilde's grandfather Antoine. The two were great friends, so when he recommended me, she paid attention.

For my first few years at the House of

Yves, I would stay after working hours to memorize the thousands of scents in the lab. Day after day, I tested myself. It became an obsession. I could — I *would* — identify them with my nose. A drop of galbanum took me back to the riverbank in Ajar where I washed my clothes. Lavender made me think of the first time I saw Jiji in Jaipur; her hands were scented with the oil she used on the bodies of her ladies.

When Michel and Ferdie took a holiday or sick day, I offered to fill in for them. I lost track of time in the lab, the way I used to lose track of time when I ground Jiji's henna paste to a satiny smoothness; I would experiment with different ingredients like geranium oil, rose water and sandalwood paste until the texture and the scent felt just right and Jiji pronounced the henna finer than anything she had ever produced. As a little girl in Ajar, I would help old man Munchi collect the mango leaves or cow urine or lemon juice to mix with his paints until he was satisfied with the color's intensity. It fascinated me that a mixture of unrelated ingredients could produce something so tantalizing, so appealing, so intoxicating.

My hours in the fragrance lab were sweeter for the new identity it provided me. Old man Munchi had befriended me in my village back when no one else would, before I knew Lakshmi as my sister, when I was known as the Bad Luck Girl. The gossipeaters talked openly about how my birth had coincided with my sister's desertion of her marriage, how my father, a former schoolteacher, had drowned and how my mother had gone blind. There were those who claimed I was to blame for the locusts eating the crops or the drought that persisted for three years or the calf born without a tail — all because Lakshmi had shamed us all by abandoning her husband. All my life I'd heard rumors about this shameful sister: she dressed in men's clothes! No, she ran away with a dance troupe! No, she'd become a prostitute, some claimed. When their salacious imaginings squeezed my heart so hard it hurt, I would escape to Munchi-*ji*'s hut at the edge of the village. There, I spent hours helping him prepare the *peepal* leaves he needed for his miniature paintings of Krishna and the milkmaid Radha, my namesake — paintings so fine I could see the tiny dots on the milkmaid's sari and each finger of Krishna's hand on his flute. Mixing paints was my sanctuary. Eventually, after Maa and Pitaji died, I found Lakshmi in Jaipur, making her living as a henna artist

— not as a dancer or harlot or any of the other rumors. I learned that she merely wanted a life of her own, one which she was in charge of. She took me in without a word.

Now, Pierre cuts into my thoughts. "I thought it would be different with us, Radha. Everyone else is having problems —" He stops.

I spear a green bean, chew slowly, wait. I know what's coming.

"Muriel left Guy because she said he is an irresponsible capitalist. He's been a banker for fifteen years and she only just noticed? He's supposed to change what he's been doing just because of a few student protests — students who hadn't worked a day in their lives?"

The younger me would have argued with him — *when did I lose that Radha?* I would have said it was more than a few student protests. Six years ago, almost half a million protestors challenged the establishment and its rules, causing President de Gaulle to flee France in secret. But I don't want to let my anger get the better of me, so I say nothing.

"Bertrand and Marie Laure are arguing because he won't let her work outside the home. They have three children. Why would she want to?"

My eye begins to twitch. He's really talking about us. I have two children and I dare to want more from my life? It's the same argument we've been having for several years now.

He shakes his head. "Do you feel I don't respect you enough? Am I not allowing you to do what you want? First, you went to work for Antoine without telling me. Fine, you wanted something to do. Then you were pregnant with Shanti, and I thought you would stay home to take care of her, but you started taking her to work with you . . ."

After I came to Paris with Pierre, I was bored sitting at home, so Mathilde talked her grandfather into hiring me for a few hours a day to help out at his *parfumerie.* I knew Pierre prided himself on being able to support me financially, so I didn't want to tell him at first. But once I was at Antoine's, I found myself in a familiar world, once again in the company of nature's scents, each of which had a separate identity, but when blended in distinct combinations produced a sublime experience.

Rockrose mixed with oak moss and patchouli created a sweet, airy bouquet — just like the fragrance of the park in Shimla where Pierre and I used to picnic. Sweet lime mixed with mint and mango reminded me of my favorite afternoons with Mathilde at the *pani-walla* in Shimla. A blend of orange blossom, cedar wood and sage had me picturing Lakshmi meandering among the plants of her Healing Garden in her peach sari. At Antoine's, the scents of my India surrounded me. Only then did I realize how much I'd missed those fragrances that conjured up fond memories of my youth, my home. I was hooked.

I began quizzing Antoine. Where did the raw ingredients for these fragrances come from? Did scents change over time? How did they evoke feelings in the wearer like joy, nostalgia and romance — as they did in me? And when Antoine told me how many perfumes wouldn't be possible without the essential oils that come from India, I understood why I felt at ease in his boutique. After a few months, I worked up the courage to tell Pierre about my work at the *parfumerie,* but I tossed it off as something I was doing to keep myself busy until our first child came along.

Now, I set my fork down on my plate with more force than I intended. "Pierre, Antoine asked me to bring Shanti when she was a baby. He wanted me at the shop — I was good with the customers. Remember how much she used to cry? With him, Shanti was always quiet." I stop myself from saying that

72

Shanti was a difficult baby, one I could never satisfy. Antoine's boutique was only two blocks from our apartment, on Boulevard Saint-Germain. He loved holding her, showing her off, strolling with her in her pram to the Jardin du Luxembourg, maybe because he had no grandchildren of his own. And she was fascinated by his white beard, his black glasses, the little hat he wore. If it hadn't been for Antoine, I might have gone crazy, so exhausted was I with insomnia and my inability to soothe Shanti's incessant crying.

Pierre holds up his hands in surrender. "*Et bien.* But then you started studying chemistry at the same time. It was . . . as if you were looking for an escape. From being a mother!"

"But Shanti was old enough for the *école maternelle.* Remember? And then I was pregnant with Asha. It was just as well that I could squeeze in a year of chemistry before Asha was born."

My voice has risen. Why do I have to defend myself? Do I ask Pierre why he chose to become an architect? Why he wants to work in Paris when he could work in India? He'd been helping Indian architects design the Le Corbusier buildings in Chandigarh when I met him. If Pierre decided to work

73

in Chandigarh again, I could be near the people I felt closest to: Jiji and Dr. Jay and Malik and Nimmi. And the girls could grow up with Malik's children.

But we never really discussed it. It was just understood that I would go to Paris with Pierre after I graduated from Auckland House School. Another job was waiting for him there. And I was caught up in the adventure. But I hadn't given any thought to how I would spend my days while Pierre was at work. So I was relieved when Mathilde returned home to Paris and introduced me to Antoine. She had never taken more than a passing interest in the *parfumerie,* and her grandfather was only too happy to have someone share his passion. He began teaching me everything he knew, and it opened up a whole new world. He was originally from Grasse, home to fragrance manufacturers and perfumers. He grew up surrounded by fragrances, as I had, albeit different ones. He began as a salesman in a pharmacy and developed relationships with the perfume salesmen who dropped by to showcase their latest offerings. Eventually, he established his boutique *parfumerie* in Paris by offering exclusivity to a handful of fragrance creators, like the House of Yves.

Antoine always said, "If you like people, Radha, you will do well in this business. It's all about finding out what they want. Ask and they will tell you. It's that easy."

Of course, it was never that easy for me to meet new people, especially here in the center of Paris where the color of my skin marked me as an outsider. But once I became comfortable with the products in his store and more fluent in French, I could talk to customers endlessly about them. With tourists, I conversed easily in English, a language that intimidated Antoine. When Antoine wanted to take a vacation, I took over the shop, catching him up on all the comings and goings of his customers upon his return.

Why couldn't Pierre see that I needed Antoine the way I needed a father? My father preferred a bottle of *sharab* to my company and died before my thirteenth birthday. And didn't Shanti and Asha need a de facto grandfather, the man who had spent so much time with them in their first few years? After I began working for the House of Yves, I still took them to see Antoine, whom they called *Grand-pére.* When he died four years ago, Shanti was inconsolable, and I felt as if I'd lost my father all over again.

Pierre turns away from me in his chair.

He taps his fingers, the ones holding the cigarette, on the table. I had resolved not to get angry, but I've broken my vow. I push my half-eaten dinner away and clasp my hands under the table to keep them from shaking. I keep my voice low; I don't want to wake up the girls. "What would you like me to do, Pierre? Quit my job? Wait all day at home for you and the girls?" I love my girls, but if I had to stay home all day I'd suffocate.

Pierre stabs the dining table with his index finger. "I make enough for all of us. You don't need to work! We don't even have to pay rent like everyone else."

Of course. His grandmother had owned this apartment outright. He has family money. His mother lives in Neuilly-sur-Seine in a mausoleum of a house. Pierre would prefer I stay here, cooking a hot dinner, my girls freshly bathed and fed. Did he always want me to be a full-time mother or has that idea grown with the arrival of two children? Didn't I also believe at one time that having children and taking care of them was all I needed in life? Then I met Jiji and understood what it was to create something larger than yourself. That thing that wasn't as easy as making babies but came from a deeper yearning. Shaping free-floating ideas into something concrete. Ideas no one had thought of yet. I *knew* I could do that with fragrances.

Pierre leans toward me, the wine strong on his breath. "Much of what you earn goes to pay for nannies anyway, which we wouldn't need if you didn't work!"

I swallow bile. If the next words out of his mouth are the suggestion that I should let his mother take care of our daughters, I will throw this plate of food at him. I have so much I could say. *Is allowing me to do what I want the same as me making my own decisions? Why are the girls completely my responsibility? Isn't he their father? When did I give up my right to decide what to do with my life?*

But I feel drained. I don't have the energy to start so I keep my mouth shut. Instead, I rise and pick up my plate and glass. Pierre looks up at me. His glass is empty. I reach for it.

"I promise to find another nanny tomorrow." I walk to the kitchen to wash the remainder of the dishes.

Pierre and I make up in bed. A kiss on the shoulder means *I'm sorry.* One on the back means *I've missed you.* One on the neck, just below the ear, means *I need you.* The

77

journey from the edge of the breast to the hip is reserved for *I can't always find the words to tell you what you mean to me.* A circular kiss around the belly button means *We'll find our way back to each other.* The area just above the pubis — and below it — says *I love you, all of you.* When our lips meet, I'm tingling with fire, with an urgency to forgive and forget. And my kisses say, *Yes and yes and yes and more and more and more.*

If my mother-in-law had her way, the girls would be in a private Catholic school. But I want them to learn more than just the French language. My English is better than Pierre's, and I want my girls to speak it fluently so they can go anywhere in the world and work wherever they'd like. I also want my girls to know children from various cultures so they don't feel isolated being half-Indian and half-French. That's another big advantage of their International School. At the Catholic school Florence would prefer they attend, they would mostly encounter French classmates.

The next morning, Pierre has a big meeting about the Pompidou Center. So many architects are working on the six-story complex that promises to be an arts mecca.

Pierre usually talks about his work over dinner, but I only listen with half an ear. It makes me uncomfortable for reasons I can't share with him. I don't like thinking about my failed first love, but it's hard to forget when my own husband is designing buildings just as I imagined Ravi would one day. Ravi had always known he was expected to take over his father's architecture practice. When I saw Malik in Shimla five years ago, he confirmed that Ravi had followed the path that had been mapped out for him since birth. He'd even married the girl his parents, Parvati and Samir Singh, had picked out for him.

After Pierre leaves for work, I check my watch. I have enough time to ask Shanti what happened at school yesterday. I cut off two thick slices from a baguette and spread a generous amount of Nutella on each. I place slices of banana only on Shanti's piece. Asha doesn't like to mix her Nutella with banana. I sit at the dining table next to Shanti with my chai. (Jiji sends me a care package of cardamom, cloves, cinnamon and peppercorns every few months for my tea.)

"Shanti, can you tell me why you hit Nanny Yasmin?"

Shanti takes such a big bite of her bread

that it's impossible for her to answer. Asha watches us, swinging her legs under her chair. I ask her to stop. When Shanti reaches for her bread again, I place a hand gently on her forearm to prevent her from taking another bite. "Shanti?"

Asha speaks up. "Nanny Yasmin told her to stay out of the sun or she would become as dark as you."

"Tattletale!" Shanti pinches Asha's forearm, making her sister cry out.

"Shanti!" I make her apologize to Asha, who narrows her eyes at her sister. But it makes me sad. I want to take Shanti in my arms and tell her I'm sorry she felt she had to defend me.

Being called out for the color of my skin is nothing new. When I was attending the Maharani School for Girls in Jaipur, one of the most popular girls, Sheela Sharma, took every opportunity to whisper *Kala kaloota baingan loota* in my ear. *You're as dark as an eggplant.*

In India, the fairer the girl, the better her prospects for a good marriage. I have more of my late father's coloring. Lakshmi has more of our mother's fairer skin. Even though Shanti's skin tone is somewhere between Pierre's and mine, it's still a tiny shade darker than Asha's. Because of my

80

green-blue eyes, some people in Paris think my olive skin is the result of a vacation to a sunny resort. I suppose that's understandable; I could be of Latin descent like many French people, perhaps with a tad more Italian in my blood. And I do take care to wear dresses and trousers and style my hair like *it*-girl Jane Birkin to appear more French. Even so, there are those who assume I must be one of the newly arrived Indian immigrants from the former French colony of Pondicherry. On the Métro, I try to ignore the glares that seem to be warning me not to steal French jobs or take advantage of their generous social services. The double takes of the proprietors in boutiques remind me to make sure my hands are free of any bags into which I might be accused of stashing merchandise I haven't paid for.

Does Shanti experience the same scrutiny? With their fluent French, I thought my daughters were safe from the type of judgment usually directed at me. To realize that I've been the cause of her aggressive behavior toward others is like a punch to my gut. Here I've been feeling sorry for having a difficult child only to find that she's been trying to protect *me* from unkind remarks!

I look into my daughter's beautiful *café au lait* face, free of blemishes, free of the lines that come with years of heartache and worry and sickness and betrayal. I tuck a few loose strands of hair behind her ear (she insists on fixing her own hair in the morning, but she hasn't quite mastered the ponytail). "Come with me."

She follows me to the large vintage globe on the living room bookshelf. I point to India on the globe. "You know this is where I was born, *n'est-ce pas?*"

She scratches her nose and nods.

I turn the globe again and point to France. "Your father is from here, much farther north." Asha has followed us to living room. I gesture for her to come closer and position her next to the globe. "Asha is the sun, and the sun is very hot."

Asha giggles and starts revolving.

I point to the equator. "See how much closer Indians live to the sun than the French? That's why we have something special in our skin that protects us from getting burned, and it makes our skin darker. You are both lucky because you have some of that special ingredient in your skin. Just as Lord Ganesh has superhuman strength built into his body." I raised the girls on *Tales of Krishna* and fables of Hindu gods, which were my favorite stories growing up.

My daughters examine their hands, turning them over in wonder. Shanti frowns. "But I don't live in India. Why am I not the same color as Papa?"

"Because Papa and I made you together, so you have a little of both of us. *Ça va?*"

A thin line forms between her brows. She's trying to understand.

"If anyone says anything to either of you like Yasmin did, come tell me. Just don't hit them. We don't do that."

My daughters look at each other.

"Now, Shanti, the girl you pushed at school yesterday. Was that the same reason or different?"

Asha, still playing the sun, pokes Shanti in the stomach and makes a sizzling sound. Their laughter reverberates throughout the apartment as Shanti starts chasing Asha. I look at the wall clock. I didn't get an answer from Shanti, but I need to get them to school and get myself to work, so I let it go.

Michel is already in the lab when I arrive. I greet him with a *bonjour,* put my lab coat on and settle down at my worktable. The tray of scents I presented to Delphine yesterday is sitting at my station with a note in Delphine's handwriting: "Refine No. 4 and 6. Noon meeting. *Bien fait.*"

My heart jumps wildly in my chest. My

knees start to shake. I steady myself against the desk and sit on my chair to calm down. She liked my suggestions for the fragrance! Delphine doesn't praise lightly, and we all await her *bien faits* with baited breath. In many ways, I crave her approval as desperately as — and perhaps even more so than — I craved Lakshmi's. Jiji's blessing was partly to be expected because we shared the same blood, but Delphine owes me no such favor. I must be beaming because just then Ferdie walks into the lab and says, "You look like you just won the Tour de France!" He sets down his satchel and rushes over to me, pulls me from a sitting to a standing position and twirls me. I'm laughing until I catch a glimpse of Michel's face. His lips are pulled into a straight line, just as the headmistress of Auckland House School used to do if we laughed during morning assembly.

"Arrete!" I gently push Ferdie away. But I'm still smiling.

"Alors?" He wants to know what I'm so happy about.

I shake my head as if it's nothing and sit down at my table. I want to get started on the refinements. Ferdie shakes his finger at me playfully and walks to his work area.

I start by reading the brief again to focus

on what the client wants. One of the first things Delphine taught me is to always go back to the starting point. I close my eyes and dip scent papers into the bottles labeled *4* and *6.* But . . . wait . . . these are not the same scents I created yesterday. I open my eyes and sniff again. Once again, there's more vetiver in them — the same ingredient I'd tried to tone down. Scents do take some time to mature (Antoine used to say, *Like fragrances, ratatouille tastes better the day after*), but the difference wouldn't be this noticeable. I look around the lab. Michel is rummaging in the refrigeration unit. Ferdie is measuring a formula.

I leave the lab and approach Celeste. "Has anyone besides you been at my station?"

Celeste looks at me wide-eyed. Today, she's wearing blue eye shadow that covers the area from her lashes to her eyebrows. She shrugs her shoulders. "When I got here, Michel was already in the lab — he's always the first one in. And, of course, Delphine was in before me." She looks left and right before whispering, "I don't think she sleeps!"

I'm about to step back inside the lab when Celeste says, "Oh, Radha. Delphine would like you to meet her at five p.m. today at the Jeu de Paume."

85

I frown. "Doesn't the museum close at five?"

With reverence, Celeste says, "Madame has friends in high places."

Why would Delphine want me to go to a museum with her? I nod at Celeste and return to my work area.

Looking at the tray of ruined samples, I'm embarrassed to have suspected those I work with. My insufficient knowledge of chemistry must be to blame. How else could the scents have changed overnight? I shudder at having to tell Delphine that my skills are not what they should be. One year of chemistry wasn't enough — I should have completed the two-year course. But Asha came along before the second year, and, finding myself with two small children, I had to take a break from my studies.

I force my attention back to my samples. Well, I can always recreate them; I'm careful to record my trials. I pull open the drawer where I keep my notebook. It's not there. I pull it out farther and rummage around. Perhaps I put it in another drawer? I open another, then another. It's disappeared! My heartbeat is racing. My hands are clammy. How could I fail Delphine now?

Ferdie approaches my desk, holding my red notebook. "Radha, isn't this yours?"

I look up at him. He's wearing new corduroy bell-bottoms and a formfitting black turtleneck. His brown eyes are guileless. When he sees my expression, he looks alarmed. "Are you all right? Just a few minutes ago, you were *à la tête.*" Suddenly, he leans in and whispers, "Are you pregnant?"

I'm so relieved that I'm neither pregnant nor have I lost my notebook that I let out a nervous laugh. "Where did you find it?"

He puts his hands in the pockets of his lab coat and nods his head at the corner of the room. "On the floor . . . there."

How would it have landed in the corner of the room? Wouldn't I have noticed if it had fallen out of my hands? I smile at Ferdie. *"Merci."*

"Now you really do owe me a dance. My friends and I are going clubbing on Friday. Even mothers are allowed to have fun, *non?*"

I give him a look that says *when monkeys turn blue.* We laugh.

One time, I did go with him to a dance club. I told Pierre in advance it was a work event and asked if he would watch the girls. The disco was crowded with men and women my age and younger, packed into this tiny rectangle of space. The floor was brightly lit from below in blinking red, white and blue lights. Ferdie got our drinks. He was a great dancer, and even though it was all new to me, I held my own. But after twenty minutes, he disappeared. I didn't know anyone else there, and I felt foolish standing on the dance floor, getting jostled by everyone, so I flattened myself against the wall. It was hot inside, the bodies of a hundred people exuding sweat, sex and Pernod. After waiting for half an hour, I'd almost made up my mind to leave, but then I heard my name being called.

"Radha! Meet Silvano." Ferdie had his arm around the waist of a slim man with olive skin and very white teeth, wearing tight white flared pants and a fitted striped shirt. The shirt was so thin I could see his nipples.

I shook hands with the young man.

Ferdie looked at his new dance partner with fondness. "I thought he'd be here. Last week, he skipped out on me, didn't you, naughty boy?"

Silvano kissed Ferdie's cheek and drew him back onto the dance floor. I left them to it. It only occurred to me on the way home on the Métro that Ferdie had used me as an excuse to find Silvano. *Pas grave,* I reasoned, everyone deserves happiness. But I never accepted any more invitations from him.

With relief, I turn to the page in my notebook to review the results of my latest trials and get to work.

I'm a few minutes late to the Jeu de Paume. I skipped lunch to finish the refinements to the samples Delphine wanted, then left early to get to the girls' school and take the Métro home with them. (Once again, I couldn't spare the time to call around for a nanny.) Asha had wanted to stop at the Jardin du Luxembourg to watch the ducks, but I rushed the girls home. Shanti held on tight to my hand, as if she was afraid I'd fly away. I gave the girls some yogurt and waited anxiously for Mathilde to take over for me until Pierre got home. She didn't have an aide for Agnes tonight, so she brought her mother with her.

I walked as quickly as my feet would carry me the seven blocks from my house to the museum. (The French never run — Pierre has often commented on the horrific sight of Americans who jog along the Seine.) Parisians walk quickly and with purpose, and I've adopted that habit.

I envied the mopeds whizzing past me on Boulevard Saint-Germain. I turned right onto Rue de Bellechasse, strode past the former Beaux-Arts railway station, which rumor has it will be turned into a museum. I crossed the Seine, entered the Jardin des Tuileries and finally arrived at Jeu de Paume.

The last of the museum's visitors are exiting the building. A security guard at the entrance asks for my identity before letting me in. Delphine is waiting just inside.

I breathe out a raspy, *"Désolé, madame."* It's all I can do to not pant. I need water but don't dare ask for it.

Without speaking, Delphine turns on her heel. I follow. The museum is small. One long rectangular building. It smells of stone, iron, bronze and linseed oil. There's a faint top note of the last few bodies who were leaving as I entered. Built originally for court games of indoor tennis, the building is as handsome inside as it is outside. Three stories of glass and iron windows allow natural light to flood the interior. I remember coming here with my mother-in-law thirteen years ago, when I first arrived in Paris and Pierre asked her to take me to the museums. He thought it might help us bond. I read on the Jeu de Paume brochure that many of the paintings had originally belonged to Jewish families but had never been returned to their rightful owners. Florence was not pleased when I read this aloud to her, and our outings were abruptly curtailed.

Now, Delphine's heels clickity-clack on the stone floor as we stroll past paintings by Monet, Degas and Cézanne, finally stopping in front of a large painting of a nude reclining on a divan. The label next to the painting reads *Olympia, 1863. Oil on canvas. Edouard Manet.* I remember it from my ill-fated outing with Florence years ago.

Delphine says, "We're here in service of a new fragrance project. I'll explain after you tell me what you see."

"In the painting?"

"Yes. What does it tell you?"

I have no idea what she's expecting me to say, but I don't want to get it wrong. I glance wildly from one corner of the painting to the other. What am I supposed to notice? What does this have to do with fragrances? Or the House of Yves?

When I say nothing, Delphine says, "Take your time." I hear the echo of her heels as she walks away from me.

I step closer to the painting. The young woman depicted looks to be in her twenties, naked except for one hand covering her pelvic area — or did the artist place it there for modesty's sake? I recognize Olympia's beige silk mules; they're like the ones the ladies of Jaipur wear to match their silk and satin saris. The shoes are embroidered and lined with velvet, exactly the way the wealthy noblemen of India would have worn them centuries ago. And that embroidered shawl Olympia is lying on? I think Jiji has one just like it. The shimmer on the fabric and the tassels tells me that it's made of satin. But Olympia doesn't look Indian. I look at the date of the painting again: 1863. Perhaps a French, Dutch, Portuguese or British trader brought the shawl back from his travels and gave it to her. Or was it a studio prop the painter — Manet — used often? To the right of Olympia is a Black maidservant offering a large bouquet to her mistress. A present from an admirer? It's hard to identify the flowers because the brushwork is Impressionist, deliberately vague. I identify a dahlia, peonies and perhaps violets? And is that an orchid?

I look around the museum for Delphine, still unsure what we're doing here. My boss is standing in front of a Monet painting of water lilies, talking softly with the museum guard who stayed behind to lock up after us. She puts a hand on his arm. She's smiling! What would Delphine have to say to a museum guard? Just then, she glances at me, and I turn quickly back to Olympia, contrite, reminding myself of my task.

The model gazes coolly at me, appraising me as I appraise her. She's attractive but not beautiful. Her auburn hair is modestly pinned to the back of her head and adorned with a . . . hibiscus? Her earrings are simple drops as is the thin velvet choker around her neck. The gold bracelet with an onyx charm is by far more elaborate. She wears no makeup. The woman in the painting asks nothing of me. She is neither embarrassed about her nakedness nor is she resentful of my clothed status.

Am I looking at a wife whose lover has just left her bed, someone she's not sorry to see go? Or a woman used to entertaining men? If it's the latter, why isn't she flaunting her talent for passion, captivating us with her sexual prowess? Olympia's gaze seems to say, *I know who I am. It matters not what you think.* I'm reminded of a French expression — *Ça m'est égal* — and I think that's what Olympia is saying. I wonder if she was the painter's lover. If so, why is her gaze so sexless?

Who are you, Olympia? Why are you in this painting? If she were real, I feel Olympia would answer all my questions without reserve, frankly and completely. Or would she answer my questions with riddles? If I were to ask, *Did the artist place your hand there or did you decide to cover yourself?* she might answer, *What do* you *think?* The whole demeanor of this woman screams a maddening indifference. I want her to tell me something — anything — about her, to give me a sign.

"Captivating, isn't she?"

My body jerks at the interruption. I've been so absorbed trying to bring Olympia to life that I've forgotten where I am. Delphine stands beside me in her beautiful cashmere jacket with a rolled collar and matching skirt, a two-strand pearl necklace at her throat, her arms crossed in front of her. She wears the scent of her cigarettes and her personal mimosa and lime fragrance like a cloak (she's never shared her private formula with anyone).

Olympia's gaze draws me back. That's when I notice the sadness in her eyes.

"She's misunderstood," I say. I don't know what makes me say that, but I'm convinced it's true. If Jiji were with me, we'd talk about the herbal remedies my sister might apply to lift Olympia's melancholy. Candied lemons? A sweet made of milk and laced with cardamom and clove? Perhaps a henna application on her tiny hands and feet that would cause her to curl her lips in a private smile?

I sigh. "She would inspire an incredible *parfum.*"

When Delphine turns to me, it's with one of her rare impish grins, the ones she reserves for things she considers truly delightful.

She takes my arm. "I was hoping you'd say that."

As we emerge from the Jeu de Paume, Delphine explains that she's taken on a new client, one who wishes to remain in the shadows for now, but who wants the House of Yves to create a fragrance that captures the essence of Olympia. The client empathizes with Olympia, finds her unforgettable.

Ever since I first laid eyes on the painting, scents have been whirling around in my mind. Dark base notes. Pungent middle notes. But also bright top notes. After all, her body is the only object that glows in the otherwise dark painting. And what about the bouquet of flowers? Does it reveal narcissism in her personality or is it merely a ruse, an artist's whimsy, meant to confuse the viewer?

Even as we sit down to tea at Ladurée on the Rue Royale (Delphine doesn't drink coffee, only tea), and she lights up her Gitane, textures and colors are flitting through my vision, much as they used to when I made Jiji's henna paste or Munchi-*ji*'s paints. My fingers are fidgety. I can hardly wait to get back to the lab and explore all the scent possibilities that are dancing around my brain. I force myself to pay attention to what Delphine is saying.

"I think it's time for you to take the lead on a project. Michel can help extend the formulas you create into colognes and *eau fraiche*." She taps her cigarette in her teacup, not seeing an ashtray on the table. "*Ça va?* Radha?"

I blink my eyes rapidly. Did she just say I would be the lead assistant on Olympia? All those long hours and late evenings and missed dinners at home, all those hours spent memorizing scents and mixing and measuring someone else's formulas — it was all worth it! She thinks I'm capable of creating my own formulas now instead of just mixing hers! I remember Antoine telling me that I might become a perfumer in less time than Delphine had. Wait till I tell Pierre! Perhaps we'll laugh at all the arguments about my work like the one we had last night. Will he finally recognize that my work could be as valuable as his? How soon after this could I wear the mantle of master perfumer, like Delphine? I'm getting so far ahead of myself! *Hai Bhagwan,* I'm only a lab assistant. But wait: How will Michel react to the news? Hasn't he been waiting to become an apprentice perfumer? He's not going to want to work under me —

Delphine is snapping her fingers. "Radha!"

I jerk back in my seat, as if she's a hypnotist who has just brought me back from a trance.

"I hope you're not going to do this every time you're handed a large project." The corner of her mouth lifts in a smile. She reaches in her clutch for her lipstick and signals to the waitress. "The check, *s'il vous plaît.*"

It's been twelve years since Mathilde's grandfather first told me about Delphine Silberman and her renowned reputation as a master perfumer. Antoine's boutique had long been contracted by the House of Yves to sell their fragrances. Whenever Delphine stopped by the *parfumerie,* they would leave for lunch and, I assume, a gossip session about the industry and how well the House of Yves's fragrances were selling against the competition.

Then one day, she brought an elegant woman with her and asked Antoine if I might help her.

I stepped forward and addressed the younger woman. "*Bien sûr, madame,* do you prefer fragrance in the daytime, in the evening or only for special occasions?" Antoine had been surprised that I always asked this question of customers before asking which scents they favored. I told him that people may ask for a popular scent, but it may not be the appropriate fragrance for them. By finding out whether a client enjoyed wearing it for pleasure (all day), for seduction (evenings only) or because it was expected of them (special occasions), I could move on to questions about scents they preferred and then recommend a few (three at the most) that they might want to try.

Delphine's friend appeared to be in her midthirties. Her brown hair was pulled back tightly in a sleek ponytail. Her skin was the same color as Asha's. I couldn't see her eyes because she wore dark Chanel sunglasses. It was summertime, and she was in a short, sleeveless linen dress that hugged her lithe frame. The muscles of her arms and calves were defined, as if she regularly played tennis or squash, or perhaps she swam. She held herself erect, her shoulder blades meeting across her back.

She laughed lightly. "I don't wear scent

except in the evenings. We do a lot of entertaining." She spoke beautiful French, but I could tell it wasn't her native tongue. The accent sounded similar to mine. She could be Indian.

"You wear it to bed?"

She seemed surprised. "Yes, of course."

I smiled. I suspected from the moment this woman walked in that she kept herself fit for her husband, who might have a wandering eye. She wore perfume in the evening to remind him she was there. She was looking for a scent that encouraged romance. But nothing overpowering. Her skin was clear, her style minimal and her heels sensible.

I said to her, "Describe your mother's scent."

For me, scent had always triggered memory, and my earliest memories were of Maa's scent. Any woman who left the scent of lime in her wake always reminded me of Maa; she loved *nimbu pani* and plucked limes off every tree in her path. I conditioned my hair with coconut oil every week (I do the same to Shanti's and Asha's hair) because it reminded me how good it felt as a little girl to have my mother close, her fingers gently massaging my scalp. Of course, all that was before my mother took to wearing bitterness and regret as her daily fragrances.

At my question, Delphine's friend removed her sunglasses. Heavy kohl lined her brown eyes, which took on a faraway look. She looked up and to her left; she was remembering. I stayed quiet. "My mother chewed parsley after meals. She loved to bathe in water scented with orange blossoms." A pause. "I remember her standing by the stove boiling milk. You know that smell? It's like comfort. Like your body is warm all over. She would be making rice pudding, and she would pour a little hot milk in a glass and add sugar to it. Before giving it to me, she would blow on the glass to cool down the milk." Her smile was pure joy. "Almonds. I remember my mother always smelling of almonds."

I wondered whether she might be Lebanese or possibly Turkish. Or was she Afghani? The scents she favored were not so different from my India. But her people might use honey in their desserts, eat more meat and drink coffee instead of tea. What I'd picked up from working with Antoine, whose parents came from Morocco, is that much of the preference for scent was in the wearer's heritage, as much a part of them as the color of their skin.

After about forty-five minutes, Delphine's friend walked away with a purchase she was pleased with: essences of bergamot, carnation, lavender, orris root, musk, amber and cedar trailing behind her. It was one of Delphine's creations, but that wasn't why I'd recommended it. Before walking out the door with her, Delphine turned and gave me the first of her dazzling smiles.

A week later, I received an invitation to lunch with Delphine. When I showed it to Antoine, he said, "*Bien sûr.* You will go." Two weeks later, I was working at the House of Yves as Delphine's third lab assistant. A month after that, Antoine told me he was dying.

After Delphine leaves Ladurée, I buy a box of raspberry (Shanti's favorite), lemon (Asha's favorite) and vanilla (Pierre's favorite) macarons to celebrate my first solo fragrance assignment. I remember when Pierre received his first big promotion, we splurged on a bottle of Veuve Clicquot, but I don't have time to stop elsewhere today. It's almost seven o'clock and I'm late starting dinner as it is.

When I unlock the door, peals of laughter and the scent of turmeric, garlic, cumin and onions greet me. From the foyer, I can see that the dining table is crowded with people.

"Maman!" Asha screams with delight and runs to me, hugging me tightly around the hips, practically knocking the Ladurée box out of my hand.

Then Mathilde rushes down the foyer with her arms wide to envelop me in an embrace, kissing me on both cheeks. *"Ma petite puce!"* She helps me off with my coat and grabs the box out of my hands. "Macarons! *Genial!*"

She takes my arm and shepherds me down the hall to the dining table. "We're celebrating! You said it was your night to cook Indian, so I went to La Passage Brady and asked the Pondicherry to cook everyone's favorites." In my ear, she whispers, "I may have to sleep with Monsieur Ponnoussamy one of these days for all the favors he has done me!" She laughs gaily.

Cher Mathilde! She remembered it was my turn to cook and she's saved me the trouble! But how did she find out about my new project?

I nod eagerly. "Yes, Manet's painting —" I start to tell her about the Olympia project, but as we arrive at the dining room table, Shanti scrambles out of her chair to kiss my cheeks. Pierre is at the head of the table, his usual place, pouring more wine into his mother's glass. He gets up to kiss my cheeks and hand me my glass of wine. Florence busies herself pouring mineral water for everyone from the bottle. Mathilde's mother, Agnes, is asking Pierre for wine, but he knows not to pour any for her. I kiss Agnes's cheeks, and she gives me a vague smile as if to say, *Do we know each other?*

Mathilde says, "Go on, Pierre! Radha doesn't know yet." She grins at me.

I'd assumed we were celebrating *my* news. Pierre has news, too? "*Chérie,* what is it?" I ask my husband.

The wrinkles around his eyes are tight even as his lips are curved into a smile. "A promotion. I'll be in charge of fifteen people instead of six. Looks as if I'm cut out to be management, after all."

I know Pierre's dream has always been to design his own buildings instead of managing projects for a large firm, as he has been doing for the past nine years. A promotion will invariably mean more money, but will it make Pierre happier? His eyes tell me no, it will not. Have I pushed him into accepting this position because of my insistence on working? He's trying to tell me there will never be any need for me to earn my own income. *Oh, if only I were a master perfumer already!* I could make twice what Pierre

103

earns and take that burden off his shoulders. I want to help him establish his own architectural firm. I'd love to see him happier doing what he loves. But we can't have that discussion with everyone around us, so I lift my glass, sip and ask him to tell us what he'll be doing in his new job.

He shrugs. "More of the same." He doesn't want to talk about it. "Now, shall we eat what Mademoiselle Mathilde brought for us?"

Mathilde removes the lids from each of the steaming stainless steel bowls Jiji sent us from India as a wedding present. She must have transferred food from the restaurant's dishes to mine. She announces each dish as if she made it herself: *baingan burta,* juicy *rogan josh, biryani* with cashews and raisins, creamy chicken *korma, saag paneer, puri* and *aloo parantha.* I look at Mathilde, gorgeous Mathilde, my oldest friend, who loves to honor everyone's successes. I'm overwhelmed with gratitude and tell her. She throws me a kiss.

I realize I'm still standing, my news about the Olympia project dying in my throat.

"Maman, ici," Asha orders, and pats the chair next to her. I think she's going to grow up to be the bossy one. Ever since she could walk, instead of carrying her Bella doll like

104

a baby, she has always lugged it around by the hair, like a caveman.

"Asha, that's my chair!" Shanti, whose ponytail Florence was straightening, slides out of her grandmother's reach to reclaim her seat. Florence is about to reprimand Shanti when I cross my arms across Shanti's chest to hug her from behind. I bend down to whisper in her ear, "Why don't you ask Mathilde if you can take her chair so you can sit on the other side of me?"

She looks anxiously at Mathilde, who says, "As you wish, *chérie*! Now I can sit next to Pierre and steal his *papadum.*"

"Only if I can steal your *samosa,* you *voleuse!*" Pierre teases as he starts passing around the dishes.

I take my place between the girls and spoon creamy spinach and *paneer* on their plates.

"Now that we are all seated, tell us about your tea with Delphine," Mathilde says.

I would have preferred to tell Pierre alone. I steal a glance at him. He's not smiling. But I can hardly contain my excitement. I tell them about Manet's painting, my lead role on the new fragrance project.

Mathilde screams delightedly, then claps her hands. *"Félicitations! À ton santé aussi, ma puce!* Soon, you'll have your name on a bottle of *parfum!*" She raises her glass. Agnes flashes a tentative smile, not sure what we're celebrating. The girls clap their hands. Mathilde's enthusiasm is infectious, so they know the occasion is significant. Pierre has put a small amount of wine in their water, enough to give it a pink color, and they extend their glasses in the air.

I'm scared to look at Pierre again. When I do, his expression tells me I've just grown three heads. Pierre and his mother are the last to raise their glasses.

"To the woman who can do it all!" Mathilde says.

Florence looks at me. "Everything except hire a nanny."

I look guiltily at Pierre, who is refilling his glass, deliberately avoiding my eyes. His expression is grim.

Florence digs in deeper. "Mathilde wasn't aware you were looking for one."

My *saas* has called me out on my lie. I keep a fixed smile on my face. *"Non?"* I glance at Mathilde, who shrugs and rolls her eyes.

Pierre's mother shakes her head. "Pierre, you know you can always call me —"

Agnes says, "Mathilde has a good nanny." She looks at her daughter. "What is her name again, *chérie?*"

106

Mathilde pinks with embarrassment. "I haven't had a nanny since I was eight, *Maman.*"

"Oh?" Agnes frowns. "I must be thinking of my daughter's nanny." Mathilde is an only child. I throw a sympathetic glance at Mathilde; her mother is getting more confused by the day.

Mathilde is determined to enjoy herself. She raises her glass again and urges the girls to do the same. "To nannies!"

The girls giggle. The adults chuckle. It's difficult for me to swallow my food. A promotion for Pierre means more business trips. He'll be home less than he is now. Where does that leave me? I look at Florence, who is discussing the way she makes crepes with Agnes. I listen to the girls tell me about the advent calendar Florence is going to give them this year.

That night, after Mathilde, Agnes and Florence leave and I put the girls to bed, I slip into bed and turn to Pierre to talk to him about his career and mine and where we want to go, but he's already snoring. During dinner, I noticed he opened two bottles of wine. He and Mathilde drank most of the second. Mathilde can hold her liquor; Pierre can't.

I'm coming to terms with what I've been

hoping wasn't true: my marriage has boundaries, my husband isn't happy and my moment of triumph isn't shared.

The citrus oil used in fragrances comes from the mist that stings our eyes when we peel the skin of the fruit, not from the juice of the fruit.

Paris
November 1974

"If only she could talk," a voice behind me says.

I turn away from Manet's *Olympia* to see a *gardien de musée* of the Jeu de Paume limping toward me.

"She was a painter, too, you know," the guard says with a smile.

For several weeks, I've been alternating my work time between the lab, the *bibliothèque* and the *musée.* I want to know as much as I can about Manet the painter and his muse, both of whom fascinate me more and more as the days go by. I arrive at the museum as early as possible before tourists flock to the galleries. Today, I'm standing directly in front of Olympia, holding one hand up to cover the right half of her face. I'd done the same with the left half of her face just a few minutes ago. In Hinduism, the left and right sides of the body carry different meanings. The left is the feminine, the right the masculine. The left is temporal and earthly, the right pure and sacred.

I hadn't realized the guard had been watching me. *"Bonjour."* I glance at his badge. Isn't he the same museum guard Delphine was talking to when she brought me here to look at Olympia three weeks ago?

He sees me looking and does a little bow. "Gérard. Not many people come to look at the same painting as often as you have, *madame.*" He's shorter than I am, perhaps just a little over five feet tall, and slight. He has a neat, close-cropped beard and wiry gray hair. His shoes are polished to a high shine. His eyes twinkle with pleasure.

I smile. "You've been watching me?"

"I'm watching her — Victorine Meurent." Gérard nods at Olympia. "A hundred years ago, she was a favorite model of many Impressionist painters. She did it for food and art supplies."

"And she was a prostitute?" I'm merely

110

parroting what I've researched.

He makes a face. "*Pah!* That's the *menace* they spread about her. Don't believe it." He considers me. "I'm a painter, too. The lengths we'll go to pay for that next tube of indigo or a fresh piece of canvas to brush it on!" His eyes twinkle again. "I've been known to do some things I'm not too proud of." Just then I notice paint around the cuticles of his left hand. When he sees me looking, he puts his hands behind his back. "Most likely the other Impressionist painters were jealous. Manet most certainly was. She was exhibiting at the Paris Salon years before his work was admitted."

Goose bumps travel down my arm, and I turn to regard Olympia again. *Did Manet fail to see you? Was he jealous of your talent?* I hide the right side of her face with my hand. Then the left. I see it now. The left recognized what Manet did to her. The right *felt* what he'd done. Betrayal. There was sadness there. Resignation.

Gérard said, "A poor woman doing what those other artists had the money and means to do. *They* didn't have to model. She did."

"Manet came from wealth?"

The museum guard nods. "As did Monet. Cézanne. Pissarro. Sisley."

111

I hold out my hand for the guard to shake. "I'm Radha."

He offers me his left hand. That's when I notice that the right hand is a claw, and that his right arm hangs at an awkward angle.

"You know my *chef,* Delphine Silberman? I saw you talking to her before."

Gérard smiles and nods. "Old friends. We attend the same synagogue. Madame Delphine patronizes many museums, including this one."

Now I seek out Gérard every time I come to the Jeu de Paume. He tells me about Victorine's last twenty years, when she lived with a female companion. She survived to her eighties, which would have been unusual for her time. I can't get enough. It's as if I want to crawl inside the painting, lie on the divan as if I were posing for that painting, feeling Victorine's devastation, her thwarted career, the jealousies damning her talent.

At my inaugural lunch with Delphine five years ago, my boss said, "When you smell your lover, you're consuming their essence. You want to absorb some part of them. That's what I create. Fragrances that make people want to consume some part of the wearer." Then she'd lifted her teacup and waved it at me. "You're going to help me do that." She was sure I would say yes to her job offer. So was Antoine.

When I got back to work that afternoon, Antoine took one look at me and said, "Say yes."

My eyes had filled. Did he want me to leave? Wouldn't he miss the girls? "But — I don't want to go. I love it here."

Antoine walked toward me and put his hands on my shoulders. "Most people work for ten years to become a master perfumer. Delphine did it in seven. Learn from her, and I think you can do it in five."

"But I've never even said I wanted to be a perfumer."

"You didn't have to." The wrinkles around his eyes settled in for a smile that made me want to hug him. I did.

My arm aches from reaching for the bottles of magnolia, bitter orange, cinnamon, pear, vanilla, ambergris and violet on my perfume organ. My hand is cramped from writing out hundreds of potential formulas over the last month. When I first started working at the House of Yves, Delphine impressed upon me that as a perfumer begins creating a new fragrance, she should forget what she personally favors and start afresh. Even the best fragrance designers can get attached to certain palettes and limit themselves without realizing it. I haven't yet had the opportunity to develop preferences. But I've been experimenting, creating scents on my own, for a while now. In my second year at the House of Yves, I came in very early in the morning to test a formula I'd created. I was using a pipette to measure an essential oil when, suddenly, my nose was assaulted with the smoke from a Gitane. I froze, my hands in midair, not sure whether Delphine could tell that I was mixing a personal formula, not one she'd specified.

I dared not look at her, but I felt her eyes scanning the scent bottles on my table. She stood still. I imagined she had a sixth sense; she could catch out lab assistants who were creating their own fragrances. I held my breath. After a long minute, she said, "Tell Michel I need to see him when he comes in." I thought I detected a smile in her voice. Then I heard the tap of her heels and the opening and closing of the lab door. When the cigarette smell receded, I exhaled. She never mentioned the incident; neither did I. That day, I finished creating my very first scent, the one I put in a vial and hung from a gold chain. The one I carry in my pocket everywhere.

The creative brief I've been given is vague: *Develop a fragrance for Olympia.* I start with a wide palette. I know Olympia needs milky, luminescent notes; her skin practically glows in the painting. What about her raw nakedness? Does it call for animalic notes like Guerlain's Jicky — musk and ambergris? And what about heavy molecules like frankincense and myrrh? I ignore the green notes like eucalyptus, sage and cedar; Olympia is an indoor creation, not an outdoor one. Instead, looking at her embroidered shawl and satin mules, I reach for the scents of my India: cardamom, cinnamon, ginger, patchouli. Wouldn't Maa be surprised to learn that patchouli leaves, which she inserted in the folds of her best sari to keep insects from eating the silk, had come to be such a favored ingredient in French perfumes?

Thinking of Maa makes me wonder: Would she and Pitaji be pleased with how far Jiji and I have come from our dusty village? Would Pitaji have stopped drinking if he could have seen what the future held for his daughters? My breath has become shallow. My father used to say: *One man's house burns so that another may warm himself.* Perhaps Pitaji's quest for India's independence was not in vain, not if it resulted in rosier futures for my sister, my daughters and me.

I realize I've been sitting perfectly still for several minutes, with my hand over my heart. I look around the lab. Michel is busy at his station, compounding Delphine's formulas. Over my right shoulder, through the interior glass wall, I see Ferdie talking on the phone at Celeste's desk. Must be a personal call. Ferdie is frowning and gesturing wildly with one arm. A boyfriend canceling their date for tonight? I can't hear what he's saying, but I know Celeste can. Her fingers are busy at her typewriter, but she looks concerned. She keeps stealing glances at Ferdie, whose face is turning pink.

I stretch my neck. I'm tempted to visit Gérard at the museum again — I find such peace in his presence — but I stop myself. I need to concentrate. Delphine wants to see some progress and she's coming to the lab later to check my work. There's one way I've found to get myself back on track: I recite the scents on my perfume organ in alphabetical order without looking at them. When I get to clove oil, I smile, thinking of Jiji. It's the calming oil she massaged on her ladies' hands after the henna paste had dried and flaked off. Only a drop or two was needed to pacify an anxious client just as only a single clove in my morning chai is needed to wake me up gently. My sister also had me add fragrant ingredients to the treats we made for each patron — lemon zest in the *pakoras* or coconut in the *burfi* — ingredients that incited desire or calmed frayed nerves or bolstered inner strength. Because of Jiji, I can no longer think of a scent without also thinking of the effect it will have on the wearer.

Alors . . . what if I started with fresh top notes of orange blossom, lavender and bergamot? Those will be first scents the wearer will discern, but top notes only last for the first quarter hour. For the heart notes, I can see Olympia in tuberose, pink pepper and cardamom, those heady scents that entice and draw us into the wearer's orbit. Sandalwood, a large, heavy molecule, is the base note of almost every perfume, as it will be in Olympia's fragrance. It will last throughout the day and night. Could the model's glowing nakedness be asking for vanilla, her indifference for amber and her sex for patchouli? What about ginger, for her unabashed stare? But even as I imagine these combinations in my mind, I know one major ingredient is missing. Liquid. Her fluid, adaptable nature. Isn't that what's made Victorine so easy to betray? Her forgiving femininity? Her naked vulnerability? Where is that wetness? Which scent would I have to add to bring that to the fore?

"Let's see what you have for us, Radha."

I look up. Delphine is at my elbow. Michel is standing just behind her. Ferdie hangs up Celeste's phone and walks back into the lab to join us; his face is still flushed. Today, my work is the only one being critiqued. I quickly pull together the blotters of the three variations with the most potential so far. Everyone takes a sniff, waving the blotters under their nose. I watch their reactions greedily.

Michel picks up the brief on my table and scans it. He sniffs the papers again. His blue eyes meet mine with a subtle apology. His glasses glint in the fluorescent lights as he shakes his head once, ever so slightly, at Delphine, who has been waiting for his reaction. She turns to Ferdie, who has been watching Michel's reaction as if to take a cue from the most senior lab tech. Ferdie forces a smile on his face and nods his head at me, as if to say *good effort.* But he seems distracted, probably still smarting from his phone call.

Delphine says, "Keep trying," before turning to leave the lab.

I try not to show how defeated I feel. My first fragrance assignment, and I'm failing already. Shouldn't I at least have produced one trial that Delphine might have considered promising? I wonder if Delphine regrets having assigned the project to me. Would Michel have done a better job of it with his chemistry background?

I want to keep working, but I'm angry with myself for being no closer to discovering Olympia's essence. And my nose is tired. Antoine told me that master perfumers never stop training their noses; they're constantly learning new scents. That's always easier to do in the first part of the day than the last; by day's end, my mind is too full of fragrance. I hang up my lab coat, stuff my notebook in my bag and say goodbye to Michel and Ferdie. Without a nanny, I have to leave work earlier than I'd like to pick the girls up from school.

As I'd guessed, Pierre will be traveling more in his new position. I've tried to ask him how he feels about the increase in management responsibilities, which will cut into his design time, but he's always on his way out the door or too tired to discuss it. Now, he's in Nice for two days on a business trip. He has hardly spoken to me since I made the announcement about the Olympia project. We've been focusing on the girls, and he's been busy preparing for his presentation. I'm embarrassed to admit I'm relieved every time he puts me off because I'm afraid it will only lead to another argument.

The girls and I make dinner together. I show them how I let the cumin seeds sizzle in the oil before adding the onions. When the onions are nicely browned, I ask Shanti to add two teaspoons each of turmeric and cumin powder and salt, one teaspoon each of *garam masala* and black pepper, the four cloves of garlic I minced, one cup of fresh cilantro and a tiny bit of red chili powder. Asha can eat spicy food but Shanti can't. Asha stirs the spice-onion mixture. I strain the water from the plump garbanzo beans, which I left soaking overnight, before adding the beans to the pan. I ask Shanti to stir the curry, turn down the flame and cover the pan. When the rice is cooked, I ladle the steaming curried *chole* on top, set out the hot mango pickle for Asha and me, slices of a freshly cut tomato, and we're ready to eat. Shanti tells us about the *Tintin* adventure she will be acting out with her fellow students in class tomorrow. She's dying to act it all out for us, but I make her finish her dinner first. She's a lively actor, and Asha and I laugh at her theatrical gestures, clapping wildly when she finishes.

I clean up the kitchen and get the girls

settled in bed. I'm feeling nostalgic for home, so I read to them from *Tales of Krishna,* wishing Jiji were here. I haven't spoken to her since she called me in early September. And it's been months since I wrote her a letter; I never seem to have the time. My sister is a fastidious writer; I'm not. But I love reading her anecdotes about Malik and Nimmi and their children, wishing Shanti and Asha could grow up with them. Although they're not related by blood, I refer to Rekha and Chullu as my daughters' cousins. Malik has been like a brother to me ever since I first met him (was it almost twenty years ago?), so I think of his children as my nephew and niece.

After turning out the light in Shanti and Asha's room, I make myself a cup of chai and remove my notebook from my satchel. With a sigh, I read the formulas I created today. Jiji would know exactly what to suggest for the ingredient I'm sure is missing but can't put my finger on. I look at the clock. Long-distance calls are exorbitant. But it's almost midnight, when the rates are lowest. It must be four-thirty in the morning in India. I know everyone in the house will be asleep except Jiji, who often wakes up early to read.

She picks up on the first ring. "Radha?"

I smile. She always seems to know when I'm going to call. "*Namaste*, Jiji."

"*Theek hai?* Shanti and Asha are healthy? Pierre is fine?"

"I'm fine," I say. "Everyone is." I don't want to talk with Jiji about the tension between Pierre and me. "I have news. I've been given my first fragrance assignment!"

"*Shabash*, Radha!" Her enthusiastic reaction rivals Mathilde's. The pride I feel is like a warm blanket. Having run a successful business as a henna artist on her own, Lakshmi understands the satisfaction a woman feels when she is recognized and appreciated for skills she has taken care to develop. I wish my husband could have reacted the same way. But I set aside my disappointment and focus on what I want to ask her about the missing ingredient in my formula.

Once I explain the Olympia project, she can barely contain her excitement. "The courtesans of Agra would know exactly how to help you!"

"Courtesans? As in . . . dancing girls?"

"*Arré!* They're far more refined than that. They know how to create whatever mood you desire with scents. They've spent a lifetime perfecting that art. But they won't talk to you on the phone. You'll have to go to them."

"In Agra?"

"*Hahn.* When can you come?"

I let out a sigh. "Jiji, I'm just a lab assistant who's been awarded my first fragrance project. It would be too much to ask Delphine to spend that kind of money on me."

I hear the smile in her voice — and a dare. "Pitaji used to say, *He who does not climb will not fall either.*"

I have never been able to resist a challenge. I'm not sure how Pierre will react, but it is worth a conversation. Besides, putting a little distance between myself and Pierre's disapproval would be a welcome relief. And maybe my worries about possible sabotage at the lab mean I'm putting too much work pressure on myself. Getting away can only help.

Delphine is at her perfume organ when I approach her about my idea the next day. It takes her a moment to focus on my request. "You want to go to India?"

"*Oui.*" I push my hands in my pockets so I'm not tempted to wipe them against my lab coat. I try for a voice that sounds more confident than I feel. "I'll be able to source ingredients that I don't think exist here. There are so many scents I remember from

123

India that aren't used in French perfumery. And the Oriental fragrances that have become popular in the last few years have only scratched the surface of what I believe we can create. I'm convinced Olympia needs something wet, fluid. But I can't find it in our scent library."

Delphine's mouth tries to hide a smile. Have I said something amusing?

"Do you know why I hired you, Radha?"

I blink. "Because Antoine recommended me?"

"Because you've been living with scents longer than I have. Remember I asked you what your earliest memories were? I still remember what you said. The smell of the mud hut where your mother gave birth, her wheaty breath, the sari she had lain in for a week and the incense the midwife lit. Radha, you were born of fragrance. It's in your blood, bones, hair, breath. You eat fragrance in your food. You wear it from the inside out. You understand it in a way Michel, with his chemistry degree, and Ferdinand with his family's wealth, never will. You are working on Olympia because you're the only person who can create a wholly unique scent for her." She turns around to her organ to reach for a bottle and resumes her work.

I'm too stunned by her words to move. Did she just say I will make a better perfumer than Michel or Ferdie, who have been here longer? Did she just approve my trip to India? Will the House of Yves pay for it or is she expecting me to? *Hai Ram,* if I'm to pay for it, will Pierre agree to let me go?

As if she has heard my questions, she says, focused on the pipette in her hand and the small bottle of alcohol in front of her, "*Bon voyage.* Celeste will take care of the details."

I nod — even though she's not looking my way — and walk out of her office.

I'm getting ready to go home when Celeste drops an envelope on my table. I look up at her. Her cheeks are pink and she's bursting, as if she can barely contain a secret. She leans closer to my ear and whispers, "Your ticket to India."

Michel looks up sharply from his station. Did he overhear the words or just the excitement in Celeste's voice?

Celeste shoots me a radiant smile. "You leave next Tuesday and come back on Friday. Take pictures!"

Tuesday is four days from now.

Pierre's train from Nice arrived in the afternoon. He called me at work and offered to bring the girls home from school so I wouldn't have to. That gives me time to walk home instead of taking the Métro after work. I need to figure out how to approach Pierre and break the news to him.

How will I tell my husband that I'm leaving for India on a research trip in just four days? Who will take care of the girls? Oh, why haven't I hired another nanny already? Because I haven't had time to conduct a proper search! I can't entrust the care of my daughters to just anybody. Maybe I can still interview a few candidates this weekend and find someone appropriate.

What if I asked Mathilde to take them? *For almost a week?* How can I even think of doing that? Mathilde has her hands full these days with her mother. She used to be able to jet off on a whim to London or Cyprus or wherever her most recent flame took her, but she's been relatively homebound since her mother has required more and more of her time.

I'll have to call Florence to help. She'll probably want the girls to stay with her in Neuilly. Is that so very bad? Florence may have issues with me, but she does love the girls. She always makes herself available on short notice — even if she lets me know she had to cancel a board meeting for one of the arts organizations she supports. For the girls' birthdays, she always plans a special trip. The Palace of Versailles for Shanti's seventh birthday. Climbing the stairs of the Notre-Dame Cathedral to show a five-year-old Asha what the gargoyles see from their perch. For each of their sixth birthdays, Florence took them to the Musée Jacquemart-André, followed by *chocolat chaud* at the café in the mansion's former dining room.

But every time I leave the girls in my mother-in-law's care, I worry that she will take over my children and transform them, consume them and turn them into little French Catholic girls I won't recognize. A voice in my head blares a warning: *You've already lost one child! You can't let that happen again!* Florence has the money and the means and the time to spend on Shanti and Asha. But what if she turns them against me, against India? I can't let that happen! I want my girls to know their heritage. I want them to know India. I want to take them to Shimla again to play with their cousins and get to know their aunt and uncle better. Florence would never take them to India. She thinks of my birth country as hot and dirty, disgusting even. How can I entrust my girls to such a person?

127

The walk home takes me more than an hour, but still I hover at the entrance of our apartment building, just out of view of the concierge. Even though I'm wearing a warm coat on this chilly November night, my underarms are soaked and my forehead feels hot. My heart feels like it's bursting out of my rib cage. I take deep breaths and try to slow down my pulse. I'm not ready yet. I double back to the corner of Rue de Sèvres and Boulevard Saint-Germain. My mind races down another track. This will be the first business trip I've ever taken. When Pierre leaves on a trip for his work, as he did this week, I'm expected to understand and adapt. He makes an announcement, not a request for understanding or permission. While he's away, I am to make sure the girls eat a healthy dinner, do their homework, get fresh air and exercise and tell me about their day. Of course, it's what I want them to do, too. Nowadays, they're even old enough to do many things for themselves; just last week, Shanti collected her clothes and asked me how the washing machine works. If only Pierre could do the same! But how could I ask him to take on tasks that he thinks are beneath a husband? I think about the working women I know: Lakshmi, Delphine, Celeste. How do they handle their job and the work at home? With a start, I realize none of them have children! So whom do I turn to?

Slowly, I retrace my steps back to our building.

I think about Pierre's grandmother — Florence's mother — the woman I never met but would love to have known. Her travels around the world are in evidence all over our apartment. The *berimbau* she picked up in Recife, Brazil, sits on the living room bookshelf; a photo of her in Kenya with her friend Beryl Markham, next to Markham's single-engine monoplane, hangs in the hallway; a Rajasthani miniature court painting — a gift from the Maharani of Udaipur — graces the foyer. Pierre told me it was her lively stories of India that inspired him to go work in Chandigarh. His black-and-white drawing of the Punjab and Haryana High Court in Chandigarh was so impressive that I had it framed; it hangs in the living room. Given his grandmother's wanderlust, maybe Pierre will be excited about the opportunity this trip to India will afford me. It would be wonderful if I could take the whole family with me, or at least the girls, but it's such short notice and a quick trip at that, with a lot for me to accomplish. Besides, Pierre's recent promotion makes it unlikely he can get away right now anyway.

I find myself standing in front of my apartment building again. I look up at the third floor. The lights are on. The girls will be doing their work for school and telling Pierre all about their day. They'll be ready for their dinner.

I take a breath and enter.

The apartment glows with soft light. Nina Simone sings "Ne me quitte pas" on the record player. The pleasing odor of chicken steeped in rosemary and *herbes de provence,* one of Pierre's specialties, makes my mouth water. At this hour, just before dinner, the girls will be in their room.

I hang up my coat in the foyer and take off my shoes. I pad in my stockinged feet to the kitchen and pause at the entrance. Pierre has his back to me. He's sautéing the chicken. The sizzling fat bubbles as he turns over a thigh. His love of cooking is one of the things I adored about him from the start. He's taught me how to make a French cheese soufflé, a Moroccan tagine and a Peruvian ceviche — recipes he picked up on travels with his *grand-mère.* I think about those cooking lessons in this very kitchen, Pierre pressed against my back, his arms reaching around my body as he mixed sauce in a bowl, stopping to nibble my ear, me laughing. I look at his slim back. He's wearing the sky blue cashmere sweater I bought him for his birthday. All at once, I feel such a rush of love for him. Why was I so filled with dread about talking to the man who swept me off my feet thirteen years ago?

Gently, I wrap my arms around his chest and kiss the area between his shoulder blades. He tenses — I've surprised him — but he quickly relaxes into the hug. We stand like this without moving for a minute until Pierre says, "I have to turn the chicken." But he cranes his neck so I can reach up and kiss him on the lips.

"I'll say hello to the girls," I tell him.

Shanti jumps up from the desk she shares with Asha. *"Maman, regardes!"* She holds up a drawing she has made for class. It's a replica in her nine-year-old's hand of the Rajasthani court painting that hangs in our foyer, the one belonging to Pierre's grandmother.

I kiss her on both cheeks and walk around the desk to kiss Asha as well. *"Genial, ma chou-chou!* What was the assignment?"

"We had to bring in something that was important to us." Shanti pulls her rubber band tighter over her ponytail.

That surprises me. "And why was that painting important to you?"

"Because —" she smacks her lips, a new habit she's picked up "— you explained to Asha and me about India."

My eyes well up. I hug Shanti so hard her feet lift off the ground. Sometimes, as a mother, I have no idea if what I teach the girls sinks in. I have an urge to tell them about my trip. "Come, I want to show you something."

I lead them to the standing globe in the living room. "Guess where *Maman* is going next week?" I turn the globe until India is in the center and I'm pointing to Agra.

Asha's amber eyes go huge. *"Inde?"*

I nod my head.

Shanti asks, "Are we going, too?"

"Not this time, *chérie.* This is for work."

Asha asks, "Will you bring us back an elephant?"

"That's silly!" Shanti says. "Whatever *Maman* brings back has to fit in a suitcase."

My younger daughter twirls the globe. "Could it be a very small elephant?"

Shanti rolls her eyes. I hide a smile. My big girl — only nine years old and she thinks she knows the world. I hug them close. There's so little there to hold on to, but their bodies are warm and soft and their hair smells like coconut oil. And they're mine.

Asha wiggles out of my arms. "What will you do there?"

"I'm going to find some amazing scents."

Asha pouts. "You don't have to go *that* far to find them. The boys at school are smelly. And the metal slide on the playground smells weird."

Shanti is thoughtful. "Asha's right, *Maman*. Chalk has a smell, too. Did you ever notice?" She looks at Asha. "Madame LaCroix smells good, though, doesn't she?"

Asha nods, "Like butterflies."

"Your *maman* smells good, too." It's Pierre. I hadn't heard him come into the room. He's standing right behind me. He places his hands on my hips and kisses my neck. All the nerves in my body come alive. He hasn't touched me like this in weeks. I want to reach behind and push his lips farther down my neck, across my shoulder, the front of my neck —

Still holding on to my hips, Pierre smiles at the girls. "Time to wash your hands for dinner."

The girls hurry to the bathroom, Asha trying to reach the sink before Shanti. Pierre turns me to face him so he can kiss me properly. His tongue is warm and wet. I taste the *herbes* and the white wine. He's hard. I feel the wetness between my legs.

"Is it my chicken or just that I am irresistible?" he asks.

"Oh, definitely the chicken," I murmur.

Shanti calls from the bathroom, "*Maman,* there's no more soap!"

I sigh. Pierre drops his arms. I leave to attend to my daughters.

The girls are in bed now. Pierre and I are in the living room, trying to keep our voices soft, a bottle of wine on the coffee table between us. A record revolves on the turntable — Dinah Washington singing "What a Difference a Day Makes." The pleasing odor of our dinner lingers in the air.

During dinner, Asha blurted out that she wanted to go to India with me so she could pet baby elephants. Pierre, who'd been about to take a sip of his wine, looked at me with an uncertain smile. "We're not going to India anytime soon."

"*We're* not. But *Maman* is," my younger daughter explained patiently. "She showed us on the globe. She's bringing back smells."

When my husband frowned at me, my heart sped up. I took my time chewing my chicken while I willed my heart to slow down. Shanti, who seemed to sense her father's disapproval, looked from one to the other of us, then pinched Asha on the forearm.

"It's only for four days. For . . . Olympia. Research for my new project." I'd been about to say *for Delphine*, which I knew would immediately incite his displeasure. "We can talk about it after dinner." I looked at the girls, avoiding Pierre's narrowed eyes, the way he set his fork on his plate, with finality. "I promise to bring back something for you both," I said to Shanti and Asha. "Something much smaller than an elephant. What do you think I should bring back for Papa?"

The girls spent the rest of dinner coming up with suggestions, giving me a little reprieve before my conversation with Pierre.

Now, as we sit with the coffee table and the wine between us, Pierre says, "It just comes as such a surprise."

We're alone. It's late. I'm tired. "A good surprise or a bad surprise?"

Pierre purses his lips. "A surprise that you would put your work before your family, the girls . . . and me, Radha." He sips his wine.

My head feels like it's on fire. "How can you say that, Pierre? I have been the major caretaker, housekeeper and chaperone for the majority of their lives. I take care of all their needs. I help them with their school-work when they need it. I help them under-stand what's important and what's not. Did you see the drawing Shanti made of Rajas-than? Did she tell you about anyone picking on her because she's darker than they are?"

I know by the confusion on his face that he's not aware of the drawing or the issue at school. "What about you?" I ask. "You're busy working and traveling for your new position. You just came back after a two-day work trip. Don't *you* put your job first?"

He rears his head, a look on his face of disbelief. "That's different!"

"How?" My voice is louder now and my hands are shaking. I take a breath. "How is it different?"

"*You're* the one who told me you wanted children. Remember? You wanted to be a mother."

"I did. I do. I *am* a mother. That hasn't changed."

He looks at me, incredulous. "How often in the last year have you picked them up from school? How often do you go into work on a weekend? You take on more work than Delphine gives you! You do Michel's and Ferdinand's work, too, when they're on vacation."

He's right. But what does that have to do with how well I mother my daughters? I rub my forehead and beg Bhagwan for patience because what I really want to do right now is scream. *This is all so unfair! Why is there one set of rules for Pierre and another set of rules for me? I need to calm down.*

"*Chérie,* I want to be as good at my job as you are at yours. You know that takes extra time, extra effort. I hire nannies to help when I'm overloaded. The girls are doing fine —"

"The girls are *not* doing fine." Pierre's whisper is loud enough to wake the girls. He points a finger at their closed bedroom door. "Shanti is lashing out at other children and getting rid of nannies as fast as you hire them. You don't seem to notice what's going on in your own family."

"She's going through something. We talked." I think back to the conversation with the girls about the color of our skin. Shanti wasn't being difficult, as Pierre and I had thought; she was merely being protective of me, of us as a family. We will always stand out because we're different from other French families.

I soften my tone. "It won't always be like this, Pierre. There will come a time when I won't have to work so hard to prove myself."

"That's not going to be the end of it. You'll spend more and more energy getting to the next level and the level after that. Like an *Américaine*!"

The French have always pitied the Americans for their long work hours and minimal vacations.

I grit my teeth. The anger that has been raging inside me threatens to boil over. "What would be wrong with that, Pierre? Aren't you moving up the ladder, too? If I start making more, we can take more family vacations abroad. The girls can go to colleges in another country if they want."

My husband glares at me. I've gone too far. It's as if I'm saying I don't trust him to provide for our family. But that's not what I mean. I close my eyes. I can feel myself losing the thread of the argument. Weren't we talking about my first-ever business trip? Why is that not a cause for celebration? Why do I have to defend the pride I feel in my work, in me, in my ability to also provide for my family?

Pierre jabs the coffee table with a finger. "I don't want them to go to another country or even to another city. I went to boarding schools when I was eight. I don't want that for my own children. I want a full-time mother for them — a normal life." He finishes off his wine and refills his glass. "I want you home more."

"What's the purpose of keeping me at home idle while they're at school?" Although I'm not shouting, my voice oozes contempt.

"You can work part-time."

"*Part-time?* What I do isn't a part-time job. It's a career! And I'm good at it. I'm lucky enough to have found something I'm passionate about and want to keep doing. And keep getting better at. It doesn't make me any less a mother or a wife." I know my anger isn't helping. My control on this conversation is slipping away from me, but I don't know how to wrest it back in my favor. "What is wrong with *you* sharing the responsibility when it's my turn to go on a business trip?"

"I do plenty to help out, Radha. I cook several times a week."

"And I work. And cook. And clean and do the laundry. I hire the nannies and supervise them. I make sure the girls do their homework. And get them signed up for school and other activities. I make sure the bills are paid on time and the concierge gets a Christmas bonus. And take the girls to the doctor. And plan what to do on the weekends."

Pierre throws up his hands. "You make it sound like a competition, Radha."

That's what it feels like, Pierre, I think, my head pounding. I want to tell him that women have moved on in other parts of the world. The best-selling perfume on the market right now is Charlie. It's American. It's about confident women on the go, wearing pantsuits, going to work in an office, carrying briefcases. And perhaps even pinching a man's *fesse* instead of the other way around. But if I bring up perfume or America, he'll roll his eyes.

This is the point in our discussions about my work where I usually stop. It's as if Pierre doesn't want to understand. He's not even trying. What good would it do to press my point? Instead, I stand up and collect my wineglass. "I'll call your mother and see if she can take them while I'm gone. It's only a few days and she's closer to their school anyway. I'm not leaving until Tuesday. I'll be home Friday night. She'll be delighted and you won't have to leave work early to pick them up."

After that, my next call will be to Lakshmi, to let her know I'm going to Agra, after all, as she had originally suggested. And to ask if she will come with me and introduce me to the courtesans and the secrets of the scents that keep their patrons coming back for more.

The girls have a half day of school on Saturdays, so I accompany them on the Métro and decide to work a few hours before school lets out. The House of Yves is only a twenty-minute walk from their school on Avenue Victor-Hugo. I've been neglecting the other formulas I need to compound for Delphine; creating Olympia's fragrance isn't my only responsibility. And I'd rather stay out of Pierre's way for a while. Last night, he came to bed long after I did. When I reached for him, he was on the farthest edge of his side of the bed. This morning, I found the empty wine bottle on the coffee table. I hadn't even finished my first glass.

The trees lining both sides of Avenue Victor-Hugo have lost most of their leaves, but it's still a pleasant walk past the cafés, shops and elegant Haussmann buildings. Despite the cold, Parisians are lining up for their fresh baguettes. The butcher is also doing a brisk business. Paris has more pigeons than I've ever seen in India, and they're milling about the sidewalks, looking for a stray morsel. An old woman in a plaid coat is wheeling her shopping cart while her terrier strolls patiently beside her. He pauses every time she stops to gaze at a shop window. She shakes her head when she sees a pair of shoes on display. Curious, I stop, too. The shoes are red patent leather platform boots with three-inch Lucite heels. Inside each heel is a live goldfish swimming in water. Picturing Ferdie on the dance floor in those shoes, I bark out a laugh. The woman turns to me, smiles and says, *"Exactement."* Still smiling, I wish her a good day and move on.

The lab is freezing when I arrive. The heat has been off since last night. The door to the lab is unlocked and through the glass wall I can see that the door to the refrigeration room is open and the lights are on. That's odd.

"Michel? Ferdie?"

Celeste pokes her head out the door.

"Celeste? What are you doing?"

Her nose and cheeks are pink from being in the refrigeration room where we keep raw materials that will spoil if they're exposed to higher temperatures. "Delphine told me the bottles are not in order. I just didn't have time to finish yesterday, and we have a big group coming in on Monday for the Rivanche project so I won't have time to do it then either. *Alors* . . ." She disappears in the room and just as quickly pops out.

"Why are *you* here on a Saturday?"

"Work I have to tidy up before I leave."

"Oh, Radha! We're all so excited you're going."

I raise an eyebrow. "Even Michel?"

"You know Michel! One never knows what he's thinking. Will you please bring back one of those beautiful Indian scarves?"

She's talking about one of those tie-dyed ones Jiji always told me to stay away from, just as she advised me to avoid saris with sewn-on mirrors. "Tacky," she'd say. "Stick to embroidery — by hand, not machine." But Celeste looks so happy just now and it might go a long way toward brightening her wardrobe.

"*Avec plaisir,* Celeste."

When the girls and I get back to the apartment, I finally reach Florence on the phone. She can barely contain her delight as she agrees to take the girls while I'm gone. Tomorrow, Sunday, I'll pack their school uniforms and clothes. Do their shoes need to be polished? Anything need ironing? I put clothes in the washer and hang up the damp ones on the line in the building's atrium. It's winter, so it will take longer for them to dry. Pierre will have to take them off the line while I'm gone. At the moment, he's at the open-air market with the girls, picking up vegetables for tonight's dinner.

The phone rings. It's Mathilde.

"*Maman* fell down a flight of stairs today."

"Oh, no!" I lean against the washing machine. "What happened?"

"Nothing is broken. My concierge found her at the bottom of the staircase. She was dazed but not hurt. She kept saying she had to go home. When she was told she lived in the building with me and that she *was* home, she got very angry at the concierge for *lying* to her. Oh, Radha, I don't know how much more of this I can take."

Usually full of verve and laughter, Mathilde sounds as if she's about to cry. I wish there was something I could do to ease her burden. Even when she's breaking up with a *mec* who showed potential, she's never this dispirited.

"Where is she now?" I ask.

"Sleeping. She sleeps a lot these days, but also wakes up abruptly at all hours and goes wandering."

"Can you get help for tonight? And go do something fun?" I ask.

"Can you join me? We could go see *Emmanuelle* — it just started showing yesterday."

"I wish I could, Mathilde, but I'm getting

144

the girls ready to stay with Florence for a few days during the week, and I have so much to do before I leave." I tell her about my work trip to India. I would invite Mathilde, but with her mother's dementia, it would be impossible for her to leave on such short notice.

"Of course." Mathilde is disappointed. And, I sense, a little annoyed. I hear her lighting a cigarette. I wait. "Everything was so much simpler when we were girls, wasn't it?" she says.

In my mind, I exhale the long stream of smoke along with her, recalling our nights in the Nun's graveyard.

"Remember that time we met Agnes in Goa, Radha?"

I can picture Mathilde twirling and un-twirling the coiled telephone cord, a sly smile on her face at the memory.

"She was with that crazy guru who drank his own urine, so she tried to get us to do it, too. We refused and hid until she stopped pestering us."

I chuckle. When Mathilde's mother latched on to something, she held on tight. "All those gurus. What was Agnes searching for, do you think?"

"Who knows?" Mathilde sounds exasperated. "All I know is that I'm stuck mothering a woman who couldn't be bothered to mother me. Ever since I can remember, she would leave me at *Grand-père* Antoine's or *une amie folle* or at some boarding school. What kind of mother does that? And I'm supposed to take care of her now that she needs me?"

I realize it was different for me when I boarded at Auckland. Lakshmi and Jay were nearby. My sister visited often or I went to their house on weekends, often bringing Mathilde with me. My sister felt that I had been isolated enough as a child in Ajar and would enjoy dormitory living. I needed the camaraderie and social etiquette that came from close quarters with other students. Mathilde, who had been at Auckland longer, took me in hand. She told me who was Queen Bee and whom to stay away from. She was a natural at field hockey and tennis. I was not. But she would make sure I'd be assigned to her team, which stopped the more competitive girls from complaining about my mediocre performance.

Mathilde took care of me, of herself, and now she's having to take care of Agnes. It doesn't seem fair.

"Mathilde, why did you adopt me at school?"

"Somebody had to. You looked so sad and

lost, *ma puce.* I remember thinking something awful must have happened to you, but I didn't want to pry." She takes a moment with her cigarette.

In that pause I could have told her what I've never shared with her. Ravi, my pregnancy, Niki. The shame, sadness, the loss. When I met Mathilde, I was still smarting from Ravi's abandonment, from having to give up Niki. I'd been foolish. I'd been a dupe. I'd been a stooge. How could I admit all that to a girl I'd just met? Especially one so savvy. Now, seventeen years later, it's too late to confess that I've kept the most significant secret of my life from my best friend. I say nothing.

Mathilde sighs. "You were the only girl who had no mother, Radha. I didn't feel I had one either. Not a real one anyway. And who knows who my father was — Agnes never did. I think you and I adopted each other."

We're quiet for a little while, listening to each other breathe, Mathilde smoking quietly.

I think of her mother and how she was never still for a moment. In her current state, she sits for hours, staring off into space, worrying her fingers and then taking flight suddenly, like an agitated bird who has no idea where she's going. "Do you think Agnes ever found peace?"

Mathilde doesn't answer right away.

"Do any of us?" is her reply before she rings off.

In India, everyone — mother, father, aunts, uncles, cousins, even neighbors — piles into a car, sitting on each other's laps or on top of the luggage to accompany their loved one to the airport. In Paris, we call a taxi. Early Tuesday morning, Pierre brings my luggage down the stairs and waits with me at the entrance of our building for the taxi. I make sure he has the name and phone number of where I am staying in Agra, in case of emergency. And remind him to take the laundry off the line. Then the cab pulls up, and as the driver puts my bag in the back, Pierre leans in and kisses me goodbye.

The girls have been with Florence since last night, Monday, when she came to get them and their luggage in her Peugeot. It will be the first time I've been away from them for so long. When they were climbing into her car, I had a desperate urge to pull them out, press them to my breast and not let go. Instead, I leaned my head through the window to plant a dozen kisses on their cheeks as they waved goodbye to Pierre and me.

It was quiet in the house without our daughters. When we came upstairs, Pierre settled in the living room with his records and a book. I went into our bedroom to finish packing for my flight the next morning. We hadn't made up since Friday night. Instead, we'd concentrated on the girls over the weekend, taking them to Luxembourg Gardens, stopping for Nutella crepes along the way and a movie with Catherine Deneuve, *Peau d'Âne.*

When I was just about to shut my suitcase, Pierre came into the bedroom. He stood in the middle of the room, looking at me, until I raised my eyes to his. I could hear the soothing notes of Nat King Cole's "You Made Me Love You" wafting from the living room. Pierre walked toward me then, took my hand and put his left arm around my waist. His touch sent a jolt through me. He smelled good, familiar, comfortable. We danced in a slow circle in our bedroom until the song ended and another began. I could feel the strong, steady rhythm of his heartbeat against my ear.

He pressed his cheek against my forehead. "My mother smothered me when I was little. She wouldn't let me breathe. So I asked *Grand-mère* if she would send me to boarding school." He paused as we moved against each other. "I want our daughters to know good mothering, Radha. I don't want them to fly away from home sooner than they need to, the way I couldn't wait to get away from my house."

His words loosened something inside me. I could imagine him as a young boy — in knickers and school tie — carrying a small suitcase into the boys' dormitory. How scared he must have been! He'd never told me that it was his choice to go to boarding school. Florence had made it sound as if it was what all boys of his class did. I let my body soften, melt into his.

He released me and went to his night-stand. From the drawer, he removed *Notre-Dame de Paris,* the book he'd spent hours reading to me before the girls were born. I don't think we'd taken it out of that drawer for years. Just seeing it made me remember our first days together. I couldn't help but smile.

Pierre placed the book on top of the folded clothes in my suitcase. Then he clicked the suitcase shut and lifted it off the bed. He was apologizing without saying the words. Perhaps it's the best he could do.

He came and stood in front of me, locking his eyes with mine. I was still in my work clothes: black tights, red turtleneck and black wool skirt. He placed his hands on my behind, squeezed, then unzipped my skirt from the back. It fell to the floor. My breath quickened. My mouth opened and my eyes fell to his lips, wanting to taste them. But he moved his head away. He pulled my tights down to my thighs and tested my wetness with a finger. Satisfied, he slid his hands under my sweater and pushed my bra up over my breasts, rubbing my nipples with his thumbs. He was breathing as heavily as I was, but still he wouldn't kiss me. I flung off his hands so I could remove the tights myself. Then I slid across the bed on my back, knees up, to show him how ready I was. He groaned, unzipped his trousers and slipped inside me. The girls weren't here. I didn't care if Georges or Madame Blanchet heard us. All I wanted in that moment was Pierre, his taste, his smell, the feel of his hands. Him.

Yet, as much as I wanted to come, I couldn't. Afterward, I lay on my side, wide awake.

■ ■ ■ ■

PART TWO

■ ■ ■ ■

Part Two

In 400 BC, the Kama Sutra encouraged wives to create the perfect ambience for love by growing roses and perfuming their houses with them.

Agra
December 1974
I'm home.

Eight hours to fly from Paris to Delhi. Jiji's journey from Shimla — first in a taxi, then a train — took almost as long. She arrived in Delhi before me and had a hired car waiting for us. I saw the driver holding up a sign bearing my name as I exited the doors of the airport into the four o'clock maelstrom. Three girls in bright *salwar kameez* — hot orange, red violet, parrot green — and tight hair braids are waving to relatives coming out of the international terminal. A *chai-walla* expertly pours tea into tiny glasses from a saucepan high in the air to quench the thirst of the new arrivals. I'm surrounded by the smell of coconut hair oil, sweet betelnut *paan,* diesel exhaust from the planes and the overpowering scent of sweat, anticipation and happiness at being united with loved ones. I breathe in a lungful.

India, how I've missed you.

Until I saw Jiji get out of the back seat of the Standard, I hadn't realized how much I'd also missed seeing my sister. I last visited her in Shimla five years ago. She smelled of the chrysanthemums in her hair, the henna on her hands and her husband's lime and antiseptic scent. I held on to her far longer than I usually do, and she let me. It's as if Lakshmi is the part of India that I miss most at odd moments of my days in Paris — when the sky is gray and I long for the bright color of a woman's sari, or when I'm eating an asparagus salad, wishing I were enjoying a spicy *pani puri* snack or when Pierre is listening to melancholy jazz and I'm craving the livelier beat of Asha Bhosle's "Aaja aaja main hoon pyar tera."

As always, Lakshmi looks composed. She's wearing a pale green sari, hand-embroidered with tiny white flowers. I'm sure she must have knit the delicate sweater-blouse she's wearing underneath. My sister's long black hair, shot through with more silver than five years ago, is parted to the side and rolled into a chignon at the nape of her neck. Early this morning, before she left her house, she must have plucked the pale pink flowers to tuck around her bun. Her eyes looked a little red — probably from getting up so early this morning — and there are more lines than before at the corners of her mouth when she smiles, but she looks content. She's forty-nine this year. Dr. Jay lured her to Shimla years ago because he saw that she had a talent for practicing herbal medicine — just as her *saas* had. Not only has she been doing that in Shimla, but she's married to a man who encourages her to keep getting better at it. I feel a stab of jealousy, wishing Pierre could be a little more like Dr. Jay.

During the one-hour car journey to Agra, I squeeze Jiji's hand every time I see something that delights me. A scrawny man, his bent head wrapped in a yellow kerchief, pulling a rickshaw piled high with burlap sacks of wheat. The chatter of schoolgirls being driven home from school in an auto rickshaw. A MemSahib squabbling over the price of guavas being sold from a cart on the street. A boy in ragged clothes pocketing fruit when no one is looking (it could have been Malik, as I first met him!). The fruit seller yelling *Badmaash!* after the thief. A vendor unhooking a turquoise sari from the rows of jewel-colored saris hanging in his stall. Along the roadside, magenta cockscomb flowers bloom brilliantly despite the drought, despite the poverty, despite the hordes of people jostling for their rightful space in an overcrowded nation.

This is my second time on Indian soil since my marriage to Pierre thirteen years ago. The only other time was when Malik and Nimmi were married in 1969, and Pierre and I traveled with the girls to Shimla. We weren't able to see much more on that trip because I had recently started the job with the House of Yves, and Delphine expected me back.

On this trip, I'm in the state of Uttar Pradesh (UP, as we call it), in North India, next to Rajasthan. Lakshmi and I were born in UP, in Ajar, a tiny village I have no desire to see. I don't want or need to recall my bitter memories as the Bad Luck Girl of Ajar.

My sister assures me once again that the high courtesans of Agra are sure to further my knowledge of the raw materials I need for Olympia's fragrance. "They know which scents soothe, which entice, which whet the appetite and which mirror the mood of their patrons," Jiji promises. "They'll point you in the right direction for Olympia." These are the same courtesans who took Lakshmi in when she showed up on their doorstep at seventeen, barefoot, bedraggled, with a few rupees and a handful of cotton root bark knotted in a corner of her sari. If not for them, she would never have learned the intricate art of henna. They came from cities with radically different styles of *mehndi:* Bangkok, Cairo, Isfahan, Istanbul, Calcutta, Kuala Lumpur. She combined her natural artistic talent with what she learned from them to become the most renowned henna artist in Jaipur.

Today, Jiji was careful to hire a Standard, a modest Indian-made automobile, to make us less conspicuous on the road. She has also brought along a chiffon *chunni* and a shawl to cover my hair and clothing. As soon as she got out of the car to greet me at the airport, she draped the *chunni* over my head to mark me as an Indian. With my French bangs, flared jeans and fitted polyester blouse — not to mention the same bluegreen eyes we inherited from our mother — she felt I might be identified as an NRI — Non-Resident Indian — vulnerable to

159

pickpockets, overpriced merchandise and a hostile reception. She tells me that the growing outrage over the shortage of food, the astronomical prices of wheat, rice, sugar and oil and lack of medicines, antibiotics and basic toiletries have led to ill-feeling against those who have more — as well as brawls, knifing incidents and thievery.

"Sometimes they hijack cars, demanding money. They hurt the drivers and passengers. We have to be mindful," she says.

I gesture to a fruit and vegetable market we drive past. The pickings look sparse, and I tell her so.

My sister nods. "It's been a hard couple of years. I remember how excited we all were when the government started the irrigation projects right after independence. But we didn't know at the time that those projects were only suited for commercial farms, and India is a nation of small farmers. Now those farmers are demanding to know why so much money was spent on something that helps them not one jot."

As we approach Agra, the Red Fort looks dull, lackluster. I ask her why the historic buildings have an unkempt look about them.

Lakshmi says, "It's so dry, Radha. For two years now, the monsoons haven't brought enough water to make electricity. The farmers can't grow anything. There's not even enough water to turn pulp into paper. In Shimla, we're lucky. We get moisture from the Himalayan snows, not monsoons." She shakes her head. "But here . . . the poor suffer the most, and the middle class is also feeling the pinch."

She takes a breath and shifts her attention to me with a bright smile. "But we are here to help you be a successful perfumer. Your first big assignment!" She gently brushes my bangs out of my eyes. "When I look at you, I'm always amazed that you're the same girl I met all those years ago. You're so . . . sophisticated."

"So French?" I laugh.

"So . . . brilliant." She smiles. I hear the pride in her voice, and it makes my eyes moist. Things weren't always easy between us; it took me a long time to realize that even when we disagreed, my sister had my best interests at heart. She has always tried to coax the best out of me.

Nineteen years ago, I was the girl that Jiji's estranged husband, Hari, brought with him from Ajar, after Maa died. At the time, Lakshmi didn't even know that Maa and Pitaji were no more. How could she? At age seventeen she had fled her marital home and her husband in order to begin a life none of them knew about. It was the same year I was born. She never even knew I existed. When Hari and I found her years later in Jaipur, she was so different from what I had imagined. The village gossipeaters used to whisper that Lakshmi made her living on the streets or that she had succumbed to *sharab*. But the Lakshmi I met was worldly, confident, composed — and understated — a woman who wore expensive saris but never upstaged her clients. She made a very good living as a henna artist to the upper classes. She divorced Hari, but she took me in without a word. She made sure I was properly dressed and groomed and found a way to enroll me in the Maharani School for Girls, an institution founded for privileged young women. One day, I accompanied Jiji to the home of her wealthiest client, Parvati Singh; I was to help Lakshmi with a henna party for girls his mother considered suitable candidates for her son Ravi's marriage. It was there that I saw Ravi for the first time. He pursued me. I fell in love.

After his mother found out about my pregnancy and sent Ravi to England, she dropped Lakshmi like a hot *jalebi* and set about ruining Jiji's business. She wanted to banish us as far from a potential scandal as possible, a scandal she felt would scald her family and her son forever. It was the reason Jiji and I left Jaipur to start over again in Shimla.

My sister squeezes my hand, bringing me to the present. "Tell me more about your Olympia."

I explain my assignment again. From my handbag, I extract a postcard I bought at the Jeu de Paume: Manet's *Olympia*. "See how she's looking at us with confidence but also sadness, a sense of loss? That's what I want to capture. I've completed the base notes of the formula, and I'm close to designing the scent. It's still missing something . . . vital. I can almost smell it, Jiji, but I can't identify it. And when I come across it here in UP, I'll know it."

"I'm sure you will. Hazi and Nasreen will be a great help. I still remember how much sandalwood and vetiver oil they would buy to scent the rooms of the *kotha*. And, of course, they didn't spare a penny when it came to floral scents. We don't see frangipani or lavender or damask rose so much in the Himalayas, but Hazi and Nasreen do down here in Agra." She shifts in her seat to face me. "By the way, you told me your mother-in-law is taking care of the girls. How does Pierre feel about you being gone for a few days? Is he excited about your new project?"

I look out the window on my side to avoid her scrutiny. "He's getting used to it." Then I turn and smile. "Which fruit is in season right now? I've missed the lychees and loquats that are hard to find in France."

She knows when I'm being evasive. And I know we'll be circling back to the subject of my marriage before my trip is over.

I've never been to the house of a courtesan, although Lakshmi has told me a lot about them over the years. She praises the two remarkable women, Hazi and Nasreen, the courtesans who gave her food and shelter when she first arrived in Agra. "I had no intention of selling my body — just my skills," Jiji told me. Lakshmi's mother-in-law — her *saas* — was the herbal healer that women relied on from the surrounding villages to cure their children's earaches, stomach upsets and their own bruises and burns. Many pleaded: How could they bring another child into the world whom they couldn't feed? To these women, Lakshmi's mother-in-law would give ground cotton root bark in a paper packet. They were to make a tea from it and drink the bitter potion to expel their husband's unwanted seed.

On the night I discovered my older sister's clandestine business of delivering cotton root bark tea to the women of Jaipur, I was shocked and disappointed in her. Here she was constantly correcting my village ways, upbraiding the crude way I dressed, talked and interacted with others! When I confronted her, she confessed: the contraceptive teas were how she supported herself during her first few years in Agra after fleeing her abusive marriage. Her sachets kept the courtesans childfree. "The women of the pleasure houses were only doing what they needed to do to survive, just as I was," she said. She grew close to them — these women from lands as far away as Morocco, Afghanistan, Thailand. She felt safe with them.

"If they hadn't taken me in, who knows where I might have ended up? I owe Hazi and Nasreen more than the kindness they showed me, Radha," Lakshmi told me once. "I owe them my life."

By the time we arrive in Agra, it's early evening. We stop in front of a three-story house on a busy commercial street. There's a bicycle repair shop on the ground floor. A boy of seven or eight rests his arm on the seat of a bike that looks too big for him. He's watching a henna-haired man, who squats on the ground below, fix a flat tire on the bike. The boy is barefoot; the man is wearing red rubber *chappals*. A yellow mutt snoozes in one corner of the shop. An older man in a red turban, seated behind a soapstone counter toward the back of the shop, fans himself while he reads a book by the light of a single bare bulb. Along the counter are ten bikes in various states of disrepair.

Next to the tall house is a spice shop. Red chili powder, ground black pepper, orange turmeric powder and pink salt have been shaped into large cones and capped with silver tops to keep their shape. Housewives are haggling with the male vendor, who looks annoyed.

A stout woman in a cerulean blue sari who has tucked her *pallu* behind her ears says, "I paid you eight rupees for that yesterday and now you're asking fifteen?"

The vendor spits the red juice from his *paan* on the ground before answering, "Do you think we can give it away for free? Find me someone who is charging less and I'll turn the store over to you, MemSahib."

The woman says, *"Bakwas!"* waving a hand as if to swat a pesky fly and moves on, her shopping bag empty.

As we step out of the Standard, I inspect the house with its peeling paint and shabby ground-floor shops. I hope my disappointment doesn't show. Jiji had always told me of the wealth these courtesans had accumulated: houses, luxury goods, orchards, jewelry shops, expensive saris, cashmere shawls, ivory combs, jade glasses, brocaded shoes. Some courtesans were supposedly so rich they helped finance the businesses of their patrons.

My eyes travel to the second floor, which holds more promise; it's all mogul arches and stone latticework. A shadow moves behind the honeycomb pattern. I'm embarrassed to be caught staring, and I look away.

The boy and the man working on the bicycle turn their gaze on us. The man behind the soapstone counter puts down his *khus* fan and walks in our direction. He extends an arm to indicate we should follow him up the side stairs and into the building. I can't stop looking at his mustache, which has to be the most elaborate I've ever seen. It extends from his upper lip to his cheeks, flares out and then up into the folds of his turban. He whistles and the young boy runs to pick up our suitcases. They are almost half the boy's height, but even so, he manages. Jiji and I exchange a look. We smile. I know we're both thinking of Malik at eight, the age he was when I first met him. He carried Jiji's heavy tiffins and vinyl totes from one henna appointment to another across Jaipur. It was the boy Malik who slipped a tamarind candy into my palm or brought me a *besan laddu* whenever Lakshmi was too wrapped up in work to think about food.

Upstairs, we turn into a dark hallway that opens onto an atrium spanning three floors. Looking down at the ground-floor courtyard, I see the back wall of what must be the bicycle repair shop. It comes to an abrupt stop where the courtyard starts. A gray-haired woman sweeps around the elegant columns of the ground-floor colonnade; another is watering tulsi plants in large stone planters. The colonnades are Islamic in design; the balcony railings far more elaborate than the building's exterior would suggest. We take off our shoes where we see a row of sequined *padukas,* leather *chappals,* closed-toe shoes and silk mules (just like Olympia!).

On the opposite side of the atrium is a large open hall with a beautifully patterned marble floor. At one end, a heavy-set woman bedecked in a red sari and necklaces of pearls and gold is sitting on a thick Persian carpet, smoking a hookah and playing cards with another woman, whose back is to us. Our guide gestures for us to continue around the balcony to the hall. He folds his hands in a *namaste,* and we return the greeting. He mumbles something to the boy, who leaves our suitcases against the wall. Both the older man and the boy turn around and walk down the stairs. Not a word has been exchanged between us.

The aroma of sandalwood fills the atrium and wafts into my nostrils. The scent is so intense that my body vibrates with the most extraordinary sensation. Episodes I've long forgotten suddenly come to me. A *puja* for Goddess Lakshmi at Diwali; Malik lighting cones of sandalwood incense at Jiji's rented lodgings in Jaipur. Another image takes its place: the moving-in ceremony at the house Lakshmi worked so hard to afford — when the *pundit* placed one ingredient after another into the smoking pot of *ghee.* I worried the flame would catch his white *dhoti* on fire. Yet one more episode I'd rather not remember elbows its way in: accompanying a pregnant Kanta — Jiji's closest friend, the one who took care of me when *I* was pregnant — to her temple and lighting incense as she prayed her baby would be

169

healthy. The prayers didn't help; her baby was stillborn, and she ended up adopting my Niki.

My hands are clammy. I rub them against my trousers. These are memories I'd prefer to keep buried. I've worked hard to separate my life into two distinct parts: *before* giving birth to Niki and *after* Niki's adoption by Kanta and Manu. If I think of the before time, I'm reminded of Ravi's betrayal and my naivete. How could I ever have been fooled into believing an upper-class boy like him would marry a poor Bad Luck Girl like me? And how silly I was to think I could raise our baby by myself — without schooling, without a job, without parents to support me. Being in this part of India, so close to where it all happened, it's as if the memories I've kept at bay for so long are demanding to be released from their prison. I feel my face flush. I shut my eyes tight. *I do not want to think about all that!*

"Radha?"

I've been so absorbed in my own thoughts I haven't noticed that I'm being introduced to the chief courtesan of the *kotha,* the house of pleasure. When I open my eyes, I see a woman with an elaborate *pallu* covering her head. It's the same woman I saw playing cards when we first entered this house. She has a long nose with a large diamond stud, fleshy cheeks and wide-set eyes lined heavily with kohl. Thirty years ago, she would have been stunning. Jiji introduces her as Hazi and reaches for the woman's feet. I'm surprised my sister would perform this gesture of respect to a courtesan, but I decide to follow suit because I think Lakshmi would want me to.

Hazi looks at me with concern. "*Beti,* your cheeks are red. Are you feeling well? Shall we get you some water?" Without waiting for an answer, she instructs a woman on the far side of the room in rapid-fire Urdu to bring us refreshments.

Next, I'm introduced to her sister, Nasreen, Hazi's partner in the card game. The crinkles around Nasreen's eyes and the dimples on her cheeks tell me Nasreen smiles easily and often. She's slightly smaller in stature than her companion and dressed just as elegantly. The beauty she could once claim is evident in her button nose and large, round eyes. She waves off our *pranama.* "Welcome, welcome! We were so excited that our very own Lakshmi was coming to visit. And what a beautiful sister she's brought with her, *haih-nah,* Hazi? Look at those green eyes!"

Hazi wags her head and the two women

share a look. Hazi gestures for us to sit on the carpet. She leans against a silk bolster and takes a puff of her hookah. "How long since my sister and I have seen you, *beti*?" She looks at Lakshmi. "Not since you left us for Jaipur, *nah*?"

Nasreen grins. "Twenty-seven years, I think! And may I say how wonderful you look, Lakshmi?" Her plump hands grasp Jiji's. That's when I notice all the solid-gold bangles decorating her forearms from her wrists to her elbows.

Jiji laughs. "That's because you're looking at a mirror, *Ji,* not at me." The old courtesans tilt their heads in acknowledgment of the compliment.

My sister has no argument with getting older. She is still slim; she rides horses and works at the Lady Reading Healing Garden with Malik and Nimmi and with her husband at the Community Clinic. But fine lines cross her forehead, and there are deep grooves between her eyebrows. Soft pouches have formed under her eyes. She's never been a good sleeper; I know she wakes up several times a night to write a letter or read a book or talk to Madho Singh, the parakeet who overhears every conversation and repeats it to the delight or embarrassment of Jiji's household.

172

I've come to talk about scents, but Jiji has prepared me to expect at least half an hour of pleasantries before getting down to business. *The branch of patience bears sweet fruits,* she reminded me. In India, one has to allow the person to whom a request is being made to introduce the order of business. It's the same in Paris where coffee and tea and light conversation are offered first, but the time period for getting down to business is shorter. Patience has always been in short supply for me, and the unhappy memories of my past aren't making it any easier to maintain my composure.

I'm distracted by the tinkle of ankle bells. I see a young woman (who I assume is also a courtesan) emerge from a doorway behind us, carrying a brass tray of cut-crystal glasses containing a thick, rose-colored drink. She bends elegantly from the waist to offer each of us a glass. *Falooda!* I haven't had this sweet treat since my Auckland days when Mathilde and I would sneak off to the *falooda* seller in Shimla. A cold glass of milk drizzled with rose syrup, crushed nuts and vermicelli was the perfect reward after a week of spelling tests, math quizzes, etiquette lessons and frequent corrections by matrons. Mathilde and I would work our way slowly through the glass, savoring each mouthful. As I take my first sip, I'm back in Shimla with a young Mathilde, our backs to the Himalayan mountains, the pine-scented valley spread out below us, as we marvel at Sophia Loren's image on the cover of *LIFE* magazine and wonder if her beauty mark is real.

"It's good to see you both looking well," Jiji says.

Hazi makes a face. "But not at our best, Lakshmi. No maharajas. Few nawabs come now. Even Westerners, who were so taken by our talented girls, are staying away. *Katham.*" She brings the fingers of her right hand together, then spreads them apart as if she's sprinkling water on us. "Because of the looting and the uncertainty in the air, the rich *baniyas* aren't coming. We see a lower quality clientele than we were used to thirty years ago." She takes a few quick puffs of her hookah. A stream of molasses and rose-flavored smoke fills the air.

Nasreen nods. "It's a good thing our guards have been with us a long time. You can't trust servants these days not to turn on you."

It dawns on me then that the men working in the bike shop and the spice vendor below are their bodyguards. No wonder the spice vendor wasn't concerned about losing a customer!

Hazi raises her eyes to address someone behind us. "Yes, *beta?*"

I turn around to see a thin young man with glasses standing some distance away. His manner is deferential, as if he does not wish to interrupt us.

Nasreen beams with pride when she tells us, "My son, Ahmed."

Ahmed comes forward and *salaams* us with his free hand. His other hand is holding a large black binder. He hands the binder to Hazi, opens it to a page and points to something.

She wags her head. "*Theek hai.* But make sure he pays up front."

Ahmed smiles at us and leaves.

Hazi turns to Lakshmi. "All these years, you've kept us supplied with your sachets, but every now and then —" she points to Nasreen "— a girl falls in love and wants to have his child."

Nasreen laughs. "*Zuroor!* My nawab was so handsome. He was my only for —" She looks to Hazi for confirmation.

The old begum says, "Nine years you were with him."

"Nine good years!" Nasreen and Hazi both laugh lustily. "I had Ahmed first. Then Sophia." Nasreen points to the same woman who served us the *falooda* and has now come to collect our empty glasses. "She's going to university. She'll be a doctor. *Our* doctor."

So the young woman is *not* a courtesan. Now I see the resemblance between Nasreen and Sophia as the young woman smiles shyly, exposing her dimples. She's wearing a lovely chiffon sari in yellow with green embroidery.

Hazi scratches her neck. "If only Ahmed had been a girl." She explains that the birth of a girl in a *kotha* is celebrated with fanfare while a boy's birth is not. What can he offer, after all? Daughters will inherit their mother's wealth, are privately tutored and educated and can choose to follow their mother's profession or not. Sons of the *kotha* have few options and no inheritance. With the economy down, Ahmed doesn't have job prospects outside of the house so he is employed by the *kotha* to keep the books.

Sophia asks us politely to move next to Hazi and face the far side of the room while we eat. Another woman brings each of us a *thali* with *rotis, rajma masala,* tandoori chicken with mango chutney and *toor dal* sprinkled liberally with fresh cilantro. The aromas of onion, garlic, ginger and *ajwain* are tantalizing, and I realize I'm famished.

Nasreen claps her hands three times. Five women dressed in embroidered *lehengas* file into the room and assume their positions. Each wears the heavily decorated skirt in a hot color with a matching blouse. A chiffon *dupatta* with a gold border is draped modestly across the fronts of their bodies and tucked into their *lehengas*. Bangles of all colors adorn their arms. Jewel-studded chokers grace their necks. Fingers and hands are covered with sparkling *haath phools* and a golden *tikka* is mounted on one side of the part in their hair.

I hear the opening chords of a harmonium. I'm surprised to see Sophia sitting behind the instrument, pumping the bellow. The man sitting next to her with a *tabla* is none other than the spice vendor we saw below. Nasreen's voice accompanies the music with a *raga*, coaxing the notes of the harmonium to climb higher. I'm entranced by the clear, fluty melody. I haven't heard Indian classical music like this since that holiday party at the Singhs' long ago in Jaipur, the first time I met Ravi. I look at Lakshmi to see if she shares my memory of the Singh party, but she seems completely engrossed in the performance. She's stopped eating to tap her hand against her thigh, matching Nasreen's rhythm.

Oh, how I wish Shanti and Asha could be here with us, watching, listening, dancing! I know Pierre's grandmother would have loved bringing them to the *kotha* and meeting the courtesans, but I don't think Pierre or Florence would have approved.

The harmonium speeds up as the vendor's fingers and the flat of his hand start stroking the *tabla.* Nasreen begins calling out the footwork for the dancers, who fly into action. Every time they execute a turn or a jump, their vermillion leggings peek out from under the twirling *lehengas.* I marvel at their dizzying footwork. How different this dance is from the waltz or the fox trot I was taught at Auckland House School (and the Maharani School for Girls before that) when India was still shaking off its colonial stranglehold! Schools like Auckland were built for British girls and boys whose families were part of the Raj. When independence became inevitable, Britishers started to leave in droves and were replaced by students from Thailand, Ethiopia, Turkey, Australia, New Zealand, France — and, of course, India. That's how Mathilde came to study at Auckland. Her mother brought her from Paris and deposited her at Auckland, promptly wandering off to an ashram run by the Maharishi Mahesh Yogi. Sometimes,

Agnes would send for Mathilde on a whim (and Mathilde would invite me) to join her mother wherever she happened to be: a hugging ashram in Kerala or a yoga awakening in Goa or a laughing retreat in Dehradun. As Mathilde was saying a few days ago, we both were motherless. Together, we felt less isolated.

By the time the courtesans finish their *kathak* routine, they're breathing heavily. We cheer and clap. Hazi jokes about how well Lakshmi took to the henna painting but not so much to the dancing. Nasreen's eyes twinkle when she tells me, "Try as hard as she might, Lakshmi would put a lot of spirit in her dancing but the steps were always off." She cups my sister's chin and kisses her cheek. Jiji's face pinks with embarrassment, but I can tell she's pleased by the grand reception they've given her.

I've seen my sister dance. The night I came to tell her that I'd decided to leave my baby with Kanta and go with my sister to Shimla, Jiji was dancing on the floor of her house, the same one where we'd held the moving-in ceremony. Lakshmi had designed the pattern on the terrazzo floor as intricately as she designed the henna patterns on the bodies of her clients. That night, she'd placed *diyas* along the walls. I

179

had caught her in a private act; she'd been saying goodbye to her life in Jaipur, celebrating her accomplishments so she could move on to the next phase of her life. I never told her this, but in that moment, she appeared to me as the Goddess Lakshmi.

One by one, the dancers come to Jiji and touch her feet before leaving. Even Sophia does a *pranama* to my sister. Jiji may only have spent three years of her life here after leaving her marriage, but she has been remembered. I didn't know she'd been sending the *kotha* her contraceptive sachets all these years. It makes sense, though. Women who make their living from their bodies would need them. I certainly needed them at thirteen, when Jiji tried to give them to me, but I resisted; I foolishly thought Ravi would marry me. And look what happened: I ended up with a baby I couldn't support.

My head starts to throb. Memories like these are the reason I don't return to India more often. The food I've barely digested threatens to come back up again. My stomach roils noisily. My throat is dry. I reach for my water glass, but it's empty. To take my mind off the nausea, I ask Hazi, "Auntie, how many girls work for you?"

The smile on her lips disappears. Nasreen

looks as if she's been struck across the cheek.

Immediately, I know I've made a *faux pas*.

The old begum casts a stern gaze at my sister as if to say, *Have you taught her no manners?*

I rush to apologize for my rudeness. I dare not look at Jiji, who has always cautioned me to think before I speak. My natural impulse is to be direct, plainspoken. When I was younger, she would try to make me understand that asking for something directly wasn't as effective as being oblique. But it had always been hard for me to hide my anger or sadness or revulsion. I'm better at it now. After thirteen years as a wife and mother, I've become more adaptable, better at masking my true feelings. I've let Pierre think that I agree with him on most issues. It's just easier that way. I've done the same thing with Florence. I stifle my retorts, swallow my bile, because I'm afraid what I might say if I gave voice to my true feelings.

Hazi nods her head at me slightly as a gesture of forgiveness. "Twelve girls *live* here. All ages. Three were widowed before they were fifteen. Two had husbands who beat them. Four are daughters of former girls here. One woman always wanted to sing and dance but her orthodox Brahmin

181

family wouldn't allow it. And two left jobs that paid nothing for a job here, where they can make more money than they ever dreamed." She smiles once again at Lakshmi. "Remember when we had thirty girls living here? Maharajas begging for admittance. It was a pleasure to provide the kind of entertainment they couldn't get elsewhere." She pauses, her eyes glistening with fond remembrance.

To me, she says pointedly, "Our girls play music, recite poetry, dance classical styles and save their money. When they have enough for a house or simply feel it's time to leave, they leave."

Chastened, I lower my eyes in apology. I'm surprised that Jiji hasn't intervened. With her clients in Jaipur, any time I made a blunder like this, she would rush to smooth over the awkwardness. Maybe she doesn't feel the need to correct me now that I'm older. Or maybe it's marriage to Dr. Jay that has mellowed her. She pays less attention to the minor irritations.

Lakshmi touches my arm lightly to let me know there was no harm done with my remark. Slowly, my stomach unclenches. "Our Radha," she says, "has done well for herself. She is now working for a major perfume house. So I said to her, who better than my friends Hazi and Nasreen to guide her in her latest assignment? Isn't that right?"

My sister is giving me a chance to make up for my gaffe. I move my head from side to side. *"Hahn.* Jiji said there was no better guide when it comes to fragrances, Hazi-*ji."*

Hazi melts a little. "We have been using scents to great effect for hundreds of years." She looks at Nasreen. "Remember that old man who came around to advise us which *attar* was beneficial for what kind of body?"

Nasreen laughs. *"Hahn.* He told me to always wear *shamama attar,* and I have for over forty years. He claimed all those herbs, woods, spices and flowers mingled together in one scent would bring me luck."

"Have they?" I ask, curious.

By way of an answer, Nasreen holds up her gold-clad arms and snaps her fingers. She releases a lovely giggle.

Lakshmi says, "But why would you need an *attar* adviser when your own knowledge is so extensive?"

Hazi leans forward, exposing her generous cleavage, *"Beti,* we *know* how to entice. The old man just provided a little boost." She and Nasreen burst into laughter.

Nasreen's cheeks dimple with glee. "As soon as you let us know you were coming,

Lakshmi, I got in touch with our favorite fragrance vendor. He's arriving tomorrow to show you his finest samples."

Hazi is lighting her hookah again. She sucks on the pipe a few times. "He's coming to see Nasreen more than anything." She winks at Nasreen and the two women chuckle. Lakshmi smiles at her old friends fondly. I think I understand what was just said, but I don't want to make another *faux pas,* so I say nothing.

Our room for the night is on the topmost floor. Jiji says it's the same floor where she stayed when she lived here. Children of the courtesans live on this floor — boys in one room, the girls in a much larger one. They have tutors for reading, math, music and etiquette. They play games — badminton, *kabaddi,* skipping rope — up on the roof. This floor is farthest from the entertainment hall on the first floor, but I can still hear the faint melody of a sitar and its mournful accompaniment, the harmonium, floating up the atrium. I wonder if Sophia plays for the audience in the late evenings. Maybe not. She probably needs to study for her medical degree.

My sister and I are sharing a bed, the kind of narrow cot we used to sleep on together at her Jaipur lodgings. In Paris, I'm used to sleeping on a plush mattress. When I turn on my side toward Lakshmi, my hip bone collides sharply with the hard jute. Tomorrow morning, we'll take a bath on the rooftop where someone will bring up the hot water. Tonight, we're sleeping in our traveling clothes.

Lakshmi is lying on her back with her arm behind her head. "There was a time when those ladies would have served five kinds of sweets and ten kinds of savories."

"There seemed to be plenty of food."

My sister turns on her side to face me. Her eyes are full of sadness. "That's not the point." Her face reminds me of Maa's — the same eyes, the same long hair twisted into a bun, the pointed chin. I know my eyes remind her of Maa, too. But we don't talk about our mother. Jiji continues. "The *kotha* way of life is so different now. The women spent years perfecting their classical dances, memorizing poetry. Training their vocal chords. Noble families sent their sons to *kothas* for training in social etiquette. And now . . . there are few who appreciate what Hazi and Nasreen know. The ones who do are afraid to be seen here."

"Why?"

"It took them a while, but the British

ultimately discovered that wealthy *kothas* were financing India's fight for independence. After that, the *Angreji* started referring to courtesans as common prostitutes. What better way to ruin their reputation? Once the British left, noblemen who added to the *kotha*'s coffers lost their titles or their wealth and could no longer support the courtesans."

We think our thoughts in silence for a while.

With the lightest touch, she brushes my arm. "Radha?"

"Hmm?"

"Why don't you tell me what's happening at home?"

I close my eyes, turn to my right side, away from her. If I start talking, I'm afraid I'll never stop. All day, conflicting thoughts have been swirling around my brain. *I want more for myself. I'm a bad wife for wanting more. I love Pierre and I want us to be happy. I resent Pierre for not understanding me or even trying to understand me. I love spending time with my daughters. I'm conflicted when I have to spend time with them and it cuts into my work on the Olympia project. I like it when we're all together as a family. Sometimes, I wish I lived alone and had no one to look after.*

Lakshmi waits patiently for me to begin.

"Remember when I was thirteen and you warned me that motherhood wasn't as easy as I was making it out to be? You were right — at that time. But now I'm older, and it's actually okay. Not perfect, but okay. The girls can do many things for themselves. It's just that I want more — more than just being a mother. Now that I'm in India, you'd think I could just forget about my daughters, as if I were flicking off a switch, but I can't. We passed a girl on the street with red ribbons threaded through her braids, and I wondered if Shanti's hair is long enough for us to try that. When we saw the boy watching that bike being repaired, I wondered if I should get Asha the bike she keeps asking for or is she still too young? Then I worry if Florence is feeding them the foods *they* like or only the foods *she* likes."

I crane my neck around to look at her. "I love my daughters. *And* I love my work. It feels as if Pierre is asking me to choose one over the other."

Jiji puts her arm around my belly and hugs me from behind.

I turn my head back and let out a sigh. "I don't want to admit it, but since the girls came into our lives, Pierre is not the one I think about the most. I love him — it's not

187

that. But I think I'm changing in ways that he's not."

"How?"

I grab her hand with my free arm and hold it against my chest. "When I was graduating from Auckland, I wanted an adventure. And there was Pierre willing to take me on one. All the way to Paris. So I went. And what an adventure! I loved walking the streets of each *arrondissement,* trying the falafel in the Marais, the fresh crepes from the street vendors, the croissants in every bakery. Admiring the architecture, the ancient buildings — so different from ours here at home, Jiji. My French improved. I was able to carry on conversations. Then Mathilde introduced me to her grandfather Antoine and I discovered perfume. You can't imagine what joy it was to be immersed in all those lovely scents again! It conjured up India and brought it back into my life in a tangible way. Until then, I hadn't realized how homesick I was. I loved going to Antoine's *parfumerie* with its aroma of *jasmine sambac* as I entered and *ruh gulab* as I walked to the back corner and saffron by the display cases on the side. I had no idea so many of the ingredients in those perfumes would seem so familiar! I missed them all, Jiji."

I pause, remembering that happy over-

188

whelm of scents, homesickness and belonging. Paris has its own unique and beautiful charm, but the city lacks the crush of a rainbow of saris, the brightly colored spices and the thousands upon thousands of smells that India produces naturally. I was so excited this year when the first Indian grocery opened in La Passage Brady, but it was like finding the tiniest chip of a diamond rather than the whole stone. It wasn't the same.

I shift my body so I'm lying on my back again. In the dark, I turn my face and search for her eyes. "Why should I feel guilty about finding something I love to do and want to keep getting better at? I want to be the best perfumer — as good as Delphine. She thinks I can do it. Why is it so wrong to want that, Jiji?"

The tears come of their own accord. They run down my cheeks. They drip into my ears. They wet my hair. Jiji uses the edge of her sari to wipe my face. She makes cooing noises. I adjust my body to bury my face in Jiji's neck, and she puts her arm around me. Her skin smells of coconut oil. For the hundredth time I wonder why she didn't have children. She has a way about her that makes me feel safe, cared for — the way my girls must feel when I'm tending to their hurts. Jiji has been more like a mother to me than our own mother was. Maa was so disappointed in her marriage to Pitaji, who promised her family he would keep her in the comfortable city lifestyle she was born into. Instead, his penalty for advocating the return of the British to their own homeland was to be sent to a nowhere rural village to teach poor children who, more often than not, didn't come to school. He sold Maa's gold to keep himself in *sharab* and self-pity, and for that, she couldn't forgive him.

As if she wants to soften my sadness, my sister sings to me the lullaby she suggested I sing to Shanti at bedtime. *"Rundo Rani, burri sayani. Peethee tundha tundha pani —"*

"Lakin kurthi hai manmani." I finish it for her, slobbering the words through my sobs. It calms me.

"Tell me what you would like to have happen."

I sniffle. "It's 1974, Jiji! The women's revolution started a decade ago. But it feels like the changes took place only in the newspaper — not in our homes." I get off the cot to fish for a handkerchief in my bag and blow my nose. "I want Pierre to understand me. I don't want him to resent the time I spend on my career. I want him to do as much as I do. I don't want to argue with him about it — I just want him to see me as an equal partner. I know I only make half of what he makes now, but I will make a lot more when I'm a perfumer. But even that shouldn't make a difference. Because I do a lot of the work when it comes to the girls and the laundry and cleaning and shopping." I sit down again on the cot, cross-legged. "He thinks doing any of that will make him *un mari américain.*" I lower my voice to imitate Pierre. "*Un homme qui est mene par le bout du nez.* A man led by the tip of the nose."

Jiji is quiet for a moment. "What about Florence? Has anything changed between you two?"

"Hah!" I stifle a laugh. "If anything, it's worse. Every year, the same fight. She wants the girls to go to Marymount, the Catholic school. How can I raise my girls in a religion with only one God when I've grown up with Swaraswati and Vishnu and Durga and Lakshmi and Ganesh and Hunuman? I would rather let the girls decide what they want to believe when they're older."

"And that's what Pierre thinks, too?"

"Pierre never stands up to his mother. He leaves that to me."

She raises her brows. "Now who's being led by the tip of his nose?"

I let out a giggle. I know I'm being disloyal to Pierre, but it feels good to be naughty like this — in private.

She smiles. "I used to worry about you, but with each step you take, it's obvious you're growing, challenging yourself in all sorts of ways."

I feel the hot tears of guilt building up again. All those times I resisted Lakshmi's suggestions and pleas when I was younger! She is my older sister. She raised me from the age of thirteen. And what did I do in return? I slept with the son of her biggest patron and ruined her business! Jiji may have moved beyond it, but I still feel the searing shame of my betrayal. It's almost as if her forgiveness makes me feel worse.

She taps my knee. "You have found gold. That thing you want to do, that compels you to get up in the morning and keep getting better and better at. There's nothing like that feeling, is there?" She takes my hands into hers and kisses them. "Tomorrow, we'll plan. Tonight, we'll get some sleep. *Accha?*"

I nod and lie down again, pulling the *rajai* over both of us. I know she'll sleep only a few hours. She'll probably lie awake thinking about what I've just told her. Having finally shared what's been bothering me for so long, I feel more relaxed than I have in years. Within minutes, I'm asleep.

Four hours later, I'm the one who's wide awake. I check my wristwatch. Here in Agra, it's three in the morning on Wednesday. I would normally just be getting to sleep in Paris. My body doesn't know whether to sleep or get up. I get off the *charpoy,* quietly. Perhaps I can make myself some chai down in the kitchen. I walk four stories down the stone steps to the ground floor. The lights are on in the kitchen. A girl with a long braid hanging down her back is washing dishes in the deep stone sink. When I clear my throat to get her attention, I startle her. I take it she's not used to the people upstairs coming down to the work areas.

She turns to see who's there. "Can I get you something, Mam?" She wipes her hands on a kitchen towel. Her complexion is dusky and her demeanor is servile. But her smile is genuine happiness. "Chai? *Subji?* Chef has left some *atta* for *chappatis.*" She seems eager to please. She must be around twelve or fourteen. If she didn't get enough food in her belly as a baby, she's probably small for her age.

"Chai, please."

"Right away." She wags her head and gets

193

to work. She strikes a match to light the burner, pulls a saucepan off a shelf lined with multiple pressure cookers, adds milk to it from the container in the refrigerator (only the wealthier households have a fridge) and water from the tap. Along the walls, stainless steel plates, bowls, tiffins and utensils are another testament to the *haveli*'s wealth. On one side of the room is a floor hearth with a clay oven where I assume *chappatis* and tandoori chicken and lamb are cooked. There is no furniture in the room. I would imagine that most kitchen staff, whether they're shelling peas or peeling potatoes or making *atta,* sit on the spotless stone floor to do their work.

"You can go back to your room, Mam. I will bring it to you," she says, when she sees me looking around for a chair.

But I don't want to wake Jiji by going back, so I lean with my back against the kitchen counter. "What's your name?"

She smiles, pleased to be asked. "Binu, Mam."

"How long have you worked here, Binu?"

Without interrupting the process of adding whole spices to the chai, she says, "Since four years, Mam. My mother worked here before me. But her legs give her pain now."

Binu wears no makeup, and her *salwar ka-*

meez is cheap cotton. The red sweater over her *kameez* has holes under the arms. Neither she nor her mother are courtesans. Of that, I'm certain.

"Are you in school?"

She giggles, as if I've said something funny. "No, Mam. I work here all night. From midnight to ten in the morning. I wouldn't be able to stay awake in school."

This could have been *my* fate if I'd stayed in Ajar after my parents died. I would have been married off to an older widower or young farmer and filled my days drawing well water, cooking food, beating laundry on rocks along the riverbank, looking after my many children — some still crawling, others playing hopscotch or jumping rope. Inwardly, I shudder.

"Do you like this work?" I ask.

She doesn't look up from the saucepan. She shrugs.

"What would you like to do instead?"

She turns to me with a smile full of joy. "Spaceman! I want to be like those people who go to the moon. My brother — he goes to school — told me about it. They do it in *Amreeka*. And Soviet Union." She dances on her tiptoes to reach the loose-leaf-tea bin on the top shelf and drops two spoonfuls into the saucepan. The familiar scent of black tea infused with warm, fragrant spices coats my nostrils and makes my mouth water.

"You'd like to be an astronaut?"

The English word makes her a little uncertain. Finally, she wags her head *yes*.

The tea is ready. She pours it from the saucepan into a strainer atop a porcelain cup without spilling a drop. "*Le lo,* Mam." She hands it to me and waits for my review.

The tea is very good, and I tell her so. "Why don't you join me?"

Binu holds up her palms as if I'm asking for too much, smiles and goes back to washing dishes.

I lean back against the counter and sip my chai. "Binu, wouldn't you make more money working in a factory?"

She lets out another giggle. "Who would hire me? Factory jobs are for men. They would laugh at me if I showed up looking for work, Mam."

There's so much fire in this girl. So much exuberance. Is her life limited to working in a courtesan's kitchen for the rest of her life — until her legs give out, too?

Today, the perfume vendor from Kannauj is expected. It's about a four-hour drive from Agra, so he should be here by lunchtime.

From my vantage point at the latticed window of the performance salon, I'd been on the lookout for a man in a *dhoti* arriving on a moped. Instead, I see a handsome Indian man of around fifty years of age emerge from a black Mercedes. He's wearing a dark linen suit with a cream shirt. He's clean-shaven with a strong, square jaw, a receding hairline. He nods at someone below us, probably the bike shop owner who showed us into the *kotha* yesterday. His driver removes a large wooden case from the trunk and follows his boss to the stairs.

We are seated in the main entertainment hall. Nasreen takes the lead this time. She introduces the vendor to us as Rajkumar Mehta. It's obvious that Mr. Mehta can't keep his eyes off the lovely Nasreen. She must be at least ten years older than him, but her coquettish manner transcends age. She removes his suitcoat and motions for him to sit on a velvet, tasseled cushion. Both he and his driver removed their shoes upon entering. The driver set the oblong case down next to his boss before being escorted to another part of the house, to eat with the cook.

Lunch is now brought in on *thalis,* just as our meal was yesterday. Nasreen doesn't eat. She sits next to Mr. Mehta, fanning him with a *khus* fan, the fragrance of natural vetiver filling the room.

While we eat, Hazi asks after his health and his family's health and the health of his business. He regales us with dramatic stories and funny ones. "Would you believe that if you want to send a letter today, you have to wait in one line to buy the stamp, another line to get the stamp and a third line to make sure the postal clerk puts the seal on the stamp before the scoundrel pockets it for his own use?"

After half an hour, Hazi nods at Jiji, who turns to me to indicate that I may ask questions now.

I turn to face Mr. Mehta. "*Ji,* I am so honored to meet you. I work in Paris for the House of Yves." I address Mr. Mehta.

"I know it," he says pleasantly, taking a sip of water from his glass. I notice the gold ring with a large, fiery opal on his pinky finger.

"We use many essential oils — you call them *attars* — that remind me of India. But I am looking for something that I haven't found in our lab. Could you please tell me about some of the ones you make that even the French may not be aware of?" I feel as if I'm groping in the dark for something, and I'm not sure what it is.

He studies me for a moment while he finishes chewing. He looks amused. "In India, you know we have been making *attars* for thousands of years?" I notice he pronounces it *ittirs*. "Long before your Grasse became known as the perfume capital of the world." He's putting me in the category of French perfumers who combine essential oils with alcohol to dilute the scent. "Our Indian and Middle Eastern customers wouldn't dream of putting alcohol on their person. They believe in rubbing the oils directly on their skin for the most beneficial effect." He turns to Nasreen with a sly smile. "Isn't that right, *Ji?*"

She puts a hand to her throat and looks coyly at the carpet. I imagine the two of them on her bed, her skin glistening with the *attar* from his magic box of scents.

Mr. Mehta mixes a handful of rice and *dal* on his *thali* with his fingers and scoops it into his mouth. "I've brought some of our finest *attars* — scents they would never be able to duplicate in the West."

I want to hurry him along because I'm impatient to sample his fragrances, but that isn't the Indian way. I tamp down my eagerness. I take a bite of my *parantha* and ask, "Why is that?"

"We use thick copper pots. We use bamboo

pipes. We seal the containers airtight with clay and wool to distill the essence of roses or what have you. All by hand. In the open air. We have men working night and day tending to the stills, feeding the fires cow dung, not kerosene. The scented vapor goes directly into the sandalwood oil — sandalwood that's grown right here in India!" He points his hands at the earth for emphasis. "We store the oils in bottles made of camel skin, not glass. You use enormous vats, sometimes copper, sometimes steel, gas fires, rubber closures — *bakwas!*" He pushes his hand to one side as if throwing something away. "It's not the same."

I wish he wouldn't keep referring to me as *you,* the foreigner. But that's my fault. Jiji brought a *salwar kameez* for me to wear in India, but, without thinking, after my bath up on the roof, I put on the same hip-hugging bell-bottoms as yesterday and a full-sleeve blouse covered in a flower print. Now I notice that Hazi and Nasreen — and Jiji — look far more formally dressed in their saris than I do. I realize I've embarrassed my hosts by dressing in such casual, immodest clothes. Have I disrespected our guest, too? Hazi's and Nasreen's bodies may be loosely shrouded in five yards of silk with only a smidgen of brown skin on display, but they allow a man enough latitude to fantasize what lies beneath. I've spent almost half my life in France, and I'm making the same mistake foreigners make when they visit India. Have I changed so much? I chastise myself for yet another *faux pas.*

Lunch is cleared. We are all given a warm bowl of water and a fresh towel to wipe our hands and dry them. I love all this — the luxurious pace of a meal, the silk carpet we're sitting on, the gentle smoke from the *bakhoor* in the corner dispensing the sweet scent of *oud.*

Mr. Mehta now takes a key from his pocket and unlocks the oblong case. He pulls out an intricately carved rectangular box. At first, I think it's marble, but if it were, he would be carrying the weight differently. This box seems lighter. I lean in for a closer look. The box is constructed from pieces of bone that have been sanded, trimmed and glued together. I glance at Lakshmi, who I'm sure has also noticed the carvings of flowers, deer and persimmon trees on the lid. It's a design she might have painted with henna on a woman's body. Mr. Mehta lifts the lid. Inside, eight glass bottles, no more than three inches high, with elaborate finials, are set into eight round holes. The ninth hole contains long cotton swabs. Each bottle is filled with an amber liquid — a few are more green than gold, a few are reddish-gold. Each bottle is labeled in Hindi.

I pull out the scent papers I've brought from Paris. Mr. Mehta frowns. He wags a finger at me, then beckons me to sit by his side. I put the scent papers back in my purse and do as he asks. He pushes my sleeve all the way up my forearm. He does the same with my other arm. It's strangely intimate. I look to Lakshmi as if to ask: *Is this improper?* She smiles calmly at me.

"You should smell the scent on your skin. Today, tomorrow. Notice the difference over time." He looks around the room at our eager faces as he lifts the first bottle from the case. "In the *Book of Delights,* the emperor recommended rubbing perfume separately into each joint. Into the armpit. Behind the knee. Each part of a woman's body." He holds the tiny bottle reverently with both hands, as if he's making an offering to the gods. "*Gulab.* The roses are grown in the fields around Kannauj. They're picked first thing in the morning, then quickly brought to our distillery." From the case, he pulls a long-handled cotton swab.

He unscrews the cap of the bottle, dips the swab inside and passes it to me. I rub the cotton on my wrist.

"Avoid rubbing your wrists together. That will dilute the essence." He has me close my eyes and wait a moment before sniffing.

When I do, it's as if I'm drunk on scent. It's strong, and I feel engulfed in a field of damask rosebushes. I want to keep sniffing; it's so addictive. But the vendor pulls my hand down. He's ready with the next swab. "See if you can tell me what this is." He dabs a little farther up my forearm.

It's vetiver! But not like the diluted one I was working with a week ago on Delphine's formula. This one is clean and green and fresh. And intoxicating.

Mr. Mehta is delighted by my response. We go through the next four bottles, which I identify easily: fig, kewra, saffron, and henna. I give my sister the henna swab to try. She'll be most familiar with the scent of the small white flowers of the *mehndi* plant.

He pulls out the second to last bottle from the case. "This one is called *shamama.* What do you smell?"

I steal a glance at a grinning Nasreen, the one who has been wearing *shamama* for forty years. I close my eyes as I inhale the oil on my arm. "Clove. Cardamom. Vetiver . . . juniper berry, *chameli,* bela and . . . perhaps jasmine?"

The vendor laughs. "*Shabash!* You really do know your scents."

I feel my cheeks redden with pleasure and steal a glance at Hazi and Nasreen, who are smiling at me. I don't want them to think I'm wasting their time.

"I've saved this one for last. Tell me what you think." He uncorks the last bottle, hands me the swab.

I close my eyes.

I inhale.

My eyes spring open. Four pairs of eyes are waiting for my reaction. I look at Jiji. I had high hopes for this one being the ingredient I was looking for. I don't want to disappoint her by telling everyone that it's not.

Mr. Mehta appears triumphant, thinking he's finally stumped me.

Hazi's sharp eyes turn to me.

I swallow. "Geranium. Frangipani. Sage?"

The vendor's face falls. He frowns. I can tell I have angered him by not playing coy, the way Nasreen does. Perhaps he thinks she really is as meek as she pretends to be — around him.

Hazi saves face by asking, "How much for half a kilo of the *gulab* and *khus*?"

He hands the two bottles to Nasreen, who passes them to Hazi. The older sister makes a show of inspecting the bottles, holding them up to the light.

The vendor mentions a sum that sets Hazi's body jiggling with laughter. She wipes her eyes delicately so as not to smear her *kohl*. "*Bhai Saab,* please do not embarrass me in front of my oldest and dearest friends. That girl —" she points to me "— is like a daughter to me. Now, how much?"

Like a daughter? I keep my smile to myself. Is this how she usually negotiates?

Mr. Mehta protests gently, appeals to Nasreen to intervene, tells us he'll hardly make any money and do we realize how many hours of labor have gone into those bottles? Their workers know precisely the right time to gather the flowers and roots, exactly what temperature is needed to cook the mixture. Nasreen smiles and shakes her head piteously at him.

Hazi says forget the *gulab* and *khus attars.* "It's too much."

After another round of negotiations, he throws up his hands and halves his original price.

I try to signal to my sister with my eyes that these are not the scents I'm looking for. But she ignores me. I'm furiously converting rupees into francs, realizing how expensive they are (this is India, after all).

205

But the figure pleases Hazi, and, it seems, it pleases Jiji, too.

"Jiji, I don't —" I protest.

My sister places a cool palm on my arm to still me. She unhooks a cloth pouch from her petticoat. As long as I've known her, that's where she's kept her money. She looks at Hazi and grins. *"Ji, may we present you with the gulab attar?"*

The begum *salaams* my sister, her lips curling into a lazy smile. She motions to a girl standing behind us (they seem to come out of nowhere whenever she needs something). The girl brings a silver wine jar with tiny glasses and pours pomegranate wine for all of us.

Mr. Mehta says his uncle will bring the larger quantities tomorrow. No one other than the family is trusted to deliver the precious oils. Nasreen and Mr. Mehta retire to her room; Hazi to hers; Jiji and I to ours.

The heavy lunch and the wine have made me sleepy, and I yawn. "Jiji, where are you getting all that money?" I ask when we get to our room.

She's taking the pins out of her hair before she lies down for a nap. "Malik turned our herbal remedy business into something much bigger. I've told you how Nimmi and I propagate the plants and Malik sells the products we make to herbal practitioners? Well, it was a modest enterprise until just a few months ago, when a distributor put in the biggest order we've had yet."

I let out a happy squeal and hug her. "*Félicitations,* Jiji!" I say, mixing my languages, as I often do with my girls.

"Nimmi and Malik work really hard, Radha. She has Malik tending the Healing Garden on the days she and I go riding with the kids. Can you believe he's scared of horses?"

I let out a laugh. I can't imagine Malik, the boy who would eagerly fight *goondas* to protect Lakshmi, being scared of anything. I'll have to tease him about it the next time I see him.

Lakshmi sits on the *charpoy,* her hair loose around her shoulders. Suddenly, she's twenty years younger, the sister I met in Jaipur for the first time.

"Radha," she says, "do you ever think about Maa?"

I shrug. I never like to talk about our mother with Lakshmi. For so long, my sister had been hoping that Maa and Pitaji would forgive her for running away from her marriage — so much so that she'd been building that house in Jaipur hoping she could bring them to live with her. What she didn't know was they'd gone to their funeral pyres still ashamed of a daughter who failed her marital duty. A daughter who humiliated a family already steeped in shame. Jiji never received the absolution she sought. I think there's always a part of her that will feel the loss of a final parting with them.

She's studying me, watching the thoughts rolling across my face. "It's all right, Radha. I've made peace with it all. And I made peace with Hari. We were both young. We'd never been taught how to talk to each other, listen to one another. Hari and I are better off with other people."

I think about that for a while, but something else is nagging at me. I sit on the bed with her. "Jiji, those essential oils you bought from Mr. Mehta? Like the *gulab* one for Hazi. They're so expensive. Why did you buy them when I don't need them?"

"We had to show Mr. Mehta that Hazi was the most important person in that room. We are going away, but she and Nasreen live here. We have to show our respect." She finger-combs the tangles out of her hair. "I was only seventeen and on my own when I got here. They saved me. Little gestures like that are the least I can do to thank them."

That's what I was wondering down in the kitchen with Binu last night. What would have happened if Jiji hadn't come into my life?

I sigh. "I understand why you bought the rose oil. But why the vetiver?"

Her face brightens. "It's the best *khus* I've ever smelled. I expect you to create something phenomenal with it."

Why does she still believe in me when all I've ever done is defy her? I wouldn't drink the cotton root bark tea when she asked me to. She advised me not to get attached to Niki after I gave birth because she had arranged for an adoption; I didn't listen. She'd begged me to wait before marrying Pierre because I'd only known him for seven months. *Didn't I want to go to college?* she asked. Again, I didn't listen.

I always thought she was trying to control me, so in the end, I ran away to Paris. Was I trying to show her — or myself — that I could make the right decisions on my own? At seventeen, hadn't she decided, on her own, to leave her marriage all by herself? What made her so very different from me? I can't seem to rid myself of that strain of resentment, the vein staining a perfect slab of soapstone, that makes me want to project an image of competence to her. I want her to see me not as the little sister who needs her guidance but as a woman who can handle whatever comes her way, as she has.

I slide my hand over the cot's undulating jute. I want to confide my conflicting feelings about my life, but I'm loath to admit that I may have made a mistake marrying Pierre. I don't want to tell her that as much as I love him I'm not sure how I feel about my marriage. When he kissed me goodbye in Paris just before I stepped into the taxi, I had the strange feeling that I was embarking on a journey that would last far longer than half a week. Even more bizarre was that I was looking forward to the separation from the familiar. Now, as I sit in Agra at Hazi and Nasreen's house, what I'm feeling is excitement, the same excitement I felt when I ran to Paris with Pierre. As if I'm about to start a new adventure, one which promises to shed old skin, like a king cobra. Maybe Jiji's right. Maybe this trip will result in something remarkable, something magnificent.

I look up at my sister and realize she's been watching me. Her green-blue-gray eyes are thoughtful. It's as if she's privy to the thoughts flitting across my brain, making me wonder if I've spoken them out loud. I look away, shielding my eyes from her gaze.

She taps my knee. "You know, Radha, I don't always know what I'm doing. I try something. If it doesn't work, I try something else. None of us are perfect, are we? But we have to keep trying to be our best selves. You are on your way to the top. You'll make some missteps, but that's normal. Mostly, you're going to do things you didn't even know you were capable of."

With relief, I realize she thinks I'm worried about my project, my career in the fragrance industry. I smile and nod.

We lie down for our afternoon naps. I dream of a rosebush that grows as high as the sky. I need to get to the flowers at the top where Shanti and Asha are sitting, calling to me, but every time I try, a new thorn emerges to prick me. I keep falling to the ground, where I turn to place my nose against the wet earth.

Four o'clock chai is served in the entertainment hall. All the courtesans are present. Hazi suggests the women act out a play they've been rehearsing for the *kotha*'s customers. Nasreen, the house choreographer, tells Lakshmi and me that it's a scene from *The Little Clay Cart,* the two-thousand-year-old Sanskrit play. The tallest woman in the house plays the male character, Charudatta, who, along with a royal courtier, vies for the affection of a rich courtesan. In elaborate costumes, the women of the *kotha* are unrecognizable. They act. They dance. They sing. We laugh uproariously at the mistaken identities and the bungling ne'er-do-wells, as we know the *kotha*'s patrons will this evening. Not for the first time do I wonder if Shakespeare had seen a Sanskrit play before he started writing his own.

Again, at night, I find I can't sleep. I liked Mr. Mehta's offerings, but I haven't found the humid, wet scent I'm looking for.

Why did I think it would be so easy to find it in India? Just because I'm familiar with the scents of my homeland? What if I return to Paris empty-handed? I'll look like a fool on my first big assignment. I will have let Delphine down. Pierre will be proven right: my work has no value; it's frivolous. And the time I've spent away from home, the hours I've logged at work instead of being with my daughters — will it all have been for naught? Have I cheated Shanti and Asha of my attention without good cause the way Maa cheated me of hers? Will they grow up resenting me for my neglect? Or will they seek attention in all the wrong places, the way I did with Kanta and with Ravi, when I felt ignored?

I glance at Jiji, sleeping peacefully next to

me in her sari. I decide to get out of bed, but I don't want to disturb the inhabitants of the *haveli*. I don't want to bother Binu in the kitchen again so I wrap a shawl around my sweater and make my way to the rooftop. When I step onto the roof, dawn is sending her first pale ribbons across the horizon.

Hazi and Nasreen's *kotha* is located less than a mile from the Taj Mahal. Theirs is one of the tallest houses, and I'm looking across forty other rooftops to catch a glimpse of the famous marble tomb at first light. All I can see now is the graceful silhouette of the Taj Mahal against the blackened sky.

As my eyes adjust to the darkness, I'm startled by the sight of humped shapes moving on the rooftops below me. In the distance, I hear the first call to prayer by the muezzin. The huddled bodies now bow rhythmically, in sync with the incantation.

The sky turns a deep indigo, then purple. Ribbons of cream give way to pale pink, amber, turmeric. The Taj Mahal begins to glow like a pearl. In the foreground, the enormous sandstone entrance to the marble tomb mirrors the two tiers of niches, the domed entrance and the four minarets of the majestic monument. The call to prayer ends and women begin gathering the clothes they left on the clotheslines the day before. Wood smoke from the first cooking fires perfumes the air.

"Impressive when you consider the empress gave up her life for it."

The husky voice can only belong to Hazi. Given that she stays up late to welcome and chat with guests, I'm surprised to see her up so early. "Who do you mean?"

"Mumtaj, Emperor Shah Jahan's wife. Surely you know that the Taj Mahal is his memorial to her." Hazi's smile is wry. She's chewing on something. She comes to stand by my side at the edge of the roof. For her bulk, she moves lightly, almost ethereally. Now I can see she's cleaning her teeth with a neem twig. She spits over the side of the roof. "Mumtaj died giving birth to their fourteenth child. They were only married nineteen years, which means sometimes she didn't even have a year between babies!"

Hazi looks at the lightening sky, her eyes narrowing. This close, I notice that her eyes are golden, like Pierre's and Asha's. "That poor woman's body just gave out. Building that monument was the least the emperor could do for what he put her through!" She spits again, then laughs, making her belly — and her sari — jiggle.

I smile.

214

"Have you been to the Taj Mahal?" she asks me.

I shake my head, turning my gaze back to the tomb. I imagine Lakshmi went there many times when she lived here. Perhaps she and I could go there with my girls someday.

Hazi looks thoughtful. "Many would argue with me, but I've often wondered whether Mumtaj herself was in a tomb during her life."

"Mutlub?" I'm interested.

"What I mean is that she was a woman prized solely for her eligibility for marriage, sold to the highest bidder, with no control over her body or her money. She had to compromise her dignity every minute of every day. My mother and grandmother taught Nasreen and me — and we teach all our girls — to unlearn the ways of centuries. To perfect their skills in classical dance, poetry and literature for their own edification. To satisfy their own physical desires while satisfying another's. To manage their dignity and their money equally." Her tone of voice is neither defensive nor righteous.

"But they'll always be courtesans. Not accepted into polite society."

"Yet, polite society still wishes their sons could be educated in the art of etiquette, music and poetry by us. Given the choice, I would rather be the jailer than the prisoner."

We're the same height, Hazi and I, but there's a pride in her bearing that makes her appear taller. I decide I like her more than I could have imagined. I can see why Lakshmi felt safe here at the *kotha*. The courtesans have a keen sense of their worth. A fierce pride in their ability to look after themselves. They are not bound by conventional roles like wife, mother, caretaker. They live by their own rules.

Hazi leans closer to me. "I want to show you something. Come with me." She throws her neem stick from the rooftop and turns as deftly as a cat.

"Abhee?" I ask. It's barely daylight. The women who sweep the streets are just beginning to start their chore.

Without turning around, she crooks a commanding finger in the direction of the door we took to get to the rooftop.

I follow.

Outside the *haveli,* we take a left. Hazi nods a hello or *namaste* to various shopkeepers who are just opening their stalls. She asks after the health of the broom salesman who is hanging up his long-whiskered *jharus* on the ceiling of his shop. To the Muslim in a white skullcap who is trying to keep his spotted goat from climbing on top of a motorcycle, she says, *"Salaam alaikum."* To which he responds, *"Walaikum salaam,"* with a smile. His goat bleats at us. Two women walking ahead of us are arguing about the recipe for vermicelli *kheer*. The one in a purple cotton sari with yellow stripes thinks you should add a little butter at the end, but the woman in the chartreuse sari says, *"Arre!* How can I afford *ghee* for *kheer* when he needs it for his *chappati?"* She's referring to her husband, of course, but won't use his name out of respect, the way Maa never referred to Pitaji by his first name. Both women stop to examine the bananas a street vendor is laying out on his table. As we pass them, I see the turmeric marks on the women's foreheads that confirm their early-morning visit to a Hindu temple.

A colorful overhead banner spanning the width of the street promotes the movie *Prem Nagar.* The image features an Indian man in a Western suit flirting with a beautiful woman in a sari who seems to be enjoying the attention. When we pass under the banner, Hazi turns right. A man in a pink shirt is facing away from us, urinating against a wall marked by his fellow relievers. Hazi and I pull our shawls up to our noses to avoid the stench. Immediately after we pass the *doodh-walla,* his motorcycle weighed down with four heavy steel canisters of fresh milk as well as his teenage son in a school uniform, we take a left and arrive at a smoke-filled warehouse.

The center of the *godown* is open to the sky. Barefoot men in T-shirts and shorts or *dhotis,* their skin much darker than Hazi's or mine, are already at work. They glance at us briefly and return to their labor. One squats on the floor tossing cow dung into two clay ovens that are already ablaze. Have the men been tending to those fires all night? There's a hole at the top of each oven. Embedded in each hole is a man-sized copper vessel. Two other, identical ovens are dormant. The lid of one of the active copper pots has been sealed with what looks like a mixture of clay and cloth. A bamboo tube rises out of each lid, then angles down, toward a leather bucket. A thick liquid, the color of olive oil, spills from the tube into the bucket. One of the workers squats before the bucket and carefully pours the mixture into smaller glass bottles.

I know, now, where I am! This is a fragrance factory — but unlike any I've seen in France. In Grasse, water is distilled in huge copper stills that sit on pristine cement surfaces; nothing like the hard-packed dirt Hazi and I are standing on. There is no smoke in the Grasse factories, just clean steam. But the result appears the same in both India and France: an essential oil so pure that people will pay enormous sums to blend it into the fragrances they're creating.

I must look shocked or baffled because Hazi is laughing. "Like it?"

"Bilkul!" I walk around the perimeter of the room, studying each still, each component, aware of a faint, familiar scent in the room that's delicate, humid, watery and sweet. All my senses feel alive. My spine tingles.

Suddenly, the door to the back alley opens and a man walks through it, pushing a wheelbarrow filled with . . . *cow pats*? He upends the lot in a corner of the room next to a larger mound of similar cow pies. Just as I'm about to turn my attention back to the essential oil, I see two of the workers using large buckets to scoop the cow dung into the copper vessel without a lid. The worker at the hearth stands and places both his hands on the metal pot. He seems to be testing the temperature of the water inside the vessel *with his palms*? In Grasse, the workers would be using a temperature gauge. I watch, fascinated, wondering why they're cooking manure.

As if she's read my thoughts, Hazi says, "It's not cow dung. It's soil, collected after the first monsoon rain."

Patties made of soil? I walk over to the pail of essential oil and tap the worker on the shoulder. He steps aside to let me sniff it.

Hai Bhagwan! Suddenly, I'm back in Ajar, seven years old, my hair hanging in a messy braid down my back. The monsoons have come and left the earth bleeding water. I'm stepping out into the open area in the back of our hut to look at the sky. Patches of blue fight for space amidst pregnant clouds. On the ground in front of me, the three metal pails I'd left out overnight have filled with rainwater, which means I won't have to fetch water from the farmer's well for several days. Steam rises from the ground. The air is dense with tiny particles of water that haven't yet been dried by the weak sun. All around me is the scent of promise and potential. I spin in a circle, let the drops wash over me. What Maa and I could grow before the sun bakes the soil! The clothes I'll wash today and hang to dry will use this energy, this possibility, of making something new. Maa is behind me, kneading dough for the *chapattis.* Her eyes haven't clouded over yet. The scent of *atta* merges with the scent of my surroundings, creating something moist and sugary. An earthy fragrance.

Hazi is grinning at my reaction. "This, Radha, is the scent of rain. *Mitti attar.*"

Ten years ago, she says, a couple of Australians gave this scent a new name — "petrichor" — but Indians, for centuries, have known it as *mitti attar.* The soil is harvested, baked and finally distilled to extract the earth's essential oil.

I close my eyes, thinking of Olympia. How unknowable she's been. The one ingredient I've missed: water, rain, mist. The very veil that makes it difficult to see her clearly. This is why she's never been appreciated, why she's been misunderstood. In my mind's eye, I'm blending the top notes, heart notes and base notes that I've isolated. And then I add in this precious new — to me — ingredient: *mitti attar.* The scent of rain.

From her divan, a glowing, nude Victorine smiles at me.

My eyes spring open. "Why didn't you tell me about this yesterday, Hazi-*ji,* when Mr. Mehta was here?"

The old begum tilts her head and studies me for a moment. "I didn't know you well enough yet, Radha. You and Lakshmi are

221

very different." She picks something from her pinky fingernail. "She was fragile when she came to us. Nasreen and I could see she needed help. She was covered in bruises. She needed us." Her amber eyes look directly at me. "You're a harder person." She splays the palm of her hand on my chest, near my heart. "You've been taken care of. Lakshmi paved the way for you. We trust her. In my world, we only do business with those we trust." She had taken the measure of me upon first meeting and found me wanting.

I feel a sharp stab in my heart. I want to tell her about the years I spent alone in Ajar. The years I spent deflecting Maa's barbs, making excuses for Pitaji's drinking, ignoring the gossipeaters and their insults — all because of Lakshmi! Because she did the unthinkable: she deserted us all. She didn't have to face the aftermath, the judgmental stares of the villagers, the mothers who kept their children away from Pitaji's school. How they always crossed the street when they saw us, barred me from using the village well, forced me to walk two more miles to the farmer's well with my empty *mutki*.

Jiji didn't have to shield her tender feelings every hour of every day as Maa, Pitaji and I had to. If I told her all of this, would

Hazi see me differently? Would she be more sympathetic? But why do I want her to be?

Or do I want her to admire, and respect, me as she does Jiji, the seventeen-year-old waif who showed up at the *kotha*'s doorstep, asking for room and board in exchange for her prized cotton root bark sachets?

I'm the one who suffered when she left her husband. My sister is the reason why I always told myself I'd never leave my marriage — no matter what. Often, the urge is there, but I suppress it. When Pierre and I are fighting. When I don't feel like making up, but I don't have the energy to argue. When I'd rather be blending Delphine's formulas than negotiating Shanti's tantrums. When I'd like to crawl under the coverlet and sleep instead of cooking dinner. When I feel I can't breathe unless I get out, get out, get out . . .

There's a ringing in my ears. I can no longer hear the noise of the men moving around the factory, the crackling and hissing of the fire or the sound of my own breathing. The ringing gets louder, the pitch higher. Hazi is looking at me with concern. I can't hear what she's saying. Her hand is on my arm.

As quickly as it started, the ringing stops. I shake my head to clear it, as if — any minute — it might start again.

I nod to let Hazi know I'm fine. The wrinkles across her forehead ease. She takes a deep breath before she lets go of my arm.

I stuff my hands into the pockets of my bell-bottoms so she can't see how they're shaking. I turn away. I try to think about something — *anything* — to change the subject. *"Ji,"* I ask her, "did you ever try to talk Lakshmi into joining the *kotha*?"

Hazi sucks her teeth. "Do you think Lakshmi didn't already know that the life society dictates for women wasn't just? She came to us fully aware. She kept herself child-free on purpose. She didn't want to sell her body for food. What she wanted was to run her own business. So, no. There was never any reason she should want to join us."

I turn to face her. Her eyes are filled with pain. "Some of the other women you've met here used to work for others — cooking, cleaning or hauling dirt from construction sites. They had to sleep with their employers or bosses just to keep their jobs. With us, they make more in a few hours dancing in civilized company than they used to make in a month. And they don't have to sleep with anyone they don't like."

I don't know why I'm skeptical, or why I

feel the need to challenge her. "Surely not all businessmen and high-ranking officials are likable?"

She offers me a wry grin. "*There are men and men and every stone is not a gem.* Likability is in the eye of the beholder."

That makes me laugh.

She says, "Seen enough?"

"*Hahn.* But where can I buy this scent?"

Hazi takes a moment. "We own this factory. Nasreen and I. We remember this *mitti* scent from our childhood in Lucknow. At my mother's *haveli.* She was also a courtesan. We were happy there."

The surprise must be evident on my face. She arches a painted eyebrow at me. "Even courtesans are allowed happy childhoods, *beti.* When it rained, we would dance in the courtyard and splash our feet in the mud afterward. If my mother had allowed me to bathe in that mud, I would have." She grins, revealing tiny, even teeth. "Now I bathe in water scented with *mitti attar.*" From the shelter of her woolen shawl, she extends a plump arm and pushes back the long sleeve of her sweater blouse. She waves her forearm under my nose. "See?"

I sniff. It's the scent I've been catching a whiff of every now and then but haven't been able to identify. And all this time, I hadn't noticed it was Hazi's fragrance!

Again, she crooks a finger at me, turns and leads me out of the factory. "How much will you need?"

I haven't thought about it, until now. I've studied the creative brief but haven't asked Delphine what will happen once the client approves the final fragrance formula.

Hazi must understand what's going through my mind. She smiles kindly. "We'll make you a good deal, my friend."

On the way back, she makes us stop for chai at a street stall. I haven't eaten or had any chai since I woke up, and now I'm hungry. The boy behind the stall pours caramel-colored chai from a saucepan into small glasses, managing not to spill a drop.

"How long have you owned the factory?" I ask.

She wrinkles her nose. "About ten years. The man who used to own it — along with several other businesses — went bankrupt." Again, she shows me her sly smile. "He owed our *kotha* quite a sum of money. Entertainment is not free, *beti.* Nor is it cheap."

I wag my head in agreement.

"In the end, we ended up owning every-thing he owned."

I drink my tea, thinking. "Hazi-*ji,* why

does the factory only employ men?"

She shrugs, lifting her eyes to the sky. "It's the way it's always been. Men tend to the fires, pour the raw material into the pots, strain the oil out of the vats. It's dirty work."

"But couldn't women learn to do it?"

She cocks her head and blinks. "I suppose they could. I've never thought about it."

We set our empty glasses on the counter of the stall. I start to take out some rupees to pay the boy, but Hazi puts a hand on my arm. She tilts her head to indicate we should move on.

As we continue down the street, I keep looking back at the *chai-walla,* who is now helping another customer. Hazi notices my confusion (there's no Frenchman who would let you walk away without paying). She lets out a loud guffaw, bending at the waist to lean on her knees. When she straightens, she wipes the tears from the corners of her eyes. She points back at the stall with her thumb. "*Beti,* that was one of the businesses our patron used to own."

Now I laugh along with her, and we continue walking back to the *kotha.* Two women in *salwar kameez* and shawls, sitting on a stoop, chatting with one another, stop to stare at us. We must look a strange sight: a courtesan — face painted, in elaborate sari and jewels at nine o'clock in the morning — and a woman young enough to be her daughter with French bangs, bell-bottoms and no makeup.

As we're removing our shoes at the threshold of the *kotha,* one of the older servants hurries to Hazi. "A visitor, madam," she whispers.

Hazi raises her brows. She must not have been expecting anyone. "Bring us some breakfast, Shalini."

The servant walks downstairs to the kitchen. I wonder if Binu is the one who will be helping Chef cook the breakfast. We walk around the atrium to the great room where two women in saris are seated on bolsters next to one another, engrossed in conversation.

One of them is Jiji.

Seated next to her is a woman I haven't seen in almost seventeen years.

I stop, frozen, as if I've suddenly grown roots in the marble below my feet.

Her hair is darker than it used to be; she must be dyeing it black the way many Indian women do when they start to go gray. When we first met, her hair was cropped into a short bob, but she wears it longer now, in a bun, the same way Jiji does.

Gone, too, are the capris and midriff blouses she used to wear when she was younger. In their place are an embroidered silk sari and matching blouse, marking her as a comfortable middle-class Indian matron. The deep grooves from the edge of her nose to the corners of her mouth and the wrinkles around her neck give away her age as midforties.

Hazi walks into the room with her hands in *namaste* to greet the guest at the same time that Lakshmi lifts her eyes to meet mine.

I glare at my sister. I'm trying to control myself, but I let loose before I even know what I'm about to say. "How dare you?" My face feels warm. Spit flies out of my mouth.

Lakshmi scrambles to stand, rushes toward me. "No, Radha. It's not what you think."

Hazi is looking at us, aghast. For once, she seems not to know what she should do. No doubt she isn't used to outbursts such as this. Not in her elegant *kotha*.

Kanta, my former friend from Jaipur, the one who took my baby boy from me, rises and stands before us in a red and gold sari.

"Hello, Radha." Her eyes are wet. She's wringing her hands.

229

I back away, fighting off my sister's attempts to keep me in the room. "I can't imagine why you'd do this!" I yell at Jiji.

"I didn't, *choti behen*!"

Kanta has to raise her voice to be heard above the din. "It isn't Lakshmi's fault. She didn't know I was coming. I had to find you so I could tell you myself, Radha. It's about Niki."

"No!" I scream. Not since I was fourteen have I uttered his name out loud. To hear his name spoken, now, on someone else's lips, is every bit as painful as it was back then.

I start to run from the hall, but Lakshmi grabs my arm, pulls me to her and wraps her arms around my shaking limbs. She holds the back of my head in her hand and shushes me like a baby. I hadn't realized until that moment that I was crying, my fat, sloppy tears running down my face and onto her shoulder. My body heaves with the effort. I'm thirteen years old again, wanting my big sister to take care of me. "Make it stop, Jiji. Just make it stop."

Kanta is twisting and untwisting her *pallu* around her hand. "I didn't mean to disrupt —"

My sister reaches a hand behind her to still Kanta, who stops talking.

Jiji rubs circles on my back. "Baby, I didn't know Kanta would be here. I didn't invite her. She called me in Shimla and Jay told her where I was. She came because of Niki. He didn't come home two nights ago. They searched everywhere in Jaipur for him."

My voice comes out wet and bubbly. "Wha-what's that got to do with me?"

She gently eases my head from her shoulder and wipes my cheeks with her thumbs. "Yesterday, he sent a telegram to let Kanta and Manu know where he is." Jiji's eyes are full of concern. "He's on his way to Paris."

My mouth flies open.

Lakshmi glances at Kanta, then turns to me. "To your house."

My house? In Paris? I imagine Pierre opening the front door, a young man explaining who he is, the confusion on Pierre's face! I fumble in my pants pocket for my necklace with the magic vial. My hands are trembling so much that I can't get to it fast enough. I almost drop it, grabbing the chain in time to save the glass vial from shattering on the marble floor. I've never opened it in front of other people, but just holding the tiny vessel and rolling it in my hands soothes me. Jiji sees it, but she doesn't say a word.

Now Hazi is at my elbow with a glass of

pomegranate wine. "Drink," she commands.

I down the entire glass in one swallow. It coats my tongue, my throat and my stomach with its warmth and sweetness. A gentle numbness follows.

I let myself be led to a bolster, where I settle. Lakshmi and Kanta sit down on either side of me. Hazi issues instructions to bring us sugared chai, along with the rest of the breakfast. I sit dumbly while an array of hot *puris,* spicy *toor dal,* curried okra *subji* and *jalebis* dripping with sweet syrup are set in front of us. Normally, I would attack this meal with fervor, but, for now, I have no appetite. Nasreen, who oversees the making of the daily breakfast with their chef, joins us, filling a *thali* for me and setting it in front of my bolster.

Lakshmi glances at Kanta. "It might be best if you tell the story."

Kanta's eyes are troubled. She unwinds and twists her *pallu* around her palm again. I think she's always held out hope that she and I might reconcile someday and be the close friends we once were. It's not her fault that we're not. She did nothing to create this rift except adopt my baby. I'm the one who cut off all contact to ensure I would stay out of Niki's life with his new family. If I'd stayed in touch, I would have made sure

Niki would have loved me more; I would have hoarded his attention, demanded it and kept his love for myself.

Kanta is crying. She takes a moment to wipe her eyes on her *pallu.* "It all started with his applications for college. Oh, Radha, you would be so proud of how smart he is. He aces all his tests — he's ranked second in his class out of forty!" She holds up a palm as if to say, *Sorry for the digression.* "He'd asked me for his exam results — I'd taken them from him because I wanted to show Sassuji. But I forgot to return them. He decided to look for them himself. In my dressing table." She glances nervously at Jiji, who encourages her with a smile. "He found other things — letters I'd been keeping. One of them was a letter Manu and I received from a lawyer in the UK."

Kanta picks up her handbag and rummages through it until she finds a bright white envelope. She hands it to me.

It's expensive paper. Heavy. The envelope flap is open. There are four pages inside. I look at Jiji with a frown. She nods. I start to read.

Hazi commands, "Aloud, please." With a start, I remember the old begum is in the room, too. How does anyone refuse her?

I do as she says.

April 4, 1974
Hazelton & Dunnwitty Esq.

Dear Mr. Manu Agarwal and Mrs. Kanta Devi Agarwal,

This letter is to inform you of an educational trust formed for the benefit of a minor, Nikhil Agarwal (hereinafter referred to as Beneficiary), a citizen of India born in Shimla, in the state of Himachal Pradesh, on September 2, 1956. Our firm has been contracted, on behalf of an anonymous benefactor, to administer the trust and to specify the conditional requirements. They are as follows:

1. Beneficiary must show proof of identity;
2. Beneficiary must attend a four-year educational institution of his choice in the United States of America;
3. Beneficiary must show proof of admission to said institution. As the admissions process is lengthy and complicated, it is suggested that the process be initiated immediately. Lists of acceptable institutions are included in this communication;

234

4. Summer employment will be provided by the trust in the United States of America;

5. Beneficiary will be required to work in the United States for two years upon completion of his bachelor's degree. Details of employment will be sent upon graduation. We will file the official paperwork for a US passport on his behalf.

In order for us to administer the trust, you will need to sign and notarize the contract herein within sixty days. If I can be of further service or answer any questions except those related to the benefactor, please do not hesitate to contact me.

Yours sincerely,
Jonathan Westerlin

I glance at the contract on the next few pages and pass it to Jiji. She has more experience reading contracts now that she and Malik are running their own business. From the corner of my eye, I see Hazi and Nasreen exchange a look, piecing the story together in their minds.

"But what does this have to do with me?" I ask Kanta. Even now, I find it hard to look directly into her eyes, focusing instead on her forehead or her hands or the crimson glass bangles on her arm. Is it guilt I feel for abandoning her as a friend? For secretly hating her because she got to raise my baby and I didn't? For ignoring her pleas to resume our former friendship?

Kanta sighs. "He found something else next to the letter." Her dark brown eyes, naked with sadness and regret, regard me. "All the letters you sent back — unopened. Every one of the photos of Niki I sent to you these last seventeen years."

Those letters! Why did she insist on sending me photos of a baby whose existence I needed to forget? I returned them unopened so she would get the message. Why should I be forced to look at something I never asked for in the first place?

Only Lakshmi understands. Kanta also sent her photos of Niki. The last time I was in Shimla, my sister asked me if I was ready to look at them. I'd shaken my head. Now, she places an arm around my shoulders and squeezes gently.

Kanta sighs, her breath shaky as if she's about to cry again. "He wanted to know why we'd kept the letter about the scholarship from him. The deadline for a response to the letter had passed. He wanted to know why I'd been sending his photos to a woman in Paris all these years. And why she'd returned them without opening them. He was confused — and we could understand why. But Manu and I didn't know how much to tell him so we said nothing. That's when he got angry. He knew that we were holding back. But after seventeen years, how do you tell a young man that his parents aren't really his parents? Or that he was supposed to be the next Crown Prince of Jaipur? But never got the chance?"

I choke on my inhale. "*What?* What did you just say?"

No one makes a sound. The room is quiet.

I spin around to face Lakshmi, whose eyes are shut. The color has drained from her face. "Jiji, what is she saying?"

My sister opens her eyes. She reaches for my arm, but I pull away. Her words are slow and measured. "Niki was supposed to be adopted by the Jaipur Palace. We had a contract. The maharaja was looking for a crown prince who would eventually succeed him. And Niki checked all the boxes. He had royal blood from Ravi's side. But you didn't want to give him up, Radha."

I remember the arguments Jiji and I had in the hospital before and after I gave birth to Niki. I was thirteen and unmarried. Lakshmi tried to convince me to let the baby be adopted, but never told me she knew, already, who the parents would be.

I told her I had no intention of giving up my baby, and certainly not to strangers. Instead, I dreamed up all manner of crazy scenarios: I would wrap Niki in a bundle and run away; I would hop on a train headed for Chandigarh with a sleeping Niki; I would be hired as an *ayah* for some woman whose baby was the same age as Niki. Eventually, though, Jiji's voice would interrupt my fantasies: Where could a thirteen-year-old girl go unaccompanied? People would wonder what such a young girl was doing with the baby. They might think I had stolen him. Who would give shelter to a thirteen-year-old carrying a baby? The nuns? If I went to a convent, I would be asked to become part of their order. Respectable families would turn their backs on me. Everywhere I turned, I would be shunned. And so would my baby. I had no choice but to agree to an adoption.

Now, I'm stunned to think the Jaipur Palace was planning to adopt Niki. "You're saying Niki could have been crown prince? He would have been raised by the Maharanis of Jaipur?"

Jiji looks down at her hands. "Yes and no.

238

He would have been raised by governesses and wet nurses and tutors. The maharanis would hardly have been involved. You made the best decision to have Kanta and Manu adopt Niki. I'm the one who forbade everyone from telling you about the palace adoption. Including Kanta and Manu. Even Jay."

"You mean Dr. Jay knew about it, too? What about Samir and Parvati Singh? Am I the only one who *didn't* know?" A cold shiver shoots up my spine. "Were you going to get money for him, Jiji? Did you plan to *sell* my baby to the highest bidder?"

"*Nahee-nahee!* It wasn't like that. You were to be paid, but I intended that money to be used for your college education. None of it was for me."

Jiji looks miserable, but I'm too upset to let her off lightly. "How much? How much were you selling him for?"

"I didn't know they were going to pay anything until I read the adoption contract."

"How . . . much?"

"Thirty thousand rupees." My sister glances at Hazi and Nasreen as if she's begging them to understand. Even they know that while it doesn't seem like much now, given how low the rupee has fallen, it was a lot of money in 1956.

Another thought comes to me: "Wait —

how did you get out of the contract?"

My sister sighs. She pulls her knees to her chin, wraps her arms around her legs. "I talked Jay into doctoring the baby's physical evaluation. Any variance — no matter how small — from the palace's requirements would make the contract null and void. But, Radha, it was all because you refused to give up the baby. It's not Jay's fault. He only did what I asked him to."

There it is again. Everything comes back to the choices I made — sleeping with Ravi, choosing to have the baby, giving him to Kanta to mother. Is it my fault that Niki didn't become the new Maharaja of Jaipur? That another sits in his place? Is it my fault that Jiji was forced to cheat the palace and Dr. Jay had to compromise his ethics? I put my hands to my head.

My sister scoots closer to me, bringing her calming scents with her. She lifts my hands away from my head. Her voice is as soft as the petals of magnolia blossoms. "You made the right decision. To have Kanta and Manu raise him. The palace would have hired nannies and governesses who wouldn't have cared for him the same way. They wouldn't have coddled him the way Kanta and Manu have. Niki has had such a good life. He has wanted for nothing. He's smart. He's healthy. He plays cricket and draws landscapes and loves festivals and dances to film songs." She lowers my arms by my sides. "You did what was best for your baby."

I feel another set of arms envelop me. I smell Kanta's rose-milk scent. This is the closest our bodies — hers and mine — have been in seventeen years. Her mouth is close to my ear. She says, "Thank you for leaving Niki with us, Radha. I've always wanted to say that to you. And I would repeat it a thousand and one times if it would make you feel better."

I hear the words but they don't quite register. I look at the letter on the carpet in front of me. "Why didn't you tell Niki about the scholarship? It sounds like a once-in-a-lifetime opportunity."

Lakshmi says, *"A wolf may lose its teeth but not its nature."*

"Bilkul," Kanta says. "Manu and I suspected who was behind that letter, and we doubt they've changed: the same people who refused to acknowledge Niki's blood as their own — Parvati and Samir Singh. They left for America five, six years ago. Remember that scandal about the Royal Jewel Cinema collapse in Jaipur? They ran with their tails between their legs, but now . . ."

She makes a face. "Seems everything they touch turns to gold. They built a real estate business in the States. Even with the economy as bad as it is the world over, people are still buying houses in America. Manu and I are convinced they want Niki back in their fold, not because they love him but because they need a male heir. Ravi and Sheela only have daughters."

Ravi Singh. Thinking of him isn't as painful as it used to be. Once Pierre came along, I could move to Paris and leave my unhappy memories of Ravi behind.

I turn to Lakshmi, ignoring Kanta. "But we can't know for sure it's the Singhs who hired that attorney. The address is in —" I look at the envelope "— the UK. What if it's not them?"

Kanta comes around to sit next to Lakshmi so I can't avoid looking at her. The two women consult one another silently. I steal a glance at Hazi and Nasreen, who are eating quietly, pretending not to hear every word.

"We have friends in England, people we know from college," Kanta says. "They're lawyers. They agreed to do some sleuthing for us. And we're almost certain the benefactors are the Singhs. Who else would remain anonymous? If the letter had come directly from them, we would have torn it up without hesitation. So they got an intermediary to do it. You've read the letter. You know they want Niki to work in the US for two years after graduation. Manu and I worry that once he's in their clutches, they'll never let go."

I narrow my eyes, thinking. "But what about Ravi? Isn't he taking over the business? And Ravi has a brother. Govind, I think. What about him? Why would the Singhs need Niki if they have two sons?"

Kanta blows air from puffed cheeks. "The Singh sons have been a disappointment to them. From what we hear Ravi likes to drink and carouse. American girls find him appealing." She rolls her eyes, and I understand what she means. That curious cocktail of self-confidence, humility and beacon-like focus on whoever he's with is what attracted me to Ravi even when we were young. I'm not surprised American women are attracted, too.

She continues. "His brother, Govind, had already decided he doesn't want to be involved in the family business. He's working in the movies in Los Angeles now, which is as upsetting to Samir and Parvati as if he'd turned into a *hijra*."

"How do you know all this?" I ask.

243

"The Indian grapevine spans the globe, *beti.*" Hazi is the one who's uttered this. We all turn to look at her. "My nephews in Dubai can tell you the state of my next-door neighbor's colon here in Agra!" Her bellow of laughter infects Nasreen, whose shoulders are jiggling with mirth.

My chai has gone cold, but I drink it anyway. Hazi asks one of the girls to bring me a fresh cup, but I shake my head.

"So what does Niki want from me?" I want to know and don't want to know. Both.

Kanta scratches her forehead. Her glass bangles tinkle delicately. "We suspect that he has somehow combined two ideas in his head and decided *you* might be behind the scholarship. You might be the anonymous benefactor. We've never told him he was adopted. He has no idea. Maybe he just wants to know who you are and why you mattered so much to me."

I color at this. Do I still matter to Kanta? There is no rancor in her eyes. Unlike me, she's not holding on to the past.

Kanta's hand moves to touch mine, but something holds her back. She retracts it. "You've grown into such a lovely woman. I always knew you would be special. You've done more with your life than most." She smiles fondly at Lakshmi. "Your sister has

244

kept us up to date on your doings. You make us all so proud, Radha."

I feel a burning behind my eyes. I have a sudden desire to apologize for all the times I deliberately gave Niki a bottle in those first few months of his life so he'd be too full when Kanta offered him her breast, the milk that was intended for her stillborn baby. I want to tell her I'm sorry for ignoring all those letters she must have spent hours writing, carefully choosing which details of Niki's life I'd be interested in hearing about. I want to sit on her bed as I used to when I was thirteen and drink rose milk and read to her from *Mrs. Dalloway* and talk to her about *National Velvet* and how stunning Elizabeth Taylor is. If only I could go back to that more innocent time before Ravi, before the pregnancy, before I ran away to Paris.

"When will Niki arrive in Paris?" I ask.

Lakshmi answers. "Maybe tomorrow. Maybe the day after. We don't know if he'll try to contact you as soon as he gets there. We have no way of contacting him. He doesn't want us to."

Oh, Bhagwan! Do I call Pierre now? What do I tell him? That I had a child at thirteen? That I was a silly girl who knew no better? That my illegitimate son is all grown now and wants to know me? While I've given Pierre two daughters, I gave my first love a son. Will Pierre consider that a shortcoming? In France, a boy is worthy of heartier congratulations than a girl. I try to picture the fallout from Niki's arrival. I don't know if Pierre has assumed I was a virgin before we married; we've never talked about it. Perhaps Pierre will just think Niki is a part of my family that he hasn't met yet. Or he'll accept a stepchild as easily as —

No, that is as unlikely as Pierre throwing a party for my promotion to apprentice perfumer.

Kanta starts to say something, then stops. I look at her narrow face. She has never been a beautiful woman, but her unflagging energy and enthusiasm for life has always made up for it. I recognize the familiar fire in those eyes of hers now. "It's up to you whether you decide to tell Niki you're his mother. But he'll want to know what our connection — yours and mine — is. Whatever you decide to do, Radha, please encourage Niki to come back home. He's *our* son, Radha. Yours and mine. He belongs to both of us. That's why I sent you those letters, those photos."

So much time has passed. How can I talk to a boy whom I only knew as a baby? A boy I left forever when he was only four months old. I can't undo my pregnancy any more than Kanta can undo her care and feeding of Niki for the last seventeen years. But it's unfair of them to ask for my help now. It's not right. From the pit of my stomach, I feel a rage so profound that I want to pick up Hazi's brass hookah and smash it against the floor until the marble cracks or the hookah splits in two.

"You and Manu are too scared to tell him the truth about his adoption so *I* have to be the one to tell him? After all these years, you want to open up those old wounds? To remind me that the Ravi I loved rejected me so roundly?" I turn to Jiji. "Why not you, Jiji? Why don't you talk to Niki? You're the one who talked me into giving him away. I wanted to keep him, remember? I loved that baby! You could have helped me keep him, Jiji. You, who always found an answer for everything, could have figured out a way to help raise my boy. If you had, I could have raised him. But you didn't try hard enough, did you? You just made me feel bad about wanting to be around him even after Kanta adopted him. What was so bad about wanting to be close to my own flesh and blood?"

Lakshmi looks as if I've struck her with

Hazi's hookah. Finally, I've said it out loud. Did she really have no idea how I felt all these years? How the part of me that has resented her was hiding just under the surface? She's my sister, and she took me in when I had no one, but she's also the one whom I hold responsible for wrenching me from my firstborn. She's never been a mother. How would she know what it feels to talk to your baby for nine months while he's inside you, describing a ladybug and why he's going to love her, or sharing with him the crisp scent of a blue spruce with every inhale, or telling him how you're going to show him how to play five stones. Jiji took all that away from me. She said I had no means to take care of a baby. I still had school to finish. I had my whole life in front of me. But deep down, I've always felt she could have helped. Look at how she's helped raise Nimmi's two children, how she dotes on them. Why couldn't she have helped raise mine, too?

I whirl around at the assembled company, who are staring, horrified, at my wet face, my runny nose. I swipe at my eyes with my sleeve. I can't stop them from welling up again as I turn to Lakshmi.

"It hurt so bad to leave him. Your compresses helped me dry up my milk, Jiji, but not my tears. I missed him so much. I cried every night for a year. At boarding school, there was only Mathilde to comfort me. I never told her why, and she never asked. She had the decency not to poke a wound. But you two —" I point my finger at Lakshmi and Kanta. "You want to pierce that scab with a knife and make it bleed again. You can't ask me to do this! I've moved a million miles away so his memory won't suffocate me. I have my own life now. With my own family. My own daughters. I don't want to meet him! I don't want to talk to him!" My blood is pumping so furiously that it feels as if my heart is about to burst out of its cage. I'm breathing as if I've just run from Jaipur to Agra.

My sister and Kanta are looking at me with wounded expressions. Is that pity in their eyes I see? Or shame? Are they sorry for what they did or sorry for me? Are they thinking of my feelings or theirs? I need to get out of this room. I need to go. I stand up, a little unsteadily.

My sister clears her throat. "Oh, *beti.* I'm sorry for all this. We didn't know he'd come back into your life. But he's coming whether you like it or not."

Hazi raises her hands as if she's about to

palm a cricket ball. "*Aaraam se. Aaraam se.* Leave it, Lakshmi. She needs time."

I'm lying on the cot facing away from the door when Lakshmi comes into the room. She's the last person I want to see; I close my eyes, trying not to snivel. From the story just below this one, the dance instructor calls out the steps as the harmonium player slows or speeds up the music. I hear the rhythmic sounds of the courtesans' *gunghroos*.

But the smell isn't Lakshmi's — that peculiar blend of henna, frangipani, coconut oil and cardamom. I recognize the strong musk and tobacco as Hazi's, with a base note that I now know is *mitti attar.* The cot shifts with her formidable weight as she sits. I feel the heat of her body against my back.

"Did you know heavy women can roll their hips faster than an old man can roll a *beedi*?"

I'm irritated by her intrusion. I speak into the jute. "I'm not in the habit of rolling my hips or *beedis.*" I may as well have asked, rudely, *Why are you here?*

"My mother despaired of my weight when I was younger. She worried that my body wouldn't appeal to the nawabs or maharajas who came to our *kotha.* But she was wrong.

I had . . . something. I was popular with the men. My first patron gave me two boys — this was before we knew Lakshmi and her magic sachets. My mother sent my babies to the local hospital. There was nothing at the *haveli* for them. I've always wondered who raised them, where they are, what happened to them. You're lucky, *beti*. You've always known where your boy was. Kanta-*ji* seems like a good sort. He has been fed, schooled, loved."

She rests her ringed fingers on my hip. In the window facing me, I see a glittering reflection of her gold and glass bangles.

"This isn't about you, Radha. It's about the boy. Put yourself in his place. He wants to know what's going on in his life. If you were his age, wouldn't you be curious? Ease his mind. Tell him the truth. He'll know if you're faking it — unlike my clients." She chuckles and pats my hip. She lifts her wide girth off the cot, but before she can step away, I grasp her hand, tightly. I crane my head around to look at her.

Hazi turns her eyes on mine and squeezes my hand. *"Khush raho, beti."*

Be happy? I watch her leave the room and close the door.

Someone is shaking my arm. I open my

eyes. They feel gummy. Jiji is sitting on my cot with a cup of tea in one hand and a damp cloth in the other. She sets the tea on the side table. Tenderly, she presses the cloth against my eyes. It's warm. I smell lavender and chamomile. I let her wash my face; I don't have the energy to move.

"Come," she says. My body feels like a rag doll as she pulls me up to a sitting position. She hands me my chai. Then she sits behind me on the cot and begins combing my hair with a sandalwood comb. We share our mother's hair: thick, wavy. (I'm starting to see strands of silver in mine these days, too.) Her touch is light as she pulls the strands into position.

With every stroke, I feel her love for me. The pads of her fingers gingerly separating a tangle. The care she takes never to hurt, only to enhance. Like her sweet breath blowing on a design of henna paste. She's always been able to *show* me how she feels about me more than she can express it in words. Now, she's telling me that I needn't worry about my outburst earlier today. That it will not affect our bond, our feeling for one another.

"How long have I been asleep?"

"Several hours."

She goes about her business while I sip

my chai. "The Kashmiri vendors come south every winter to sell their embroidered goods. Will you come with me to pick out a wool jacket for Shanti and one for Asha?"

I nod. I feel so drained that I don't know whether I'm still angry at Jiji or mortified at having aired my grievances so publicly. I don't know how to feel or what to say. Should I apologize or wait for Jiji to apologize to me? Are apologies even necessary?

The chai's soothing perfume of cardamom, cloves and cinnamon begins to revive me.

Finished with my hair, Lakshmi massages my neck and shoulders with her fingers. She says, casually, "Kanta has gone back to her hotel. She returns to Jaipur tomorrow."

Kanta! I was so harsh with her this morning. I feel sick. My neck flushes with embarrassment. Jiji's dearest friend was there for me when my sister was too busy with work. Kanta introduced me to her own books: *Vanity Fair, Lady Chatterley's Lover, Jane Eyre.* She took me to see American films — *Some Like It Hot* and *The Last Time I Saw Paris.* I looked up to her, so chic in her capris and bobbed hair. Unlike the Jaipuri matrons Jiji serviced, Kanta was modern and so much fun! When I was with her, I felt like I was with the sister I'd been looking for in Jaipur instead of the one I ended up with. At times, I sensed that I was a burden for Lakshmi to feed, clothe and house, but I never felt that way with Kanta.

Jiji asks me to wear the Indian *salwar kameez* she brought for me. I don't object. I've disrespected the *kotha* enough with my Western garb. I also know that when we go to the Agra bazaar, I must not look like a tourist or we will be besieged by hawkers.

It's quiet in the *kotha* when we pass the entertainment hall. The dancers and singers must be resting before their evening performances. The courtesan way of life is to work late, get up early, practice their routines and rest in the afternoon. There's no sign of Hazi or Nasreen anywhere.

Outside, it's already dark at five o'clock. Our auto rickshaw driver has his *filmi* music turned up loud, so Jiji and I are silent on the fifteen-minute trip to the night market. There's a chill in the air, and we're both wearing sweaters over our *kurtas*.

As soon as I see the overhead lights strung haphazardly across the lanes of the bazaar, I feel excitement mount. It's been years since I've been to a night market. I stay close to Jiji as she leads us through the crowded stalls selling potatoes, beans and *karalas*. Here, too, the pickings are slim. We turn into another lane busy with shoppers. Here, the vendors specialize in knives and steel tiffins and plates. I try to prevent my eyes from settling too long on any one object lest a vendor notice my interest and latch on to me. There's very little haggling in Paris, and I'm a little out of practice when it comes to bargaining.

Jiji seems to know exactly where she is going; I imagine the market has grown since her time in Agra but probably has the same general layout as before. If nothing else, our noses can tell us which part of the market we're headed toward; I catch a whiff of leather when we arrive at the *juti* vendors. Would Asha and Shanti wear the maharani shoes if I found them in their size? Closer to the fruits, I catch the odor of overripe loquats. A bull meanders from stall to stall, looking for a sweet morsel. The vendors throw a little offering his way, and he stops to eat. A cat darts out from nowhere to join him.

Next, we see the vendors selling saris. Stack after stack of delicious jewel colors, each one as breathtaking as the last. How can India produce such vibrant color — and so much of it — when color seems to be in short supply in France? I want to stop, buy up an entire silk stack and decorate my apartment with it even though I know it will seem as foreign there as pale beige and lackluster tans do here.

Jiji slows down, looking for someone. She looks right and left until her face breaks into a smile. We approach an incense vendor. Who should be sitting behind the narrow stall but Hari, her ex-husband?

I'm so shocked to see him I stop in my tracks. He's surprised to see us, too, but he recovers quickly with a grin and a *namaste.* He's clean-shaven, the sleeves of his starched white shirt rolled up to the elbows.

He's surrounded by boxes of incense sticks and cones stacked neatly behind him and in front of the stall. Samples of five *agarbatti* sticks waft their fragrance in our direction. I practically moan with pleasure. I smell the *mogra* flower, rose, *chameli,* saffron and — could it be? — *mitti attar?* Jiji laughs at my response as if she's been anticipating it.

My sister seems completely at ease with Hari. "Hazi told me you were now working with the women of Agra. Running an incense factory," she says. "You remember Radha, don't you?"

His eyes grow wide. He greets me with a high *namaste* and smiles.

How odd it is to encounter Hari after

almost twenty years! This man I barely knew but who traveled with me so long ago from Ajar to Jaipur in search of Lakshmi. She'd left him after he started beating her; he wanted children, but she'd long been drinking the cotton root bark tea she learned to make from his mother to keep herself child-free.

Munchi-*ji* was the one who told me where to look for Hari after Maa and Pitaji died. When I found Lakshmi's estranged husband, I talked him into accompanying me almost a thousand miles from Ajar — all the way to the Jaipur train station (how bold I used to be!). I remembered seeing that name — Jaipur — on the envelopes that the postman delivered to Maa, the same ones *she* would throw on the fire, unopened. At the station, Hari and I started asking anyone we saw where we might find my sister. At first, Jiji didn't want to believe that her husband had changed, but he had. He'd picked up where his late mother had left off: healing injured women and children who had no money to pay doctors. Nonetheless, my sister hadn't wanted to stay married. A 1955 law allowed her to divorce him. By the time she, Malik and I left for Shimla, she was a single woman again.

Hari calls to someone behind the stall. A

woman in her twenties, wearing a pale green sari and an emerald-green sweater blouse, walks into view, carrying a sleeping baby. A boy of four or five follows her. Hari picks up the boy and introduces his family to us.

"My wife is the reason I came to Agra," he says. "I met her in Jaipur, but her family is from here, and she wanted to return."

His wife smiles shyly at us.

Hari leans toward us as if he's sharing a confidence. "Don't let her fool you. In the daytime, she manages forty women who roll the incense paste into sticks or cones while I tend to their children. Lakshmi, I have more children now than I ever wanted!" He laughs, and his wife and my sister join him. Lakshmi asks after his children, and the wife proudly replies with their names and ages. Hari tells us he buys the *mitti attar* from Hazi and Nasreen's factory. That's how he knows them.

My sister's ex-husband seems happy, and so does she. Gone is the rancor of their first meeting in Jaipur, the wariness in Lakshmi's voice when she spoke of him, and the bitterness in his before he realized she was never meant to be his property.

Hari is eager to send us off with several boxes of his incense. Lakshmi puts her hands together and wags her head to let him

258

know that we appreciate the gesture, but it's not necessary. Instead, she pulls some rupees out of the pouch inside her petticoat, hands them to Hari's wife and picks up a box of the *mitti attar* incense.

For whatever reason, when we've said our goodbyes, I feel lighter. The weariness in my limbs is gone.

As we leave Hari's stall, Jiji says to me, "I was telling Hazi I've often wondered what became of Hari after we left him in Jaipur. She told me he was here, in Agra, at the night market. He's still helping the poor, healing them with the herbal poultices he learned to make from working with his mother. If the women are in need, he gives them jobs at his incense factory."

"Is that how he met his wife?"

My sister shrugs. "Maybe. Some of the women who work at their factory used to be prostitutes. Some were runaways or orphans. Nasreen said all the women who work there make enough to feed their families." She grins. "He's done well. I'm proud of him."

Long ago, she'd told me of the times when she could barely get up off the floor after one of his beatings. I feel a twinge of resentment on her behalf.

"Jiji, how could you forgive him after

259

everything he did to you?"

"It's over, Radha. He hasn't hurt me for a long time. And I think he pays the price for those beatings every time he helps a woman in unfortunate circumstances." She turns to look at me. "The measure of us isn't in the day-to-day. And it's not in our past or our future. It's in the fundamental changes we make within ourselves over a lifetime. *Samaj-jao?*"

We look at one another for a moment before my sister turns and leads the way.

When we arrive at the clothing stall Hari recommended, Jiji and I examine the craftsmanship of the woolen goods, the embroidery detail and the polyester or cotton lining of each handmade coat. Hari was right: this vendor carries merchandise from Kashmir far superior than that of his competitors. I pick out two coats. For Shanti, I've chosen one in a creamy red wool decorated with tiny yellow embroidery. The other — olive green with darker green stitching on the collar — will highlight Asha's amber eyes.

"Should we get something for Pierre?" Jiji asks.

I think of Asha's requests. "Yes! Hand-carved sandalwood elephants. For his desk — the girls will love them, too."

Jiji leads the way. Once we've purchased Pierre's gift, Lakshmi takes my arm and directs us to the snack aisle. Men, women and children are munching on fried mung *dal*, spicy peanuts, *sev*, *chakli*, salty cashews. "Let's get something to eat," she says, scanning the rows of sacks filled with tasty savories.

We walk around, carrying our newspaper cones of fried snacks (the kind Jiji would never let me eat when I was younger), admiring the aisle of colorful lac and glass bangles. Each row of glittering bracelets unique in its design, so different from every other row.

Lakshmi slows and turns to me. "Radha, I don't want you to leave without us understanding one another," she says. She's speaking carefully, choosing each word as if it's a pearl.

"I've never been a mother. You're right about that. It made me sadder than you can imagine to think of you crying and feeling so alone the year after you left Niki. I do remember trying to get you to talk to me during your weekend visits with us, but you wouldn't. And I didn't know how to make you. I feel so bad about that. Try as hard as I might, you refused to answer my questions. Do you remember? Jay took you riding, hoping you'd feel comfortable enough to talk to him. We saw that you were bottling up your feelings, and we knew you needed to air them. But we failed to find a way to help."

My sister picks a chili peanut from my cone and pops it in her mouth. She's giving me time to respond. I remember her taking me for Sunday morning walks in Shimla before dinner, laughing at her failures in the Healing Garden or telling me about her attempts to mend the sagging window on her cottage by herself. Always, she kept the conversation light, asking me about my friends and classes at school, how I was feeling. It occurs to me now that she never once said Niki's name, hoping *I* would bring him up. I never did, and she honored my silence. Even when we hiked on his birthday, we never spoke about him. I would deflect her attention from my sadness, tease her about Dr. Jay's infatuation, suggesting she give him at least some sign of encouragement. She would laugh. "Why would I trouble myself with him when I have you and Malik to keep me busy?"

Once, at Auckland, I came close to telling Mathilde. It was the middle of the night. I was having a fitful dream, trying to count how many teeth Niki had. I kept starting over and over, never finishing. I must have cried out in my sleep because Mathilde had to shake me awake. I was crying. She combed her fingers through my hair until I fell asleep again. In the morning, she looked at me hopefully. Perhaps today would be the day I shared what haunted me. But I never did.

Now, I take a deep breath. "I thought I could make him disappear. If I didn't think about him."

"Niki?"

"Hahn."

"You couldn't help but think about him! Because he happened. He happened, Radha, and he was lovely. And he *is* lovely. You did nothing wrong. An older boy took advantage of you. He knew what the consequences would be but failed to tell you. You know that now, don't you, *choti behen*?"

"I was stupid to let Ravi get so close. It's embarrassing to think how silly I was, how naive." As I'm saying this, I feel my cheeks grow warm. I know they're turning pink. "I was the dumb village girl who didn't know any better. I felt as if everyone was calling me that behind my back."

"Who?"

"You. Kanta. Malik. Manu. Ravi. The Singhs —"

"None of us thought you were dumb, Radha. If anything, we all felt guilty. I failed in my duty as your older sister to teach you about sex. Kanta failed in her duty to guide you toward books and movies more appropriate to your age. Malik felt bad that he hadn't come to me sooner to tell me he'd seen you with Ravi. *We* failed, Radha. *You* didn't. And for that, I'm profoundly sorry. *We* failed *you.* Do you understand?"

I shake my head. "Even right up until the end, when I had Niki, I wanted to prove to all of you that I wasn't naive. I was sure Ravi would do the right thing and claim our baby as his own. He would marry me. He'd come charging through the door of my hospital room and rescue me. I thought he'd be my Mr. Rochester, Jiji. But he wasn't, was he? So when he never showed, I felt more stupid, more naive, than ever. Everything you had already thought about me was true. I was impressionable. A silly village girl."

"Oh, *choti behen.*" Jiji removes a handkerchief from her handbag to wipe my eyes. I hadn't realized I was crying. "I never once thought of you as simple. You've always been so bright. All I could think about, back then, was how Jaipur society would shun you and your child. A pregnant girl can't go to school. In 1956, no one wanted unwed mothers in their classes. It frustrated me that a smart girl like you would allow yourself to succumb to Ravi's advances. I did resent you for that. I admit it. I knew Parvati would hold me responsible for the fact that you slept with her son. She, of all people, knew what he was like. I knew, too. I should have known to protect you from boys like him. But I didn't. And for that, I am so very sorry."

Oblivious to the shoppers who are having to move around us, my sister folds me in her arms and holds me tight. It releases something in me I've been holding on to, like a balloon deflating. Why couldn't we have said these things to one another years ago? Why has it taken so long for us to tell each other how we felt seventeen years ago? Why have I been waiting all this time for her to share the blame with me?

Over my shoulder, Lakshmi is saying, "We can't go back and change anything, *beti.* Let the past go. But think of what it's taught you. What does the present tell you? You've given Niki the best life possible. You made the decision to let Kanta and Manu raise him. You did right. He's happy, Radha. He's a lovely boy."

I release her and search her face. "You've

265

seen him?"

She wipes my eyes again. "After Jay and I got married, we started going to Jaipur in the winter. I missed Kanta. And I wanted to see Niki — *my* nephew, Radha. That's how I think of him. He is such a delight. He loves reading as much as you do. He draws the most beautiful sketches. These are all things you should learn about him. And then you'll see the good you did."

I feel my heart speed up. "But, Jiji. How do I explain to Pierre that I had a child before I met him? That I abandoned that child? Pierre grew up Catholic. He has no idea. What if he asks for a divorce?"

"Because you had a child at thirteen? As if the French don't have girls that age with babies?" Jiji scoffs. "If Pierre is angry with you for having Niki, he'll have me to talk to. You've given him two gorgeous daughters. He'd be a fool to give all that up! You yourself said this is 1974. It's no longer 1955. Times have changed."

Vendors and shoppers stop to stare at us, two women embracing in the middle of a crowded lane with cows, dogs and cats slinking by. I feel her strength, the way she makes me feel safe, always, and I will that strength to become part of me.

"Do you want me to come to Paris with

you?" she asks. "I'm sure Nimmi would take over for me in Shimla for a few days."

As tempted as I am to say yes, to have Jiji make everything better, I shake my head.

Niki is coming to see me. This is something I need to handle by myself. I take the vial out of the pocket of my *kameez,* uncap it and inhale. I hold it out to my sister. Jiji frowns, an uncertain look on her face, but brings her nose to the vial, gingerly, and sniffs. Her face clears.

"Ah," she says.

She cups my chin. *"Shabash."*

■ ■ ■ ■

PART THREE

■ ■ ■ ■

PART THREE

Used for thousands of years in India to calm the mind and soothe the skin, sandalwood was introduced to Europe only two hundred years ago.

Paris
December 1974

In the taxi from the de Gaulle airport to our apartment, I smooth my hand over the precious rosewood box of *mitti* and *khus attars* in my lap. Jiji wanted me to go back with her to Shimla and stay with Jay and the family for a few days. She refers to Malik, Nimmi and their kids as *the family* now. How odd that when I first arrived in Jaipur, Lakshmi was my only family, and now I have my own — a million miles from hers. But I needed to get back to Paris for Niki — and for Pierre and the girls. And for my work.

271

The overcast December sky in Paris makes me long for the bright white heat of India. On the coldest day in Agra, it was seventy degrees. Here, at six in the evening, it's forty-seven degrees, and huddled in only a sweater, I'm shivering. I wish I'd kept the shawl Jiji offered me.

I called Florence's house once while I was gone. I wanted to hear my daughters' voices, their incessant chatter, where their *grand-mère* had been taking them. They said they'd played pétanque, and badminton, and eaten chocolates from their Advent calendars (Christmas is something we only celebrate at Florence's house).

I didn't call Pierre. I was afraid to know if Niki had shown up at our apartment or if he and Niki had already met. If they had, I figured Pierre would have phoned me right away. I imagined Niki showing up in the daytime; Pierre would have been at work. I doubt the concierge would have let Niki go upstairs, never having met him before. Even if she had, no one would have answered when he rang the bell to our apartment.

In the evenings, Pierre would have been at Florence's having dinner with the girls, or else he would have been out with friends. I imagined Niki losing hope and, finally, deciding to go home. Perhaps I would be spared the awkwardness of introducing Niki to my husband and my daughters.

But, even then, I knew that this was wishful thinking.

And when Pierre does meet Niki, well . . . I'll have to figure something out. Right now, I'm exhausted from my trip, and I don't have a clue what to tell either of them.

I lug my suitcase and the box of scents to the third floor. Before I turn the key in the lock, I hear voices, which is a relief; it means I won't have to be alone with Pierre or brace myself for the Discussion. At least not tonight.

I hear Pierre say in an overly cheerful voice, "Ah, this must be her." He's smiling as he comes down the hall to kiss me on both cheeks. As he picks up my suitcase, he whispers, "You didn't tell me you were expecting company?"

My heart skips a beat.

Niki is already here.

I feel dread squeezing my chest like a vise.

Pierre takes my suitcase down the hallway to our bedroom. I hang my coat on the wall hook. Slowly, very slowly, I remove my shoes. That's when I notice men's white Adidas with red stripes, the tops covered in dust, sitting alongside my family's shoes.

273

It's as if Niki has walked through the Rajasthani desert to get to me. I lean a hand against the wall.

Like an old woman, I shuffle toward our living room at the end of the hall.

I see the back of a man's head. He's sitting on the couch. His neck is slim and vulnerable, like a boy's.

"Hello?" I say.

He stands up and turns around in one smooth motion. I notice everything at once: the peacock eyes, luminescent in the center, blue turning to green turning to brown at the rim. His nose is all Ravi: straight, without the bump on mine. Lips like mine: heart-shaped at the top, plumper on the bottom. My cheekbones, thick eyebrows like Ravi. His hair: black, curly. It was curly as a baby, too. Would I have recognized him on the street? I don't think so. But I would have stared because he's so handsome, and his eyes are so striking.

Niki hasn't moved. Neither have I. I'm still holding on to the box of scents from Agra, my grip on it so tight that my fingers are turning white.

Pierre comes into the room carrying a tray of glasses with pineapple juice. "Here we are." I'm aware of him setting down the tray, handing a glass to Niki. All at once, we hear the front door opening and the high-pitched voices of the girls, Florence telling them to hang up their coats and take off their boots. Pierre excuses himself to greet his mother and help the girls.

Niki is holding on to his glass but hasn't taken a sip. Neither have I.

I hear Florence saying, "I figured Radha would be too tired to make dinner. So I made some *coq au vin.* We can all have dinner together . . ."

"Maman!" The girls come rushing into the room, putting their arms around my waist. They're vibrating with excitement, energy. In their young lives, a thousand and one things have happened since they last saw me four days ago.

"Josephine got a rabbit. Can we get a rabbit, too?"

"Maman, I won three times at *un, deux, trois soleil* today!"

"Grand-mère played *barbichette* with us!"

"Did you bring us anything? What's in the box?"

Niki looks around, suddenly embarrassed. His cheeks are flushed. He takes a sip of his drink, then sets it down on the tray. He rubs his palms against his black jogging pants.

Florence appears to my right. "Ah. *Bonjour.*"

I feel my mother-in-law's eyes on me, on Niki. I can't speak. Can't open my mouth. Can't move. All I can think is: *He's more beautiful than I imagined he'd be. Taller, too. Is this real? Am I having a dream? Or is this a nightmare?* But I can feel my feet on the hardwood floor, my hands on the box. *I need my vial.* But I can't seem to connect the vial with a movement of my body that would take me to it.

Pierre is in the room now. He's telling his mother that my cousin has come to visit. He introduces Niki. The girls smile shyly at him. Asha steps forward to take him by the hand. She wants to show him her Advent calendar. Shanti races Asha to the room. Niki blushes as he walks past us. Florence's gaze is on me again, on Niki again. Now Florence is prying the box out of my hands and setting it on the dining table.

I clear my throat. "When did he get here?"

Pierre is setting the table for dinner. "Just a few hours ago. He seems nice. His English is very good. He admired my drawing of the Chandigarh building. Apparently he's been there. He's been studying French." He lowers his voice. "You know, *Je m'appele Pierre. Comment allez-vous?* Like you used to talk before I met you." He winks at me.

He's in a good mood. I'd expected him to

be a little peeved with me for not calling him from India, for going off to Agra, for working, for having a family member show up at our doorstep, for any number of things.

"Surely he's not staying here?" Florence asks, scanning our small apartment. She goes to the kitchen to get water glasses and a bottle of mineral water.

"He's staying at a hostel. Kind of far from here. In the twentieth, I think." Pierre removes the cover off the dish with the *coq au vin* and sniffs. *"Magnifique, Maman."*

Florence smiles graciously as she comes out of the kitchen. *"Salade?"*

Pierre walks to the kitchen to make it.

Niki and the girls come out of their bedroom. Asha runs up to me. *"Maman!* Niki has the same color eyes you do! I have Papa's eyes." She pulls down an eyelid to show off her golden-hued irises. "And Shanti has brown eyes. Where does she get those from?"

I steal a quick glance at Florence, who is watching us intently. She has a puzzled expression on her face. I lower Asha's hand away from her eye. "Eye color can skip generations. Shanti's eyes are like my father's. Florence, where does Pierre get his unusual eyes?"

Florence, whose eyes are blue, looks at me as if I've just slapped her. I'm so startled by her reaction I don't know what to say. She surprises me by looking away and addressing Niki. "Why don't you join us for dinner, Niki? You look like you could use a good French meal."

Normally, I would have rolled my eyes. As if French food is the be-all and end-all. But Niki looks at me with a lopsided smile. I realize he's expecting me to translate Florence's rapid French. I speak in Hindi. "She's asking you to dinner, but I would prefer you didn't stay. Your parents are worried about you. They want you home."

Niki's mouth falls open. He hadn't anticipated my rudeness.

Pierre walks into the room with a watercress salad. He says in English, "Radha, he speaks English. You don't have to use Hindi." To Niki, he offers a friendly smile and speaks in English. "We would love for you to join us for dinner."

Now Niki looks confused. Which invitation should he respond to? The girls decide for him. Asha takes his hand and leads him to the table. "You'll sit by me." She says it in French but in English she adds, "Please."

The meaning is clear enough. And with an apologetic glance at me, Niki takes a seat. Shanti runs to the kitchen to set another plate for him and takes a seat next to him before Asha can sit down. I call Asha to me to avoid an argument. Before long, Pierre is offering him a glass of wine (which he accepts). Florence is offering him a helping of *coq au vin* (which he also accepts; does Kanta know he eats meat?). The girls are using their English to ask him what grade he is in, where he lives and if he has any brothers and sisters. Before he answers, he often looks to me as if seeking permission. I refuse to engage with him. Having him under my roof is like having pebbles in my shoe. I want him gone before he figures out that I'm his birth mother. Before my family finds out. Before the voices that simmer just below the surface of my conscience scream: *Radha is bad. She did bad. She couldn't help herself. She let herself be used and discarded, like a dirty handkerchief.* No, I can't allow that to happen. But my family is being so kind and welcoming that Niki barely has a chance to refuse.

Taking a sip of wine, Pierre tells the girls in French, "Niki is a distant cousin of your mother's. I'm sure we can learn a secret or two about her if we ask him nicely." He translates for Niki.

Niki blinks, not sure if this is meant as a

279

joke. But everyone at the table laughs. Except me. I look down at my plate. The sooner he leaves, the better.

In her halting English, Florence says, "You can stay with me, Niki. I have room." She gestures with her hands like a magician, as if conjuring space, which makes Pierre and the girls laugh. She joins them, as does Niki.

Pierre says, "*C'est genial!* My mother stays in a very big house. You could sleep in two bedrooms instead of just one!" He chuckles.

Florence waves her hand at Pierre as if to swat a fly, but she's smiling.

I'm so startled by Florence's offer that I turn to study her. What could possibly have prompted that invitation? Her eyes crinkle as she grins at Niki. She likes him. She likes my son!

Did I just think of him as *my son*? No, he's just Niki. *I can't call him that again. I'm not allowed. He's someone else's son.* All at once, the room starts to tilt. I grip the edge of the table to keep from sliding off my chair.

"*Maman?*" Shanti reaches for my arm.

Florence is telling Pierre, "She's just gone through two different time changes within a week. She must be jet-lagged, exhausted. Maybe she picked up a bug traveling."

I hear chairs being scraped backward. I'm

being guided to bed by Florence. My *saas* is telling me to take deep breaths. My head is on the pillow. My legs are being lifted. Is this the same mother-in-law about whom I was just complaining to Jiji? Why is she being so nice to me?

"We'll take him sightseeing tomorrow. You rest . . ." she's saying now.

Then I'm under the covers. There are hushed voices around me. *Maman needs to rest. She'll talk to you in the morning. She's been working very hard. Have you eaten all your salad?*

Everything goes dark.

When I wake up the next morning, the apartment is quiet. I walk into the hallway, call for the girls, but there's no answer. I have to shade my eyes from the sun pouring through the living room windows; Pierre must have opened the drapes. I look at the clock. It's eleven o'clock on a Saturday morning. The girls have school for half a day.

On the dining table is a note in Pierre's handwriting.

Took the girls to school. Didn't want to wake you. Afterward, Maman, the girls and I are taking Niki sightseeing. He's never

been to Paris! Back for dinner. Rest up.
Bisous.

Niki! It all comes rushing back. Him in
our apartment. Telling everyone he was my
cousin from Jaipur. Florence offering a bed
at her house. Where is he now? I should see
him. Convince him to go home. That will
be the end of it. Then my life can go back
to normal.

The phone rings. I look at it as if it's alive.
As if it might burn my hand were I to pick
up the receiver. Gingerly, I answer.

"Have lunch with me." It's Mathilde. "I
have a nurse for *Maman* today. I really need
to see you, *ma puce.*" She sounds so desperate that I do a quick calculation. If Pierre
has the girls and keeps Niki busy all day, I
can spare an hour for Mathilde.

I usually bring a book to keep me company
when I'm meeting Mathilde at L'Atlas Café
on Rue de Buci. She's always late, sometimes showing up with shopping bags filled
with clothes or shoes or a handbag she happened to see on her way to meet me. Today,
I was too preoccupied with thoughts of Niki
to stop at the *bouquinistes* along the Seine
and pick up another dog-eared book in
English that a tourist left behind.

282

With a flourish, a cheerful waiter in a white shirt, black tie and black apron sets my *menthe à l'eau* on my little round table. The sparkling peppermint drink is what I always have, and Thomas knows it. He tucks the small black tray under his armpit.

"No book today?" he asks.

I smile. He knows me too well. "I might just watch people."

"Until Mademoiselle Mathilde arrives." I think Thomas has a crush on Mathilde because he makes a point of always serving us when we meet for lunch. But I know he has a wife and son in the *banlieu* so flirting is as far as he's going to go.

"Let's hope she doesn't keep us waiting too long or we'll be ordering dinner," I tell him.

A middle-aged couple sits down at the table next to mine. They are looking at a map and arguing in English about what to see next. But it's not British English; they're Americans. The woman lifts her heel out of her low pumps and massages it. The man, balding at the crown, folds up the map and fans himself even though it's cold outside. His shirt collar is unbuttoned. There are two cameras hanging around his neck. I'm sure the couple has already covered three tourist sites on their list and it's not even two o'clock in the afternoon.

I know better than to tell Thomas he has more customers. He's well aware, but he'll keep them waiting for another ten minutes — or even twenty. Perhaps it's the fact that they don't greet him with a *bonjour.* Or the fact that their voices carry; they speak more loudly than the French. Or he doesn't like their ill-fitting clothes. Whatever the reason, I can see them giving his back sidelong glances, waiting for him to notice them.

"Shall I get your lunches started?" he asks me now. I always have the *moules frites* and Mathilde has a *salade Niçoise.*

I nod, and he hurries away, seemingly oblivious to the American man raising his hand to stop him. I offer the couple a sympathetic smile.

Mathilde and I always sit outside, even on chilly, overcast December days like today. There's something comforting about watching people walking, lounging, talking, flirting in Paris. It takes my mind off my troubling thoughts. I sip my *menthe* as I watch an older matron across the street talking to her little white poodle. The dog has stopped to sniff something interesting on the sidewalk. She's saying, *"On avance?"* but the dog is not budging.

"Désolé, désolé, désolé!" It's Mathilde, car-

284

rying her large caramel-colored handbag, bringing with her the smell of tobacco, lemon, patchouli, leather and amber. But no shopping bags.

She kisses my cheeks. Today, she's wearing a slate blue cashmere dress tied across the waist with a matching belt under her navy blue coat. The dress matches her eyes. As usual, heads turn to stare at her.

"Are you wearing Gentleman?" It's the newest men's fragrance from Givenchy.

She gives me one of her wide gap-toothed smiles. "Do you like it?" She takes her seat, hanging her purse behind her chair, and sniffs her wrist. She holds out her wrist for me to inhale.

"Strangely enough, it suits you."

Mathilde removes the pack of Tigras from her coat. Her hands are shaking. I reach across the table, pick up her box of matches and light her cigarette. (Mathilde refuses to get a lighter; she loves the sudden flare of a match head as it's scraped against the phosphorus strip.)

After her first inhale, she says, "The scent is not mine. It's Jean-Luc's. He left it behind."

"Hoping for a repeat visit?" I hope she doesn't notice how desperately I'm trying to keep my tone light. My mind is otherwise busy with what I'll say to Niki when I see him. *Hai Bhagwan,* what if he says something to Pierre about those letters? Is today the day I should tell Mathilde about Niki? Will it make me feel better the same way my talk with Jiji did? How will Mathilde react when she finds out I've kept Niki a secret all these years?

But Mathilde isn't smiling. She wrinkles her nose and taps her ash in the tiny black ashtray on our table. "I wouldn't have minded. But . . ." She takes a drag of her cigarette.

"But?"

She blinks her eyes, the mascara so thick I can see the clumps. At Auckland, she and I would swoon over Twiggy's big-eyed, big-eyelash makeup. Mathilde had a cousin in Germany who would send her the latest cosmetics, and we spent many happy hours imitating the model's signature look when we were supposed to be studying. I cut back on the dark eyeliner and mascara when the girls were babies. I just didn't have time to fuss with it. But Mathilde has remained faithful to her idol, who graces the cover of *British Vogue* this month.

Mathilde taps thoughtfully on her cigarette again, rolling it on the rim of the ashtray. "Jean-Luc dumped me." She looks at me

286

then, and her pale blue eyes tell me how deep a wound he left. She looks wan, fragile. For once, a man had met her expectations, and for whatever reason, she hadn't met his. She isn't used to rejection from men; it's a new experience for her. How fragile our hearts are when we open them wide to allow love that never arrives!

I want a happy life for Mathilde, one in which she's the center of someone else's world. God knows how hard it's been for her with a mother who was more focused on herself than on her daughter. "Oh, I'm so sorry, *cherie*, I —"

She cuts me off, suddenly clearing her throat and straightening in her chair. "Let's not be sad. Make me happy. Tell me about India. What did you eat? What were the courtesans like? Was it fun being back?" Mathilde loves India, the crazy quilt of business hustle, larger-than-life celebrations and the fiery cuisine. How she loves the food!

Just then, Thomas brings our lunches and a glass of chardonnay for Mathilde, the same drink she orders whenever we come to L'Atlas. Thomas blushes as he greets Mathilde.

While we eat, I tell Mathilde everything, from seeing Lakshmi again (who fascinates Mathilde; my sister painted henna on

Mathilde's hands more than once), to meeting the intimidating Hazi and the demure Nasreen. I have her laughing about the curious Mr. Mehta and his obvious lust for Nasreen. I catch her up on the scents I've brought back from India and how I hope to use them in the Olympia project.

Mathilde spears an anchovy. "And what about this mysterious visitor of yours? When were you going to tell me about him?"

I'm opening my first mussel with a fork. My hand freezes. How did she know about Niki coming to Paris? Did Pierre tell her? I've never even had the courage to tell her about my pregnancy at thirteen. "Who told you we had a visitor?" I ask cautiously.

Her mouth opens and closes. She sits back in her chair. Her eyes drift to her glass of wine. "*La Reine,* of course. Florence called me this morning to invite Agnes and me on their sightseeing outing." She takes a sip. "She seemed surprised you hadn't told me about his visit."

My pulse starts to race. "My cousin. He only arrived yesterday just before I got back. We had no idea he was coming. Just showed up at our doorstep." I can tell Mathilde is hurt that I haven't shared something as important as a visitor from India with her. She is my best friend, after all. I set my fork down and help myself to one of her Tigras. Mathilde watches me curiously. I haven't smoked since our student days at Auckland. The swift charge of nicotine to my brain leaves me light-headed, but it's a welcome contrast to the heaviness in my chest. "He's run away from home. His parents have asked me to send him back." I tell myself I'm not lying, just not telling the whole truth. I take another puff. "He'll be gone by the end of this week. Now, tell me, how is your mother?"

I knew the change in topic would take the heat off me. But Mathilde is no fool. She's taken note of my sudden nervousness. She pushes her plate away and folds her arms across her waist, as if she's cold. She must have decided not to question me further because she says, "I don't know how much longer I can take care of *Maman*. I had to have a special lock put on the door so she doesn't escape in the middle of the night while I'm sleeping. I have to watch what she eats. She's put on twenty kilos since she came to live with me. She doesn't even know when her stomach is full." Her blue eyes are full of misery. Mascara from her lower lashes is melting into the folds below her eyes. "Radha, I don't remember when I've been so tired."

"But the aides —"

"Yes, they help, and I can leave the apartment for a few hours at a time. But if I hire them every day for twenty-four hours, the money will run out before we know it. Agnes already ran through hers before she came back to Paris."

Antoine had left Mathilde and Agnes very comfortable. He had owned the narrow building where his *parfumerie* occupied the ground floor, and it had fetched a pretty sum upon his death. I know Mathilde missed her *grand-père* as much as I did. If he were still alive, he would know what to do, how to help my friend.

I put my hand over hers and leave it there. There's not much else I can do.

An hour later, I find myself alone before Manet's *Olympia* again. I don't want to go home where I'll have to face Niki and my family together in the same room.

There are no benches in this narrow museum, so I sit cross-legged on the cold stone floor as I look up at Victorine. From the corner of my eye, I see Gérard limping toward me, dragging his chair behind him. I breezed past him as I entered the Jeu de Paume, too preoccupied to greet him. Not until now does it occur to me that Olympia acts as a sedative, calming me, soothing my frayed nerves. As much as my vial of scent does.

My lunch with Mathilde has left me downhearted. For my friend's predicament. For Agnes's failing memory. For their uncertain future. And I still have no idea how to handle the questions Niki will ask me. *How are you related to my mother? Why did you return all her letters unopened? What's in them?*

Gérard offers me the chair. But I shake my head. I want the discomfort of the hard stone. He sets the chair next to me and sits down. He gives me his handkerchief.

When did I start crying again? I hastily wipe my eyes, my cheeks, my chin, with my fingers. "Did Victorine ever have children by Manet?"

He looks surprised by my question. "I've never heard that. Mrs. Manet was very possessive. I don't believe she would have tolerated a romantic liaison between her husband and one of his models."

Unlike me, Victorine wasn't silly enough to get pregnant by the painter. "But Victorine was his favorite model, you told me?"

"*C'est ça.* She was the favorite of many. Dégas. Lautrec. Stevens. You can see her face in about thirty paintings around the world." He pauses while I blow my nose.

291

"She was petite. And red-haired. Friends called her *la crevette.*" He smiles fondly. "She came from a working-class family. Started modeling at sixteen."

We're quiet for a while. Then I ask, "Do you think he disappointed her? Manet, I mean."

"*Bah* . . . who knows?" Gérard scratches his beard. "Perhaps she was disappointed by men in general. They wouldn't admit her to the Fine Art Academy, you know. They didn't admit any women for that matter — for a very long time. The painters didn't take her seriously. Manet told her he didn't care for her painting style."

Victorine/Olympia is studying me. I cast my eyes to the floor in embarrassment. The words that have been building up inside me now bubble to the surface. "I had a baby when I was thirteen."

Gérard turns his head to look at me. I meet his eyes.

I can't read his expression. I offer him a smile. "I thought I was in love with his father. We used to meet at the polo grounds in Jaipur. At the shed where they kept the tools to shoe the horses. We would practice his lines for the Shakespeare plays his theater class was studying." It had been so easy to go from studying lines to acting them out. From Romeo romancing Juliet to Romeo making love to Juliet. It was a sweet time. I still remember every glorious kiss, caress, sigh, thrust, squeeze, bite, lick. No one was there to tell me what to do or what to say or how to act. I just *was.* I just *did.* I just *felt.* Is it like that for everyone's first? Do they never forget it? Can they ever repeat it?

We sit in silence for a while.

Gérard asks, "And the baby's father? What happened to him?"

I shrug. "His parents shipped him off to school in England. I didn't even know. And I don't know if he knew about the baby. Like a fool, I was going to his house and leaving notes with the gateman." My face colors just thinking about how the Singhs must have laughed at me. I can't bear to look at Gérard. He must think me such a simpleton.

"That must have felt terrible," he says. His voice is sad, as if he's feeling what I was feeling all those years ago.

I gaze at Victorine. I wonder if the expression she wears is the one I would have worn if I'd come face-to-face with Ravi. *Why are you betraying me? Can't you see how much it hurts?*

"What of the baby, Madame Radha? You

kept him?"

I shake my head. "I cut him out of my life."

"Ah," is all he says, as if he understands. He has no idea how it felt. How could he? Niki came from my body — I made him! Separating myself from him was like chopping off an arm or a leg from my own body. How dare Gérard pretend to empathize? I feel the blood pulsing in my neck. I know my cheeks are reddening. I tell myself to calm down. It's not Gérard's fault. He's just being kind. I've never talked to anyone in Paris about the baby I gave birth to seventeen years ago — until now. Gérard has listened. He has not judged.

"You see this hand?" Gérard holds up the claw that is his right hand. "I used to be right-handed. Now this hand is useless. So I learned to paint with my left hand. When the disease progresses, my left hand will be useless, too." He smiles down at me, which is when I notice how electric his blue eyes are. "But in my dreams, I still dream I paint with my right hand. In my dreams, everything is as it used to be. I have not forgotten."

He regards me with those shocking azure eyes until I have to look away. I realize I have not forgotten either.

■ ■ ■ ■

I close the front door as quietly as I can and stand in the foyer of our apartment. I can hear the girls and Pierre chatting, but I don't hear Florence and Niki. A shudder passes through me. Is it relief or fear? I pad down the hall in my socks.

"Maman! J'adore mon monteau!" Asha says as soon as she sees me step into the living room. She twirls, arms extended, like a ballerina. Both girls are wearing the embroidered coats I laid out for them on their beds before I left for my lunch with Mathilde. It's now almost six in the evening.

Shanti smiles shyly and approaches me for a hug. *"Merci, Maman. Tu m'as manqué."* I squeeze her tightly. How I missed the love of their small bodies! The delicate ribs I can feel through their clothes. The silk of their hair.

Not to be left behind, Asha runs up for a hug, too.

Pierre, who'd been sitting on the sofa, comes to standing, his face full of concern. "Radha, where were you? We thought you'd be resting today. There was no note. I didn't know where you'd gone."

I release the girls and walk to the sofa to

295

kiss him. "Mathilde called. She needed to talk."

Pierre blinks. "Is it her mother?"

I sigh. "That and other things. I think —"

Asha grabs my hand. "What smells did you bring back with you?"

"Not smells! They're scents," Shanti corrects her, then turns to me. "What did you bring for Papa?"

"Papa didn't show you?" I raise my eyebrows at Pierre. "I brought him five elephants from India." Of course I'm talking about the sandalwood carvings, but Asha's eyes widen in surprise.

"Where are they, *Maman*?"

Pierre laughs. "I'll get them." As he passes me on his way to our bedroom, he whispers in my ear, "They smell better than real elephants."

"*Mes choux,* tell me about your day." I sit on the sofa and the girls curl up on either side of me.

Shanti says, "Did you know Niki can draw? We went to the Louvre and he did these sketches of the art he liked. He did sketches of Asha and me, too, when we weren't looking." She gazes at me solemnly. "He carries his sketchbook with him all the time. *Maman,* I'd like to carry a little notebook, too." Oh, how I love her serious expressions.

"What would you put in it?" I straighten the collar of her red coat. It's perfect on her.

She answers right away, as if she's been thinking about it for a while. "What we did with Niki today. How we went to the Louvre. We also took a *bateau-mouche* around the Seine. Asha and I fed the seagulls."

Pierre returns with the sandalwood elephants I brought for him. The girls want to sniff them. Asha asks if she can take *les éléphants* to school to show her teacher. I look at Pierre, and he nods. "But be careful not to break off the tusk, *d'accord*? That's the elephant's tooth, and it never grows back." Asha looks gravely at the carved animal in her hand.

Pierre offers to make omelets for dinner. He says he wants to know about my trip, about Agra, what I saw, what I ate. "I know it won't compare with omelets, but I can dream, can't I?"

I smile at him. It's good to be home.

Especially since I've avoided having to talk to Niki for another day.

The next day is Sunday. I slept dreamlessly and woke up early, determined to put Niki in the compartment where he's been all these years. But it's especially difficult when my family thinks he's my cousin and treats him as such. I called Florence while Pierre was in the shower this morning. I told her I'd heard from Niki's parents. They said there had been a disagreement about where Niki could go to college. Niki had been upset and ran to the only other family he knew about: me. "His parents have asked me to send him back home."

"Does he have to leave right away?" She sounds disappointed. "I was taking him with us this morning. I want him to see our beautiful *église.*"

Twice a month, I agree to let Florence take the girls to morning service at l'église de Saint-Germain-des-Prés — around the corner from our apartment — and to Les Deux Magots café afterward. Sometimes Pierre joins them.

I'm surprised Niki agreed to go too.

"He's a most accommodating young man," Florence continues. "He helped me make baguettes last night at my place. I'm sending some home with the girls. And Asha wants him to see the gargoyles at the top of Notre-Dame. We'll walk over there after church, then have lunch at the café."

Florence sounds . . . *happy*? I'm trying to remember when I last heard her sound this

way. For the first time, it occurs to me —
why has it taken me so long to realize? —
that Florence is lonely. She's happiest when
the girls spend the night at her house and
she can show them how to make *financiers*
or plant tulip bulbs in her backyard or read
the latest *Astérix* with them. It looks as if
Niki might fulfill the same need for her as
the girls: children who can take the place of
Pierre, whom Florence must have missed
terribly when he went to live at the boarding school. I don't ever remember Pierre
sharing fond memories of Florence doing
any of these things with him. Or has he just
forgotten?

"I do need to talk to him today, Florence.
His parents are anxious to hear from him.
Perhaps after Notre-Dame?"

In the pause that follows, I sense she
wants to say something but decides against
it.

"Could you tell him to meet me at the
Jardin du Luxembourg? At three o'clock?" I
need a neutral place. Without family. "Between the *palais* and the pond?"

"D'accord." Florence doesn't ask me any
questions, which is puzzling. I've always
found her prying to be as natural as her
breathing.

I make myself say it because she deserves

it. "Florence? Thank you for last night."

She's silent for a moment, but I hear the smile in her voice when she says, *"Bien sûr."*

Pierre needs to put in a few hours at work today, as do I. I'm anxious to try the *mitti attar* in my formula for Olympia, and I know Delphine will be waiting to hear about my progress tomorrow, Monday. Since the church is on the way to his office, Pierre has offered to accompany Shanti and Asha there and hand them off to Florence.

Paris is quiet on Sunday mornings. The cafés are not yet full. The Métro is relatively empty. Across the seat from me, a Black woman in a blue work uniform leans to one side, asleep; she must have just gotten off work. A foreign couple, probably tourists, sit close together, afraid to let go of their belongings. I wonder what they've heard about pickpockets. I get off before my regular stop at Pont d'Alma and walk the twenty minutes in the brisk air to Place Victor Hugo. The air is a mélange of odors — banana peels, urine, a patch of diesel oil, hot coffee, sleep.

It's ironic that my office, Florence's home in Neuilly and the girl's International School are within two or three kilometers of each other. Our apartment in the sixth *ar-*

rondissement is the anomaly, five kilometers away from the hub. Really, my practical brain reasons, it would be far more convenient for Florence to pick up the girls after school and keep them with her until I leave work and can take them home. I could forget about hiring yet another nanny. Then my fear of being left behind, of Florence taking charge of my daughters, worms its way in and tells me how ridiculous that sounds.

In the lab, the lovely scent of rain, *mitti attar,* fills the air as I add it, drop by drop, into my test samples. My formula contains the sharp blend of hibiscus, marigold and mango, calming cardamom and clove oils and the sultry allure of musk and frankincense. But I've been varying the quantities of each ingredient these last few weeks. Now I'm working with a consistent base that feels right, and only varying the quantity of the scent of rain. After a dozen trials, I think I may have found the right formula. I close my eyes as I wave the blotter in front of my nose to inhale the result. Finally, I can see and feel Olympia! I can't believe it. After a hundred trials, I've found her. I urge her to react. Is she pleased? Does the scent curve her lips into a private smile? Does it make her eyes blink in recognition? Is the fragrance *her*? Is *she* the fragrance?

I'm so pleased I sit back and survey my perfume organ. I used to have a tiny brass statue of Ganesh, the Remover of Obstacles, hidden among the bottles of scent. Lakshmi sent it to me when I first began working for Delphine. But I felt self-conscious in case Celeste saw it when she did her monthly inventory. I take it out now from my bottom drawer. Lord Ganesh gazes at me placidly from his perch on a rat. In his four hands are items that have meaning for me and the significance I have given to each: a lotus flower for the knowledge that has led me to this place in time; *laddus* for the sweet results of my efforts; a hatchet to clear what stands in my way; and the blessing of his hand that I need for each project. Not everyone would agree with my interpretation, for there are many images of the Elephant God, and they all differ in some way. I cannot perform *aarti* for him here at work, but on this occasion, I take his benediction into my hands anyway and bring it to my face. What I'm doing is no different from what Florence is doing this morning at mass — accepting the blessings of her chosen God.

I glance at the clock. Two-thirty. If I leave

now for the Métro, I'll make it to the Jardin du Luxembourg in time to meet Niki.

I'm sitting in front of the pond at the *jardin*. Behind me are the *palais* and the *musée*. To my left, the Fontaine Medicis. Despite the cold, the park is full. I see two women in coats, gloves and boots, their handbags in their laps, talking in soft tones. A group of Japanese businessmen and their wives are being led by a guide to the far end of the pond. A pair of young lovers huddle together as they stop to admire the statue of Marie de' Medici, the queen who made this extraordinary *jardin* possible. Families wander the grounds chatting, the children in yellow slickers and yellow rubber boots or pea-coats, their cheeks flushed pink, their energy boundless.

I watch the ducks gliding across the pond. The chilly breeze on this December day ruffles their feathers. I pull my coat tighter around me as I watch a small child place his boat in the pond. He turns around to make sure his grandfather is watching from his chair a few feet away. Did Niki ever have such an outing? Would I have brought him here if I'd been living in Paris when he arrived in the world? I could imagine him steering that toy boat. But which color boat would he have picked? I don't even know if he likes boats or ponds or fishing or what his favorite color is. I know so little about him. If only I'd read Kanta's letters!

Suddenly, my view of the boy navigating his boat with a long-handled paddle is blocked by someone wearing black jogging pants. I notice his shoes — white Adidas with red stripes, the tops covered in dust.

My heartbeat thunders in my ears. I want to look at his face, but I can't find the strength to lift my eyes. *I can't do this!*

"Look at me?" It's a young man's voice, a plea. I smell hurt, loneliness and something else. Fear? Disgust? "Please."

I'm shaking my head no. *Make this stop. Make it go away. This is not happening.* I cover my eyes with the palms of my hands, start rocking back and forth.

A disturbing crunch of gravel. He's moved closer, so close that I can feel the heat coming off his body. I smell bergamot, neroli. Niki no longer smells the same as he did at four months, the last time I saw him.

He says, "I just want to know why my mother wrote to you all those years."

What do I tell him? Why is this happening?

I feel the whoosh of air, rustle of clothing, hear the squashing of gravel. Is he squatting in front of me? *Why won't he go away?*

Now his warm breath is on my fingers. I smell honey and sesame seeds. Has he just eaten *til ki laddu* or does he always smell this way? Surely Florence wouldn't have fed him an Indian sweet? She doesn't cook Indian food.

Fingers, slightly sweaty, pry my hands away from my face. A quicksilver memory: me playing hide-and-seek with baby Niki, his tiny fingers reaching for mine. I realize my eyes are still closed. Slowly, I open them.

It's like looking at Ravi all those years ago. He was also seventeen when I met him.

All at once, my head is spinning. I try to take a gulp of air.

"Put your head between your knees," he says, and sounds just as commanding as Delphine when I was dizzy in her office. "Take deep breaths."

I do as he says. I feel his hand on the ridge of my spine.

"That's what our coach tells us to do when we've had the wind knocked out of us." I hear the smile in his voice. The smell of daffodils, vanillic in tonality.

The spinning slows, stops. My breathing becomes more regular. But now I'm shivering. "Thank you," I murmur.

He sits on the gravel, cross-legged, next to my chair. I can see all of him now. His dark green sweater, a black jacket made from some shiny material. All wrong for France. He pulls something out of his jacket pocket. "This might help." Niki offers me a *til ki laddu*. Now where did he get that in Paris?

I take a bite and close my eyes. The sugar goes right to my brain, shoots through my nerves. Once again, I'm thirteen years old, in Lakshmi's lodgings, making this treat for one of Lakshmi's ladies in Jaipur. Sesame seed warms the body, and it's mainly eaten in the winter, but that particular client of Jiji's suffered from cold hands and feet all year round.

I chew and steal a glance at Niki, struck by his beauty. Long lashes. The same rosy cheeks I remember on Ravi. And those eyes! My eyes. Jiji's eyes. Maa's eyes.

"Baju makes the best *laddus.*" He smiles. "Have you ever met him?"

I make a noncommittal noise. I remember Kanta's old servant. In his spotless white *dhoti.* Kanta's mother-in-law was always chiding him for one reason or another, but I think he enjoyed the attention, no matter how crusty her comment.

"My mother was always a hopeless cook," Niki says cheerfully.

Mother. He says it so casually. Of course he's referring to Kanta. But — just once —

306

what would it feel like to have him call *me* that?

"Why are you here, Niki?" I hadn't meant to blurt it out so gracelessly. But there are so many voices inside me. *Talk to him! Tell him everything. Don't say anything! But he deserves to know. What will happen if I do? He'll hate me for abandoning him. He'll want to be part of my family. What would Pierre say to that?*

"My parents —" he stops again. "We got this letter. It says I can go to school —"

The dizziness returns. I close my eyes and lower my head again.

"It's from a lawyer. I'm not explaining it well." He starts from the beginning. The benefactor's letter, Manu and Kanta's unwillingness to let him go to America. "I searched my mother's desk for answers. I found all these letters you'd returned to her — unopened. She won't tell me why she sent them to you or why you returned them."

"Why is it important for you to know?"

His head jerks backward, his expression one of disbelief. "Because she sent you so many with photos of *me* inside. Why would she want you to know about me? Who are you to her? I've never even heard of you. You're not one of my aunts, her sister or

307

her sisters-in-law. And you're obviously not a friend since you keep returning the letters. I thought . . . maybe . . . you're my anonymous benefactor?" He ducks his head, sounding sheepish, embarrassed.

"Well, I'm not," I say, looking away. I sound harsh, as if I'm scolding him for thinking such a thing.

"Oh." He chews his lip. "So . . ."

"*Hahn*. So." I notice the little boy and his grandfather are no longer at the pond. I see them walking up the wide stairs to another part of the garden.

"So why all the secrecy?"

"I asked Kanta and Manu never to tell you about me."

"What? Why?"

"Because I didn't want to know about you. Or for you to know about me. I wanted your mother to stop sending me those letters. I thought she would get the hint if I never opened them. I told Lakshmi — my sister — to tell Kanta to stop."

Why did she keep the letters? If she hadn't, he may never have come to Paris. I turn to look at him. He's frowning, concentrating. The smell of bewilderment — cold and dark — surrounds him.

"Lakshmi Auntie? Who lives in Shimla? You're sisters?"

I nod.

"But why would you do that? You're obviously angry at my mother. Why? Why would anyone be angry at her? None of it makes sense! She won't tell me. I've come all this way, and you won't tell me either?"

There's a fire behind my eyes. My face feels hot. *I can't take much more. And I can't lie to him. He doesn't deserve it.* "Because I . . ." I stop. "Because I'm . . ." I'm going to pass out! My hands are fists. I push my fingernails into my palms. I take a deep breath. "Oh, Niki! Because I brought you into this world."

He looks even more perplexed. "You were the nurse? Or the doctor? Were you there when I was born?"

Tears fill my eyes and roll down my cheeks. I nod.

"What were you — ?"

"Niki, your parents want you to go home. I want you to go home. Why won't you just go home?"

Those beautiful blue-green orbs get wider. "I'm not going anywhere till you all tell me what you're hiding."

"I — Niki — I gave birth to you. And your parents, Kanta and Manu, adopted you as a newborn. But I'm the one who had you."

His body twitches as if I've just flung a

match at him. "No. No." He stands, tum-
bling over his feet. "Kanta is my mother."
But he sounds less sure now.

I wipe my face. If I look up at the sky, will
my tears go back in my head? It's something
I used to wonder as a kid.

"Yes, she is. But you wanted the truth. So
there it is. Your mother and father adopted
you." Through my tears, I look at the pond,
the ducks floating slowly. Out there, everything looks so peaceful. Inside, my body
feels like it's being pried apart the way it
did when I gave birth to the boy before me.

He pushes his hair off his forehead and
walks around in a small circle, stops, stares
at me. "I'm *adopted*? Why didn't they tell
me? Ever?"

This is not my responsibility. "You'd have
to ask them. They adopted you when you
were just a day old. To them, you *are* their
son. What good would it do to tell you? How
would it help?"

He puffs up his cheeks and blows out the
air. Walks back and forth in front of my
chair for a few minutes. He stops moving.
"You didn't want to keep me?"

*I'd never wanted anything so much in my
life.* "I was thirteen!" My voice has risen.
"How could I keep you?" Why do I sound
so defensive?

"But you — you returned all those letters. It's as if you didn't *want* to know anything about me." His eyebrows knit together. "Did you — do you hate me? Is that why you gave me away? Why you want me to leave now?"

Hate him? I love every hair on his head more than he can ever know! How can I explain a lifetime of pretending not to care? How do I tell him I couldn't have moved on if I had cared too much?

This was a mistake.

I get up from the chair too quickly and have to hold on to the back of it to steady myself. I need to go home, to the girls. All at once, I have an overwhelming desire to hold them, to feel that I'm a good mother, regardless of what happened with Niki.

"You're leaving?" He sounds incredulous. "I come all this way to see you and you're leaving? What's so important that you need to go right now?" He's shouting at me. People are turning their heads to look. The two women chatting on a nearby bench stop to stare at us.

"Go home, Niki," I shout back.

I reach in the pocket of my coat and feel the chain, touch the vial. I pull it out. I reach for his arm, unclench his hand and thrust the necklace in his palm.

311

He looks at me with wild eyes, bewildered. "What's this?"

"You, Niki. It's you."

Coconut oil. Tangerine. Arrowroot. Lychee. Saltwater. Rosewood. Myrrh. All the scents that remind me of you.

I turn and step quickly away, unsure my legs can hold out long enough for the fifteen-minute walk home.

All the way to the apartment, I chastise myself for how badly I handled the meeting with Niki. Surely I owed him a fuller explanation? Or a gentler letdown. Why was I so careless with his feelings?

Pierre doesn't even wait to scold me when I enter the apartment. Normally, he would hold off until the girls were in their room.

"Where have you been? First you were in Agra for most of the week. Then you rested yesterday. I was hoping we could spend time as a family this afternoon. I called Mathilde. I called *Maman.* I couldn't find you. I leave you notes to let you know where I am. You can't even extend me the same courtesy? What's going on with you?"

I'm so drained from my meeting with Niki that I don't know how to answer my husband. I stare at him, dumbfounded. Surely he notices that my eyes are puffy and my nose is congested. Can't he tell I've been crying? If I tell him I've been with Niki, he won't understand and will ask what happened. I am not ready for that conversation. Not yet.

Behind him are my girls. Shanti is standing with a large piece of paper in her hand. Is it a drawing? Asha is right behind her with a similar piece of paper. Both girls are in their tights and plaid skirts from church this morning. They look uncertain; they're not used to their father shouting at their mother.

I put on a smile. "*Mes poussins,* did you make me something?" I hang up my coat and walk past Pierre to hug them. I hold on to them longer than I usually do. Their wiry bodies relax under my embrace. And, once again, they're radiating the energy of little girls who have made a discovery and can't wait to tell me about it.

"*Maman,* Niki drew gargoyles for us. Look!" They hold up the charcoal drawings for my inspection, pointing out that the mouths of the beasts are actually waterspouts. The drawings are good. There's life in them. Vibrancy. How did Niki make silent statues come alive on the page?

"They throw water off the church!" Asha says.

Shanti puts a hand on her hip, looking so

adultlike it makes me smile. "Asha, they don't *throw* water. Rainwater comes out of their mouths so it doesn't hit the walls," she explains patiently.

I turn to Pierre, who is still standing in the hallway, and smile. *Look at our daughters,* I'm saying. *If they can be this excited about gargoyles, what's next?* I think of Binu, in the kitchen of Hazi and Nasreen's *kotha,* telling me she wants to be a spaceman.

But Pierre is not moved. His mouth is pinched in irritation. He shakes his head, as if to say, *What's the use of talking?* He walks into the kitchen to make dinner.

Dinner is a quiet affair during which Pierre and I barely speak. I put the girls to bed that night, reading from the Madeline series. It's a little young for Shanti, but it was her turn to pick, and she knows it's Asha's favorite. Asha drops off to sleep before I've turned the second page. I'm sitting with Shanti on her bed, propped up against the pillows, but I can tell she's not really interested, so I close the book.

"It was nice of you to pick a book your sister likes, *chérie,*" I whisper. Frankly, that was a first since Shanti doesn't usually go out of her way to help Asha. But at least there haven't been any more incidents at school involving my older daughter.

314

Shanti smacks her lips, her new habit. "I have to be a better sister."

This is a first, too. "What makes you say that?"

Shanti puts a strand of her hair in her mouth and chews. I gently remove it and pull her hair behind her ear. "We went to see the gargoyles at Notre-Dame because Asha wanted to."

"And you didn't?"

She raises a shoulder and lets it drop. "I didn't mind. Asha is the one who suggested it, so we went. We usually do what Asha wants because she has all the ideas. But then I went to the other end of the terrace where you can see Montmartre."

I'm not sure where this is leading, so I grab her hairbrush from her side table and run it through her hair. It's thick, like mine. Brown, like Pierre's. I part it down the middle and form two rows. I start braiding the first row.

"I was just looking around and Niki joined me. It was like he came to be with me." She sounds pleased . . . and proud. I smile.

"He asked if I liked being a sister. I told him it was all right. But I wished I was the little sister. Then everything would be easier. Everyone wants to help Asha."

My fingers slow their braiding. It's as if

she sees the ugly undercurrent of my guilt laid bare: I feel Asha is much easier to handle, less complicated than my older daughter. Does Shanti think I love her less? I let go of the braid and turn her by the shoulders to face me. "Oh, *chérie!* Why would you say that? We love you just as much as Asha. Your papa loves you. Your grand-mère —"

"No, *Maman.* It's not like that. It's just that I have to be the one to look out for her. That's what big sisters do."

"You feel you have to protect her?"

"It's what I do. When a girl tries to pick on her at school, it's my job. She knows that." Her brown eyes are solemn; they always have been. Shanti hardly smiled as a baby, making me wonder if she was going to be like that all her life. She was and is so much like me, brows furrowed, focused on the task at hand — whether I was drawing water from the well or collecting grain from Prem and his mill, or teaching two plus two to the kids at Pitaji's school. I'm looking at the eyes of the woman Shanti will be some-day, someone who thinks deeply about things and can't always find the words to describe her feelings.

"*Beti,* what happened that day at school with that girl? When they sent you home?"

She doesn't speak for a moment, and I wonder if she heard my question. Then she turns her head toward me to whisper into my ear. "Asha didn't even know that girl was about to pour water on her head. And it was cold outside! I had to stop her. I don't think she likes Asha."

I know I shouldn't agree with what Shanti did, striking her classmate, but I can't help it. I would have done exactly the same thing at her age. I remember, at thirteen, when I almost threw rocks at pretty, spoiled Sheela Sharma in the courtyard of her house because I was mad at her for being rude to Malik. Even if Sheela deserved it, I'm glad Lakshmi stopped me from lashing out at her that way. My sister taught me that, eventually, everyone gets their due in one way or another; physical retaliation, while it feels just at the time, is never a good idea.

I go back to braiding my daughter's beautiful hair, feeling the glossy strands sliding around my fingers.

"Know what Niki said to me?" she asks.

My breath catches. Did he tell the girls I was his mother? No, he was with the girls *before* I met him by the pond and told him, so that's impossible. My chest relaxes.

Shanti says, "He said I was lucky I had a sister. He doesn't have one. He doesn't even have a brother. He says he wishes he had a sister." She puts a hand on my knee and turns around to face me again. "Can I be a sister to him? I would let him pick the book he wanted to read at night."

It's moments like these that make me cherish my role as a mother. I wrap my arms around my older daughter and plant a thousand kisses on her cheek. With my body curved around hers, I slide down the headboard, taking her with me. I pull the covers over us, and we fall asleep together.

By Monday, my trip to Agra already seems like a distant memory. My thoughts are still with Niki and our conversation at the *jardin*. He must have gone back to Florence's with more questions than answers.

At the House of Yves, I stop at Celeste's desk to give her the tie-dyed scarf in maple, periwinkle and sky blue that I brought back from Agra. She tries it on immediately. The colors of the delicate muslin brighten her eyes. Her smile is wide as she jumps up from her chair to kiss my cheeks.

"I have to show Ferdie!" she says, leaving her desk and bouncing into the lab.

For Michel and Ferdie, I've brought back sandalwood pens with carvings of the Taj Mahal minarets. Delphine doesn't care for trinkets, and her obsession with midcentury objects keeps her from adding anything to her environment that doesn't fit. I assume bringing back the *khus* and *mitti attar* essential oils will be present enough. Celeste told me Delphine is at a client meeting outside Paris all day today so we won't see her till tomorrow.

I unlock my desk and pull out the samples I worked on yesterday. The fact that I've brought back something so exotic for Delphine — and, of course, Olympia — takes my mind off Niki for a while. The dried scent papers from this weekend smell wonderful! Exactly as I remembered them with the varying quantities of the scent of Indian rain. Last minute check: insert fresh blotters into the vials and sniff.

But . . . something is wrong. There's an odor of . . . *benzene*?

I try again. Definitely benzene.

Where is that smell coming from? I smell my hands. No benzene on them. Could the chemical combination of ingredients in my samples have simulated benzene? But the scent papers from yesterday don't smell like benzene. Could someone have added an ingredient to my work since yesterday? I've been so careful to lock everything up; how could anyone have accessed my vials? Who?

Delphine is the first one at the office in the mornings. Could it be her? Is she setting me up for failure because she secretly wants me off her payroll? But then why would she have sent me to India? And why would she tell me how good my work is and why she's given me this opportunity? She could just fire me instead of creating such an elaborate hoax.

Michel has long been the person I have felt the least kinship with. He's never made any effort to get to know me — although I made the effort with him when I first started working here. I've often wondered if he might be upset that Delphine gave the Olympia project to me. He works silently, barely speaking more than five or ten words a day to anyone except Celeste, whom he lunches with sometimes. I've seen him glancing my way every now and then, regarding me with his cool blue eyes. Is he jealous?

No way could it be Ferdie. When I joined the lab, he was the first one to welcome me and invite me out to lunch. He's always sharing his escapades with Celeste and me, bringing us treats from the café next door, adding levity to our day.

That leaves Celeste. I hate to think it, but she might want me to fail so Ferdie could have the chance to work on Olympia. Even though she knows he dates men and her chances are slim, she hasn't given up hope. She moons after him. Still, who am I to judge her? Didn't I once invest all my hopes in Ravi, a boy with whom I had the slimmest of chances?

It's silly to even suspect my coworkers. Could the odor of benzene be coming from the note of melon in my formula? Sometimes a ripe melon can smell like petrol. Or is it the miniscule amount of fennel I added? Does the combination of melon and fennel create that sweet benzene scent? Not for the first time do I chide myself for not completing that second year of chemistry. Whom should I ask for help? If I ask Michel, he will tell Delphine I don't know what I'm doing.

That leaves Ferdie.

When Ferdie goes to get coffee from the reception area, I follow him. While he pours his drink, I make my tea and we chat about Agra. He has so many fond memories of his travels in India. He wants to know if the Taj Mahal is as spectacular as he remembers it. We joke about the taxi drivers having to weave between pedestrians and livestock, narrowly missing both.

I finally work up the courage to ask.

"Ferdie, would you mind looking at something for me? It's probably nothing, but I'm either losing my sense of smell or something is way off in my samples."

He smiles good-humoredly. What a relief! "Lead the way," he says.

As we walk past Celeste's desk, I think I see a flash of envy — or is it jealousy? I smile at her as if to say, *I'm no threat.*

At my worktable, I tell him, "It's for the Olympia project." He nods. When he sniffs the fresh blotter, he draws back and chuckles. "Are you creating the essence of petrol?"

So it's not my nose that's off. It *is* benzene. I know it didn't smell like this yesterday when I went to meet Niki. I nod my thanks to Ferdie. He gives me a sympathetic smile and ambles back to his station. Michel was watching our exchange. His brows are raised, as if he might be volunteering his services, but I smile politely at him and take a seat on my chair. I sigh. Should I tell Delphine what's going on? No, I don't want her to think I can't handle it.

I take out my notebook and start again. I remix my samples. Now my mind keeps drifting to my talk with Niki. I hear his voice. *Why didn't I care to read the letters or look at the photos Kanta sent me?* I keep seeing the dazed look on his face, the uneasiness of discovering that the two people he has called Mummi and Papa all his life are the ones with whom he shares no blood. I try to shut the images from my mind. The more I try, the more they boomerang back. And I wonder: How would I feel if I'd learned that Maa and Pitaji weren't my birth parents? It would upend my world, make me question everything I took for granted. That's probably how Niki is feeling. How could I have left him in the park like that? Alone. Confused. I should have been kinder, softer, more understanding — as a *real* mother would have been.

I can't work anymore. I leave early to get the girls from school. But instead of taking them home, I bring them to Florence's, where I suspect I'll find Niki. I haven't quite worked out how I'm going to talk to him while the girls and Florence are in the same room, but I take a deep breath and think of Jiji's words. *We can't go back and change anything,* beti. *But think of what the past has taught you.* What it's taught me is that keeping secrets has a cost.

Florence's house is on Boulevard Victor Hugo in the area called Neuilly-sur-Seine. I don't often come here — Florence usually comes to our house — but when I do, I'm always startled by how large a house Pierre grew up in. For the majority of his life, it was just him and his mother. Did they spend most of their time in separate rooms? Separate wings? Separate floors? Each of the three stories has large windows overlooking the boulevard, but the ten-foot-high *fleur-de-lis* iron fence and the rhododendron hedge keeps passersby from view.

Florence answers the buzzer. The girls kiss her cheeks and walk in as if it's their house. To be fair, it's been more their house for the past few months; Florence has picked them up from school when I couldn't. Shanti and Asha begin to take off their coats and shoes before I can tell them we're only here for a little while. They've grown used to spending time here, and they're settling in. Florence is in a camel wool skirt, long-sleeved striped blouse and a cream sweater vest. She's wearing an apron and carrying a large wooden spoon. She's pleased to see the girls, but she seems subdued.

Before I can get a word out, the girls ask, "*Grand-mère,* is Niki here?"

I should have known they'd be excited to see him again. At breakfast, it was *Niki this* and *Niki that* and what they would like to show Niki. On the way here, they were asking if they could take Niki on the carousels.

It's something the girls love to do in December. They have their favorite merry-go-rounds. The one at the Place du Trocadero, not far from their school, is a good bet because there are fewer tourists in winter. There's the little one at Saint Sulpice, the elaborate Italian carousel at Place Willette. At the Tuileries, the carousel is right where the girls can visit the menagerie. Asha says, "It's almost Christmas, and we can ride for free!"

Shanti adds, "Let's get sugar crepes. Niki's probably never tasted them before."

We follow Florence to her kitchen. She says, "Sugar crepes later. Yogurt now. Niki is resting so keep your voices down."

She doles out two small bowls of thick yogurt and hands them to the girls. They take their snacks to the dining table, where they've already dispatched their bookbags. From the living room, I hear the voice of Jacques Brel singing "Ne me quitte pas."

Florence's face looks strained. She's not in good humor. I can tell she wants to say something to me, but in the next moment, she brushes past me to the stove, where the aromas of saffron and paprika dominate.

"I'm making paella. It's something my mother loved, so I learned how to make it for her." She removes a lid from the cast-iron pot on the stove and stirs it with her spoon. "Still didn't make her like me." She gives me a wry smile that makes her cheekbones fuller. "Do you think Niki likes paella?" she asks me.

"Well, you know he's Indian, not Spanish, right?"

Florence's nostrils flare. Her look says, *I'm not daft.* "I don't know how to cook Indian food, and I don't want that smell about my house." Gone is the Florence from the past two days. Perhaps it was too good to last.

There was a time when Pierre and I were first married and she came to dinner at our apartment. I'd spent all day cooking four or five Indian dishes for her. Pierre had warned me that, unlike his grandmother, Florence refused to travel outside the country and hated anything *étrange.* "She is French through and through," he said. But how could the woman who came from the womb of Pierre's bohemian *grand-mère* be so unadventurous, I reasoned. That evening, Florence stared at her plate and asked if I had any salad. I was crushed.

I'm about to ask if I can go upstairs and see Niki when she says, "He was really distraught when he came home from meeting with you yesterday." It sounds like an accusation. She pours sliced sausages into

326

the rice mixture and stirs.

What business is it of hers? "Did you ask him why?" I'm afraid of the answer. What if he did tell her?

"Couldn't. He ran upstairs and slammed the bedroom door." She puts the lid on the pot again and turns down the heat. She turns to me with a hand on her hip.

"How old were you when you had him?" It's as if she's just asked me which movie I'm going to see tonight.

She knows? How? Did Niki tell her? I try to feign surprise, but she narrows her eyes and tilts her head, waiting. When I say nothing, she says, "I've never met two cousins who look that much alike. You must have been very young."

It's a statement, not speculation. She does know. I remember how closely she was looking at us that first night she met Niki. I'm too tired to lie, too defeated to cover up the biggest secret of my life. Why deny it? "Almost fourteen," I reply. I wonder if that somehow makes it less scandalous than saying thirteen?

She crosses her arms over her chest. "Pierre doesn't know?"

I shake my head. Why am I confiding in her? This woman has done nothing but criticize me — the way I cook, the way I raise my children, the country I'm from. She'll use this against me. It'll be another way for her to drive a wedge between Pierre and me.

Florence is regarding me thoughtfully, assessing me. "Here's another thing Pierre doesn't know. He's not my husband's son." She lifts a glass of wine from the counter next to the stove. She waves it at me to ask if I'd like a glass.

I'm so startled by her revelation I don't answer.

She takes a sip of her wine and leans against the Formica counter. She's keeping her voice low so the girls don't overhear. "I didn't have a lot of experience with men. I was twenty-five when I met his father, Vincent. Oh, I was foolish with love for him. It was the first time I'd really felt like that. Pierre's amber eyes? They're Vincent's. When I told Vincent I was carrying his child, he denied it was his." Her nostrils widen. "As if I'd spread my legs for every man I met! *Connard!* I never saw him again." She pours herself more wine. "Sure you won't have any? It's your favorite red."

I wasn't aware she knew my preference for red over white. I shake my head.

"Philippe Fontaine was an old family friend. He always liked me. I told him I was pregnant, half hoping he would marry me. And he did . . . because he felt it was his duty or to save me the embarrassment or because my family had money — who knows? Maybe he felt sorry for me." She takes a gulp from her glass, wipes the rim with her thumb. "You know what my mother said when I told her I was pregnant?"

Her hand is shaking slightly. That's when I notice her eyes are bloodshot. Not enough sleep? I look at the opened bottle. It's almost empty. *Is Florence drunk?* Her smile is full of irony. "*Maman* said, 'Well, let's hope it's not a girl.' She hated the female species. Even tried to talk me into getting rid of it. But I wouldn't. If I couldn't have Vincent, I wanted what we had made together.

"So I had Pierre. And my life became all about him. There was no room for Philippe. Eventually, he left. And then, because I smothered Pierre, my obsession with him drove him to my mother, who took him away — all the way around the world. In the end, I lost them all. Vincent. Philippe. Pierre."

Florence drains her glass. She lifts the lid on the pot and stirs the paella some more. "You, Radha, had a baby and gave him up for adoption. And look how different your life has been. How much better for you and for him. You have a husband who adores you. Together you started a new family. You have two lovely daughters. You have a career. Something you love. From what Niki's told me, he has loving parents. He's had everything he could want."

Is she saying I was right to give up my son? She knows I had Niki out of wedlock, gave him up for adoption and went on to marry her son without telling him, and she's not shocked?

Did she just also acknowledge that I work because I like it? I don't just do it to torture Pierre and the girls? Have I been so sensitive to her remarks that I twisted them to mean one thing when they meant another? Have I been so worried that she's been judging me — and so harshly, too — when I've really been judging myself? Now that I think about it, she's never actually said I shouldn't work outside the home — only that she could look after the girls while I do. When I talk about my work, she doesn't ask any questions, but she does listen.

She looks annoyed. "Oh, don't look at me like that. I know better than Pierre how you love being in that lab and creating all those scents. What woman wants to stay home all day? That's just a fantasy men make up. I envy you. This passion you have. And the talent. They make you come alive."

I blow air out of my cheeks. If this is how Florence sees me, why is she always saying and doing things to get a rise out of me? But . . . maybe that's exactly what she's doing. She wants me to react, to show myself. She senses the many parts of myself I keep hidden.

She's still talking. "Being a woman is difficult. I can see why my mother didn't like her own gender. We can do so much. Give so much. But not everyone wants what we're offering. And in the end, we're left with . . . pieces of a whole. Shards. Splinters. Chips. Pick them up, they cut our hands. Leave them on the ground, they cut our feet. It's hard for us to just walk away." She waves her empty glass in a circle to make her point, but it catches the handle of the pot, shattering the stem. Her finger starts bleeding, dripping blood onto the stovetop.

I grab a dishtowel and wrap it around the finger as I ease what's left of the wineglass out of her hand. Her mouth seems frozen in an "O" and she's blinking rapidly. She seems to be in shock, so I help her to the sink, remove the dishtowel and run cold water over her hand. The girls come into the kitchen, wondering what the crash was.

"*Grand-mère* cut herself. Don't come any closer. There's glass." I ask Florence, "Where are the bandages?"

She points with her good hand to the bathroom.

I tell the girls to get the bandages. They scamper off, happy to be of use.

When I'm satisfied there's no glass left in the cut, I pat it dry. The girls return with bandages, binding clips and gauze. I smile at them, proud that they've learned well at school. I tell them to go back to the dining room.

I wrap a gauze bandage around Florence's finger and fasten the end with a binding clip. She looks forlornly at the stovetop, which is now covered in glass. I clean it up with the ruined dishtowel and put all of it in the trash. The heavy lid on the Le Creuset pot would have prevented anything from getting into the food.

Florence still hasn't said a word. I walk her to the dining room and help her sit down on a chair along the dining table. The girls are already seated, watching all of our movements in silence. Florence has had too much wine; she's going to be dehydrated if she doesn't drink something. I run to the kitchen and return with a glass of water for her.

Then I remember why I came here in the first place. I go down the hall in search of Niki. He's not in any of the bedrooms on the first floor. I go up the stairs but he's not there either. The beds are undisturbed. I look in the backyard. No one. I return to the dining room. Florence is sitting quietly, gazing into the distance at nothing in particular.

"Florence? Which room?"

Her eyebrows come together, as if she has also just realized that we have heard no noises from upstairs. "Top floor. On the right."

I shake my head. "He's not in any of the rooms."

She looks off to the side, thinking. "I went out to get ingredients for the paella. Could he have slipped out then?" Her words are slurred.

"Did he have any luggage?"

"No. He only had a backpack. One change of clothes. He took a bath last night, and I gave him an old pair of Pierre's pajamas to sleep in."

"I saw those lying on one of the beds."

"And the backpack?"

"I didn't see one."

I run back upstairs and make a round of the rooms again. Nothing. I hurry back to the dining room.

Florence and I stare at one another.

She speaks first. "Where would he have gone? To your apartment?"

I reach for the yellow wall phone with the long ringed cord in the kitchen and dial our home number. Pierre picks up.

"Pierre? Is Niki there?"

"Bah . . . non. Isn't he with *Maman?"*

"No. Please call your mother's if he turns up at our place."

"Maman? Is Niki all right?" I turn around at Shanti's voice. She's standing next to me now.

I stare at my daughter, but I'm thinking of Niki. Why didn't I tell my beautiful boy I'd never stopped thinking about him? Why didn't I tell him I never wanted to give him up? Now he's out in this city somewhere or on his way to who-knows-where wondering if anyone cares about him. But surely he knows how much Kanta and Manu love him? Jiji's friends wanted him from the first moment they saw him at Lady Bradley Hospital nursery in Shimla. I should call Lakshmi! I don't even ask Florence's permission to use her phone. I dial the long-distance number, glancing at the kitchen clock. It's evening there, so my sister should be home.

"Hello?" It's Jay.

"*Bhaiya,* is Jiji there?"

Normally, he would chat with me pleasantly, ask after the girls. And Asha would be at my side, jumping up and down, dying to talk to her favorite uncle. But he must sense the urgency in my voice because he says, "I'll get her."

And then Jiji's on the phone asking what's wrong.

When I tell her we can't find Niki, she asks a million questions. When was the last time we saw him? I check with Florence. About two hours ago. What did he have with him? Only a backpack. Did he have enough money to take a plane back? A train? I don't know. I ask Florence. She doesn't know either. Jiji is silent. I know my sister's wondering what she hasn't yet asked. What other clues could help us find Niki's whereabouts. Finally, she says, "Let me call Kanta. I'll get back to you."

I replace the receiver in its cradle but my hand lingers. I can't seem to let go. My mind is full of places Niki could be and how he must be feeling right now and why *didn't* I and what *could* I and what *should* I have said to him instead of what I did say. Isn't that what Florence was trying to tell me? If Pierre had known the truth about his birth

— how much she fought to keep him in her life — perhaps he wouldn't have hardened his heart against her.

On the way home, the girls and I are quiet. On the Métro, they huddle next to me, and I put my arms around them. I can't stop thinking about what Florence told me. That Pierre was also born out of wedlock. That he chose his grandmother over his mother because Florence wouldn't let him breathe. That's what Pierre told me the night before I left for Agra. Every summer, his grandmother would take him to another part of the world. There are pictures of the two of them climbing Machu Picchu, gazing up at the giant stone statues at Easter Island, catching *bacalau* off the Portugal coast, marveling at the Yasaka Shrine in Kyoto. After university, he ran off to India to work on Le Corbusier's projects in Chandigarh. All this time, I thought Pierre traveled because he loved discovering the unknown. I thought he married me, a woman from another culture, another world, because to him I was mysterious, the unknown. But what if he was just running away from Florence?

I tighten my hold on the girls. What was *I* looking for when I married Pierre? Yes, I loved him. But I wanted to get away from India, too, from my memories of Ravi and Niki, from people I might encounter who would know about my past, the mistakes I'd made. Getting pregnant was a mistake. Falling for a boy I couldn't have was a mistake. Thinking I could master love at thirteen was a mistake. How foolish I was! Involuntarily, I shake my head.

On the subway, a young woman across the aisle from us looks startled, as if I'd been talking to her. Have I? I look away.

Florence doesn't regret having Pierre. I don't regret having Niki either. Like my girls, he is a pure scent, with the intensity of juniper, the tartness of tangerine and the sweetness of figs. But she does regret the secret she's kept and made Philippe keep. It created invisible walls that even a small child can detect — just as I know my girls can feel the tension between Pierre and me even when they don't see us fighting. Niki has probably sensed those invisible walls his whole life. He deserves better. I promise myself I will talk to him (if I get another chance!) and tell him what I've been thinking.

I close my eyes. I let myself imagine a life in which Niki has a place with my daughters, with Pierre and even with Florence.

337

Why couldn't he come visit us regularly here in Paris? Maybe even go to university here if he wants to? Why couldn't we take a family trip to Shimla where we could all stay at Lakshmi and Dr. Jay's house? The girls can be with their cousins, Rekha and Chullu, again.

I can almost imagine the girls asking their big brother for advice about colleges and trips abroad. We could visit India more often, something I would welcome. I want the children to have a foot in both countries, not just one. Already they've lost so much Hindi since they started going to school. It was easier to speak Hindi to them all day when they were little and we were together — even at Antoine's.

We arrive at our Métro stop and the girls tug at my coat to tell me to get up. I take their small hands in mine and we walk up the subway steps to the street. I know that none of what I was imagining will be possible until I tell Pierre the truth about Niki.

I know now that I liked Pierre because he was everything Ravi wasn't. At eighteen, I was still smarting from Ravi's complete abandonment. No letters. No messages passed to me via friends or servants. As soon as I realized I was pregnant, I even tried sending him notes through the Singh *chowkidar,* who wagged his head and made me believe he would pass the envelope along, but I doubted he did. Perhaps Parvati Singh had instructed her servants not to accept messages from me or admit me into their home. I cringe with shame now when I think about the fountain pen Jiji gifted me and that I messengered to Ravi's house to get him to talk to me again. What I didn't know at the time was that Ravi wasn't even in the country. He'd been sent to England as soon as his parents found out about the pregnancy.

Pierre was quiet and kind where Ravi was gregarious and impulsive. His hair was a pecan-brown while Ravi's was ink-black. Pierre's eyes were the color of honey; Ravi's were dark chocolate, mysterious. Pierre was a few inches shorter than Ravi and slight in stature. The night I first met Ravi, at his mother's winter holiday party, he was shirtless, his chest muscles gleaming in the blue makeup they had painted on him to play Shakespeare's Moorish king. What a long time ago that was.

When the girls and I get home, Pierre is cooking dinner. The phone rings, and I pick it up. Florence tells me that Niki has come back. I'm so relieved. Apparently, he had gone out to send a telegram to his parents. I would love to know what he said to Kanta and Manu, but Florence didn't ask him, and he didn't say.

Florence's parting shot before hanging up: "Niki likes the paella, by the way." She must be feeling better.

I take a bath and wash my hair, think about what to say to Pierre. We have dinner and the girls tell Pierre all about how Florence cut herself. "There was blood everywhere," Asha, ever the dramatic storyteller, says. All Shanti has to do is look at her sister a certain way, and Asha retracts the exaggeration. Pierre laughs.

Once the girls are in bed, he offers to make chai. He doesn't usually make Indian tea. But I understand; he wants to make peace.

I come up behind him while he's at the stove. He's already heated the milk and water in the saucepan. Now he adds the loose-leaf tea. And drops the cardamom seeds, the cloves and the peppercorns in the milk mixture. I taught him how I make it when we were first together. Now I think he makes better chai than I do.

I lean my cheek against his back. At first, he resists; his torso stiffens. Then I feel his body relax into mine.

I'm in my pajamas. The ends of my hair are still damp from my bath. As always, Pierre radiates heat. I've always liked that about him. I sigh into his shirt. "I have to tell you something."

I feel the muscles of his back constrict again. There's a pause. I take a step back.

He reaches for the cabinet above his head to put the ingredients away. "Chai is almost done. Then we can talk."

I walk to the girls' bedroom and watch them. Asha is reading. Shanti is drawing. They look up.

"Ça va mieux, Maman?" Shanti looks concerned. There it is again. The innate radar of my girls, picking up what I'm feeling.

"Oui, chérie." I plaster a smile on my face to make her feel better. Then I tap the doorframe twice, the way I used to right before I turned out the light when they were younger. I did it then to scatter any ghosts who might live in the building. Today, I'm scattering my own ghosts.

Then I go to our bedroom and sit crosslegged on the bed. Pierre comes in carrying two steaming cups of chai. He shuts the door with his foot.

"This is nice," I say. We rarely do this anymore. When the girls were little and crawled into bed with us on Sunday morn-

341

ings, Pierre would sometimes bring chai to bed. Shanti would be trying to braid my hair. Asha would have brought her *Babar* storybook for Pierre to read to her.

Pierre pulls his pillow up against the headboard and sits against it, his legs stretched out in front of him. "You'd like to tell me something?"

He lowers his head to his cup and takes a sip. I smell ammonia: fear. Does he think I'm about to tell him I'm having an affair?

I rub a hand over the *rajai* Lakshmi sent us as a wedding present. It's quilted red velvet, soft as butter after thirteen years of washings. "A long time ago, I did something that I've felt bad about ever since."

I steal a glance at him. His raised eyebrows give him an earnest expression. He's listening.

"Before I ever met you. When I was thirteen." My finger catches on the bedspread where the quilting thread has unraveled. I meant to fix it a few years ago, but never got around to it.

"I had a baby. And I gave him up for adoption."

Pierre sets his cup on his lap. I'm not sure how I want him to react, and perhaps he doesn't quite know how to react either. It's not as if there's a rule book about this sort of thing.

"You had a baby at thirteen?"

"Almost fourteen. He was seventeen. We were too young."

He is frowning now. "You were in love? He didn't force you?"

I can't look at him when I say this. The shame makes my cheeks warm. "I thought we were. He wasn't."

"Where is he now?"

Is he asking about the baby or about Ravi? I must look confused, so he asks, "The boy. The one you were in love with?"

I shake my head. "I found out much later that his family had sent him to England most likely before he even knew I was pregnant. Five years ago, Malik told me his family had moved to the United States. That's all I know."

He looks at the chai in his cup as if it holds all the answers. "What happened to the baby?"

My lips tremble and I think I might cry when I tell him. "He's here."

"Here where?"

"In Paris."

"In Paris?"

I meet his gaze. Try to tell him without words. I can't make myself say it.

His eyes search mine. He blinks one, two,

three times. His lips have parted in a silent gasp. "Niki?"

Pierre looks at my hand on the *rajai,* the stripes of my cotton pajamas. His eyes travel to my face. He is scanning my features. I can almost hear his thoughts. *I see it now. The long slim fingers. The resemblance in the eyes and around the mouth. The rounded chin. The way he laughs.*

My husband's golden eyes are guileless. "I didn't know. I thought he . . . But . . ." He pauses. "I put it out of my mind . . ." He pauses again. "Who adopted him?"

I tell Pierre about Kanta and Manu. How Kanta practically raised me when Lakshmi was too busy with her henna business. How Kanta used to take me to see American films at the Jaipur cinema and get beautiful dresses made for me. I tell him what happened to Kanta's baby in Shimla. How Niki came a month early. And then, how I took care of baby Niki for four months in Jaipur as his *ayah* before leaving for Shimla.

"So why has he come here? Why now?"

I set my cup on my nightstand and sit with my arms wrapped around my knees. I tell him all that I learned from Lakshmi and Kanta in Agra.

"You found out in Agra?" He sounds angry. "But you've been back for days. You didn't think to tell me until now?"

"I was just getting used to it myself. Besides, *chérie,* what difference does it make *when* I told you? It would have been a shock regardless. It's been a shock for me, too."

He considers this. "Did you know he was your son right away?"

"I wouldn't have recognized him had I met him on the street. But in Agra, Kanta told me he had come to Paris to find out who I was. So when I arrived and saw him . . ."

I reach for my chai. It's lukewarm now. I don't even taste it. I take another swallow. I drink the whole cup. Chew on the cardamom seeds that arrive with the last gulp.

Pierre taps my forearm with his finger. It sends an electric shock up my arm and down my spine. "Radha, why tell me now? You've had thirteen years to do it." His eyes hold hope, as if I might ease his pain with my next reply.

"*Mon coeur* . . . I had hoped never to tell you. I wanted to keep it from you as much as I've kept it from myself. I thought if I left India, I could leave it all behind. And we've made a lovely life here in Paris. We have the girls. We have our work. Why would I want to burden you with things that have nothing to do with you?"

His eyes narrow. "Radha, this has every-thing to do with me. The girls —" He sets his cup on his nightstand before he spills the chai. When he turns to me, his voice is an octave lower. "They have a brother. They need to know about him. And *Maman*. She needs to be told."

I sigh. "She knows."

He looks as if I've just told him I'm Père Noel. "What? How?"

I shrug. "Mother's instinct?"

I look at the man I've slept next to for thirteen years. The mouth that curves deliciously around words like *chou-chou* and *bonne nuit* and *toujours.* The hair that curls just at his forehead and around his ears. The skin that freckles in the sun. He looks disoriented, as if he doesn't understand the world he's suddenly found himself in. I want to erase the patina of disquiet, the unease, from his face. And I worry. Where do we go from here? Will Pierre want to leave me? Will he leave? Can he? Does he hate me? But it's out now. The secret I can't take back. And I feel the air lift around me. The way I do in the mornings when I draw the drapes open on the living room windows to let the light in.

After a while, Pierre lets out a slow breath.

"What does he want from us? Does he want to live here?" Then, as if it's just hit him: "Does he want money?"

"Pas du tout." I shake my head. "His parents want him back home. I think he just wanted to know who I was. Kanta has sent me letters and photos of him over the years. Every one of which I returned unopened. He found the unopened envelopes."

There's a silence between us as we hear a toilet flush in the apartment above us.

"And he knows now?" Pierre asks.

I squeeze my eyes shut and nod. I remember the shock in Niki's eyes when I told him. I cringe. How roughly I shoved the necklace in his hand.

He nods. "Is there . . . anything else I should know?"

"Like what?"

"Other children? Other marriages?"

My hands go cold. "No, Pierre! How can you even ask that?"

"How can I know unless I ask?"

"And what about you? I've never asked who you were with before me. That was your past. It's yours, not mine. All I care about is our life now."

Pierre looks at his hands and rubs them together slowly. "He's a nice boy. Niki. He's been raised well. The girls love him."

347

My eyes follow him as he gets off the bed and picks up our cups.

With his hand on the knob, he turns to me and smiles. "You know I've never liked chai? I only drink it to keep you company?"

I return his smile. "That's how I feel about wine."

"Ah." He shakes his head and leaves the bedroom. When he comes back, he is wearing his coat.

My heart misses a beat. "Where are you going at this hour?"

"For a walk. I feel like I need one."

I stand up. *Is he going to leave me?* I follow him to the foyer. He's putting on his shoes. "Pierre, have you never kept secrets from me?"

His hands still for a second before he resumes lacing his shoes.

A pain shoots up my ribs. Why doesn't he say something? "Pierre. I was so young." My voice is a whisper, plaintive and pleading. *Please don't make me feel like the Bad Luck Girl again.*

He stands with his back to me. Puts one hand on the knob. After a pause, he opens the door and closes it gently behind him.

I feel hollow. I'm not sure if I'm sad or angry or hurt or confused. Am I supposed to apologize? For what? For falling in love?

For doing what my flesh so desperately craved? For being duped by the charm of an older boy? For being gullible and easy to deceive?

Or am I responsible for making Pierre feel good about this, too? For soothing his bruised ego? And the shock he must be feeling? Am I supposed to make everything okay for Niki as well? To assure him he did the right thing by finding me? Or tell him I'm delighted he found me, showed up to surprise me and my family and end my marriage? Why should something I did so long ago in the name of love be my undoing?

I crawl back in bed. I'm still awake when Pierre returns. I hear him moving about the house quietly, brushing his teeth, taking his clothes off and hanging them in the closet. He lies down on his side of the bed as far from me as possible. I want to reach for him, wrap my arms around his chest, but I don't dare. It's as if he's created a fence around himself with a caution sign that says *Défense d'entrer.* Do Not Trespass.

We are startled in the night by a phone call. Immediately, I'm awake. Perhaps it's Jiji or Kanta or Florence telling me Niki has run away again. I hear Pierre rustling in the sheets. I tell him I'll get it. I run to the phone near the dining table and pick up the receiver before the trilling can wake up the girls.

"Sorry to disturb you at this hour, *beti*." It's Hazi. "But Nasreen thought I should call."

"Is everything all right, *Ji*?" My voice is a croak. I take a seat on the closest dining room chair.

"Hahn. Theek hai. We had a call today. Asking about our *mitti attar*."

"From who?"

"A company that wants to use it in their beauty product."

Instantly, my senses are alert. If another company wants what Hazi is offering, we'll need to put in a proposal right away to ensure we get the quantity we need. That means we have to step up our presentation to the client. I rest my forehead in the palm of my hand. But how can I do that when all my samples seem to have soured?

"Hazi-*ji,* please give me a little more time to secure a purchase order. The scent is working beautifully in my formula." Even as I say this, my stomach roils at the possibility that my visit to Agra may have been a waste. What if I can't get the formula right?

"Aaraam se, beti." Her voice is soothing. "Remember what I told you. We only do

350

business with those we trust. I just wanted you to know."

Just before I hang up, I think of one more question to ask. "Did the caller leave a name?"

"Just a minute."

I hear the clunk of the receiver being put down on a stone surface. Hazi's voice returns, along with the jingle of her bangles and the scrape of a piece of paper. She pronounces the French name slowly, in her heavily accented English, but I know who she's referring to. *Michel LeGrand.*

Now why would Michel be calling about the scent I discovered in Agra? Could it be — as I had wondered before — that *he's* been polluting my samples? Did he take my notebook? That's the only way he would have known how to find Hazi. Or was he calling on behalf of Delphine? Why wouldn't she ask me to make the call to my contact? Does she not trust me? Or is she just checking to make sure I went to Agra to do what I said I did? I feel my grip slipping on the Olympia project. My biggest project to date, the one which would lead to my promotion as apprentice perfumer, could point the way to my biggest failure.

"Are you still there, *beti*?"

"*Hahn-ji.*"

351

"You know who has been asking about you?"

I hope it's not Mr. Mehta! "Who?"

"Binu, our kitchen maid. She keeps telling us how smart the Mam from Paris was. That's what she calls you."

Just thinking of Binu makes me smile. Her pert nature, her efficient manner. "Tell her I thought of her when I read that the Helios probe has come the closest to the sun of any satellite so far."

Hazi chuckles. "She knows. She told me all about it. Her brother reads the newspaper to her every day."

When I hang up, the damning thoughts about Michel and Delphine come crowding back and overwhelm me. I know I won't be able to sleep for the two hours until daylight. I would love to find comfort in Pierre's body, but that's not an option tonight. I head for the girls' room instead and snuggle with Asha. She's a noisy sleeper, breathing as she does with her mouth open. Even so, I place my cheek on hers and use the rhythm of her exhales to lull me to sleep.

In the morning, taped to the saucepan I use for chai, is a note from Pierre. "Snag with one of the suppliers. Overnight in Nice." The Pompidou Center he's working on isn't everyone's favorite. Unlike the historic buildings of Paris loved by visitors the world over, this one will be a wholly modern design. The guts of the structure — plumbing, elevator, air ducts, electrical tubes — will be exposed on the outside, as if the building has been turned inside out. And it's a big building. Taking up two city blocks. Not every contractor is eager to work on something so *brut* to the ordinary Parisian's eye. It's also unknown, risky; such a design has never been tried before. There's a large team of architects and engineers working on the project, including my husband. Pierre has his hands full.

Still, I breathe a little easier. I think a few days apart is better than the two of us being excessively polite to one another until he gets over the shock of my revelation about Niki.

Florence calls as the girls and I are having breakfast. Niki doesn't know anyone's phone numbers, so Florence has provided him with our number as well as her number in case he feels the urge to disappear without telling anyone again. *Bien.* I've been worried that something will happen to him while he's in my care. I feel responsible about returning him safely to Jaipur. To his parents.

"I'm showing him the carousels of Paris today," Florence says. "Why don't I take the girls, too? They only have one more day before the winter holiday. You know they love riding the carousels at Christmas. Surely they can skip school today?"

I don't know what's more surprising. That Florence is suggesting the girls skip a school day or that she's so taken with Niki. I ask, "Why not go tomorrow, when they're off for two weeks?" (At that, the girls look up from their breakfast, sensing I'm talking about them.)

I can almost see Florence raising her eyebrows to her hairline. "Niki's never been here before. So far, he's seen two churches and the Louvre. That's not all Paris has to offer. I asked him if he would like to see more before he goes back home, and he said yes. We had a very nice chat over dinner last night. He's a curious young man. And you know the girls love riding in the Peugeot instead of taking the Métro. We'll have a great time! Mathilde and Agnes are meeting us there."

When was the last time I heard Florence sound this excited about anything? I say yes.

Then another idea comes to me from the night before. "Florence, could you please take the girls for the night? Pierre is away in

Nice, and I may be late coming home."

"I would love to," she says, and, as always, she means it.

When I get to work, there's a palpable anxiety in the air. A scent of anticipation. Celeste is not at her desk, but her typewriter is uncovered, and her coat is hanging from the stand near her desk.

Ferdie is not at his station. I glance at Michel's workstation. He's not there, but I can hear someone moving about the refrigeration unit. Hazi's phone call last night replays in my head. Her careful pronounciation of *Michel LeGrand.* Slowly, I hang up my coat. With a feeling of dread, I unlock my drawers and test my samples. No more benzene. But something else. A faint aroma of *wormwood*?

Suddenly, the rapid click of Delphine's heels echoes in the hallway. Something about the way she's carrying her body tells me she's agitated. She glances through the windows of the lab, but heads to her office. Celeste follows close on her heels with pad and paper. They've come from the direction of the elevator.

Celeste opens the door to the lab. She makes eye contact with Michel in the far corner. She approaches my station. "Meet-

355

ing with Yves in ten minutes. About Olympia."

A meeting with Yves only means one thing: we're presenting Delphine's selections to him for final approval before the client meeting takes place.

My heart jumps in my chest. "But I'm not ready. Delphine hasn't approved my trials."

Celeste bites her lip. I can tell she's thinking of some words of comfort, but all she says is, *"Désolé."*

My underarms are soaked. We're not ready. Why can't Delphine call the meeting off? Why are we rushing the process? I need one more day to tinker with the samples. Maybe they're not being tampered with at all? Could it be that Hazi gave me a bad batch of *mitti attar*? Perhaps it has bacteria in it? But how can that be when I smelled it yesterday, and it was exactly what I smelled in her factory? Perhaps the scent changes over time? Is that why French perfumers haven't used this *attar* in the past? Perhaps they knew about its unreliability and chose not to use it?

My temples are tight with a headache, and I want to massage them, but I don't want Delphine to catch me looking so fraught.

When we arrive at Yves's office, his secretary gestures for us to go on in. Delphine opens Yves's door. She halts abruptly. I barely stop myself from crashing into her, carrying my tray of ruined samples.

"Pardon," Delphine says to someone in the room.

I hear Yves's hearty voice. *"Entrez, entrez."*

As soon as we're in the office, I understand why Delphine hesitated. Ferdie is sitting across from Yves.

Delphine looks confused. "Perhaps we should come when your meeting is over?"

Yves is smiling broadly. "This *is* the meeting. Last night, my nephew called me to say he had something to present — a brainstorm he had on the Olympia project." He smiles fondly at his nephew, who greets us with a nod. Ferdie's cheeks are rosy with excitement or embarrassment — perhaps both.

"I always knew Ferdinand was special. Now you'll see. Just sample this, Delphine. I think you'll like it." He picks up a scent paper from a tray in front of him. I realize Ferdie has brought his own tray of samples with him.

Delphine does not sit down. I know her well enough to know she is furious. It's the way she's holding herself perfectly still. She is a master perfumer. Ferdie is a lab assistant who works for her. He's not even an apprentice perfumer. Yet, here he is sitting next to her and across from the owner of the company as if he is of an equal rank. He looks pleased with himself. I'm shocked at his audacity; he's superseded Delphine's authority. If he had an idea for the project, why didn't he go to Delphine with it first? That would have been the correct protocol.

"Sit, sit." Yves indicates the other chair in front of the desk.

Delphine moves the chair farther from Ferdie and sits down at the edge of it, her back straight. I look around for a place to put my tray. I walk to the corner of the office, where there is a round table with three chairs. I take a seat, feeling foolish to be so far from the meeting I'm supposed to be a part of.

Yves hands the scent paper to Delphine. He clasps his hands under his chin, beaming at her. She looks from Ferdie to Yves, as if she's trying to figure out what's going on here. Is this a prank? Is it her birthday? An anniversary? She glances back at me. I can offer no solace since I'm as lost as she is.

She waves the scent paper in front of her nose. Repeats the process. She turns to me with a look of alarm. Her eyebrows have risen almost to the root of her hair.

"Well?" Yves asks. "Isn't it marvelous? I think our client will be very pleased."

Delphine pastes a smile on her face that doesn't reach her eyes. She looks at Ferdie. "What's in the formula?" Her tone is cool, only mildly curious.

Ferdie meets her gaze and recites the exact formula I've been working on — including the *mitti attar* — without blinking. I gape at him. *He's the saboteur? He's the one who's been peeking inside my notebook? Ferdie? Sweet Ferdie who dances with me after a night out with his friends?* My headache pulses with outrage, anger, dread. How could he do this to me? To Delphine? Why? But then, why was Michel inquiring about the *mitti attar*? Hazi read his name out clearly on the phone last night. Or did I imagine it? Did she say Ferdie's name and my mind substituted it for Michel's because I wanted to believe it was him? Suddenly, nothing seems as it should be. I strain to focus on the conversation that's proceeding without me.

Yves is saying, "Now, Delphine, my rising star, can you top that?"

She cocks her head at Ferdie. "Where do you source the — uh — petrichor?"

"In India. The city of Agra." He swivels in his chair and gives me a friendly smile. "It's where you just went, Radha." Without waiting for an answer, he faces Yves again. "The city of the Taj Mahal."

Now I know he's seen the address of Hazi's factory and the *haveli*'s phone number in my notebook. Are he *and* Michel in on it together? Are they both double-crossing me? I close my eyes. The bright future I'd envisioned for myself suddenly goes dark. I've made my boss, my mentor, look like a fool. There's no way to come back from a colossal failure like this. And there's no way to rectify it. If Delphine accused Ferdie of stealing my work right now, she would appear petty, jealous. What would she say if I told her about my suspicions surrounding Michel?

Delphine addresses Ferdie. "I didn't realize you'd been to Agra, Ferdie. You've kept that little secret hidden from me."

Ferdie smiles good-naturedly and waves a hand at Yves. "My aunt and uncle took me there for my sixteenth birthday. Wasn't it beautiful, *oncle*?"

"*Magnifique.* Ferdinand told me he always wanted to return. Looks like he'll have the chance."

My mentor takes no notice of Yves's comment. Instead, she focuses her gaze on Ferdie. "How much of this new ingredient can we get immediately? The client is anxious to start production as soon as they

360

approve the scent."

Ferdie looks around the room. He's on less firm ground here. "There should be no problem with that."

Now she turns to Yves. "We should also prepare at least three or four small vials for the client to take back to their people. I think all we need now is to schedule a meeting with the client. I'll get Celeste to set that up tomorrow." She stands.

Yves points to me, the silent observer in the corner with a samples tray in front of me. "Did you have something you wanted to show me?"

"*Bah,* that's for the Alsace project," Delphine lies smoothly. "Radha and I are needed at another meeting. I'll leave you to it." She nods at Yves, pointedly ignores Ferdie and tilts her chin at me to come with her.

I follow Delphine back to her office, struggling to keep up with her brisk pace. As soon as she shuts the door to her office, Delphine explodes. "How the hell did he get the formula?" She lights a cigarette and stands with one hand on her hip.

"I have no idea, but . . ." I realize I've never told anyone my suspicions. I do so now, starting with the vetiver fragrance we were working on a few months ago. The samples that didn't smell the same as the day before. The notebook that went missing for an hour. The way I'd been locking my samples in my drawers before leaving work.

"But how did Ferdie know about the Agra factory? *I* don't even know the name of your factory, Radha."

"He would have had to look in my notebook." I close my eyes, trying to remember if I locked the drawer last night. I'm almost sure I did.

Delphine is smoking furiously. She notices I'm still standing with the tray and barks at me to set it down somewhere. I look around and put it on the only surface I can: her desk. She points at me with her cigarette, the ash falling on the tray now. "Why didn't you say something earlier?"

"For a long time, I thought I was imagining it. Then I thought it was something I was doing wrong." I hesitate. "Then I thought it might be Michel's doing, and I didn't want to say anything against him." Embarrassment is making my face warm. "Because you trust him."

Her look is incredulous. "Michel? Michel LeGrande? He's always singing your praises. He thinks, as I do, that you have what it takes to become a master perfumer. No, it's

362

not Michel."

I'm so surprised by this revelation I don't know what to say. Michel has never so much as asked me where I live or how many children I have. "There's something else," I say, rubbing my palms against the coat. Her eyes follow my hands, so I shove them in my pockets. Reluctantly, I tell her about the phone call from Hazi, Michel requesting the *mitti attar.*

"Nonsense!" she snaps. "Michel would never do anything of the kind. And before you think it, I didn't put him up to it."

As always, she's three steps ahead of me.

She shakes her cigarette at me again. Ash falls to the carpet below. "Could have been Ferdie. Maybe he used Michel's name to throw off suspicion." She blows smoke toward the windows. "You said you notice the changes to the samples first thing in the morning? Not during work hours?"

I nod.

Her fingers tap the edge of her desk. She picks up the phone and tells Celeste she needs her.

Celeste walks in the office. Today, she's wearing a lilac sweater dress with a tie across the middle. With no breasts and no hips, however, Celeste looks like the hanger it must have come off of. Her pale hair is hiding half her face.

"Where are the master keys to all the desks?" Delphine asks.

"In my desk," she says.

"And when you're away from your desk, the keys are there, in a locked drawer?"

Celeste looks uncomfortable. She pushes her weight from one foot to the other. "Well, I unlock my desk in the morning when I get into the office."

"And it stays unlocked all day?"

Celeste steals a glance at me, as if to ask a question. *What is this about?* I try for a sympathetic smile. *"Oui,"* she tells Delphine. "Except for lunch, when I lock it."

"And you take the keys with you."

"Not always."

"What do you mean?"

A furious blush spreads across Celeste's cheeks. "I usually take them with me. But sometimes . . ."

"Yes?"

"When someone forgets their keys, I let them use the master key to unlock their desk. If I'm rushed, I may forget to ask for the master keys back until the end of the day when I'm locking up."

Delphine puts out her cigarette thoughtfully in her ashtray. "I see." I notice Celeste looking at the ashtray, probably thinking

364

she needs to empty it. "When was the last time that happened?"

"F-Ferdie seems to have lost his keys. He keeps borrowing my master set. I asked if he wanted me to get another set made, but he said he knows his set is at home somewhere. He hasn't had a chance to look for it." She looks from Delphine to me. "To be fair, Ferdie has a lot going on right now. His parents have cut him off —"

"Cut him off?" Delphine's voice is sharp.

"I can't help but overhear when they call." Celeste wrings her hands. "His expenses. The clothes. The discos. They stopped paying for his apartment." Her nose and cheeks have turned pink. "Please don't tell him I said anything."

Now I remember the time I saw Ferdie on the phone at Celeste's desk, his agitation.

Delphine waves a hand as if casting aside Celeste's plea. "Do you have the master set now?"

"I'll get them." Celeste exits the room and returns in half a minute. She looks like she's about to cry. "They're not there."

Delphine squeezes her eyes shut. "That Judas." When she opens them again, she fixes a stern gaze on Celeste. "A leopard doesn't change its spots. *Il revient au galop.* You realize, *chérie,* that, for Ferdie, you'll never be a replacement for Maurice or Noel or Sergio?"

Celeste looks stricken. Her cheeks and neck are crimson. It's as if Delphine has slapped her. I look down at my lap. We're all aware of Celeste's unrequited crush on Ferdie, but no one would have dared mention it openly the way Delphine just did. I wish I weren't in the room to witness Celeste's humiliation.

"Tell Michel we need him."

Celeste retreats quickly, before her tears can spill across her cheeks.

Delphine looks out the window, tapping her fingernail across her desk. I sit mute, unable to move; the last thing I want is to be a convenient target for her anger.

Michel comes in five minutes later, followed by Celeste. He looks around the room at me, Delphine and, finally, at Celeste, whose face is now a mottled pink. She tugs at her dress to keep it from clinging to her tights.

"Michel," Delphine says. "Have you noticed anything about Ferdinand's behavior recently that would concern you?"

It's hard to see Michel's eyes because his wire-rimmed glasses are reflecting the light from the window. He adjusts his spectacles before speaking. "Nothing more than usual."

Delphine raises her eyebrows in a question.

Michel blows air out of his mouth, puffing out his cheeks. "Talks of parties, boyfriends, discos, that sort of thing. Perhaps more keyed up than he normally is. On the phone more than usual."

Delphine stands up and goes to her window, surveying her city. La Tour Eiffel gleams in the distance on a rare sunny December day. After a minute, during which I know her mind is working furiously, she turns to us. She recounts to Michel and Celeste what we just witnessed in Yves's office.

"My agenda has always been clear — to create the best *parfum* in Paris. The formulas we create must be both critically successful and commercially viable. We cannot allow others to subvert our good work. That's what Ferdie has done. He has stolen Radha's work. *Our* work. We cannot allow him to succeed, *n'est-ce pas?*"

At the mention of Ferdie's name, Michel turns to Celeste, his brows raised. She hangs her head. A curtain of fine hair falls across her flushed face. Michel then glances at me. I look away, embarrassed to have suspected him, to have had all those awful thoughts about him.

Delphine is still talking. "He thinks he will prevail. Because we always trusted him before." She turns and walks back to her desk, lights a cigarette. "But we are going to make sure he doesn't get away with this." She looks from Michel to Celeste and back again. Something passes between them. *"Comprenez?"*

That's all she says before she makes a gesture telling us to leave. Celeste leaves first, closing the door after her. Michel doesn't move. I hesitate. What exactly are we meant to do?

Delphine's phone rings. She picks it up, listens, then hangs up. She nods at Michel. "It's clear." Some signal has passed between them. I wonder if I will ever know her well enough to read her as intuitively as Michel does.

Michel walks to the door, opens it and glances back at me. I realize that I'm supposed to follow him. I lift the tray from Delphine's desk and walk out with him. I take one last look at Delphine before leaving. She's picking up the phone and pressing a button for one of the outside lines.

I follow Michel back into the lab, but I'm waiting for him to tell me what Delphine meant about not letting Ferdie get away with it. How will we do that? But he says nothing to me. He sits at his desk, absorbed in his thoughts. All at once, he gets out of his chair, walks out of the lab and goes directly to Celeste's desk to talk to her.

Slowly, I settle down at my table and pick up a stack of briefs. I don't have the heart to do a new project. Instead, I take out the vial of the scent of rain. Less than a quarter of the *mitti attar* remains in the vial. That's odd. So far, I've only used a fraction of it to experiment with my formula. I look across as Ferdie's empty work area. He must have taken the remainder to recreate my formula, just as he stole the formula from my notebook.

Now, so many things make sense to me. The day he returned my notebook, claiming he had found it in a corner of the lab. The way he smirked at my sample with its odor of benzene. He'd messed with my formula! How blind I'd been! He'd always been so friendly, so jolly, so easygoing. Why would any of us have suspected he would turn on us, the way he had? What a fool I'd been to smile and laugh with him when he was planning how to use me — how to use us all — to get what he wanted. Had I only imagined that we'd been friends? Was he laughing the entire time at how easily I could be duped? I can feel my face get hot with equal parts outrage and shame.

Ferdie walks into the lab. The grin on his face makes me want to slap him. He's not the least embarrassed or ashamed for taking credit for work *I've* done these past two months. Oh, when I think of the time I robbed from my daughters! And the friction it created between Pierre and me. I set the vial of *mitti attar* back in the drawer, inside the rosewood box Mr. Mehta gave me. When I slam the drawer, Ferdie looks at me from across the room, smiles and shrugs. He begins whistling a disco tune he often resorts to when he screws up in the lab. "Bad Luck" by Harold Melvin and the Blue Notes.

As if it's all been a game to him. *No hard feelings.*

No hard feelings? *Behenchod!* I need to give that *connard* a piece of my mind! To let him know it's not all right to steal my idea! I clamber off my stool, but my coat pocket catches on the handle of the drawer that's still open. It's almost as if my work is holding me back.

Michel steps in to block my way. His face is inches from mine. I've never seen his eyes this close before. The blue is more cornflower in the center, fading to a pale turquoise at the edge. There's compassion in them. And a warning. *Don't. You'll make it worse.*

After a moment, I take a breath and go back to my chair. When Michel moves out of the way, I can see Celeste in front of Ferdie's work area, a bottle of Moët et Chandon in her hand. She offers it to Ferdie as she congratulates him.

What? Ten minutes ago, she was cowering in Delphine's office, apologizing for giving Ferdie the keys to the kingdom!

Michel joins them now, holding three champagne flutes. He's smiling. "*Félicitations,* Ferdinand!"

I can't begin to know how to react or what to say. Is perfume only the domain of people who look like Ferdie and Delphine and Michel? Is there any room for an Indian woman like me? Since she's the master perfumer, Delphine Silberman will be recognized by the industry whether Ferdie's name goes on the formula or mine does. I'd fooled myself into thinking I had a chance to become a master perfumer one day. Right now it seems impossible. I stay put, confusion and frustration writ large on my face.

Celeste hands Ferdie his champagne as she says, "I can't wait to try your fragrance!"

Michel clinks glasses with Ferdie. "I always told Delphine you were our next master perfumer."

Liar! I thought Michel said that about *me*? Isn't that what Delphine said?

Ferdie accepts the compliment gracefully. He's self-effacing. *It was luck. And intuition. I was so inspired. I know it was Radha's project; it got me thinking about India. And the scent of rain after the monsoons.*

I can't believe what I'm seeing. Ferdie is actually describing *mitti attar* as if he'd discovered it! And why not? He's one of the most accomplished deceits I've ever met. The lies roll off his tongue like beads of water roll off a *peepal* leaf. It's effortless. How could I not have seen this coming?

Celeste is all smiles. "We were trying to guess, Michel and I, what your inspiration was? Something to do with an essential oil made of mud?"

Now it's Michel's turn to grin. "In all my years working here, I've never smelled anything like it."

Ferdie can't resist. He reaches for his drawer, unlocks it and pulls out a small vial. He uncaps it and inserts a paper blotter, waves it about and hands it to Michel. "On its own, it's not a remarkable scent. But in combination with other ingredients, it's *ex-*

372

traordinaire. It's called petrichor. I remembered it from the time my aunt and uncle took me to India. That was ten years ago, but the scent made such an impression on me."

Celeste reaches across Ferdie's desk to pour more champagne into his flute and Michel's. Her arm hits the neck of the scent bottle, causing it to tip in Ferdie's direction, dousing him with champagne. He jumps up and away from his worktable. Michel tries to rescue the vial of scent, which is about to tip over. He succeeds.

All at once, Celeste is apologizing, as is Michel. Ferdie is telling them to step away so he can brush champagne off his brand-new corduroy shirt. Celeste tells him she'll clean his table. He should put cold water on the shirt before the alcohol ruins it. "That's what you're wearing to the club tonight, aren't you?" she asks.

Ferdie looks annoyed. He pushes her out of the way, roughly, to head out of the lab to the bathroom. Celeste runs to the supply closet to grab small lab towels and gets to work soaking up the mess on Ferdie's work area.

The failed celebration party has taken all of five or six minutes. I'm sickened by all of them — applauding the work of a thief! I push away from my desk, scowling. I rip off my lab coat, grab my overcoat and my purse and head out of the lab, determined to leave after only putting in half a day.

I huff down the hall, past Delphine's office in my rage. She calls out to me. I double back and stand in the threshold, my lips flattened in anger.

"Come here and close the door."

For once, I defy her order. "I'm going home, Delphine." I don't address her politely as Madame, the way I usually do.

She rises from her chair, takes me by the arm, closes the door behind me and guides me to one of her guest chairs. *"Attend."*

Wait for what? I wonder. The smell of her burning Gitane, which normally doesn't bother me, makes me want to gag. What am I doing here at the House of Yves? What am I doing in Paris? Wasn't I much happier in Agra? Back on familiar turf, with people who spoke my language, ate the same foods I loved and called me *beti* and *behen*? I have a wild desire to pick up my daughters at Florence's and take them to India today! Is there a flight leaving tonight? Is there enough money in the bank to write a check for tickets? My foot starts a rhythmic tapping on the carpet until Delphine shows me her raised eyebrows. My foot stills. Why am

I still under her spell?

"Yves and I have a meeting tomorrow with the client. We have agreed to send their team off with three small vials of each scent. Yours and Ferdie's."

"But it's not Ferdie's scent! You were there. Ferdie has stolen my —"

Without a knock, Michel enters the room. Delphine eyes him expectantly.

"All done," he tells her.

"What did you use?" she asks.

"Point zero one grams of cinnamon." Michel's eyes seek mine. He smiles.

Michel smiled at me! I throw Delphine a puzzled glance.

She tells Michel, *"Merci."*

He touches my arm on his way out. "Don't worry. *À bon chat, bon rat.*" He closes the door behind him.

"Radha, what happened to your formula is unfortunate. But Ferdie forced our hand. Two can play at this game."

She tells me they tinkered with Ferdie's formula as he'd tinkered with mine. I stare at her dumbly.

She grinds her cigarette in the overflowing ashtray and lights up another. "Michel has been with me a long time. He loves working in a lab. He likes the regular hours, and he has no desire to become a perfumer. But he is a great chemist." She taps her Gitane on the side of her already full ashtray. "This afternoon, when Ferdie recreates his masterpiece, it won't smell the same as yours. Where is your bottle of *mitti attar*, by the way?"

I reach in my purse and pull it out. "There isn't much left. I kept having to repeat my samples. And now I know where the rest of it went."

She nods. "Keep that bottle with you at all times. I won't be able to get someone to change the locks in here until tomorrow." She extends her hand for me to shake. The last time she shook my hand was when I accepted the job as her lab assistant. I look down at our joined hands. Mine: smooth, brown. Hers: pale with blue veins, a ruby signet ring on the pinky finger. I raise my eyes to hers. This close, I see the wrinkles that have gathered below the lower lid, a testament to her years of service, creating what she loves.

"It happens, Radha. Move past it." Her voice is kind.

I go back to the lab in a daze. What just happened? I'm not sure. That party in the lab was a way to get Ferdie out of the room long enough for Michel to alter Ferdie's *mitti attar*. Now, even if Ferdie has memorized the formula, it will never come out the same as my intended fragrance. But how did Delphine convince Yves to present both our formulas? Ferdie is his nephew; he barely knows who I am. Then I realize: Delphine must have told him that she had a surprise scent she'd been working on; he would make the exception for his favorite master perfumer.

All of which means I may not get any credit for my work. But Delphine will know. Michel will know. And Celeste — well, she must know now if she didn't before. I glance out the windows of the lab at Celeste's desk. Her typewriter is covered. She's gone home early. She must be feeling terrible. I'll buy her flowers and croissants tomorrow. None of this was her fault; she was as taken in by Ferdie's charm as we all were.

Ferdie seems to have gone home early, too. His jacket and bag are gone. I'm relieved. I don't want to be in the same room as Ferdie right now.

I mix my Olympia formula again. I sniff the blotter. *It's her.* The goddess of the divan herself. Proud. Wounded. But not defeated.

Belatedly, I realize Olympia is also me, isn't she? I've given my best, but I've been used. Delphine said I have to move past it. Lakshmi moved past her betrayals. So did

Victorine. Isn't that the look she's giving us in Manet's painting? There will always be a Ferdie in our lives. We have to do our best despite them.

I compound the larger quantity for the three client vials. Then I pull out the rose-wood box, roll cotton around each of the vials, insert them snugly into the box, along with what remains of the precious *mitti attar.* I take the box to Delphine's office for her presentation tomorrow. She tests each of the bottles with a fresh blotter. Satisfied, she looks up at me.

"Bien fait."

It's what I always long to hear from her. Her blessing means as much to me as Jiji's.

In her deep smoker's voice, she says, "Don't come in tomorrow until Celeste calls you. You should enjoy a morning in bed. You've earned it."

I skipped lunch so I could finish the samples. It's just past four o'clock. I decide to leave. I still need to speak to Niki.

I walk to Florence's. I have a key to her house, which I only use when no one is there. I wasn't expecting everyone to be home from their excursion, but there they all are. *My three children.* My heart bounces at the thought that now when people ask how many children I have, I can stop lying. I've always hesitated when I answer, "Two." I gave birth to *three.* Two girls and a boy. Instead of making me cringe, the thought makes me smile, freeing me in some way, lifting a weight off my chest.

Asha runs up and takes my hand to lead me into Florence's living room. She's bursting to tell me the whole story. They were taking Niki around to all their favorite carousels. At Luxembourg, they showed him the *jeu de bagues,* a medieval knight's game played while the merry-go-round is in motion.

Now I see that Niki is lying on the living room couch with his eyes closed. He has a bandage on his forehead and one on the index finger of his left hand. Shanti is sitting next to him on the sofa. She raises her finger to her lips. "Niki gets a headache if you speak too loudly."

Asha reduces her volume to a loud whisper and drags me by the hand into the kitchen. I crane my neck to look back at Niki, alarmed. If he's not at the hospital, he must be well enough to be at home.

"We saved the best carousel for last so we could show him the game. We had him sit on one of the horses on the outside of the ride," Asha says.

Florence is taking peasant bread out of the oven. "He reached a little too far to get the last ring and fell off the ride."

"Is he badly hurt?" I ask my mother-in-law.

"A small bump on the head. He'll be fine. If you ask me, that man holding the rings deliberately pulled it farther away when Niki's turn came around. *Connard!*"

For the second time in three days, Florence has sworn in front of me. She notices Asha is still in the room, looking wide-eyed at her grandmother, and says, "*Désolé, chérie.* Please don't use words like your *grand-mère* just did."

"What happened to Mathilde and Agnes?" I say.

Asha is poking the bread with her fingernail. Florence smoothly moves her hand away from the hot loaves. "They went home. The whole incident frightened Agnes. I think she's quite ready for full-time observation. Frankly, I think Mathilde will be relieved."

I scold myself for not checking in with Mathilde as often as I should. I should call her later tonight.

I address Florence. "Do you think Niki is well enough to accompany me somewhere? I need to talk to him."

380

Asha protests, "But you just got here, *Maman.*"

Florence tells Asha, "And she'll be back later. Go on, Radha."

I walk gingerly into the living room and kiss Shanti on the cheeks. Niki opens his eyes. His expression is neutral; he's neither glad nor upset to see me. There's a guarded look about him, however. He doesn't trust me.

"I want to show you something," I say.

When we arrive at Jeu de Paume, I greet Gérard and introduce him to Niki. He nods as if he's been expecting us. He makes no reference to Niki's bandages. Gérard picks up his little wooden chair and places it in front of *Olympia* for me. It's a small kindness, but it makes me want to cry.

We are going to immortalize you, I silently tell Victorine when I sit down. Her expression doesn't change. But I feel a surge of courage as I talk to her in my head.

Niki stands still for a moment, looking at Manet's painting, then he sits cross-legged on the floor next to my chair.

"I'm going to tell you a story," I say.

From the corner of my eye, I see him set a small drawing pad on his knee. He flips it open to a page. I hazard a glance at the

381

paper. There are pencil sketches of people sitting on a park bench. The statue of *Winged Victory* in the Louvre. I recognize Shanti's face, deep in thought.

Niki now starts a new sketch. Of *Olympia*. His fingers are long, the nails bitten off. I turn my attention to the painting again.

"When I was thirteen, I met a handsome, charming boy. He used to play polo at the Jaipur Club with his friends. I would watch him on the way home from Kanta's — your mother's — house. The boy was so graceful. He noticed me one day and invited me inside the grounds. He asked if I would help him rehearse his lines for the Shakespeare play they were going to put on at his school. I probably should have said no. A proper girl would have."

Now he looks at me.

"But I was raised in a village where I was known as the Bad Luck Girl. I was born the year Lakshmi left her husband. Everyone blamed me for it. I don't know why. I guess they needed a reason. After that, every bad thing that happened . . . was my fault. But here was a boy who didn't know my family's history. He thought I was smart, funny, desirable. So . . . we . . .

"It was Lakshmi who told me I was pregnant. I didn't even know. I tried to tell the boy, but his parents wouldn't let me. Your mother took me to Shimla to have the baby. She was also pregnant at the time. She was very kind to me." I find myself smiling, remembering all the walks Kanta and I took together to the Shimla library so I could load up on books to read aloud to her (her pregnancy made her nauseous). Sometimes, we'd run into Dr. Kumar (who delivered both our babies) as he was on his way to mail a letter at the post office (probably to Lakshmi, I realize belatedly).

"But your mother's baby didn't . . . he died in the womb. She was devastated." That weight, like a ship's anchor, is back in my chest.

His hand has stopped moving across the page.

"I was too young to raise a child. It would have meant giving up school and giving up childhood. So Kanta and Manu took you. And raised you as their own." I remember begging Jiji to paint Niki's eyes and feet with *kajal* so he would always be protected from *burri nazar.* Back then I believed in superstitions like the evil eye that could harm my baby. "You were one month early, but you were perfect. Perfect fingers. Perfect toes. Perfect nose. You had so much hair we joked that you were born wearing a wig." I can't suppress the chuckle, and, forgetting myself, look at him. Lakshmi and Kanta had asked me not to tell him about the Jaipur Palace's aborted adoption, dreading his reaction, so I don't. I don't want to upset him further.

Niki is staring at his notepad. Now I see that he hasn't been drawing *Olympia.* He's been drawing me. There's my profile with the small bump on my nose, like Maa's. The puffiness below my eyes. The rounded chin, not pointed like Lakshmi's. My mouth is turned down slightly. I look sad. Is that how he sees me?

I keep talking. "I held you in my body for eight months, but you wanted to come into this world sooner. I read you *Tales of Krishna* I had carried all the way from the village of Ajar. I sang songs from the movies Kanta and I saw at the Ritz Cinema. Every time I sang 'Mera joota hai japani,' you would start kicking your feet as if you were dancing along with Raj Kapoor. I imagined you smiling every time I drank rose milk and frowning when I ate *pakoras.* I loved you so much." I sigh.

"I only took four things of yours when I left you. This tiny quilt Lakshmi made for you. I still have it. And your little yellow booties. Your silver rattle — you loved to gum it! Oh, my! The day you discovered you could make it rattle by yourself. The surprise on your face! I still remember it. And the *Tales of Krishna* book. I raised my daughters on that book, too." I pause. "The vial I gave you? That's the scent of you as a baby. I created it from those four things. When I'm feeling anxious, it's your baby smell that calms me."

He still hasn't said anything. I lift the notepad from his lap and examine it. "You're good. You have Lakshmi's hand. She told me you could draw."

He lifts his head. "I like her. Lakshmi Auntie. We see her when she and Dr. Kumar come to Jaipur."

I hand the drawing pad back to him. "I like the gargoyles you did for the girls. They've got them taped up on their walls."

"All this time —" he starts.

I look him in the eye and hold his gaze. "All this time, Niki, you've been wanted by everyone. By me. I never wanted to give you up. But I was only thirteen, going on fourteen, Niki. Four years younger than you are now. You were wanted by Kanta. And Manu. And Manu's mother — the grandmother you've grown up with. And even Baju, your old servant, was charmed by you. Everyone loved you. You were special."

385

"So you do know Baju? And *Nani,* too?" Niki says.

"*Hahn.* And you're right. He is an incredible cook." I can almost see the thoughts, the memories, flitting behind his peacock eyes. And I know what he's about to ask, so I save him the trouble.

"I can't speak for your . . . birth father. It took me a long time to get over him. He was my first love. I'd like to believe he never found out about you. I'd like to believe that's why he never reached out to me. But I don't know." I think about the letter from the UK lawyer about the scholarship. "At some point, I stopped caring. That's not to say it didn't hurt or keep hurting. Just that I stopped thinking about him."

When Niki swallows, I see his Adam's apple moving up and down. I notice the darker area on his chin where he shaves. What a marvel: the baby I left at four months is old enough to have children of his own!

"Where is he now? My . . . father," Niki asks.

All I know is that his entire family moved to the United States, but even that little bit of information could be dangerous for him. I choose to tell him I don't know.

A group of noisy college students speaking Italian walk into the museum. We look at them, then turn back to *Olympia.*

I tell him, "I come here to look at her because I was given an assignment to develop a fragrance for her."

"For a woman who's in a painting?"

"You'd be surprised at the creative briefs we work on. There was one where my boss was asked to create a scent for a horse who won the Ascot races."

"A horse?"

"*Hahn.* The fragrance was called Gelding."

He grins, and the tension between us eases a little. "Wouldn't Stallion have been a better name for a fragrance?"

Now I laugh. "It was already taken." I tell him what I've gleaned from my research and from hours spent staring at *Olympia.* That her real name was Victorine. That this is a woman betrayed. She doesn't want revenge. She wants merely for her pain to be witnessed, noted.

"What will you call this fragrance?"

"I think the client is going to call it Olympia. It won't be my decision. Why? Do you have an idea?"

"Victorine. You should call her by her real name. Not the name the painter gave her. You're not after Manet's fantasy. You're after the real woman who posed for him."

I think about what he says. He's right. I'll talk to Delphine. And tell her *my son* suggested it. The idea makes me smile.

Niki rolls the pencil in his long fingers. "Do you like what you do?"

We could be strangers who met at a Métro stop or in line for baguettes. That's what I can't get over. Here is a human being I created in my own body but he is a stranger to me. He has a whole life outside of me, just as I have a whole life outside of him. What if we're two strangers who meet and grow to like each other over time? I offer up silent gratitude to Florence for sharing her secret with me.

I tell him how I started at Antoine's *parfumerie* and how I ended up working for Delphine. He asks questions, unlike other young men I've met. And he listens. I like that. Kanta and Manu raised a sensible boy. Look how he traveled from Jaipur to Paris and found me! He'd never been outside of India before. He knows who he is, which is more than I could say about myself at his age. If I'd raised him, would he be as confident? As sure of his right to belong? Kanta and Manu have always belonged in society in a way Lakshmi and I never have. My sister and I have always been on the outside, looking in. It hits me: all those years

388

ago, I did make the right choice, as Lakshmi claimed. And so did Jiji — and Dr. Jay — when they prevented Niki from being adopted by the Jaipur Palace. There's no reason to blame them and every reason to thank them for the risk they took.

"Why did you return all of Mummi's letters?"

His swift detour takes me by surprise. I'd been proud of how composed I've been for the last hour. But the tears come before I can stop them. "In order to stay alive, I had to cut you out of my life. No photos. No letters. Nothing that would make you real as you are now." I stand up, hoisting my handbag on my shoulder. "I'm sorry if that wasn't the right thing to do, but I couldn't see any other way."

He gets up abruptly, too, dropping his drawing pad, and stands in my way. "I didn't mean anything by it." When he touches my shoulder, I flinch, as if I've been burned. I step back.

From his jacket pocket (is that one of Pierre's old coats?), he extracts my necklace with the vial. I gasp and grab it from him.

I rub the necklace in the palm of my hand. I like the contrast between the cold metal of the chain and the smooth glass of the vial. "When I first started working with fragrances, the first one I wanted to create was the smell of you. Having you in my belly was the happiest time of my life, Niki. I walked all over Shimla with you inside me, pointing things out to you that I liked. The library where I got all my books. The way the crocuses hid in the ground one day and burst open the next —" I stop, embarrassed. The time Niki and I spent together feels intimate, memories I haven't shared with anyone else.

His eyebrows are raised and his eyes are bright. He gives off the smell of daffodils, happiness. Maybe these memories are worth sharing with him, after all.

I open my palm and look at the vial. "Did you take a sniff?"

"*Hahn.* Baby powder and wet diaper?" His smile is lopsided.

I offer a smile in return. "And basmati rice and neem oil and rose milk and cotton wool and the pine trees of Shimla. That's where you were born. In Shimla. At the Lady Bradley Hospital. Dr. Kumar delivered you."

"Dr. Jay?" He looks delighted.

I laugh. "You call him that, too? Malik and I have always called him that! We could all see that he was in love with Lakshmi long before she did."

We're quiet for a while. The college group laughs at something one of them says as they leave the museum.

"Shanti and Asha are good girls."

"Pierre wants them to know they have a brother."

"He knows about me?"

I nod. "You kind of forced my hand."

When I turn to him, he looks guilty, so I reassure him. "I've been carrying this secret for so long, Niki. It feels like such a relief to let go of it. I'm grateful for that. So, you have two sisters, whom you've already met. You aren't an only child, after all."

I try to let him know with my smile that I want him to be easy with all this.

His eyes hide nothing. Not the awe he might feel at finding a new family. Nor the surprise of discovering two sisters. Nor the nervousness of being accepted by them and me. I realize he wants me to also be comfortable with his presence in my world.

I think about the distance between Pierre and me just now. "It will all take time. I can't promise that it will be easy for everyone. You understand, don't you?"

"Yes." He's thoughtful. "Radha, did you name me?"

I'm startled by his use of my first name. What had I expected? For him to call me

Mummi? That title rightfully belongs to Kanta.

"No, your father did. Manu. I think Lakshmi was thinking of Neal. For the color of your eyes."

I hadn't noticed Gérard approach us.

"Vous permettez?" He points to the chair. I look around and notice the darkened evening outside the glass doors. I look at my watch. The museum closed an hour ago, but Gérard waited for us to finish our conversation.

"Merci." I place a kiss on the old man's cheeks. To Niki, I say, "Gérard is a painter."

Niki raises his eyebrows. "Really? How long have you been a painter? Where did you study?"

This could be a long conversation, so I ask Gérard in French if he'd like to join us for a drink.

Gérard looks pleased. He nods.

In Hindi, I ask Niki if he'd like to ask Gérard more questions over drinks. I'll translate. This is something I can do for him. I see how he comes alive when he draws. Art isn't a respectable profession for a middle-class Indian boy like him the way math or the sciences are. It would be reasonable to assume that Manu, whose background is in engineering, is steering him in that direction. But is that where Niki wants to go?

The light in Niki's eyes — those blue-green-gray eyes of his — tells me all I need to know.

Pierre will be away overnight for his business trip, so I decide to spend the night in the girls' room at Florence's. It's nice to wake in the morning to an omelet, and Florence's coffee isn't half-bad as a substitute for chai. It's the start of the winter holidays, and the girls want to stay with Florence, where they will make madeleines and *financiers*. They also want to spend more time with Niki, quizzing him about anything and everything.

Alone, I make my way to the Saint-Germain apartment to shower and change. Today is the big day: Delphine and Ferdie meet with the Olympia client. Throughout the project, Delphine has refused to reveal the identity of the client, per their wishes. The client must want anonymity for a reason. If the client is a celebrity, he or she may want to introduce the fragrance in a spectacular reveal. I wonder who the lucky actress or actor is this time.

The front door to our apartment building is wide open. The concierge has swept the sidewalk. I greet her as I go past her window. She calls my name. I turn around, *"Oui, madame?"*

Jeanne is wearing a housedress and sweater that stretches tightly across her ample bosom and hips. In her hand is the mail she's sorting for all the building's occupants. I'm assuming she means to give me our mail, and I step toward her.

She lifts her hand at the last minute, putting the letters out of my reach. "You told me your daughters were at their *grandmère*'s house?"

"C'est ça." I nod.

"But your friend was here."

Jeanne sets the mail down on the desk, just inside her front door, which she usually keeps open. It's cold in the entrance; the foyer isn't heated, and frigid air is sneaking in through the open front door. Jeanne is only wearing a blue cardigan over her dress, but she doesn't appear to be cold.

I shiver. Who could she be referring to? I didn't talk to Mathilde yesterday. I really should have called her, but with everything . . . Besides, I wasn't here at the apartment and neither was Pierre. "Perhaps it was one of Madame Reynard's nieces. You know they're always visiting."

Jeanne's eyes are hooded, giving her a perpetually mournful look. "No, I'm sure it was your friend. The pretty one. The one

394

who looks like Catherine Deneuve." She runs a finger across her forehead to indicate the visitor's bangs.

Inwardly, I sigh. She *is* talking about Mathilde, but I'm sure she's wrong. The *concierges* of Paris remind me of the gossip-eaters of Ajar. They know who goes in and out, how many visitors each occupant has, how often. They know where we get letters from and if we're behind on our taxes. It's their job to keep tabs on the building in the name of security. But I've caught Jeanne with her ear to Madame Blanchet's door when she's supposed to be in the middle of scrubbing the stairs or lingering too long at the planter just outside her apartment when the residents on the first floor are having an argument. Still, she's an older woman, a widow without children, and she lives here, too.

"Pas grave," I say with a smile before quickly heading up the stairwell.

There, a familiar smell lingers. Garlic. Boiled potatoes. No, this is fragrance. Is it what Madame Reynard wears? I shake my head, as if to shake off the smell. Perhaps my nose is just tired from all the trials I've conducted in the last few days.

As I round the corner to take the stairs to the third floor, I see high-heeled brown boots above me. When I look up, I see Mathilde. In that instant, I'm happy to see her, but in the next, I'm filled with guilt for having ignored her.

"Mathilde! Are you looking for me? I'm so sorry I haven't called, *chérie*!"

But the expression on her face tells me she's not as pleased to see me. Her face is pinched. There's no color in her high cheekbones. The soft pouches under her eyes mean she hasn't slept well. "When were you going to tell me, Radha?"

I'm shocked at her tone of voice. She's five steps above me, filling the stairwell with her anger and . . . her scent. So that's the fragrance I smelled earlier! "Tell you what?"

"That you have a son. You had him a year before you met me. You could have told me then. You could have told me lots of times in all these years. I tell you everything. Why would you keep that from me?"

I lower my voice, but it still echoes in the stairwell. "How do you know about . . . Niki?"

She's caught off guard. She hesitates. "Pierre."

"Pierre? When did he tell you? Why?"

"You'll have to ask him." She starts down the stairs again, brushing my shoulder as she passes me. "And thanks for asking about my mother. I put her in a facility yesterday. For good." She sobs out the last word and races down before my thoughts can catch up.

I hear our apartment door open and look up. It's Pierre, shrugging his coat on, his attaché case in one hand. He slows when he sees me. "Where were you?"

"At your mother's. With the girls. You said you were in Nice."

He sighs. "I got done early. So I came home. Mathilde showed up. She was hysterical. She's really been through a lot, Radha."

This gets my back up. "So have we all."

"She's your friend. Why am I having to console her?"

I realize how ridiculous it is to have this conversation in the stairwell where everyone can hear us. I climb the five steps to reach Pierre. "Can we talk about it inside?"

He checks his watch. "I'm late as it is." He frowns. "Why are you not at work?"

"Delphine told Celeste to call me here when she's done with the client presentation. She gave me the morning off. I thought I would get some laundry done."

He hurries past me. "Well, I need to go. Mathilde is giving me a ride on her scooter."

Slowly, I enter the apartment. He's never referred to Mathilde as *my* friend before.

She spends so much time at our place that I've always thought of her as *our* friend. Is this the way it's going to be from now on? The other day it was chai versus wine — who likes what and who drinks it to get along. We're going to divide friends, food and even the girls according to each of our likes now?

Calm down, Radha. I hear my sister's voice. *Aaraam se.* I hear Hazi's. It helps.

I shrug off my coat and look at the state of the apartment. Cleaning it up will help take my mind off Delphine's meeting with the client. I pick up Pierre's socks and the girls' tights and put them in the washer. I strip their beds and replace them with clean sheets and pillowcases. I gather the dirty bedding and go into our bedroom. Pierre has already stripped the sheets. They're in a pile in the middle of the mattress. That's a first. He's never helped me gather the laundry to take to the *pressing* before.

The *pressing* is a luxury I'm grateful for. In India, we had *dhobis* who used to come by, pick up the dirty clothes and deliver them the next day, washed, ironed and folded. Here, the *pressing* folks don't pick up but at least they'll wash and fold — and iron — all the bedding you drop off. I add the girls' used bedding to ours in a pile on the floor.

I put fresh sheets on the mattress, put clean pillowcases on. I pluck the used towels off the bathroom racks, the kitchen dish-cloth from the refrigerator handle and the apron that hangs on a hook, and take them to the washer. Next, I sort through our clothes in the laundry bin, separating the colors from the whites, and get a load started.

I look at my watch. Depending on when Celeste calls, I may not have time to hang up the laundry on the clothesline in the building's interior atrium.

And as if I've just conjured the woman herself, the phone rings. It's Celeste. Can I meet Delphine at the Hotel Bristol in a half hour?

Delphine grins at me, that reward she bestows so grudgingly. "You won, Radha."

"Won what?" I ask, looking around ner-vously. The Hotel Bristol, with its Art Deco exterior and its eighteenth-century furnish-ings, intimidates me.

We're sitting in one of the discreet recep-tion areas on an overstuffed sofa. It's velvet, in a deep magenta. Above the sofa is a painting of Marie Antoinette in elaborate bouffant wig and gown (prerevolution, when she was still a self-satisfied innocent). A low coffee table in front of us is flanked by several upholstered French armchairs with rounded backs. A centuries-old tapestry of a hunt hangs on a nearby wall. A crystal chandelier on the ceiling above us glitters in the afternoon light. The Persian rug under our feet makes me want to take off my shoes and slide them across the thick silk and wool weave. The staff, so polite and well-groomed, move about soundlessly. This is the kind of place Florence would love. I wonder if she's ever been here. And just as quickly, I realize: *I've never before given any thought to what Florence would or would not like.*

Delphine's cigarette is about to drop ash on the carpet below. Just before it does, a gentleman in a hotel uniform appears out of nowhere, placing an ashtray in front of her on the coffee table. She acknowledges the gesture with a quick *merci.*

"The client loved your formula. You should have seen the look on Ferdie's face! He had created those scent vials for the client using what he thought was the essential oil you brought back from Agra. The client took one sniff of the blotter and turned to me with a grimace. It was priceless!"

I can imagine the scene. Michel had

added cinnamon to the oil, which would have been all wrong for Olympia. There is nothing sweet about her; underneath that soft flesh, Olympia has developed a steel core that protects her from the slights of the world. Oh, how I would love to have been at the meeting to see Ferdie's face! He almost got away with it. To keep from hugging Delphine (I'm sure she would not appreciate it), I fold my hands in my lap. "How did Ferdie take it?"

My boss taps ash into the ashtray. Her smile is wry. "Not well. He will get promoted, however."

"What?" I can't contain my surprise.

"Yves believes in his nephew. He was as perplexed with the result as Ferdie was. He's going to send Ferdie to Spain to start a new branch of the House of Yves. As a consolation."

When she sees the look of incredulity on my face, she says, "It was my idea. I need Ferdie out of my lab — I can't work with people I don't trust — but I can't afford to question Yves's judgment. Ferdie will love Spain. He already loves the men there."

I think of Machiavelli, whom we had to read in our last year at Auckland. Delphine is either a master of his principles or she has tremendous instincts. And her knowledge of Ferdie's personal life comes as a surprise to me.

Delphine smokes, allowing me to sit in silence for a while, taking it all in.

"So what happens now?"

Delphine checks the gold Longines on her wrist. "You will meet the client."

I can't believe I'm finally being invited to a client meeting. "When?"

"Now."

"Now?"

"Yes." Delphine stands, collects her purse and her gloves. Now I notice that she hasn't removed her coat since we arrived.

"Where are you going?"

"To give you privacy. Don't look so worried. You'll be fine." She stands. "And enjoy the rest of the day for yourself."

She's going to leave me here alone with a client? I watch her walk away, as I try to curb my rising panic. I've never been in a client meeting before. Shouldn't this meeting be taking place at the House of Yves, in Delphine's conference room, like all her other client meetings?

I smell her before I see her: Bergamot. Amber. Carnation. Lavender. Cedar. Orris Root. Musk.

She comes into my peripheral vision and

then she's standing in front of me. Like Delphine, she's polished. Glossy black hair parted in the middle and pulled back into a sleek ponytail. Large Chanel sunglasses. Her skin has a slight olive tinge. She's wearing a white cashmere blazer — no lapels — and matching white pleated pants. Her platform shoes in suede match her ensemble. Her only accessories are a gold belt at the waist, a wide gold cuff on her wrist and large diamond earring studs. She's not carrying a purse or a clutch. She sets a hotel key chain on the coffee table: she's staying here.

She takes the seat Delphine was sitting in before she left. Immediately, a hotel attendant comes to ask what she needs. She answers in perfect, but accented, French. "Two very dry gin martinis. Up. Make sure the glass is cold, please." She glances at me. "Olives okay?"

Absently, I nod. It's lunchtime, and I've never had a gin martini, but I don't think I'm supposed to say no to a client. I'm focused on that peculiarly accented French. I'm sure I've heard it before. And why is her smell so familiar?

She finishes with the attendant, who inclines his head and disappears to my left.

Now she turns to observe me. She clasps her hands on her lap, and I notice the immaculate manicure. No rings. The polish is clear with a pearl sheen. Everything about her says she's in charge. Only the tight clasp of her hands betrays her nervousness. "We've met before, Radha. When you worked at Antoine's." She removes her sunglasses.

Of course! She's the woman Delphine brought to Antoine's boutique before I started working at the House of Yves. And the scent — it's the one I recommended for her. One of Delphine's creations from the House of Yves. Given the woman's accent and her coloring, I remember wondering whether she might be Turkish or Middle Eastern.

"I don't think I caught your name then or now."

As if I hadn't spoken, she says, "Toast first. Then I'll tell you." She waits while the waiter sets our martinis on the table. We clink our glasses.

I take a sip of my first gin martini. The glass is so cold it looks as if it's coated in frost. The liquid goes down smoothly, a cool rivulet down my throat. I feel it coat my stomach. There's a slight burn, but otherwise, I like it. Perhaps I've found something to replace the wines I merely tolerate. I'm not quite sure how to tip the glass without the olive sliding into my lip, so I take small sips.

She's been watching me. "Your first?"

I smile, as does she. What beautiful teeth. And those dark eyes lined in kohl are striking.

"I have to be so careful when I come to Paris to specify what I want in my drink. The first time I ordered a martini, I was given a sweet vermouth. Here at the Bristol, they know me."

"You come often?"

"As often as I can."

The alcohol has given me a little courage. "Did the fragrance you bought at Antoine's do what you needed it to?"

She runs a finger around the rim of her glass and smiles into her glass. "For a time, yes." She takes another sip and eyes me over the rim. "We've met other times. Once at a holiday party. In Jaipur. At Parvati Singh's house. You and Lakshmi were doing our henna. I think the year was —" she narrows her eyes, thinking "— 1955."

1955? That's almost twenty years ago. Who is she? Like a View-Master, images click rapidly through my brain. Parvati Singh's holiday party. Jiji, Malik and me arriving at the Singhs' in a *tonga*. Teenage girls, a few years older than me, in the latest frocks, dancing to Elvis Presley by the gramophone. A few sitting on couches, waiting their turn for me to oil their hands in preparation for Lakshmi's henna design. The girls barely noticed us, so focused were they on the main event: Ravi Singh playing Shakespeare's jealous Moor. There was one girl in a champagne chiffon dress who almost made me spill clove oil on myself. I look more closely at the woman sitting beside me — it's her!

She's only two years older than me — so she must be thirty-four. Gone is the baby fat on her frame; she's almost gaunt. Her jawline has slackened somewhat and some of the cushion in her formerly rosy cheeks is gone. Now she needs blush to create the illusion. There's a weariness around her mouth; the corners drag downward when she's not talking. Her hair used to be wavy — or did she have a servant wave it for her? The woman before me has hair as straight as the reeds Jiji painted henna designs with.

No wonder she looked and sounded familiar. I'm sitting at the table with Sheela Sharma, a woman I haven't seen — or at least recognized — in two decades! The woman who married Ravi Singh, Niki's father. She made my life hell at the Maharani School in Jaipur for the few months that I attended the private school. All because I was poorer than her, less refined. She would say I was as dark as an eggplant and trip me in dance class. She was rude to Malik, who was just a boy then, and made Lakshmi send him home instead of having him work on her family's mandala. She was the prized only daughter of the wealthy Sharma family, and she was determined to marry the most eligible bachelor. Before I left for Shimla to have my baby, I learned of her engagement to him: my Ravi. She eventually became Sheela Singh.

"Careful," she says, pointing to my martini glass.

My hand has loosened its grip and the glass is tilted, the liquid slowly dripping onto my wool skirt. I place the martini glass on the coffee table and try to brush the gin off with my palm. Now my palm is damp. I rub it against the side of my skirt. All the while, I'm thinking: *She's* the client? *Sheela Singh* is the woman who wanted to create a scent for Olympia?

She's been watching me with an intense expression, as if she's trying to read my thoughts. She takes a large gulp of her martini. "You remember me now, don't you?" She lifts the olive out with those manicured nails and pops it into her mouth.

She switches from French to Hindi. "I wanted to create a fragrance for my favorite painting. And I wanted *you* to do it."

"Me? Why me?" I'm trying to act normal. Trying to keep my voice steady, as if I'm really sitting down with an ordinary client. Six years ago, at Antoine's, she was just another customer I was helping. Now, she's a reminder of my unhappy past. Does she know I had a baby with her husband?

She tips her glass to her lips, realizes it's empty and looks around for someone to bring her another. As if she has pushed a button for an attendant, one magically appears. She recites her order. The attendant checks my glass, and seeing it's still half-full walks away.

I'm not sure how much more of this polite chatter I can take. "Why are you here? What am I doing sitting here with you?"

"I was horrible back then. I don't blame you for being upset. So let me explain." She leans forward. "Five years ago, I learned that my husband had a son. With you. Before he and I were married. I was devastated. His parents knew and never told me before we married."

So she does know.

She straightens and sits back on the sofa. "I can't imagine how you must have felt."

I frown. She's *sympathizing* with me?

"I came to Paris to sort myself out. I brought my two girls with me." Her eyes meet mine. "I understand you have two daughters as well?"

What is this? She's hired someone to look into my private life or has Delphine told her everything about me? I feel exposed, but I can't seem to tear myself away from her, from this conversation. She's still a client and I'm still an employee of the House of Yves. And if I'm honest, I'm strangely curious about her motivation for the Olympia project. Frankly, I'm also flattered that she — the self-centered, vile Sheela Sharma of my past — would want *me* to create a fragrance for her. Isn't that vindication?

Sheela looks down at her hands. "Anyway, I knew of Delphine — she's famous — and so I got in touch with her. The idea of this son of Ravi's — and yours — made me crazy. I wanted a scent that would make my husband forget everyone but me. We've been married a long time. I know him well. He lies. He drinks. He cheats." She glances at me hastily. "But you're well aware of that."

Her second martini arrives. She waits until the server leaves to continue talking. I look around at this lovely hotel, the sparkling chandeliers, the ancient tapestries from the Louvre, and wonder what I'm doing here, what this woman wants from me.

"When I came to Antoine's that day," Sheela says, "it took me a while, but I recognized you because your relationship with Ravi was top of mind. You, however, didn't recognize me. I look different than the girl you knew." She sighs. "The fragrance you recommended was perfect. But with Ravi . . . it only worked for a while." She looks wistful. "I was still in love with him then."

She picks up her glass and takes a sip. "Then I learned that my in-laws were thinking of bringing his . . . *son* into their business. Nikhil is his name, I believe." She says it as if she's guessing, but I can tell she's done her research. "They're not convinced Ravi is the right successor for their real estate business. He has proved disappointing — for obvious reasons." She has turned a shade darker. "I've started divorce proceedings, but the Singhs don't know that yet. I plan to move here, to Paris, eventually."

She raises her eyes from her drink to gaze into mine. "The Singhs tried to offer a scholarship to Nikhil through his adoptive parents, but there was no response. Frankly,

I was relieved."

She knows about the letter to Kanta and Manu from the UK law firm, too? Of course she wouldn't want Ravi's illegitimate child to become part of her family, and I say so.

"It's not that," she says. "It's because the Singhs are poison. Look what they did to your life. To Ravi's. He never wanted to go into the family business — it's made him so unhappy. They've disowned Govind because he's working in the movies. And he's living with an American." Her brows knit together. "The farther Nikhil stays from the Singhs, the better for him."

This surprises me. I turn slightly so I'm facing her. "If you're leaving the Singh family, what difference does it make to you whether Niki goes to America or not?"

"Ravi is not . . . kind. He can be very cruel." Her face falls, and I see what the makeup can't hide. The sagging eyelids, worry lines around her eyes, that groove from her nose to her mouth that must be getting deeper with the years. "He will make Niki's life hell. That's one of the reasons I put my daughters in boarding schools in Geneva. They're out of the reach of that . . . family. As Nikhil's mother, I thought you'd want to know." She swigs her second drink as if it will fortify her.

I'm not sure if I'm glad that her marriage has turned sour or if I'm sad for the woman whose husband neglects her. My mind is such a confused jumble. I'm angry when I think of my past with Sheela, baffled by the present conversation we're having and intrigued by where this is all leading.

I clear my throat. "I haven't been Nikhil's mother for seventeen years. Manu and Kanta Agarwal adopted him when he was a baby. Shouldn't you be talking to them?"

"I've tried. I've called several times, but they won't talk to me. They think I'm part of the Singhs' scheme. Trust me, Radha, I'm not. Like you, I'm a mother. I know how ruthless Parvati is. I fought her for years. She always won." That steely look is back in her eyes again. "This time, *I'm* going to make sure she loses." Her face resembles Delphine's when my *chef* found out about Ferdie's betrayal.

It's hard to trust someone whom you knew to be a different person in the past. Lakshmi had that issue with Hari, her ex-husband. But Hari *had* changed. And Jiji accepts him as he is now. The woman before me does appear genuinely contrite. I try to think through everything she's told me, to ferret out her true intent. She's been defeated, but there's a determination in her that tells me she has no intention of giving up her plans. She must believe the fragrance line will be the thing that sets her free.

"Why are you so sure Niki will listen to me? He's been upset with his parents for keeping the letter secret from him."

Her neck flushes. She reaches for her cocktail and gulps it. She's downing her martinis like water. "I hired an investigator. I know Nikhil is here in Paris. I know you've talked. The investigator tells me you two have a connection."

She's been *spying* on me? On us? How can I trust someone like that? "What do you gain from this?"

Her eyes bore into mine. "Revenge. I don't want the Singhs to get what they want. They think only a man can run their business. They ignore my daughters completely and despise me because I didn't give them a grandson. When we got to America, I decided to consult my own lawyers and set aside money for me and my girls. I'm starting a company that I hope will support them one day. It's called Remember Me. A line of scents for the women in classic paintings, the ones history forgot or ignores.

"Did you know I studied art history in the States? I've spent a lot of time with the paintings here in Paris. When I look at the ballerinas of Dégas or the dancing girls of Lautrec or Titian's *Girl in a Fur,* I wonder about the female subjects. They were as critical to the artist's success as his skill. They posed for hours, ignoring their thirst or hunger, their aching muscles. Who were they to the painter? What were they thinking while posing? Why did they agree to pose for him? Whom were they supporting with the money they might have been paid? So many questions come up for me. But I find few answers. Why does no one talk about these women? The focus is always on the men — the artists. I started wondering: When I die, who will remember me? I've raised two incredible girls. Yet, the Singhs place them second to boys. Who will remember my daughters? Are men the only figures to be immortalized in history?"

Sheela reaches for my hands. When her cool fingers touch mine, my instinct is to recoil. Instead, I stare at her manicured fingernails. "When you helped me at Antoine's, I didn't know Delphine was taking me to see you, Radha. I only knew that the person who could help me was someone who understood what it is to be forgotten. Then, when I met you and heard your name, I knew immediately who you were. I knew you'd understand Olympia. You'd understand the forgotten women. Maybe you'd even understand me. I didn't want to be impressed with your skill, but I was. There was no denying your talent."

Forgotten? I suppose to Ravi and the Singhs I am the forgotten woman. And I suppose I was forgotten by Niki, too. I pull my hands away and reach for my martini, now no longer cold. I swallow the remainder quickly. I feel as if I'm in a dream and can't wake up.

She hasn't stopped talking. "The House of Yves will develop the Remember Me product line. With you as the lead perfumer, working under Delphine. I'm contracting the development of the fragrance to them. I'll provide the marketing, financing, distribution and publicity. It's taken me five years to pull all the details and paperwork together. I told Delphine I have every intention of succeeding. She believes in me. And she believes in you. And now, Radha, that I've seen your work, I believe in you, too." She pauses. "Will you help the world remember these women?"

I'm so shocked that the imperious Sheela Sharma would one day be begging for my services I can't find my voice. Did Antoine have an idea about any of this the day he sent me off to my lunch with Delphine?

Somehow, I think he might have. Because he knew my worth. So does Delphine. I've brought more work into the House of Yves. With the release of Olympia, my name will be known in the industry, and talent creates its own trajectory. I could move to another fragrance house, but I know I won't. I still have much more to learn from Delphine.

I fold my arms across my chest. "Four years' free tuition at a university in the United States is hard to turn down. How do you propose I convince Niki not to go?"

I'm negotiating on behalf of Niki now, as I would for my daughters were they in his position.

It takes her a minute, during which time she stares at me to see if I'll flinch. I don't. I'm perfectly serious. I've been with Niki. I know how determined he is. Look at how he's still here in Paris after being told he's not wanted. He won't give up that scholarship easily.

She chews on her olive. "Do you have any suggestions?"

I think about the conversation last night between Niki and Gérard at L'Atlas. How Niki hung on Gérard's every word. How he couldn't tear his eyes away from the paint under the museum guard's fingernails. He wanted to know how one learns to be a true artist, to move the imagination of a viewer who is staring at a static work of art. Gérard had said, "There is no such thing as a static drawing or painting." He had borrowed Niki's pad and pencil and, with his good hand, created a swift likeness of me as he talked about lines and movement and composition.

Niki had watched in silence, his face a study in wonder and awe. When Gérard turned the pad around to show us the finished sketch, even I felt as if the figure (me!) was just about to look up or turn or pick up their glass. There was so much life in the rendering.

I know the answer to Sheela's question. "The École des Beaux-Arts, here in Paris. That's where Niki deserves to be. Five years' free tuition. That's what you'll agree to if you want me to continue working on your project."

In that moment, I feel more powerful than I've ever felt in my life. I know before she's said yes that she'll accept. It takes all my willpower to keep my triumph to myself.

Sheela raises her eyebrows. She hadn't expected me to drive such a hard bargain. "Has Niki been accepted?"

"That won't be an issue." Now I know why I've been put on the same planet as

417

Florence. She's on the board of the Beaux-Arts.

Sheela studies the carpet at her feet. She's concentrating. After a few minutes, she extends a hand toward me. At first, I don't know what she wants, but then I, too, extend my hand and we shake. This time, I don't pull my hand away. I squeeze with my newfound strength.

I'm still at the Hotel Bristol, sitting on the same velvet sofa, an hour later, going over my conversation with Sheela Singh — the girl who used to say the color of my skin was wrong, my clothes were wrong, I didn't belong. I marvel at the civilized conversation we just had. We couldn't stand each other eighteen years ago! Did I really just speak to the woman whose husband we've *both* slept with?

I pinch my wrist. It hurts. Which means I'm not dreaming.

The aroma of delicate spices and sauces wafts from the restaurant into the conversation nook, and I realize I'm hungry. It's lunchtime here at the Bristol.

I ask an attendant walking by if I might use the phone. He extends an arm courteously to have me follow him to the main desk. The gentleman behind the reception desk puts a white phone up on the marble counter and presses one of the buttons on it for an outside line.

I call Mathilde and ask her to join me for lunch at the Hotel. It will be a big expense, but I owe her.

"What's the occasion?" Mathilde asks as she drapes her napkin on her lap. She looks unimpressed. This is the kind of place she's used to frequenting. She belongs here; I don't. "This is quite a treat for you. *Trop cher.*"

I fold my hands in my lap and take a deep breath. "I owe you an apology, *chérie.* You've been going through so much, and I haven't been available. You're right. I should have told you about Niki years ago. I thought if I just didn't mention him, he would cease to exist. But, of course, that was impossible."

The waiter arrives with a lemon water for me (the martini I had with Sheela made me a little light-headed) and a glass of chardonnay for Mathilde. He returns presently with our first course: beef carpaccio for Mathilde, cheese flan for me. He is sensitive enough to know not to disturb us, and he leaves as quietly as he arrived.

Mathilde has not put on mascara today.

Without it, she looks younger, more vulnerable. It's almost as if her makeup is a shield between her and the rest of the world. She has had to guard herself from a mother and father who couldn't be bothered to tell her how much they loved her or missed her. The money has helped, but hasn't it just been another kind of shield? The hurt is always there, layers of it, just beneath her skin.

My friend is looking at me with her head cocked to one side, skeptical. Am I about to tell her everything she wants to know? Or will I hold something back as I always have? I've known Mathilde forever. If anyone would understand what compelled me to sleep with Ravi Singh all those years ago, it's her. Why didn't I tell her the truth about how I ended up at Auckland, so far from Jaipur? Where do I start?

"First, please tell me about Agnes." I implore her with my entire being to share her grief with me. If Antoine were still alive, he'd have done the same. He'd have stuck with her throughout her ordeal.

She forks the beef and chews, looking down at her plate. "There's not much to say. When we came home from the outing with Florence and the girls and Niki, she sat down on the living room floor and shat. Then she walked to the kitchen and asked if we had any cheese. *C'est la comble!*" She throws her fork down on her plate with a clatter. "I didn't get married and have children for a reason, Radha. I never wanted to be responsible for raising anyone — not a husband, not a baby, not a sixty-five-year-old woman who can't find her way to the bathroom."

She raises her eyes. I see that they're filled. "You know I love your girls. Shanti and Asha are like the nieces I'll never have. But at the end of the day, I can turn them over to you and be their favorite aunt." She uses her napkin to wipe her eyes. "Agnes wasn't always unkind. She had her moments. Sometimes she sang me to sleep if she was high." Mathilde attempts a laugh, but it comes out as a hiccup. "She did give me the experience of India and of meeting you, which I would never trade for the world." She smiles, the gap between her front two teeth on full display. "But I could never count on her to be where she said she was going to be. After a while I gave up trying. I just accepted that she would always let me down."

She runs the napkin under her nose. "I guess I stopped expecting anything." She pauses. "You and Antoine are the only people I could count on. And then Antoine died . . ." She trails off. "The thing is, Radha, I don't love my mother. I know that sounds horrible, but it's true. I know she brought me into this world — I heard enough times the story of her eating copious amounts of jaggery dipped in *ghee* to make sure I was going to be healthy — but I don't feel a connection to her. Does that make sense? And does that make me a horrible daughter?"

I put my fork down. I think of Maa. She showed her love by scolding me, pulling on my ear to reprimand me, slapping me if I spilled food. But I felt her love, always. I know Jiji felt it, too, even after Maa refused to have any contact with her. My mother was only following what centuries of tradition had taught her: a woman's duty is to be subservient to her husband; he becomes her master, protector, provider. When Lakshmi broke that sacrosanct vow, my mother couldn't hold up her head in the village. She felt Lakshmi had robbed her of her dignity and pride. It wasn't right, but it was what she believed.

I reach for Mathilde's hand. "Did you know there's a Hindu belief that the people known to you in this life are the same people you knew in your last life but in different roles? And that we're always trying to learn how to coexist with those people in a better way? Agnes was your mother in this life, but you might have been *her* mother in your past life or her best friend."

Mathilde laughs through her tears. "*Sacré!* That means Agnes might be my *grand-père* or my husband in the next life! I'm not sure I could take that!"

It feels good to laugh with my oldest friend. "We don't choose our families, Mathilde. Whatever you're feeling is a result of your personal experience. There's no need to feel it's wrong or that you're a bad person for feeling it."

Mathilde closes her eyes and sighs. When she opens them again, I see gratitude, forgiveness and something else — regret? My friend has no reason to regret anything. She's doing the best she can, just as we all are. I try to encourage her with my smile.

I pick up my fork and take a bite of the cheese flan. It's delicious. "Where is Agnes now?"

Mathilde forks more of her carpaccio. She tells me the name of a facility an hour north of Paris. "I'd filled out the paperwork weeks ago. But I kept putting it off. Until yesterday. She'll be well fed, well cared for. All her needs will be taken care of."

The waiter, who I think has been waiting

for the right moment to interrupt us, whisks our small plates away and leaves our main courses of *confit de canard* and *salmon en papillote.* He fills Mathilde's glass and, with a quick *bon appetit,* disappears.

My old friend regards me. *"Ma petite puce."* I'm happy to see her smile. She chews her duck. "So what about you?"

Even though I invited her to lunch today to tell her about Niki, I hesitate. I remember reading in history class about a particular kind of torture in medieval times called quartering. A person's arms and legs would be tied to four separate horses. The horses would move in opposite directions until each limb was torn right off the torso. That's how painful my separation from baby Niki had felt. Mathilde has never had a child. Could she understand what it felt for me to give him up? Or why I wanted to keep him separate from the rest of my life?

I place my utensils on my plate and my hands in my lap. I think about how keeping this secret from her has kept me from sharing an important part — the most tender part — of myself. When she would tell me about her heartaches, I pretended Pierre was the only boy I'd ever been with. What if I'd been able to be truthful about Ravi? Mathilde may have realized that I understood the depth of her pain. She might even have helped me feel better about his abandonment. I missed so many chances to reveal my true self to her when she has always been so forthright with me.

I finally begin. "I met a boy named Ravi Singh when I was thirteen and he was seventeen."

In the end, I tell her everything. All the details I've kept to myself for so long. Does it make me feel better? Honestly, no. It just feels as if the whole sordid history is being stretched out, like laundry left on the line too long.

Mathilde is taking the final bite of her duck. "Niki knows you're his mother?"

"Now he does."

She nods. Her smile is sad. "You were always unknowable, *ma puce*. I wondered what had happened to you to make you that way. Like you were keeping secrets you thought were too precious to tell anyone."

I want to explain. "Not precious. Just shameful. As if I'd done something wrong. Like I'd been a bad girl — depraved, immoral — and everyone would know it."

"So Pierre knows. And Florence?"

"Yes. She even told me —" I stop abruptly. Florence shared a secret with me, one Pierre is not even aware of, and I'm not sure I'm at liberty to divulge it. It's the first time in all the years I've known Florence that she has confided in me. Who am I to break that trust? I wonder if Pierre himself is aware that Philippe wasn't his birth father. If he finds out, how would he react? What if I told Mathilde before I told Pierre what his own mother told me?

When I don't respond, Mathilde leans away from me and folds an arm across her stomach. She sips her wine. She knows I'm holding on to another secret. And she's right. I can't be trusted to share openly and honestly. It's as if I'm always keeping some part of me in reserve. With a pang, I realize I've done it with Pierre for thirteen years; he must have felt the sting of my reticence just as Mathilde did.

Mathilde's blue eyes with their unadorned lashes regard me a moment longer. The sadness in them goes deep. She pushes her plate away and leans forward. "I've done something really terrible, *ma puce,* and you're going to hate me for it."

Betrayal has a smell. Burnt rubber, ginger, dandelion leaves.

I recognize it now when I return to the apartment. Without taking off my coat, I sift through the mound of bedding in our bedroom I had gathered for the *pressing.*

There they are. Blush: a color I would never wear. With elaborate lace that would look pretty on Mathilde's pink skin. Like the mascara that coats her lashes, Mathilde prefers decoration on her underwear. I hate the scratchy feel of lace, preferring cotton panties instead. My heart hammers in my chest as I slide down the bedroom wall like a marionette whose strings have been cut.

She told me all of it. How she had been hysterical the night before, distraught after leaving her mother at the old-age home. She'd sought me out, waited at our doorstep for me to come home. But I was out with Niki and Gérard at the time.

Then Pierre came home early from Nice. He brought Mathilde inside. She told him she was angry that I'd been neglecting her. Pierre told her he was angry that I'd kept Niki a secret from him, that he'd always felt I held a big part of myself back from him, from the family. Was it a mutual disappointment in me that led them to their first kiss? Or had their easy teasing always been a cover for a dormant attraction? Florence sometimes pretended Mathilde was her daughter-in-law, not even hiding the fact that she thought Mathilde would be a perfect French wife for Pierre. Had Pierre ever thought of Mathilde that way?

Perhaps. But I'd never thought it as a real possibility. It's reasonable to assume that if I like Mathilde and Pierre likes me, he finds Mathilde's qualities appealing, too. A couple we know — the husband works in Pierre's firm — actually switched partners with friends of theirs, so similar were they in their likes and dislikes. But to think that the two people I trust most in Paris would betray me like this in retaliation — that is hard to accept. Attraction is one thing. Revenge is another. That he felt the need to get even for the secret I've kept from him by sleeping with my best friend? Did he enjoy it? Did Mathilde?

Images of their legs and naked torsos twisting on my bedsheets flash through my mind even as I try to banish them. I'd like to feel angry, but all I feel is numb. I'm neither hot nor cold. I feel neither rooted to the floor of my apartment nor to my marriage. I dig my fingernails into the floorboards. I want to gouge the wood, feel the splinters pierce my skin. When I release the pressure, my fingers are red, as if they're on fire, but I feel no pain. And there's not the slightest indention in the oak floor.

Have I always been able to turn off my feelings this easily? How did I learn to do

it? When? Was I only five or six when I realized I couldn't trust Maa or Pitaji to care
for me because they were too absorbed in
their own grief? They couldn't protect me
from the stigma of the Bad Luck Girl. So
instead of asking them to insulate me from
the villagers' taunts, I built a vault around
my feelings, telling myself it didn't matter
what they said. I wouldn't let them hurt me.

What a balm it was when Ravi came into
my life and made me feel as if I actually
deserved the time, attention and love of
another. I'd been so starved for it that I tore
down that vault and said, *Yes! Take all of
me! I'm ready!*

And when Ravi's sweet talk turned out to
be nothing more than lies, I gave myself
completely to my baby. But then I was
forced to separate from Niki, and my heart
was so broken that I erected that vault
again. Not enough to keep me from my
infatuation with Pierre. Not enough to keep
me from loving my girls. But enough to seal
a small part that I kept just for myself. I
would never again give anyone permission
to take that bit.

It's that tiny nugget that I've protected
and nurtured that's allowed me to pursue
my life's work. That raw, animalic part of
me connects with fragrances the way bees

429

home in on pollen and hummingbirds on nectar. If I hadn't pursued my passion single-mindedly — despite Pierre's objections, despite the time I stole from my daughters — I may never have discovered my natural talent for — and love of — working with fragrances. I may never have come to value my skills the way Pierre values his. He's always known he'd be able to focus his energy on building his career — it was always expected of him, and it's what he expected of himself.

Why, then, does it feel as if I should apologize for focusing on what I love to do? That's what Pierre can't forgive, isn't it? I'm being selfish. Keeping the *me* part for myself instead of relinquishing it all to him. But do I have to? Delphine doesn't. Mathilde doesn't. Florence didn't. Do I become selfless and devote my entire life to my husband and children or split myself in two: one part of me surrenders myself to my family; the other part dedicates herself to growing her talents — not giving myself completely to either?

Now I do feel something: a piercing pressure at my temples, a pinch at the base of my skull. I need to make a decision. To which there is no right or wrong.

Lakshmi will understand. She's always

understood. Work I loved, something just for me — that's what she tried to tell me. All those years ago when she was the doyenne of the henna set in Jaipur and talked to me of working toward a brighter future. She wanted me to find my place in this world, not just as a wife and mother but as something in my own right.

I get up off the floor. I can do this. I *want* to do it.

But things will have to change.

I walk to our bed and smooth out Mathilde's underwear in the center of the coverlet.

I hear Pierre's key in the lock. I can picture him hanging up his coat, taking off his shoes, walking down the hall.

He enters our bedroom. "Radha, you're home . . ." His eyes stray to the only spot of color on the white coverlet.

His mouth falls open. His eyes grow round.

He turns to me slowly. "It's the first time I've ever —" He runs a hand over his mouth. "It was just a fuck. It meant nothing."

I sit down on the edge of the bed and rub my temples. "What if it meant something to her? Did you stop to consider that, Pierre?" I'm surprised at how calm I sound. My heart is beating normally. My hands are steady. In my body, there's no rage, disappointment, panic or despair.

Pierre stands uncertainly. My husband. A man I've known for thirteen years.

Now I say, "Or was this —" I straighten one edge of Mathilde's underwear. "Was this your way of telling me you're unhappy with me? I already know you're unhappy. About my job. My late hours. My need to have something separate from the family. But there was no need for you to do this to Mathilde."

He frowns and flings an arm to the side. "To Mathilde?" His face is pink with frustration. "She was more than happy to jump into bed. She's had a lot of practice, God knows! She's a grown woman. She made her own decision."

I smell cinnamon — it's considered a sweet scent, but it has a bitter edge. He's angry that I want to protect my best friend.

Pierre takes a step closer to me. "What's worse? That I slept with Mathilde or that you kept Niki a secret from me all these years? You had a son, Radha, and you never told me! How do you think that makes a man feel?"

"No worse than I felt leaving my son and keeping him a secret from everyone. If I'd told you about him, would you still have married me? Would we have had a life together? Would we share two wonderful daughters? I didn't want to risk a life without you, *Pierre.* I wouldn't trade the last thirteen years for anything."

The creases across his forehead soften. His jaw relaxes.

"I can't take back what I did and didn't do all those years ago," I tell him. "I have to keep moving forward, *chérie.* As do you. I've tried to tell you why my work with fragrances is important to me. It transports me. Excites me. Takes me to places I've never been. I *need* it. And it makes *me* feel needed in this world."

Pierre tilts his chin up as if he's about to say something. I hold up my hand to stop him. "Yes, I know the girls need me, but it's not the same. They will leave someday, start their own lives. But I'll still have this. This thing that makes me curious and keeps me wondering. What will this scent do to the wearer? How will it change the way she — or he — moves in this world? What memories will it conjure? Will they be happy ones or sad? Will the fragrance open new possibilities for that person's future? These things matter to me, Pierre. They are as important to me as a building you design for people to work or live in. Either you can accept that or you can't." I hold my hand out for him to take. A plea. "Can you?"

Pierre regards my offering, staring at my outstretched hand. His shoulders slump. His eyes fill. "I can't."

That evening, Pierre says he needs to go for a walk and think.

I make two phone calls. One is to Florence. "Can you please drop off the girls at the apartment?"

"What? Now?"

I can hear the girls in the background playing some kind of game with Niki. They're laughing and arguing at the same time, teasing each other. I think about how hard it's going to be for the girls to hear that their mother and father aren't going to live together with them. First, there will be separation, then a divorce. Two homes they'll have to shuttle back and forth from. My heart flutters. "*S'il te plaît,* Florence."

Something in my tone makes her pause. I hear her closing a door. I can no longer hear my children. *My children. All three of them.* How odd and lovely and frightening that sounds. Soon, I will have to tell Shanti and Asha about Niki. But when? How? What will my girls say when I tell them I had a baby when I wasn't that much older than Shanti?

Florence sighs. "You're leaving Pierre." She states it as a fact, not a question.

Has my *saas* always been able to read me so well? First, she figures out that Niki is my son. Now, she's guessed that I'm ending my marriage to *her* son. I hesitate. I shouldn't do this over the phone. My voice is barely above a whisper when I say, *"Oui."*

"Oh, Radha. Mathilde called me. Foolish girl. She feels very bad about it all."

"That's not the reason I'm doing this. You do understand?"

She is quiet. We listen to each other breathe. Finally, she says, "Two days ago, I told Pierre that after you returned from Agra you seemed different. I don't think it's just because Niki showed up. It goes beyond that. There's a settled feeling about you, in you. It's as if, in India, you found a piece of yourself you had lost."

There it is again. The idea that we women lose track of ourselves. Lakshmi always said henna was a way for a woman to find a part of herself she may have mislaid. Sheela said she wanted to bring the forgotten women back to life because while their painted images were famous, they themselves were invisible; they'd been discarded, like candy wrappers tossed on the ground. Is that erasure of us something other people do to us or do we women do it to ourselves?

I struggle to bring myself back to the present. Florence is still talking, "Pierre didn't want to hear it. Radha, I've spoiled him. And I let his grandmother spoil him. He's always had everything he ever wanted. He can't imagine a life where everything doesn't go the way he wants. I'm sorry."

I don't know what to say to that. A month before our separation, I would have expected Florence to jump for joy at a romantic liaison between her son and Mathilde. Surprisingly, her reaction is more sorrowful, subdued.

"Will you tell the girls tonight?" she asks.

"Yes. We'll do it together. Pierre will be back from his walk by then." He and I talked about many things this evening, including how to tell the girls. He'd cried. I'd cried. We'd been good together for so long. Until we weren't. Until I fell in love with my work. He still didn't understand, perhaps he never would. But Pierre deserves happiness, too, and I hope he finds someone who wants the same things he does. It won't be easy for me when it happens. I know I'll be jealous — I won't be able to help myself. In my most selfish moments, I want Pierre to love only me for the rest of his life. That's what I'd wished at the age of fourteen, when

I left Niki in care of Kanta and Manu. I wanted Niki to love only me. But that would have been wrong. It would have made none of us happy: not Niki, not Kanta or Manu and not me.

"Pierre will need you, Florence."

She scoffs. "I don't think Pierre has ever needed me."

Perhaps she's right. The Pierre I know has never told his mother he loves her, not within my hearing.

"*I* need you, Florence," I say quietly, and I realize it's true.

There's a pause. When she speaks, her voice is thick, wet, and shaky. *"Merci."*

I remember the other reason I called her. "Has Niki said when he's going home?"

"End of this week. He has exams back in Jaipur."

"Do you think you could work on getting him into l'école?"

"Which *école*?"

"*The* École. L'école des Beaux-Arts, of course. It's where he belongs."

"Ah."

I can almost see her smile.

After my talk with Florence, I call Shimla.

Lakshmi is laughing as she picks up the phone. In the background, I hear the talking parakeet squawking, "Pushpa, I hate tears!" Jiji tells me Malik and Nimmi just returned from the film *Amar Prem*. Malik was reenacting a scene for them in which the character says, *Pushpa, I hate tears*. Now Madho Singh has picked it up and won't stop saying it.

I hear a rustling sound and realize Malik has grabbed the phone from Jiji. "*Choti behen,* this family will see a flood of tears if you don't come see us soon. And, Radha, I hate tears!" He laughs.

Madho Singh cackles, "Radha, I hate tears!"

That makes the other inhabitants of Jiji's house laugh. As sad as I feel tonight, I find myself smiling. I hear Chullu and Rekha asking Dr. Jay if he'll take them to see the film. Oh, how I miss them. And how I wish I were in Shimla with them — right now — along with all three of my children.

Jiji comes back on the line. "Niki called Kanta. He's coming home. He still has his final exams to take before completing Senior Secondary. Then he can go to university." She pauses. "You did it, Radha."

"It was harder than anything I've ever done."

"Telling Niki that you gave him life?"

"*Hahn.*" I sigh. "I feel . . . relieved. Everyone knows about Niki now. Pierre. Florence. Mathilde —" I stop. For some reason, I hesitate to tell her about Mathilde and Pierre.

Her tone changes. "What's the matter?" My sister has always been able to hear what I don't say.

"I don't know yet, Jiji. I'm trying to figure it out."

She waits. I can hear her footsteps, as if she's finding a quieter place to have this conversation. "What about the girls? Have you told them they have a brother?"

"Not yet, Jiji. I need to find the right time."

Lakshmi must realize how much is happening all at once in my life. *Theek hai.* She changes the subject. "What happened with your project and the *mitti attar*? Did it work?"

I describe the ordeal with Ferdie, how Delphine turned it all around. "Remember Sheela Sharma?"

She doesn't answer right away. "Sheela Singh now, I think," she says cautiously.

"Soon she'll be Sheela Sharma again." I tell her it was Sheela who commissioned the fragrance for Manet's *Olympia* and that she is planning to leave the Singh household to start a fragrance line. Proudly, I relate the deal we struck about Niki. Sheela will find a way to finance his five years at the Beaux-Arts in return for my commitment to work on her fragrance line.

I hear my sister hesitate. "Do you trust her?"

My confidence falters. "What do you mean?"

"Something about it doesn't feel right, Radha. That family finds ways to corrupt every person who stands in their circle."

"Sheela said as much, too." I hear the defensiveness in my voice. "That's why she thinks Niki is better off not joining the Singhs in America." I'm sure I've made a good bargain. My voice is firmer when I tell her, "I trust her, Jiji."

After a moment, my sister says, "*Accha.* But be careful, okay?" She pauses. *"Aur kuch?"*

It's now or never, so I blurt it out. "I'm leaving Pierre."

She sucks in her teeth. "What happened?"

So many things. But all I say is, "He's not comfortable with me being a working mother. And he's only become more uncomfortable as time has passed. I've come to realize that he will only be happy if I work as a lab assistant forever or quit my job. That's what he said when we talked. And you know I won't be happy with either of those choices, Jiji."

She allows me space to say more.

"I wish I'd known back then what I know now. How was I to predict my fondness for chemistry and fragrances? And my ambition? I want to go back and finish my second year of chemistry so I understand it better. So far, I've been relying on instinct. I'm sure Delphine will support me on that."

"You work hard, *choti behen.* You always have. Don't think I've forgotten how you improved my henna paste or the sweet and savory recipes I created for my clients."

Her praise warms me. "There's something else." I decide to tell her about Mathilde and Pierre. My tone carries no emotion when I do.

"Is that why you really want to leave Pierre?"

"No, Jiji. When Mathilde told me, I felt . . . disappointed. That Pierre would have chosen to sleep with my best friend. I already knew he was upset. I just wanted him to meet me in the middle."

"I remember Mathilde as a fragile soul," Lakshmi says. "She acts tough, but she has a soft center. She missed having a mother."

"Yes, and Pierre should know that. He's known her for thirteen years! I feel bad for *her.* An affair like this at a time when she's feeling guilty and sad about abandoning her mother will unnerve her. Does that make sense?"

She doesn't answer. "And Florence? Does she know about all this?"

"*Hahn.* I'm going to have to rely on my *saas* a lot more to get the girls through this. Frankly, she's been terrific with them — and Niki, too. Did I tell you she guessed he was my son the moment she saw him? In a strange way, it brought us to some kind of understanding." With my sister so far away, I feel comfortable telling her what Florence shared with me about Pierre's birth. "That was a surprise."

Through the phone, I hear Madho Singh cry, "I love *rabri.*" Little Chullu says, "So do I!" My mouth waters. I wonder if Nimmi is making the *rabri* now. That creamy, rich dessert is one of my favorites and one I've never made for the girls because it takes so long.

Lakshmi asks, "Are you scared, Radha?"

I think about this. Is that the emotion I'm feeling? "Terrified, Jiji. I'm terrified."

Now the parakeet is saying, "Welcome. *Namaste. Bonjour!*" Somewhere in the back of my mind, I think Florence might find Madho Singh amusing. Then, a surprising thought: I wonder if she would ever want to visit India with me and the girls.

When Lakshmi speaks, her voice is soft. "Do you want me to come there? Or do you want to come to us for a while?"

I haven't cried during our phone call, but I feel the need building up in me. How wonderful to have Lakshmi in my life, to have a family here and in India. How lucky I am.

"*Nahee-nahee.* I'll be fine. I *am* fine."

"Call anytime. *Accha, Rundo Rani?*"

"*Hahn-ji.*" I set the receiver down gently. Now the tears come. I walk to my bedroom and pick up a pillow. I bury my face in its downy softness and scream as loudly as I dare. In the apartment below, Georges plays his melancholy piano melody, and it makes me mourn for my broken marriage, my bruised friendship. What will happen to the girls? How will I explain to my babies what's happening? I cry until the pillow is sopping wet and my throat burns from my wailing.

PART FOUR

The petals of the jasmine flower are so delicate that they must be picked by hand very early in the morning and rushed to a distillation facility before their scent fades.

Paris
April 1975

The knock at the door tells me Florence is here to take me to the de Gaulle airport. I'm flying back to Agra to meet with Hazi. During the last four months, Delphine, Michel and I have identified six of Sheela's "forgotten women" from classic paintings. I've been studying each one of them — Gérard had been a big help — to develop ideas about fragrances that could define them. There's van Gogh's *La Berceuse,* a portrait of Augustine Roulin, the wife of the Arles postman who befriended the painter. She's looking away from the painter, as if she's not comfortable with him; there are depths of meaning to be uncovered there. There's Berthe Morisot's *The Cradle,* where a woman watches over a sleeping baby, lost in thought. Is she the mother or the governess? What is she thinking? We are also considering Morisot's *Woman at Her Toilette* because of the beauty of the subject's half-dressed torso. Is she getting dressed or undressed? Something about the twist of her back seems resigned, and we're thinking of exploring that. We wanted to include an accomplished Indian painter, of course, and *Sumair* by Amrita Sher-Gil seems a perfect choice. And although I'm not a big fan of Gaugin's appropriation of Tahitian women, I think we do need to honor his teenage Tahitian wife and muse in *Tehamana Has Many Parents.*

Delphine has given me *carte blanche* to work on the Remember Me project exclusively. She believes it might be one of the most successful fragrance launches of the decade for the House of Yves. Certainly the most successful of my career — so far.

Back in December, when I told Delphine about my separation from Pierre — I needed to tell her while I worked out the logistics of where the girls would live and how Pierre and I could both have time with them —

she didn't make any comments about marriage being a forever state or whether we should try to work things out. After half a minute, she arched an eyebrow and asked, "Is there someone else?"

"No," I replied.

She was firm. "*Bon.* You'll stay at one of my apartments." *One* of her apartments? I wasn't aware she had more than one. As it turns out, she invests in real estate. And in me. "I'd like you to focus on the work, Radha. It will live longer than the heartache. Can you do that?"

I'd nodded. She'd put Celeste in charge of getting me settled. It was a tiny studio near Les Invalides, halfway between work and the Saint-Germain apartment. Within a few days, Celeste had moved in a bed, a desk, a chair and enough kitchen supplies to make it a temporary home.

It was Florence's suggestion that the girls should stay in the Saint-Germain apartment and either Pierre or I should stay with them on alternating weeks. That way, their routines stayed consistent. And they would have their clothes, books, supplies, everything they needed at the apartment. She promised to make herself available to help around our work schedules. Pierre stayed with his mother on his weeks away from the apartment.

The night we told the girls about our separation, they had come home from Florence's with drawings they had been working on with Niki. We asked them to join us in the living room. Asha was on the floor in front of the coffee table. She wanted to finish her drawing.

I let Pierre take the lead. When he finished telling the girls that we wouldn't all be living in the same house together, Asha, the easygoing child who had always taken things in stride, looked alarmed.

"How am I going to do my maths without Papa? Who will make our dinner? How will our clothes get washed? Who is going to put coconut oil in my hair, *Maman*? Shanti and I are going to live in the apartment alone? You can't do that to us!" By the time she finished, she was hysterical, her cheeks and forehead pink.

I sat on the floor next to her and took her hands in mine. "Everything will be as it was. Either Papa or *Grand-mère* or I will always be here to take care of you."

Asha flung my hands off and stood up. "Why can't we all still live together? You and Papa don't have to talk to each other if you don't want to."

450

I looked at my seven-year-old, then turned to Pierre. He crouched in front of her. "*Chérie*, we know this is difficult. It's going to be difficult for all of us. Don't you think *Maman* and I will miss you during the weeks when one of us is not here?"

My daughter's amber eyes, so like Pierre's, were filled with fear. She had never liked change. She'd always lived in the same house, always had a big sister, always had a grandmother, always had two parents. "That's why you *must* stay here. Both of you. Then you won't miss us. Please?"

Pierre tried a different tack. "*Grand-mère* lives in a different house. And she often comes here to be with us. It will be just like that —"

"No one in my class has *parents* who live in two places!" Sobbing, Asha took off for her room.

Pierre stood up and met my eyes. A look passed between us. *We knew this would be hard on our children. But are we scarring them for life by separating? Are we doing the right thing? Are we sure we want to end this marriage?* I wished in that moment that Lord Vishnu would magically appear to align us in our needs. He would make Pierre accept my need to do the work I love. He would make me accept Pierre's need to be the master of our household. Pierre and I would mutate into one soul, one mind, one decision-maker. There would never be another argument for the entirety of our lives together.

But Lord Vishnu didn't appear.

From the girls' room, we could hear Asha's muffled crying. After a moment's hesitation, Pierre left the room to talk to her.

Shanti, who had been quiet ever since we broke the news, got up from the sofa and took my hand. She regarded me with her solemn eyes and said, "I'll talk to her, *Maman*. She'll understand. If I had to live with that girl from class who teases me about my skin, I wouldn't like it either. You and Papa shouldn't have to live together if you're not liking it."

Tears sprang to my eyes.

"Don't cry, *Maman*." Shanti patted my hand. "I'm ten years old now. You've been teaching us how to cook. I can cook for Asha and me."

I took her in my arms and hugged her, hard. "That won't be necessary, *ma chouchou*. Unless you really feel like cooking. I promise Papa and I will try to make it as much like it was as before. *D'accord?*" I released her and wiped a hand across my

452

eyes. She looked so small. And wise. Her brown eyes were that of an old soul. "Are you scared?"

She was quiet for a moment. Then she nodded.

"Me, too," I said.

I looked at the drawing on the coffee table, the one Asha had been working on. It was our family. We were sitting on a bench under a tree. There was a pond in the background. It must be the Luxembourg Gardens, Asha's favorite park. I recognized Pierre; he had the largest head and shortest hair. Then came Shanti, whom I identified from the red dress she likes to wear. Next was Asha, the shortest figure of the four. The last figure was me, but it was only half-complete. My head and torso had been filled in but my legs and feet were yet to be drawn. It's as if the bottom half of me had already taken flight.

When I open the door to the studio where I'm living now, Florence is standing there in her belted dress, coat and handbag. She leans forward to kiss me on both cheeks. I return the gesture.

We've been joined at the hip these past five months, making sure the girls' routine is the same as it was before Pierre and I started living apart. Then came the news that Niki's portfolio was accepted by the École and he would be attending the art school this fall. Florence called in a few favors, but Niki's work spoke for itself. I could see the impact Gérard's teaching had made on Niki's drawings. He was good before, but he was even better now. Florence offered to have Niki live with her while he attends school, which seemed to please both of them. Niki joked that he would teach Florence to cook Indian food, and for once, I didn't see her wince at the mention of curry.

Now, Florence smiles at me, a smile that reaches her eyes. *"Ça va?"*

"Ça va bien." I smile back. "I've made coffee. Would you like a cup?"

Sweet-smelling violets were used in love
potions to induce fertility in ancient
Greece, but Ayurvedic practitioners used
violets to cure headaches and skin
ailments.

Agra
May 1975
I'm back in Agra, and the heat is oppressive. It's as if the sun is punishing us for a slight only it is aware of. We suffer in silence, waiting for its reprieve. The air conditioner in my hired car isn't working. Although I rolled my windows down, the air fanning my face is a balmy one hundred degrees.

Once I reach the *kotha,* the bike repair owner hurries to take my bag from the driver and ushers me upstairs to the performance room where it's much cooler. The tall windows are curtained in enormous *khus* screens. An old woman is sprinkling water on them. The wind flowing through the grass mats is releasing that lovely vetiver scent and cooling the room. When the woman finishes one side of the room, she moves to the other and starts wetting the khus all over again. Once again, I'm reminded of my childhood when we were too poor to afford large *khus* screens like these; we had to make do with a handheld fan made out of vetiver grass that we dipped in water occasionally.

Hazi and Nasreen look comfortable enough even with the scorching temperature outside. Every now and then, they swipe their upper lip with the edge of their *pallu.* They greet me enthusiastically, imploring me to sit, sit, sit. And who should bring my Rooh Afza *sharbat* but Binu from the kitchen! Her smile is wide as she carries my drink proudly into the room. I don't think she's usually allowed where guests congregate.

Hazi looks at me, raises an eyebrow and moves her head from side to side. "Binu insisted — no, she begged, pleaded — to serve the Mam from Paris."

I laugh and take the drink from Binu's tray. "*Shukriya,* Binu. What's the update on the space mission?"

Binu stands at attention, as if I were her teacher asking a question in class. "Last month, India launched its first satellite. Four days ago, *Amreeka* launched an astronomy satellite to rotate around the equator — successfully. In two weeks, Soviet Union will send two cosmonauts in a space station to perform experiments and repair damaged areas of Salyut 4." She grins at me as if to ask, *How did I do?*

I shake my head in disbelief. Neither of my daughters is this interested in spacecraft. Again I wonder: What could this girl do if she were given a chance?

Hazi turns to me. "You will eat something?"

It would be impolite to tell her I'm not hungry when I know my hosts will have prepared some extraordinary specialty, so I tilt my head in agreement.

As soon as Hazi gives Binu the order, she runs to the end of the room and down the stairs, calling to the chef below.

Nasreen asks after everyone's health: each person in Lakshmi's household and each one in mine. I assure them they're all fine. She tells me her daughter, Sophia, is back at college or she would have liked to see me again.

I've come to Agra this time for two reasons. To talk to Hazi and Nasreen about other essential oils like *mitti attar* that they might be able to produce at their factory and that I'd like to use in Sheela's fragrance line. After all, we have many more forgotten women to bring to life through perfume. Secondly, I want to explore the idea of training girls like Binu in the art of production, which would involve chemistry, math and instinct.

But first, I'm waiting for two other people to join me. They should be here shortly.

This time, the courtesans of the house are invited to join us for lunch. They sit in a semicircle around us.

Smiling, Nasreen says, "They want to ask you about Paris. They think you're very glamorous."

I laugh because *glamorous* isn't a word I would use to describe myself.

Hazi says, "And they also want to know how you got your green eyes." The courtesans nod enthusiastically.

I explain about Maa's eyes that were more of a cloudy blue and Lakshmi's eyes that turned out to be bluish-green, and mine, which have more green than blue. Our parents' families have always lived in North India, which means they might have mingled with Persians, Afghanis or even European traders, or perhaps they were just born with light eyes. Several women nod.

Just then, the first set of appetizers arrive. Tiny *pakoras* — vegetables and pieces of meat coated in batter and fried — are served with tamarind and cilantro chutneys. Then come platters of *aloo tikkas* and *papadum.*

Next, these elegant ladies, all in their silk finery and gold jewels, want to know what I do all day. I explain my profession. They seem puzzled. One of them asks, "In Paris, you sit in a lab all day in front of a desk? What about the Frenchmen and the romance and the wine and fancy food?"

That makes the group explode into mischievous laughter. I'm thinking of Pierre. How I may no longer be married to that particular Frenchman by the end of this year. I feel a sharp twinge in my chest.

"I see we have come at just the right time!"

It's Malik, and I jump up to greet him. I'm so happy to see him I have tears in my eyes. My cousin-brother comes around to greet first his hosts with a *salaam,* then takes me in his arms. I don't want to let go! Right behind him is Jiji. I pull her into a hug, too.

The courtesans are busy with their own exclamations and observations at the newly arrived guests. Malik is a little taller than me and still thin as a stalk of wheat. I've seen him devour food that would easily feed three people and never gain an ounce. His hair is thick and styled in layers so he looks more like an American than an Indian. He's wearing a crisp white shirt with the cuffs rolled back and tan trousers. Lakshmi, as usual, looks cool in a starched blue cotton sari with silver edging and a white blouse. Her hair is pinned on the back of her head, the bun surrounded with a jasmine *gajra*. She smells heavenly. She's brought several *gajras* to put on the wrists of our hosts and on mine. She folds her hands in *namaste* at everyone in the circle.

Malik puts a hand to his heart. "MemSahibs, I see that I am outnumbered." He takes out his handkerchief and waves it at the gathered assembly. "You win. Please take it all."

The courtesans tease him back — some sweetly, some lewdly — and break into laughter.

More food arrives as Malik and my sister settle down next to me.

I feel safe. I feel loved. I feel whole.

In the early evening, when the heat dies down, and before the *kotha*'s guests arrive for entertainment in the great hall, Hazi walks with us to the *attar* factory. I want Jiji and Malik to see what happens here, how the men gauge the temperature of the water, the distillation process and the logistics. I want them to smell the quality of the *mitti attar* and conjure ideas for other scents they might want to use in the herbal lotions that they're creating. I know Jiji favors the natural scents, but some of the remedies she makes could smell more appealing by adding a drop of *attar*. She and Malik thought it a splendid idea for their business, so she brought Malik with her.

As before, the men at the *attar* factory are going about their business silently. They glance and nod at us, then return to their work. Only when they need to ask a question or give a direct order do they talk. Sweat pours off their foreheads into their eyes as they slide more cow dung into the fires or place their hands on the copper vats or add more *mitti* to the pots.

"We only use two of the four ovens because that's all we need to produce right now," Hazi says placidly.

Malik watches the men. He looks at Hazi with a gesture that asks if he can talk to them. She gives her permission. I'm staying in the shelter of the overhang and trying to

461

stay cool with a handheld *khus* fan Hazi gave me. Lakshmi, more used to the heat, has covered her head with her *pallu* to keep the sun at bay.

Sudden motion at the factory rouses us. The girls are starting to arrive. They're wearing threadbare or worn petticoats and *salwar kameez*. Their feet are bare or in rubber *chappals*. They vary in age. The youngest must be ten. The oldest is perhaps eighteen. They stand in a huddle in front of Hazi.

Hazi claps her hands and calls the men over. The men are slow to respond. They're not sure what's going on. The ones who tend to the fires are reluctant to leave lest the liquid in the copper pots overheat.

"Come, come," Hazi says, encouraging them with a smile.

Slowly, the men form a group opposite the young girls. They're hunched over from squatting, tending to the ovens, carrying bags of soil. They're also dusty and barefoot.

"You work hard. These girls are here to help you. You are going to teach them everything you know."

The men eye the girls suspiciously.

Hazi fans her bejeweled hands up and down to allay their fears. "They're not going to take your jobs. They're going to help expand our factory so we have more jobs than before. *Aap samajh-jao?*"

There are a few grudging nods. One of the older men in a soiled *dhoti* and bush-shirt says, "They can't lift the heavy sacks we can. They can't push those big wheelbarrows." His bushy white eyebrows meet across the bridge of his nose. He hawks and spits on the ground to his left.

Calmly, Hazi says, "Three of them can lift the sack. Two of them can help with the wheelbarrows. One of them can pour more water in the big pots."

The men look at each other.

Hazi continues. "The girls can lighten your load. Let's try it, shall we? All of you go back to your places. When you need something, tell the girls closest to you." She claps her hands. "Girls, stand in clusters of two or three at each station. When Mister asks for something, get it for him."

The girls wag their heads *of course.*

The men run back to their work, checking temperature, water, fire. The girls separate into smaller groups, waiting. One of the men says, "Cow dung." The man who usually hauls the fuel starts to load his wheelbarrow with the cow dung. Two girls quickly use their hands to help. The man stops to stare at them. The girls work so fast the wheelbarrow is full in no time. They grab the handles from him, each girl taking one wooden arm, and push it to the waiting attendant at the oven. The wheelbarrow wobbled more than it would have had the man who normally does this job rolled it, but there was no denying the girls could do the job.

Another worker is rolling clay mixed with wool into two-inch-wide tubes. Two girls watch him flatten the clay into a ribbon and then roll it up. The smallest girl in the group takes his next tube of clay from him, flattens it with her slim fingers and coils it exactly as he did. Another girl follows suit. These clay ribbons will be used to seal the tops of the copper pots when the water and raw materials have been deposited inside.

Lakshmi, Malik and I watch as each girl takes on a helping task.

Like a theater director, Hazi claps her hands again. All the workers, including the girls, stop what they're doing to look at her. "Starting tomorrow, we're building ten new ovens. The copper pots will arrive in five days, when the ovens are dry. By then, each of these girls will be apprenticing with each of you. Because you are the masters of your craft. You have years of experience that you can pass on. *Theek hai?*"

The men, now more indifferent than resistant, incline their heads.

"*Shukriya.*" Hazi smiles widely.

Binu rushes in, bringing with her that restless energy I so admired the first time I met her. "I'm sorry I'm so late, *Ji,*" she says to Hazi. "I had to help with the food for tonight." To us, she beams a lovely smile. "This evening, it's all women. No men at the *haveli.*" Her eyes land on Malik in surprise, and she glances at me in confusion.

"Binu, this is my cousin-brother, Malik. And this is Lakshmi, my sister. I don't think you met her last time. He will be the only man at dinner tonight, if that's allowed."

She tilts her head side to side, smiling. Her two front teeth reveal themselves to be larger than the others. It's charming. She turns to Hazi. "How did they do, Mam?"

Hazi says, "You trained them well. *Shabash.*" To us, she says, "Binu recruited the girls and told them what to expect today."

Binu says, *"Hahn."*

"What did you tell them, Binu?" Malik asks. "They were very impressive."

"I told them to make themselves useful. Every girl knows how to do that," the girl says, with the confidence of a woman much older.

Walking back to the *kotha,* Hazi tells us that the girls will receive instruction in math and chemistry every afternoon, when it's too hot to work. They will be required to work only six hours a day to begin with and given food. Once their lessons stop, they will work a full eight hours.

I feel they should be in school. I glance at Lakshmi, and I know she's thinking the same thing. I look behind us at Malik, handing out toffees to the girls if they guess the answer to the questions he's asking.

"What's four plus four?"

"Eight!" they shout.

"What's the capital of India?"

"New Delhi!"

"Are you sure it's not Mumbai?"

They look at him uncertainly until they realize he's pulling their legs. "Toffee, please," they laugh.

"What's the farthest planet?"

Binu shouts her answer. "Pluto!" Then she holds out her hand for toffee.

Hazi, in her characteristic waddle, is walking a few steps ahead of Lakshmi and me. Without turning around, Hazi says in a quiet voice, "We will take as good care of these girls as we do our own. If we weren't taking them on, they might be on the street or married before they've even begun to

466

menstruate. We don't want that for any girl. So, given a choice, wouldn't you rather have them learning a skill and getting two hours of school a day?" It's as if she had heard our private thoughts.

Jiji asks, "Hazi-*ji*, will they be safe? From the men at the factory?"

The old courtesan chortles. "Binu will be in charge. She'll make sure. One of the reasons her mother sent her to us is because her own father was messing with her. Binu knifed him. Sliced his hand open. Her mother said she'd be safer with us. She is."

That evening, we feast on venison, butter eggplant, egg curry, *poha* potatoes, red lentil curry, tandoori chicken, onion *bhaji*, grilled *nan*, lamb *koftas*, coconut and spinach *paneer*. After dinner, the women dance and play their *sitar* and *tabla*. Binu's girls, as I've started calling them in my head, are transfixed by these exotic creatures. Their eyes keep roving around their opulent surroundings — the silk carpet, the feather bolsters, the gold bracelets and necklaces of the courtesans. I can tell they're never going to forget this night.

I savor the hours after dinner when Malik comes to our room and it's just the three of us, like it used to be. Malik sits on the floor against the wall. Jiji and I turn the *charpoy*

467

to face him and sit with our legs folded under us. Malik has a few toffees left in his pocket, and he tosses them one by one in the air, catching them neatly. We chat about the factory and Binu's girls. I ask after Malik's children, and the Healing Garden business (yes, that's what Lakshmi and Malik named their company).

"It's good to see you looking so good, *choti behen.* I was sorry to hear about Pierre. I always liked him," Malik says, tossing me a toffee.

"Me, too." I smile and unwrap the toffee, popping it in my mouth. "I think it was a long time coming, but I didn't know it. I kept thinking things would change." I smile. "I'm fine. Pierre's fine. The girls are fine. It will all be fine."

Malik asks, "Have you told the girls about Niki?"

I shake my head. This is the one thing I've shied away from. Once I tell Shanti and Asha that Niki is their brother, they will ask or want to ask a million questions. *You were only thirteen when you had a baby? How old was Papa then?* I picture the expression on their faces when I tell them Pierre isn't Niki's father. That will lead to more questions. *Why didn't Niki live with us? You just left him when he was born? Who took care of him?*

468

Why didn't you tell us about him before? Does Niki know we're his sisters? Are they old enough to understand my life as a girl in India? If they know how impulsively I followed my heart, will it make them want to do the same? Now that I'm a mother, I cringe at the thought of them falling for a boy who promises gold and only delivers tinsel. I don't relish being in Lakshmi's shoes all those years ago when she had to explain to me why Ravi was never going to admit that he was the father of my baby.

From the corner of my eye, I see Lakshmi lift her chin toward Malik. They often communicate this way, without words. He stands and walks to our *charpoy.* He sits next to me and gently turns my chin so I'm facing him. His eyes, the same black-brown as the bottom of the well I used to draw water from in Ajar, are full of compassion. He regards me for a moment before his forehead meets mine. It's as if he's giving me a blessing. Sweet, sweet Malik.

"*Choti behen,*" he says. "You will find a way."

My eyes fill. We sit like that for a while in silence, the rhythmic slapping of the courtesans' feet on the floor below the only sound.

After a moment, he gets up and goes back to sit against the wall opposite us.

Lakshmi takes the strand of jasmine out of her hair. She wraps it around my wrist. I take a whiff. Immediately, my body relaxes. Jiji folds my hands in hers. "These flowers release their most powerful scent after the sun sets. One chapter of your life is setting, and you are becoming your most powerful self."

But I'm not listening to her words. I'm looking at the flower bracelet she has fastened on my wrist. It's like the *Raksha Bandan* ceremony in India, where sisters tie an amulet around their brothers' wrists. Like I used to tie around Malik's wrist. It's a way of acknowledging that a girl's brother — or brother-figure — will protect her to the end of her days.

I sit up straight, looking from Malik to Lakshmi. "Jiji, can we go to the night market tonight?"

She looks surprised. "Why?"

"To buy *rakhi.*"

Malik squints. "I think they only sell them in August, when the festival starts."

Now, Lakshmi smiles. She knows what I'm thinking. "There *is* someone who might be willing to make us a few. Fancy ones using beads, tinsel and sequins." She grins.

Once again, we make our way to Hari's stall.

An age-old bonding tradition in India, massaging coconut oil into the scalp is believed to activate the crown shakra and calm the mind.

Paris
August 1975
Niki will arrive in Paris tomorrow to get settled before starting his first year at the École in two weeks. Florence will drive the girls and me in her Peugeot to pick him up at the airport. All week long, Shanti and Asha have been drawing the favorite things they did with him during his first visit to Paris. They stacked the drawings together and punched holes along the edge. Then they threaded a bright green ribbon through the holes to create a "book" for him.

It's my week with Shanti and Asha in the apartment. The place smells of the coconut oil I put in their hair this morning. We washed it off this evening with shampoo, and their hair is still a little damp. They want me to braid their hair so they can sleep on it. In the morning, it will be wavy, like the actress Isabelle Adjani's. Posters of her latest film, *The Story of Adele H,* are plastered all over Paris.

My hands are clammy. I've put off telling them about Niki as long as possible, and it's not fair to them or to him. He knows they're his sisters; surely they deserve to know they have a brother.

I'm sitting on Shanti's bed to do her hair. I've finished with Asha's. With her hair in two braids, Asha looks no older than five. She's watching us as she sits cross-legged on the bed in her pajamas.

My pulse races. *It's now or never.* I can't bear to look at either of my daughters, so I focus on Shanti's braid. "You should ask Niki about all the Indian festivals he'll be missing while he's here."

"What festivals?" Asha wants to know.

"Oh, there are so many. There's Independence Day on August 15. And there's the Birthday of Krishna. There's a festival just for women called Teej. To celebrate the start of the monsoon rains. Auntie Lakshmi and I would go to women's houses to decorate their hands with henna the day before."

"I don't like it when it rains. Why would you celebrate it?" Shanti asks.

"The monsoons mean crops will be watered — they'll grow and feed lots of people. Flowers will bloom. Everything will turn green. And the air will smell of rain. That's the scent I brought back with me from Agra, remember?" The girls had a chance to sniff the new vial of *mitti attar* I brought back from Agra in May.

Asha nods. "I liked it." She has forgiven Pierre and me for upending her world. She told me a few weeks ago that she decided not very much had changed, after all. "It's just that I miss you when it's Papa's turn to be with us, and I miss Papa when he's not here," she said.

Now I tell them, "There's one festival I always looked forward to celebrating with your uncle Malik."

Shanti pipes up. "Which one?" Malik is one of her favorite people in the world.

"It's called *Raksha Bandhan.*"

The girls try to pronounce the Hindi words, smiles turning into giggles when they can't.

"That festival is just for brothers and sisters. Each girl ties a bracelet made of string around her brother's wrist."

473

Asha wrinkles her nose. "A bracelet for a boy?"

"It's actually called a *rakhi.* When a girl puts it on her brother, it means the brother will protect her for the rest of her life."

Shanti says, "Forever?"

"Forever." I finish her braids. She leans backward until her head is in my lap. "Want to see what a *rakhi* looks like?" I ask her.

Shanti quickly sits up straight. *"Oui!"*

Asha claps her hands.

I run to my room, the girls following on my heels. From my purse, I extract a paper packet with the amulets Hari's factory made for me (they make them in July for the upcoming festival, but he had two made especially for me in May). The thick string is woven in green and red threads. In the center is a large round star made of gold tinsel. Crystal beads decorate the middle of the star.

The girls examine the amulets as if they're looking at precious jewelry. "Wow! Is it expensive, *Maman*?"

"Non. But it's very important."

Shanti scratches her cheek. "What if we don't have a brother to give it to?"

My heart speeds up. *Tell them! What are you so afraid of?* "You tie it on a cousin or the closest thing you have to a brother. Like

474

I did with Malik."

The girls consider this. They look at each other, as if silently conferring which of their classmates they should give a *rakhi* to. Shanti says, "Like Niki?"

"Yes. Like Niki. Only —" *Say it!*

Now the girls turn to me, eyebrows raised, waiting.

Do it! I feel faint. *Oh, don't stop now!* My throat is so dry. "Shanti, do you remember the day you asked if you could be a sister to Niki? Because he didn't have any sisters?"

Shanti nods.

"Well, he does." I swallow. "*You* are his sisters. *He* is your brother." My heartbeat is so loud I wonder if the girls can hear it.

Asha narrows her eyes, as if this is a trick. "No, he's not."

My legs are trembling. I sit down on my bed before I fall. "Come here. Sit."

The girls glance at each other. They approach the bed slowly, eyeing me as if I've suddenly grown two heads.

When they're comfortably settled on the bed Pierre and I used to share, I reach for their hands. They're warm. They're soft. They're trusting. I feel calmer now. I begin.

"When I was thirteen, I had a little boy."

They did ask a lot of questions. There were things I couldn't explain because they're not old enough. But they understood the important bit. What won them over was the fact that Niki, a boy they adored, was really their brother. And their brother would be here tomorrow.

At the airport, Shanti and Asha squeal in delight when Niki comes out of the terminal. They run to hug him. He laughs and lets them wrap themselves around him. His eyes seek mine. I'm standing beside Florence. He smiles. He kisses Florence on both cheeks, then does the same to me.

I whisper in his ear, "Ask the girls what they brought for you."

He does.

Shanti's face flushes. She looks at me, and I nod in encouragement. Asha doesn't hesitate. She pulls her amulet from her coat pocket. "We're supposed to put it on you, *mon frère.*" Then she grins and ties her *rakhi* to his right wrist.

Shanti looks up at Niki solemnly. She ties her amulet around his left wrist. She holds his hand. She looks so serious when she says, "I'm glad that if I had to have a brother, it's you."

His mouth forms an "O." He looks at me as if to ask, *They know?*

I wag my head from side to side, Indian-style.

Until that day, I had never seen a young man cry.

And just like that, Niki is no longer a secret.

Often used as a base note, cinnamon oil is added to ingredients like coffee and grapefruit to create an intensely masculine fragrance.

Paris
June 1980

The seventies are over. Gone is the long, unkempt hair. The style now is a little shorter on the sides, longer on top — for both men and women. Jackets are boxy, made more intimidating by giant shoulder pads. Women's earrings are outsized, too. Pants with front pleats are the rage.

Today, Niki graduates from the École des Beaux-Arts. No one knows it yet, but it's also my graduation day. My obligation to remain in Paris and complete Sheela's fragrance line ends here. We've finished the formulas and the product extensions — *eau de cologne, eau de parfum, eau fraîche,* body lotion, body powder — for the fifth and final fragrance.

In a month, I leave for Shimla. I'll decide, later, where I want to settle. I'm taking the girls with me for the summer. Pierre approves. He and his new girlfriend are off to Cyprus in August for their holidays, and his work life is exploding, so he will have little time to spend with Shanti and Asha this month and next.

I can hardly believe that Shanti is almost fifteen. Her brown hair is darker than it was when she was little. She's as tall as I am with the same slight build. Still as serious as she was as a girl, she is easier to be around now that she's more confident. She likes traveling with me on my business trips, and I like having her there. So many memories of childhood come back when I'm in India, and I love sharing them with Shanti, who loves India as much as I do. When we go to the markets, I tell her about *behl,* the custard apple fruit I love but can't find in France. We search for a beautiful quilted *rajai* to replace the one Lakshmi gave me years ago. (That one is fraying and shrinking with each wash; it barely covers the bed anymore.) I show Shanti how to determine the quality of woolen shawls hand-embroidered by the Himalayan people. No two designs are alike. On these visits, she asks a lot of questions about India's history and politics and people. She tries out her rudimentary Hindi, charming Hazi and Nasreen and the other courtesans when she accompanies me to Agra.

When she comes to India with us, Asha prefers to stay in Shimla, where she can play with her cousin Rekha. My younger daughter loves Madho Singh and Dr. Jay and the sheep in the hills and Lakshmi's horse. I usually send her there for a portion of the summer.

Today, however, we've all gathered together in Paris for Niki's graduation from the École des Beaux-Arts. Lakshmi, Dr. Jay, Malik, Nimmi, Rekha and Chullu have planned a tour of France around it. The girls and I will travel with them.

The graduation reception is being held in the small interior courtyard of the centuries-old school. Kanta and Manu are here. As are Florence and Pierre.

Florence had a new navy blue suit tailor-made for Niki's big day, and I must say he looks perfectly dashing. He's twenty-four this year. As tall as Ravi was when I met him. He has thrived in Paris. He has French friends, Algerian friends, Nigerian friends, and many of them are girls. And, living with Florence for the past five years, he's eaten well, taking to French food better than I ever did. Of course Florence is here; she wouldn't miss his graduation if her house were on fire. Now she tells everyone proudly that she has *three* grandchildren.

Five years ago, I finally called Kanta. I wanted to tell her about Sheela and the École des Beaux-Arts opportunity for Niki. It was awkward from my side, but not from hers. I also wanted to express how grateful I was that she and Manu stepped in when they did to raise Niki. It gave me the opportunity for an education and a more adventurous future. She, on the other hand, saw Niki as a precious gift she and I shared. "He has two mothers, Radha," she said. "I've never forgotten that."

She'd hesitated when I told her about Niki's pursuit of a career in art. "But how will he earn a living? How will we find a suitable partner for him? Will any family want a son-in-law who can't support a wife?"

"Kanta Auntie, every family wants a well-educated, worldly son-in-law. That's what Niki is. Does he need to follow the old ways of thinking when the world doesn't? I didn't. Lakshmi didn't. And we're doing fine. With all his contacts now, he'll always be able to work in art galleries or represent other artists or do something else with his talent. What if he ends up with a wife who makes all the money and lets him paint all day?" I teased.

Kanta groaned. I knew what she was thinking: *But you don't live in India, Radha. We do. And people will talk. People will judge.*

"Let him be who he wants to be, Auntie," I pleaded.

Who's to say Niki will or won't go back to India? He's produced some splendid work here at the Beaux-Arts, and it's on display for all to see. The graduating students showcase the best of their work, and attendees are allowed to bid on pieces they admire. Most of the art will be purchased by the student's family, who will hang it on their living room wall, a proud declaration of their progeny's talent.

But I've seen several people stopping to admire Niki's paintings this afternoon. They're in the style of the late Indian-Hungarian painter Amrita Sher-Gil, a former graduate of this school. One winter semester, Niki traveled to South India, where I've never even been, to see the landscape and the people she painted. He came back with renewed energy and completed ten canvases in a month. He talked about color, light, composition, echoes of that same conversation between Niki and Gérard I heard five years ago. (Gérard is here today, too, talking to some of the instructors who used to be his classmates years ago.) The glow on Niki's face when he talks about art is similar to the one on Lakshmi's when she talks about her healing plants. And I imagine it's similar to how bright my eyes become when I talk about fragrances to clients.

It's a hot June day, a little muggy. Foreheads glisten with perspiration. The men are wearing suit jackets, continually adjusting their ties. The midday sun is prompting many to fan themselves with the graduation program leaflets.

Asha taps me on the shoulder. She's a few inches shorter than me. Her leonine eyes glow against her golden skin. Her hair is lighter than Shanti's (Florence told me Pierre's hair was much lighter when he was a child). The effect is that of a gentle lioness. Shanti is attractive, but Asha is exotic. She's only thirteen. Whenever she's with me, I want to shield her from the stares of older boys.

"Chérie?" I brush back her bangs, so much like Mathilde's.

"Those people are looking at Niki's painting of me."

She points with her chin at a small group gathered around one of his larger canvases. The painting is of Asha and also not of her. It's the blend of her likeness with something from Niki's imagination that makes it unique. In the painting the subject stands close to the viewer, her arms leaning on the stone railing of one of the Paris *ponts,* her body turned so that we see her in profile. She looks pensive. The view beyond is of the gray-green water of the Seine, a *bateau-mouche* and a few blurred Haussmann buildings in the distance. Niki plays with flat, muted colors but manages to make his subjects come to life even without the brushstrokes of the Impressionists. It's one of my favorite paintings, and I'm hoping to buy it for Asha's birthday.

I look to see who else is interested in Niki's painting of Asha. A slim woman in a sleeveless linen shift. Large sunglasses. Black hair pulled back into a low ponytail.

It's Sheela.

With her are two girls. The younger one looks to be around ten. The older girl is perhaps the same age as Shanti. Sheela's daughters both share her dark hair and light olive skin. And, I imagine, Ravi's coloring as well.

We never drew up a legal contract for Niki's education, the sort the UK law firm promised. But Sheela has kept her side of the bargain, paying his tuition on time every year.

She knew that in order to keep me working as master perfumer on her product line, she couldn't stray from our handshake agreement. The first scent I created, which we renamed Victorine — per Niki's suggestion — has been very successful, especially with the middle- to upper-middle-income women. The second, third and fourth fragrances, in as many successive years, hit the international market at a time when excess was coming into vogue, and women bought the entire line at exorbitant prices. The fifth and final fragrance is being released this fall. Michel developed the extensions for each line. He and I have come to enjoy working together. He's less formal than he used to be, and I'm not wary of him any longer. He's been an enormous help with my chemistry homework and spent many hours tutoring me for tests.

Sheela's company, Remember Me, inspired a graceful, haunting advertising campaign. The ads for each "forgotten woman" featured an actress coming out of the famous painting and into the life she held dear. Haunting melodies by international singers were used for each television commercial. Every product in the Remember Me line has been successful, which reflects well on the House of Yves. We receive more — and more profitable — pieces of business every year. Yves added an additional master perfumer to the staff.

Delphine is retiring this year and moving to Spain with her longtime partner, Solange (who knew she had a partner? None of us, not even Celeste). As a parting gift, Delphine left me her antique perfume organ. I accepted it with reverence and a tearful embrace. If it imparts even a fraction of the professional flair it's provided Delphine all these years, I'll be a lucky perfumer! She also told Yves to promote me to master perfumer, something he didn't want to agree to. He wants to hire a man instead. But whether or not I have the title, I have the experience. And I'm known in the industry. I can go anywhere with my skills.

Now, I approach Sheela. She removes her sunglasses and smiles at me, the corners of her eyes crinkling.

"You came," I say.

She gestures to the painting of Asha. "He has a gift. You recognized it long ago."

I look at the woman whom I used to

consider my adversary. For the past five years, we've been partners in shining a light on women who deserve to be remembered and in educating the boy who brought us together. If not exactly friends, we are allies against the Singhs.

"I see you got my letter?" I say as I turn my attention to the two girls, one of whom resembles Sheela, the other favors Ravi.

"I wasn't sure, at first, whether to bring them. Then it seemed like the most natural thing." Sheela moves to stand between her daughters. "Girls, meet Radha. She's the perfumer who's been designing my fragrances. This is Rita. This is Leila." The girls smile shyly at me and mumble hello. They're dressed in matching ivory linen dresses as elegant as their mother's. I tell them how lovely they look.

I take a breath and ask Sheela, "Ready?"

She looks nervous. I take her hand in mine. She squeezes it. She nods.

I look around for Niki. I spot him with a group of his friends and call to him.

My firstborn approaches us with a brilliant smile. Sheela gasps. It's the first time she's met him in person. I imagine she's seeing the same thing I am: young Ravi Singh, a polo player who once dreamed of becoming an actor, at a time when his entire life was ahead of him.

Niki looks at us in anticipation, his peacock eyes luminous. My handsome boy.

"Niki, I'd like you to meet Sheela Sharma, your benefactor."

He can't hide his surprise any more than he can hide his delight at discovering who sponsored his education at the École; he'd been asking me for five years. He shakes Sheela's hand heartily, thanking her for the scholarship.

I know what's about to come next, and I want to give Sheela and Niki their privacy.

I take a step back, then another. I turn away.

As I walk slowly toward the three women who have been observing us — Lakshmi, Kanta and Florence — I hear Sheela ask, "You prefer Niki to Nikhil?"

Now I hear Niki say, "Niki, please."

"Well, Niki, I'd like you to meet your sisters Rita and Leila."

Epilogue

Shimla
May 1981

There's no easy way to justify a life taken. The Himalayan white-bellied musk deer lends his life to the creation of musk, the scent used in so many fragrances around the world. Sandalwood oil, a popular base note we used at the House of Yves, is produced by chopping down entire forests that take up to sixty years to grow. The forests are not being replenished. Until I started working with scents, I'd never given much thought to where *agarbatti,* incense sticks, came from. The agarwood tree becomes infected by a fungus, occurring naturally, that produces an aromatic resin used in perfumes. In India, whenever I walked past a temple or mosque or a shop with a small *puja,* I would feel soothed by the scent of incense, never once calculating the cost of that luxury. Agarwood trees are dying out. Same with the depletion of vetiver grass from India, the scent I wrestled with in Delphine's formula years ago and which led to my work on the Olympia project.

During my first five years at the House of Yves, I was only concerned with blending the right formulas. But during the last five years, since Pierre started taking care of the girls every other week, I was able to spend my evenings finishing my degree in chemistry. That's when it hit me: companies were creating molecules in labs that could simulate the natural scents of musk, agarwood, vetiver, for mass production, but why did we have to rely on synthetics for small-scale production? Could I approximate the intoxicating fragrance of musk using plants found in the Himalayas? Or devise an organic method to create the essence of a raw scent material? I loved watching the workers at Hazi's factory making *mitti attar,* doing everything by hand. No machinery involved. I wanted to work like that, too.

Jiji and Malik and Nimmi's business allowed me to realize my dream. With the plants they've been propagating in their greenhouse to produce Lakshmi's lavender skin creams, vetiver cooling water and healing hair oil, I had a treasure chest of new ingredients to work with.

So I came back to Shimla. To live and work. The city has grown since I last lived here, but the majestic pine forests and the snowcapped peaks in the distance never waver.

I bought a cottage not far from Lakshmi with the money Pierre gave me to buy out my share of the Paris apartment. There are three bedrooms here, one for me, one for the girls when they visit and a guest bedroom for Florence or whoever else wants to come and stay awhile. Shanti is now sixteen. She elected to spend her last few years of high school at Auckland House School in Shimla. I'd told her so much about my boarding school over the years that she wanted the experience of going there, too. Her roommate is from Dubai, and Shanti finds her fascinating. Maman, *did you know Dubai is planning on building the largest flower garden in the desert?* Maman, *Kayla's family burns incense using charcoal instead of lighting* agarbatti! It makes me feel good to know she has a close friend, someone she can talk to about things she's not willing to share with her mother.

Mathilde was that kind of friend for me. Despite her betrayal, I miss her. I feel a sense of loss when I think of her, but

Mathilde hasn't responded to my entreaties for us to make amends, and I haven't pushed it. I've come to think that some people are meant to be in our lives for a certain length of time and not a moment more. Mathilde may have been one of them.

My relationship with Pierre is like that, but since we share children, we can never be completely divorced in the emotional sense of the word. For the sake of the girls, we do our best to get along with one another. If we're all in Paris, we have dinner with Pierre and his girlfriend.

Asha decided to stay in Paris to complete her schooling. *All my friends are here,* Maman. I miss her and send her care packages once a week with things I know she'll like from India: a sandalwood comb, butter toffees, a hand-embroidered shirt in fine muslin. She stays with Florence now that Pierre and his girlfriend have moved into the Saint-Germain apartment. Shanti and I call her and Florence every Sunday after the rates go down. Once the girls are done chatting, I often stay on the line with Florence. Funny that I think of her as more my *saas* now than when I was married. She's always curious about the new experiments I'm conducting, and she asks thoughtful questions that make me think of new directions to explore.

Niki is now living at Kanta's family cottage in Shimla. If he is at our house for Sunday dinner, he will want to talk to Florence, too. It's only because of Florence and the five years he lived with her while attending the École des Beaux-Arts that he was able to follow the instruction in French. She was an excellent — and strict — teacher, not letting him draw or paint until they'd finished their French lessons. Not only did the board of the École buy Niki's painting of Asha (which she loves to show off to her friends in Paris!), but he received a *Prix de Dessin* monetary award that bought him a year in which to decide what he wanted to do next. Kanta and Manu want the decision to be his own. They come as often as they can to Shimla to visit with all of us.

For Asha's summer holidays, Florence is bringing her to Shimla. It will be my *saas*'s first time in India, a country she never wanted to step foot in before. But as she says now, "I have three grandchildren who are Indian. What's a *grand-mère* to do?" I get a lump in my throat when I hear her include Niki in the mix, and I'm grateful to her. I think she's excited about the prospect of exploring the buildings here in Shimla left behind by the British: Christ Church and the Viceregal Lodge, the Oberoi Cecil hotel, the State Library, the Gaiety Theater. I've promised to take her and the girls to a production at the Gaiety unless the restoration work is underway, which the city keeps threatening to start every few years. I've also told them to be prepared to see a film crew in action while they're here; so many Indian movies are shot in and around the foothills of Shimla.

Another visitor I'm expecting this summer is Michel. I can't believe how badly I misjudged him. He was so generous with his time and patient with his teaching when he tutored me for my chemistry degree. Sometimes, he'd join the girls, Niki and me for a weekend outing. Turns out, he's been divorced for years. No children. My girls like him. He says he's coming to check out my scent lab here in Shimla, but I sense he may be looking for more. I'm not sure I'm ready yet, but, these days, I'm open to all manner of possibilities.

Of course I see a lot of my sister and Dr. Jay. And Malik and Nimmi. On her visits, Asha loves spending time with her cousins (as we've all come to call them), Rekha and Chullu. All three are crazy about Lakshmi's horse and take turns riding him.

Together, Jiji and Nimmi organize the

Healing Garden and the greenhouse: selecting the plants, tending to them, cultivating the soil. Malik handles the business end: sales, distribution, coordinating the schedule of students who want to learn from the Healing Garden. I'm the chemist. I tinker. Mostly on paper, with different formulas. Once I learn about a new scent in the Healing Garden, my nose remembers it and I can recreate it in my mind as I design a fragrance for her products. I had Delphine's vintage perfume organ shipped out here. If I put my nose to the mahogany, I can still smell her Gitanes. As I create, I imagine hearing the click of her heels, the rasp of her voice and her *bien faits.* I smile.

Last month, Niki was milling around the Healing Garden (much bigger than it used to be), sketching, and he showed me his lovely pencil drawing of a chrysanthemum. I showed it to Jiji, and she asked if he would create labels for her products, featuring the plants and flowers used for each. He was so excited he went to work right away. I think he's created nine product labels so far.

As busy as she is, Lakshmi always makes time for me. We take a walk several mornings a week, when our breath makes clouds in the air, and the trees sprinkle their dew on our heads. We walk quickly to warm up, then slow down to gaze at the purple horizon, the smoke from the morning's cooking fires layering the sky with another pastel hue.

Today, on our walk, Lakshmi tells me, "Jay was talking last night about getting another horse for the kids."

"A bit extravagant, isn't it?"

She waves her hand in front of her face. "*Koi baat nahee.* Jay discovered the cause of a chronic infection in one of his patients, and the gentleman is so pleased he wants to gift him a horse. Of course Jay isn't going to accept the gift. He's going to buy it and ask the man to gift the money to the Community Clinic."

"Hand it to Dr. Jay! Everybody wins."

"Including the horse! Jay's patient is almost three hundred pounds. I imagine the horse will be relieved."

I laugh, picturing an exceedingly overweight man on a skinny horse. I take Jiji's arm in mine. "Hazi called me the other day."

"*Accha?*"

"She says her factory just signed on two more clients. Big firms from New York. They want to buy the *mitti* and other *attars* the factory is producing. Apparently, the Remember Me fragrance line has catapulted her factory into the big-business category.

And guess who's heading up the expanded operation?"

Lakshmi turns to me with a smile. "Binu?"

I grin. *"Hahn."* That girl is even more capable than I'd thought. She'll end up running the entire factory someday. "Binu has been feeding her entire family on what she makes and even sent her younger brothers and sisters to school."

"Shabash, choti behen." She squeezes my arm.

At first, the men of the factory were suspicious of the girls, afraid that their jobs were being taken away. After all, they had families to feed, children to send to school. As they began to see more and more ovens being added to the factory to produce different kinds of *attars,* they realized they needed the extra hands. Being young and full of energy, the girls assumed the additional tasks. Grudgingly, the men had to recognize the value of the labor they provided. The girls were lively and joked and teased each other and the men all day long.

I tell Jiji, "Hazi said that if she ever catches one of the men asking the girls to make them chai or go to the store for *beedis,* she docks his pay."

Lakshmi chuckles. "Did I ever tell you Hazi's nickname?"

"What nickname?"

"When I first arrived at the *kotha,* they called her Begum Hazi to her face, but behind her back, they called her Begum *Hathi.*"

"Madam Elephant?"

She raises an eyebrow. "*Hahn.* And they weren't talking about her size."

I chuckle.

"Arré!"

We break apart and look behind us to see Malik jogging up the hill, waving his hands. He has a loose, athletic stride. When he reaches us, he's breathing a little heavily. At this altitude, even the slightest exercise can elevate heart rates.

"Niki's been looking for you!" he manages to say between breaths. "Big news! He's been selected for the art restoration project in Italy!"

Jiji and I look at each other.

I say, "He didn't tell me he was applying. Did he tell you?"

"No," Jiji says.

"Who cares who he told? He wants to learn how to restore frescoes and paintings to their original state. After Italy, his plan is to come back to India to restore the art on historic sites." Malik looks triumphant. "You know what that means?"

498

"He's not going to America!" And just like that, I know I did right by my firstborn. I couldn't raise him, but I've been able to guide him to his passion. First a degree from the École. Then convincing Kanta to let him pursue what he loves. I'll never hear Niki call me Mummi — Kanta earned that title — but in my heart, I'll always be his *other* mother. And he will always be *my* Crown Prince. My heart swells. *I brought this amazing creature into this world. I did that.* I caress the amulet in my jacket pocket. It's time I gave it to Niki.

Lakshmi claps her hands. "Wait till the Singhs find out!"

Malik links one arm in Lakshmi's and one arm in mine. We begin strolling again. "But *chup-chup*. You didn't hear it from my lips. Let Niki tell you at dinner tonight. Nimmi is making a feast. Madho Singh keeps shouting for *rabri,* so she's making that for dessert. Kanta and Manu are also coming over." He casts a sly grin at Jiji. "You're not the only artist in the family anymore, Auntie-Boss!"

Jiji arches an eyebrow. "But I am the *only* Auntie-Boss."

"And you will be Auntie-Boss to one more still," Malik says, his face glowing.

Lakshmi stops walking. Since our arms

are still linked, it brings Malik and me to an abrupt halt.

My sister's face is full of wonder. "Is that why Nimmi has been making *rabri* so often? I thought she was doing it for Madho Singh."

Malik laughs. "That parakeet knew before any of us! Maybe he knows if it's a boy or a girl."

I pull his ear gently. "Well, if it's a girl, Malik, I expect you to name her Radha."

"So now I have *two* Auntie-Bosses?" He shakes his head. *"A wise man to the rest of the world is a nobody at home."*

"Do you hear someone talking, Radha?" Lakshmi asks me.

"Only the wind, Jiji. Only the wind," I answer.

Malik's laughter echoes in the blue valley as he escorts the two of us down the hill toward home.

GLOSSARY OF TERMS

À bon chat, bon rat: two can play at that game

À ton santé aussi: to your health also

Aap samajh-jao?: do you understand?

Aaraam se: easy does it

Aarti: ceremony in which a metal plate containing a sweet, an oil lamp and incense is offered in love to an image of a god or a person

Abhee: right now

Accha: okay

Agarbatti: incense

Ajwain: seed used in Indian cooking, similar to caraway or cumin

Aloo parantha: whole wheat flatbread stuffed with spiced, mashed potatoes

Amreeka: America

Angreji: English people

Arrete: stop

Arrondissement: administrative division; Paris has twenty-one arrondissements

Atta: dough

Attar: essential oil

Aur kuch?: what else?

Avec plaisir: with pleasure

Ayah: nanny

Bacalau: cod fish

Badmaash: hooligan

Baingan burta: curry of mashed, cooked eggplant, garlic, tomatoes

Bakhoor: wood chips soaked in essential oil and perfume

Bakwas: nonsense

Balayage à coton: highlights painted onto strips of hair

Baniyas: Hindu caste of merchants and money-lenders

Banlieu: suburbs

Barbichette: fun children's game played by holding the chin of your opponent and singing a rhyme until one person smiles or laughs

Bateau-mouche: an open excursion tourist boat along the river Seine

Beedis: hand-rolled thin cigar; the poor man's cigarette

Begum: a well-to-do Muslim woman

Behenchod: sister-fucker

Berimbau: single-string instrument with roots in Africa

Besan laddu: a sweet made with chickpea flour

Beti/beta: daughter/son (affectionate term)

Bhai Saab: sir

Bhaiya: brother (affectionate term)

Bhaji: spicy vegetable fritter

Bibliothèque: library

Bien fait: well done

Bien sûr: of course

Bilkul: absolutely

Biryani: spicy rice with vegetables, nuts, saffron and sometimes fish or meat

Bon voyage: have a good trip

Bonjour: hello, good morning

Bonne nuit: good evening

Bonsoir: good night

Boteh: a leaf shaped like a mango

Bouquinistes: booksellers

Brut: ugly

Burfi: a sweet made with milk and flavored with cashews or cardamom or nuts

Burri nazar: evil eye

C'est ça: that is so

C'est la comble: that beats everything! That's the last straw!

Ça m'est égal: it's all the same to me; it's fine

Ça va?: okay?

Café au lait: coffee with milk

Chai: tea made with spices

Chai-walla: tea seller

Chameli: sweet-smelling jasmine flower

Chappals: sandals

Chappatis: flatbread made with whole wheat flour

Charpoy: low-slung bed made of tightly woven jute and wooden legs

Chef: boss

Cher: expensive; dear

Chérie: dear (term of endearment)

Chocolat chaud: hot chocolate

Chole: garbanzo bean curry

Choti behen: little sister

Chou-chou: cabbage (term of endearment)

Chowkidar: gateman; caretaker

Chunni: gauzy, light scarf loosely draped across the shoulders or over the head

Chup-chup: quiet, shh!

Comment allez-vous?: how are you?

Comprenez?: understand?

Confit de canard: slow-cooked duck

Connard: bastard

Coq au vin: French chicken stew cooked in red wine, bacon and onions

D'accord: all right

Dal: lentil curry

Désolé: I'm sorry

Dhotis: white cloth, about seven yards long, worn by Indian men around their legs

Diya: small clay vessel with ghee and cotton

wick, used for festivals and prayer

Doodh-walla: milk seller

Doucement: slowly

Dupatta: large gauzy shawl worn by women over the head and around the shoulders

École maternelle: French nursery school for children three to six years old

Écoute: listen

Église: church

Entrez: enter

Et bien: so

Étrange: foreign

Exactement: exactly

Faux pas: socially improper or embarrassing remark

Félicitations: congratulations

Fesse: butt

Filmi: movie

Financiers: dome-shaped French cookie with a cake-like texture

Gajra: scented flower garland worn in women's hair

Gardien de musée: museum guard

Genial: terrific

Ghee: clarified butter used in Indian cooking

Godown: warehouse

Goondas: thugs

Grand-mère: grandmother

Grand-père: grandfather

Gunghroos: musical anklet with bells often worn in classical *kathak* dance

Haath phools: jewelry worn on the hand, spanning from the fingers to the wrist

Hahn: yes

Hai Bhagwan/Ram: oh, god!

Haih-nah?: isn't it so?

Haveli: family compound

Herbes: herbs

Hijra: eunich, intersex person

Ici: here

Inde: India

J'adore: I love

J'arrive: I'm coming

Jalebi: fried sweet filled with syrup

Jardin: garden

Jasmine sambac: strongly scented white flowers that open only at night

Je m'appele: my name is

Jeu de bagues: game of rings played on a carousel

Jharus: long-whiskered brooms

Ji: the addition of "ji" to a person's name (e.g., Ganeshji, Gandhiji) accords them respect and reverence

Jiji: sister

Juti: shoes

Kabaddi: team sport where players try to tag the opposing team's players without getting tagged themselves

Kaisa ho?: how are you?

Kajal: kohl, a black eyeliner

Karala: bitter melon vegetable

Kathak: a classical dance form from North India

Katham: it's over; the end

Kheer: a dessert similar to rice pudding

Khus: a tall, bushy grass ("vetiver" in English)

Khush raho: be happy

Kofta: a round savory made of chickpea flour or meat

Koi baat nahee: it's no big deal; no problem

Korma: dish made of meat or vegetables braised in yogurt

Kotha: a house where courtesans live and entertain

Kurta: long tunic worn over leggings/pants

La crevette: the shrimp

Le lo: take it

Lehengas: floor-length skirts elaborately decorated with beads

Les Nez: master perfumers

Magnifique: magnificent

Mais: but

Makki ki roti: flatbread made with corn

Maman: mom

Mari américain: American husband

Masala dal: spicy lentils

Mec: a guy

Mehndi: henna

MemSahibs: the respectful address for "ma'am"

Menace: malice

Menthe: mint

Mera joota hai japani: my shoes are Japanese

Merci: thanks

Mes poussins: my little chicks (term of endearment)

Mitti: soil, dirt

Mogra: species of Indian jasmine

Mon coeur: my heart (term of endearment)

Monteau: coat

Moules frites: popular french dish of mussels and fries

Musée: museum

Mutki: clay vessel in which water is kept cool

Mutlub: meaning

N'est-ce pas?: isn't that so?

Nahee: no

Namaste: Indian greeting made by bringing both palms together just below the neck

Nan: flatbread made with yogurt

Nani: grandmother

Ne me quitte pas: don't leave me

Nimbu pani: sugared lime water

On avance?: shall we proceed?

On se vend comme des pains!: it will sell like crazy!

Oud: resin of the agarwood tree used in

perfume, popular in the Middle East

Paan: tobacco- and betelnut-laced paste wrapped in a leaf

Padukas: shoes consisting of only a sole and a knob between the big and second toe

Pakora: fried savory, often filled with vegetables like potato or onion

Palais: palace

Palak paneer: vegetable dish made with spinach and Indian cheese

Pallu: the decorated end of a sari, worn over the shoulder

Pani-walla: seller of water and soft drinks

Papadum: a crispy savory made with chickpea flour and fried over open flame

Parfum: perfume

Parfumerie: a shop that sells perfume

Pas du tout: not at all

Pas grave: no big deal

Peepal: tree with large leaves that are dried and used as a canvas for oil painting

Petite puce: little flea (affectionate term)

Pranama: the action of reverential bowing in front of elders, touching of feet

Pressing: laundry cleaner

Puja: ceremonial worship and offering to an image of a god

Pundit: priest

Puri: a round fried bread

Qu'est-ce qu'il ya?: what is it?

Rabri: a creamy dessert made from milk

Raga: a musical pattern for improvisation, part of a longer piece of music

Rajai: a quilted coverlet for a bed

Rajma masala: popular curry made with kidney beans

Rakhi: amulet

Regardes!: look!

Reine: queen

Rogan josh: popular lamb curry

Roti: flatbread made with a mixture of wheat and white flour

Ruh gulab: essence of rose

S'il vous plaît: please

Saag paneer: vegetable dish made with leafy greens and Indian cheese

Saas: mother-in-law (when addressing her, the daughter-in-law calls her saasuji)

Sacré!: damn! (shortened version of sacré bleu!)

Salaam: a greeting, in Arabic

Salade niçoise: popular salad with tuna, hard-boiled eggs and anchovies

Salmon en papillote: salmon cooked and served in parchment paper

Salwar kameez: tunic and pant set worn by women

Shabash!: bravo! Well done!

Sharab: liquor

Shukriya: thank you, in Hindi

Subjis: spicy, cooked Indian vegetables

Tabla: a drumlike instrument played with fingers and palms of the hand

Thali: a brass or steel dinner plate containing many different dishes

Theek hai: all right, or are you all right? if asked as a question

Tikka: a mark on the forehead made of fragrant paste like sandalwood or vermilion

Til ki laddu: sweet made of sesame seeds

Tonga: horse carriage

Toor dal: a variety of yellow lentil

Toujours: always

Trop cher: very expensive

Tu m'as manqué: I missed you

Un, deux, trois soleil: popular French playground game

Une amie folle: a crazy friend

Urdu: language closely related to Hindi containing many Persian and Arabic words

Voleuse: thief

Zuroor: absolutely

Zut or Zut alors!: damn!

ACKNOWLEDGMENTS

I often tell readers it takes a village to bring a book into being. My charmed village includes the ever-gracious, whip-smart agent Margaret Sutherland Brown of Folio Literary, my insightful editors Kathy Sagan, Nicole Brebner and April Osborn of MIRA Books as well as VP Margaret Marbury, independent editors Ronit Wagman and Sandra Scofield, talented cover designer Mary Luna and creative director Erin Craig of Harlequin and the hardworking Harper-Collins promotional team: VP publicity Heather Connor, publicity manager Laura Gianino, international marketing manager Shannon McCain and Christine Tsai from Subsidiary Rights.

One of my goals is to immerse readers in the world my characters inhabit, which means I, too, must immerse myself in it. My fragrance education started with re-nowned fragrance developer Ann Gottlieb in New York, referred to me by executive producer extraordinaire Michael Edelstein. Ann generously opened doors for me at IFF with master perfumers Carlos Benaim and Luc Dong in New York, and Celine Barel in Paris along with scent design manager Orlane Duchesne. Ann also introduced me to the lovely Linda Levy of the Fragrance Foundation. While in Paris, I also met with: Sylvie Jourdet of Creassence; Coralie Spicher, Berenice Watteau and Marine Merce of Firmenich (courtesy of Jerry Vittoria); and Thomas Fontaine of Pallida. Principal perfumer Sophie Labbe of Firmenich indulged me with her incredible career journey during high tea at the elegant Hotel Bristol (which makes an appearance in this novel!).

The next leg of my research took me to Grasse, in southeastern France. Creative director Florence Dussuyer generously hosted me at the incredibly chic IFF Atelier where master perfumers are allowed free rein to create. Also in Grasse, Olivier Maure and Sylvie Armando of Accords et Parfums showed me how their company's manufacturing process enables independent perfumers to thrive. One of those independents is Jessica Buchanan of @1000flowersperfumer, who made time for me at her charming Grasse studio.

In Lisbon, I had the pleasure of spending a day with the debonair Yves de Chiris, a seventh-generation French perfumer. In his honor, I named the fragrance firm that Radha works for the House of Yves — even though Monsieur de Chiris is nothing like the gullible — and imaginary — Yves du Bois. Also in Lisbon, independent perfumer Jahnvi Dameron Nandan gave me valuable insights into her experience in the industry and its future going forward.

In Istanbul, I walked through the Grand Bazaar where thousands of *attars,* vials of *oud* and fragrant incense intoxicated my senses.

I owe Paul Austin a huge debt of gratitude for connecting me to Yves de Chiris and to Anita Lal, global tastemaker and founder of LilaNur Parfums, the first international fragrance brand out of India. I also want to give a shout-out to renowned perfumer Honorine Blanc Chandler Burr, author of *The Perfect Scent,* Sheba Grobstein, William Hunt and Lynda Lieb for sharing their scent knowledge, and my good friend and superfan Bhavini Ruparell, who introduced me to perfumer Sonya de Castelbajac, who in turn put me in touch with Sylvie Jourdet in Paris.

If I have neglected to mention someone who spends their waking hours making this world a little more delightfully fragrant and who accompanied me on this journey, *mea culpa.*

I consulted excellent tomes such as *Perfumes: The A to Z Guide* by Turin and Sanchez, watched many YouTube videos about the manufacture of perfume in France and Kannauj to understand the differences in the processes and watched films about *parfum* like *Nose* (2021).

It was important to me to be sensitive to adoptees, birth parents and adoptive parents in writing about Radha and Niki. To that end, no one was more helpful than Cameron Lee Small, founder of Therapy Redeemed and a spiritual soul. I'm also grateful to Therese Allaire and Teresa Drosselmeyer for their contributions.

Acknowledgments wouldn't be complete without a thank-you to my early reviewers: my father, Ramesh Chandra Joshi (always my first reader); my brother, Dr. Madhup Joshi, one of the kindest people I know; Sara Oliver; Gratia Plante Trout; Rita Goel; Ritika Kumar; Barb Boyer; Elyse Bragdon; and Jaspreet Dhillon. And thank you to Sandy Kaushal, Lisa Niver and Amy Ulmer, just because. Also Cheri and Don Cline.

Thousands of readers around the world — men and women of all nationalities and cultures — have written to tell me about the strength, inspiration and cultural tidbits they've gleaned from my novels, and I am so grateful to you all for taking the time and energy to do so.

Last, but not least, my husband, my reader, my friend, Bradley Jay Owens, deserves huge kudos for encouraging me to write and for modeling the amazing Jay Kumar!

As always, you can message me on Instagram @thealkajoshi, at my website alka joshi.com and on email: alka@alkajoshi .com.

CHICKPEA CURRY: (CHOLE)

Whether you're a vegan, vegetarian or a meat lover, chickpeas, also known as garbanzo beans, satisfy. They're hearty, tasty and, when combined with Indian spices, they're a meal in themselves. You can, of course, ladle them over rice, as my mother used to do, or roll the delicious curry into a soft tortilla and enjoy.

My mother would soak whole garbanzo beans in water overnight to soften them, but I take the easy route: cans of chickpeas from the grocer's shelf! You can also substitute water or even chicken broth for the coconut milk if you want a lighter curry.

Ingredients:
3 tbsp canola or coconut oil
2 tsp cumin seeds
1 yellow or white onion, finely chopped
4 cloves garlic, minced
1 tsp ginger, minced

1 tsp red chili powder or red pepper flakes (or to taste)

2 tsp cumin powder

2 tbsp turmeric powder

2 tsp garam masala

2 tbsp coriander powder (if not available, use more coriander leaves)

1 tsp black pepper

2–3 tsp salt (or to taste)

1 can crushed or diced tomatoes

1.5 cups water or coconut milk or chicken broth

2 cans chickpeas, drained

1 cup coriander/cilantro leaves, chopped

Directions:

1. Heat oil on medium in deep skillet or large saucepan with a heavy bottom. Add cumin seeds until they begin to sizzle.

2. Add onions, garlic, ginger and red chili powder or red pepper flakes and sauté until onions are translucent.

3. Add cumin, turmeric, garam masala, coriander power, black pepper and salt, and mix until a spice paste forms. If the paste is too dry, add a little water.

4. Add tomatoes to the spice paste. Stir.

5. Add the coconut milk/water/chicken broth and chickpeas, stir and turn heat to low. Simmer about 15 minutes until the

chickpeas are soft.
6. Garnish with cilantro leaves. That's it!

ROSE PETAL JAM: (GULKAND)

Roses aren't just an important ingredient in fragrances. In India, cooks use them in food, especially desserts. Rose water, rose sherbet, *falooda* and rose ice cream draw their heady flavor from the petals of red and pink roses. So does a particular rose petal jam that my mother used to make. It's called *gulkand*, stemming from the Hindi word for rose, *gulab*.

Every family has their own recipe for rose petal jam. I've captured my mother's version here. It was so good that we gobbled it up as soon as it was ready, never once stopping to wonder where she got the rose petals (were they growing in our yard?), when she plucked them (early in the morning when they were covered in dew?) or how she prepared the condiment. Just one day, we'd come home from school and there it would be, like magic.

And the taste? Heaven.

Like most Indian foods, *gulkand* has benefits beyond its delicious aroma and taste. It helps reduce acidity in the body, boosts energy and helps heals skin irritations like blisters, acne and wrinkles (yes, please!).

Ingredients:

1 clean jam jar with airtight lid
2 cups rose petals, red or pink, washed, dried and shredded (be careful to use only rose petals that have not been sprayed with insecticides)
1 cup white sugar (or rock sugar)
1/2 teaspoon cardamom seeds, crushed (optional)

Directions:

1. Layer the bottom of the jar with some shredded dried petals.
2. Add a layer of sugar.
3. Repeat the process until you've used up all the petals and sugar. At this point, you can add the crushed cardamom seeds if desired.
4. Close the jar tightly with a lid.
5. Place the jar in sunlight for 7 to 10 days.
6. Every day, use a clean spoon to stir the contents, which will start to become moist.
7. On the last day, stir and store the jar in

the refrigerator. It should last up to a year.
8. Enjoy on toast, ice cream, in milk or even just out of the jar! Some folks add it to *paan,* a popular Indian snack and breath freshener made with betel leaves and stuffed with areca nuts, lime paste, cardamom, coconut, fennel and other spices.

A PERFUME PRIMER

Perfume. The very word conjures an image of Cleopatra seducing Marc Antony in a bathtub filled with rose petals. Indeed, Egyptian, Arab, Indian, Greek and Chinese people were using natural scents to entice, adorn and enhance their bodies and their environments for thousands of years before European traders discovered the art of fragrance. In fact, upon first meeting Europeans, who were following the silk and spice routes in search of what the "oriental" world had to offer, Middle Easterners and Asian people thought Westerners were barbaric because they smelled; they rarely bathed or cleaned their teeth.

Evidence of the use of scents in religious ceremonies, palaces and mosques, as well as descriptions of the production process of fragrances, exists in ancient texts from Cyprus, India, Mesopotamia and the Islamic world. Not until the fourteenth century did Europeans begin using scents in daily life — primarily to mask body odor created by poor sanitary habits.

But the process of making scent was laborious and the raw materials from far-away lands were so expensive that only the royal courts, like those of Catherine de' Medici and Louis XIV, could afford such extravagance. (The French coined the word *parfum*. From the Latin *per* and *fumus* meaning "by smoke," the word *perfume* actually describes just one of many processes by which scent is extracted from plants and flowers.)

Demand for fragrances grew. Soon enough, plants like jasmine, tuberose, orange blossom and lavender were brought from the Middle East, India and the Mediterranean and planted in southeastern France, in the city of Grasse, because of the city's temperate climate. That made it possible to produce fragrances more affordably. Quickly, Grasse became the new epicenter for perfume production. Perfumed gloves, usually worn by ladies of a wealthy class, covered the pungent smell of tanned hides, which used to be Grasse's main industry.

Most perfumes contain anywhere from seventy-five to eighty percent denatured alcohol, which dilutes the intensity of the fragrance oils. As a rule, Westerners prefer these lighter scents. In the Indian subcontinent and the Middle East, the fragrant oil derived from raw materials is mixed with a base oil like sandalwood and applied directly to the body; alcohol is never used. The intense, concentrated result is called *attar*, preferred by Eastern cultures.

Kannauj, in the state of Uttar Pradesh, is considered the *attar* capital of India. Because they're extracted directly from a mere handful of plants, flowers, roots and other natural materials, *attars* are considered purer, closer to the source, by those who use them. (By contrast, today's Western perfumes may contain more than a hundred ingredients.) A little goes a long way, and that means *attars* can be less expensive to use than brand-name perfumes. Many European and American fragrance houses buy pure essential oils from Kannauj for their formulas.

THE MASTER PERFUMER

Before meeting with perfumers in the US and Europe, I assumed master perfumer was a designation awarded after the completion of a certificate, like a doctorate or a master's degree.

Not so. It's an earned promotion within a fragrance house. After the commercial success of several scent creations, a degree in the field of chemistry (or at least a profound knowledge thereof), and skill in helping clients realize their vision, a perfumer can be recognized as a master perfumer by her executive team. It may take anywhere from seven to ten years. She is then referred to as *Le Nez,* which I'm told is preferred in France to the English translation, The Nose.

In meetings with French perfumers, I was told that as of 2021, a master perfumer's salary could be ten times higher than that of a perfumer.

Why are master perfumers held in such

high regard? Because they must learn to discern over 3000 scents and store them in their memory bank. *Les Nez* create formulas for a project brief purely from memory. Those formulas are then sent to lab assistants who will blend the specified ingredients and return samples for *Le Nez* to evaluate. That process could be repeated several times until *Le Nez* feels some of the trials can be presented to the client for consideration. It may take hundreds of trials and a few years to find the perfect note.

When the client chooses one of the formulas presented, it is sent to a compounder so a larger quantity can be produced. Bottles — an essential part of the brand identity — and labels will be designed and sent to a bottling plant where "the juice" will be packaged.

Houses like Fragonard, Guerlain and Houbigant used to be the main purveyors of perfumes. Then fashion houses like Donna Karan, Halston and Givenchy, who wanted to market their own branded scent, commissioned the established houses to create one for them. Soon, celebrities joined the fray. Today, three large companies produce most of the fragrances in the world: IFF (International Flavors and Fragrances), Givaudan and Firmenich.

In 1970, the first perfume school was founded in Versailles by perfumer Jean-Jacques Guerlain. It's called ISIPCA, and it's a globally prominent institution today. Its mission is to teach technical, scientific, marketing and business principles of the world of perfume. A degree in chemistry is *de rigueur.*

According to Fortune Business Insights, as of 2020, the global perfume market was almost $30 billion. Which means there is always room for niche fragrance houses, and many young designers around the world have founded boutique firms to make a name for themselves in this exciting, enticing and exceedingly competitive industry.

ABOUT THE AUTHOR

Born in India, **Alka Joshi** is a *New York Times* bestselling author who moved to the United States at the age of nine. She holds a B.A. from Stanford University and an M.F.A. from California College of Arts. She is the author of The Jaipur Trilogy.

The employees of Thorndike Press hope you have enjoyed this Large Print book. All our Thorndike, Wheeler, and Kennebec Large Print titles are designed for easy reading, and all our books are made to last. Other Thorndike Press Large Print books are available at your library, through selected bookstores, or directly from us.

For information about titles, please call:
(800) 223-1244

or visit our website at:
gale.com/thorndike

To share your comments, please write:
Publisher
Thorndike Press
10 Water St., Suite 310
Waterville, ME 04901